'Claudia – a super-bitch who keeps us all on the edge where she loves to live . . . The Roman detail is deft, the pace as fast as a champion gladiator.'
Sunday Express

'A timeless heroine for today – you'll be hooked.'
Company

'An endearing adventuress who regards mortal danger as just another bawdy challenge.' *She*

'Terrific read . . . thoroughly entertaining.'
The Bookseller

'Marilyn Todd's wonderful fictional creation – a bawdy superbitch with a talent for sleuthing – [is] an enormous triumph.' *Ms London*

'A daring debut from a promising writer.' *Oxford Times*

'The first in a very entertaining series of mysteries.'
Lancashire Evening Telegraph

'Feisty and fun.' *Yorkshire Post*

'*I, Claudia* was one of the best and most amusing historical detective narratives of the last year, and *Virgin Territory* is a fine follow-up.' *Crime Time*

'Thoroughly entertaining mystery. This heroine will run and run.' *Richmond and Twickenham Informer*

'A murder mystery with a difference, which gives a vivid view of life in Roman times.' *Northern Echo*

'If you're looking for a romp through the streets of Rome in 13BC then this is the book to buy!'
Books Magazine

Man Eater

Marilyn Todd was born in Harrow, Middlesex, but now lives in West Sussex with her husband, one hare-brained dog and two cats. *Man Eater* is the third in her series of Roman mysteries, following *I, Claudia* and *Virgin Territory*.

Claudia's latest mystery, *Wolf Whistle*, is available in hardback from Macmillan.

Marilyn Todd

Man Eater

PAN BOOKS

First published 1997 by Macmillan

This edition published 1998 by Pan Books
an imprint of Macmillan Publishers Ltd
25 Eccleston Place, London SW1W 9NF
and Basingstoke

Associated companies throughout the world

ISBN 0 330 35407 8

1 3 5 7 9 8 6 4 2

A CIP catalogue record for this book is available from
the British Library.

Phototypeset by Intype London Ltd
Printed and bound in Great Britain by
Mackays of Chatham plc, Chatham, Kent

To Nigel
without whom I'd still be on the starting blocks

I

Would you believe it? You start off doing someone a favour, not so much as a thought for your own interests, then, before you know it, the whole thing backfires and you end up in this mess. Typical!

Claudia's mouth turned down at the corners. All right, all right; maybe the word 'favour' was not strictly accurate. A letter had arrived from her bailiff, urging her to visit the estate immediately and without delay, so theoretically, if you wanted to be really pedantic, you could argue that this was in her own interests. They were her vineyards, her problems, if you like – but a bailiff's job is to run the estate, smoothly and without fuss, isn't it? Therefore it was a measure of how seriously Claudia Seferius took her new obligations that she actually *did* set off at once. Heaven knows it was one hell of a sacrifice, she'd have given her right ear-ring to stay in Rome for the processions and the dances and the gladiatorial games, but, alas, with wealth comes responsibility – and was she a girl to shirk hers? She was not.

On the other hand, a voice inside her had argued, there was no reason why you can't cut a few corners. And Claudia was all for listening to a balanced argument . . .

Necessary as it might be to visit Etruria, equally she could see no reason why she should not be home again before the spring equinox and the subsequent rush of wall-to-wall festivals. Grabbing her cat, her bodyguard and the merest essentials, that same afternoon she rented a driver and gig from the nearest stand and set a cracking pace along the Via Flaminia. Since this was the main road linking Rome with the Adriatic, progress had been swift and she had not so much as hesitated when, at Narni, the road swept east. Claudia simply swept north.

And that was when the trouble began.

Because, instead of being ensconced in her villa by now, albeit digesting some dreary report on what damage winter had inflicted on the poor vines or sidestepping her late husband's odious tribe of relatives, she was stuck in this godforsaken backwater.

'Drusilla?' She twizzled her neck to crane out of the window. 'Is that you?'

It was not. The rustle that she'd heard was a hedgehog, stretching its stubby post-hibernatory legs, and Claudia chafed her upper arms. They say spring comes early to Umbria, and she'd seen for herself how the almond blossom was almost past and the corn was standing tall, but all the same it was really too cold to stay at this window much longer, and yet –

The new moon, so thin it had to lie on its back to support itself, was rising between two dark wooded hummocks but, below the skyline, fog rose steadily and when you held the lamp to the window, a fleecy wall glowered back at you.

Dear Diana, it's like staring into Hades. Only noisier! Good grief, you come to the country expecting peace and tranquillity and what do you get? Billeted next to a bloody great zoo, that's what. And they have the cheek

2

to say Rome's noisy! Well, it might get rowdy in the streets from time to time and the pavements might turn mucky in the rain, but at least you don't find yourself sleeping alongside half the African jungle. Brawlers, beggars and bawds you get used to. The stonemasons' hammers, the creaks of the cranes, the cobblers' lasts – that's civilization with a capital C. But out in the country one expects no more than leaves tousled in the wind, perhaps the odd bark of a fox, not this constant succession of bloodcurdling howls and menacing growls, and *certainly* none of these formidable pongs!

''Night, miss!'

Claudia's heart flipped a backward somersault and landed awkwardly as two security guards emerged from the gloom.

'Goodnight.' Her reply was a trifle croaky, but the fog, which plays tricks anyway, had gobbled them up again.

She counted to twenty then whistled two or three piping notes repeatedly. A horse doctor from Tolosa once told her that a cat had over thirty muscles in its ear, enabling it to detect the highest squeak of a dormouse, the shrillest trill of a warbler. Surely Drusilla could hear this? Claudia waited, gooseflesh creeping over her shivering frame. Nothing. Not a sign. Only when her teeth began to chatter did she drape her tunic over the sill and close the shutters, one reluctant leaf after the other, her cheek pressed against the polished beech long after the two big bruisers had finished their rounds.

Come on, kid. I know you can find your way –

Hitching the hem of her borrowed nightshift, Claudia hunkered over the little round brazier, warming her hands as light from the flickering lantern danced off the bronze. On paper, there should have been no problem with the road north of Narni, since it used to be the original Via Flaminia. However, in an effort to speed up travel and facilitate commerce within and beyond the boundaries of the Empire, Augustus had diverted this vital artery eastwards, round the other side of the mountains. So what if fifteen years had passed since then? Give us credit; we Romans build roads to last. Sure, the waysides are a little overgrown, but we're making progress, aren't we?

Then it happened. The . . . accident.

Picking up the looking-glass, a patchwork of cuts and bruises stared back at her, legacies of that . . . accident. Hmm. Claudia scanned aquatic friezes on unfamiliar walls, the garish oriental bedspread over a bed cast in silver. She smelled the heavy clover-like scent of the nightshift which hung stiff and strange from her shoulders – and vowed never to cut corners again. Never, ever, ever.

Taking one last peek out of the window, Claudia sighed. If there was ever light at the end of this particular tunnel, some smart-arse must have blown it out.

Jabbing back the bedclothes, she kicked off her sandals. This wasn't the first time Drusilla had stayed out all night, but it was the first time in their seven years of sharing secrets and sustenance and shelter that she'd physically gone missing. Claudia snatched at the cat's blanket and pressed it to her cheek, lingering over the matted fur and snagged fabric until her eyelids finally grew heavy. With one puff, the flame from the lamp flickered and died and she felt herself being sucked into sleep.

Down, and down, and down.

After a while, after a very long while, Claudia Seferius stopped fighting, and the thin crescent of the moon rose even higher in the heavens.

Thick mist, white like smoke, obliterated all vision and muffled every sound, even the hoofs clip-clopping in unison along grooves worn by countless wheels before them. The road, peeling itself back to admit them, revealed itself as little more than a ghost road. No brightly garbed Syrian merchants. No rumble of wagons. No loud-mouthed students travelling to university in Athens or Massilia or Alexandria. Gone were the actors, the athletes, the dispatch-carriers who once tramped these stones. Gone, too, the constant straggle of labourers, beggars, immigrants, in search of a better life. But in her dream, their shades lingered silently, leaving just the faintest whiff of commerce and philosophy, soldiering and whoring.

Hemmed in by the green-grey hazy hills for which Umbria was famous, home to boar and badger, wolf and porcupine, the sounds you would normally expect to hear – the rushing snowmelts, the territorial birdsong, the scrape of dead antler against bark – these sounds were deadened by the mist's embrace. Tiny pearls of moisture embroidered her cloak.

It was like a dream within a dream.

Oblivion in a white cocoon. Then –

Trumpets. Shouts. Drums. Riders, six maybe seven of them, charging in and out, in and out of the fog. She saw the mares' eyes rolling in fear, smelled the acid steam from their nostrils. They began to rear. The driver (she could see him now) was wrestling with the reins.

Abruptly the dream changed again. The riders had gone, but so also had the gig and the driver and the horses, and she was spinning through space. Thick, white, silent space. She saw the ground hurtling towards her, heard a scream . . .

Except –

The screech wasn't part of the dream. Shrill and penetrating, it shattered the night and Claudia shot bolt upright in bed. A second scream rang out, and Claudia Seferius was out of bed and kicking over the brazier before she remembered.

'Mingy, mangy, flea-bitten mishmash!'

Her voice echoed in the dark as she pushed away the curls that had tumbled into her eyes. This zoo is beginning to get on my whiskers! A big cat snarled, silencing the monkey. Well, that was something, she thought. At least it put paid to the shrieks.

She flopped back on to the couch. Ah yes, the dream. Fiction? If only! Instead her troubled mind had been rerunning the morning's escapades – events she could well have done without, thank you very much.

Small red embers glowered like a hundred eyes on the mosaic, but they would all too rapidly cool and the stars would have a long way to travel before the slaves would be up, stoking the furnace that would blast welcome warm air round the ducts under the floor. Claudia wriggled beneath the counterpane and dismissed from her mind the yobs who had forced her off the road. Make no mistake, their turn would come. She'd had a jolly good look at three of the little toe-rags!

She rubbed her throbbing temple and plumped her bolster. What did they stuff them with? Marbles? Her ears strained in the blackness and heard the thumping of her heart even above the rumpus from the menagerie.

Oh, Drusilla. Curling into a ball, she stroked the woollen blanket as though the cat lay curled upon it. Where are you?

When the gig rolled down the embankment, Drusilla's cage had burst open and the cat had bolted. More than bolted, she'd completely gone to ground, no amount of calling would coax her out. The heat from the charcoal had long since dissipated and Claudia huddled lower under the covers. Ideally she'd have left the shutters open, but the nights were too chilly and the best she could do was to drape her torn tunic over the sill and hope Drusilla would pick up her scent that way. Assuming . . .

Assuming, what? Surely you're not going to take notice of that ridiculous bit of homespun which says that when an animal's injured, it crawls away to die? Codswallop. Drusilla is sulking, and that's the end of it. Claudia closed her eyes, yet still saw the image of a blue-eyed, cross-eyed cat – and the space where Drusilla snuggled in the crook of her arm seemed suddenly huge. Claudia punched the pillow, then doubled it over. What was in here, for gods' sake? Acorns? All this trumpeting, growling, screeching and cackling; it's enough to drive a girl demented!

Still. There seems to be a law which determines that beggars and choosers must walk separate paths and, be fair, this *was* the nearest settlement. She'd staggered to the top of the hill (why hadn't someone told her this region was so lumpy?) and there it lay, the Pictor residence – salvation sprawled in the valley, four wings round a central courtyard, its terracotta tiles shimmering in the burgeoning sunshine. The Vale of Adonis, she found out later, named not after Aphrodite's lover but the profusion of glossy red flowers that sprang from his blood and coloured the meadows so prolifically during the hot summer months. Which was perhaps just as well, because Adonis wasn't the Immortal who sprang to mind in this narrow strip of land, crowded by woods and the hills so close the farm buildings had to stagger up the sides.

One's first impression was of satyrs and centaurs, of Pan summoning wood nymphs on his mysterious reed pipes . . .

Claudia's head lifted from the pillow. What was that? It sounded like . . . bugger! Just a seal. She turned fitfully, trying to blank out the problems that awaited her up at her own estate. What was so urgent – and so secret – that Rollo, her bailiff, daren't commit it to paper? Since Gaius had died, his relatives had installed themselves at the villa, no doubt plotting ways to disinherit the widow. Was that it?

The night droned on. The caged beasts struck an uneasy truce and eventually Claudia's eyelids surrendered once again. But, instead of seeing her mother-in-law's desiccated features or hearing the carping voice of her sister-in-law in her dreams, the figures of the family whose roof she shared drifted in and out of Claudia's consciousness.

Roly-poly Pallas. 'Darling girl, whatever happened? Sit down, sit down. You must drink this, I insist.' Irres-

8

pective of the blood streaming from her forehead, a glass of strong Falernian wine was pressed into her hand.

Pallas changed. He remained the same age, early thirties, but grew leaner, and a hand's span shorter. The puffing and fussing gave way to authority, and it was Sergius Pictor, head of the household, with his thick, springy curls and saturnine good looks, who was assessing Claudia's injuries and striding off to pick up her injured bodyguard and driver . . .

A pale-faced creature introduced herself as Alis, Sergius' wife, and then turned into his echo. 'Oh, yes. We must send a wagon immediately,' she was saying, even though Sergius and the slaves had left . . .

Another girl, younger than Alis, dark and sultry, could be seen in the background as she leaned against a pillar, watching, pouting and chewing on a lock of hair . . .

Pallas returned and was forcing a second glass of wine on her when Claudia heard the clatter of chariot wheels in the courtyard. Funny. She hadn't heard horses.

'Tulola.' It was Pallas who made the introductions. 'Our dear host's sister.'

There was something odd about the chariot. Richly decorated, richly embellished, it was designed for racing and now, Claudia realized, tall slinky Tulola was dressed as a charioteer. But something was wrong. And then she spotted them. The creatures who pulled it. Six Negroes, glistening with the sweat of their recent exertions . . .

Tulola was walking towards her. 'You poor creature.' She had a long, low stride, almost as though with every pace she had to step over an obstacle. 'You're bleeding.' There was compassion in the voice, if not the eyes, and when she ran her hand down Claudia's cheek, the fingers were stiff and splayed . . .

Claudia snapped into wakefulness, instantly aware of the empty space beside her. She cradled the cat's cushion then thumped and punched and rearranged the lumps in her own bolster. What was in here? Chicken bones? It was good of the Pictors to take her in, she supposed. To patch her wounds, tend the two injured men, to feed, clothe and rest her. But the instant Drusilla turns up, she thought, I am o – f – f, off!

Suddenly there was a blockage in her throat. Oh, she'd find her way here, no question of that. In fact, Claudia had no doubts whatsoever about the intelligence of her sharp, Egyptian cat, only –

The trill of a blackbird interrupted her musing. Just one or two notes and faint at that – she could barely make them out between the howls and the growls – but others would follow and the evidence was conclusive.

Juno be praised, the long night was over!

The road accident instantly forgotten, she flung the counterpane round her shoulders and fumbled her way to the window. It was going to be another dank start, she thought, easing open one narrow shutter, but at least the fog lifts quickly as she knew from experience. She unhooked the second leaf. Oh. Her tattered tunic hung limp on the ledge, but of Drusilla there was no sign. And the mist in front of her suddenly seemed denser.

'You don't fool me, you wretched feline.' Claudia's breath was white in the pre-dawn air. 'I know you're out there.'

Just because the bones of your ancestors lie in the

tombs of the Pharaohs, don't think you can put on airs and graces with me!

'Sulk all you like, but we both know that one sniff of a sardine and you'll be over this sill like a shot.' Whose was that silly, reedy voice? 'And remember, it's not my fault you used up four of your lives in one go!'

What was that? It sounded like a soft scuffle. There it was again. Claudia's breath came out in a rush. 'Drusilla!'

Tossing the bedspread aside, she picked up her skirts and raced across the room. Although the grey light of dawn was growing paler by the minute, it was nowhere near sufficient and Claudia cursed the upended brazier as bronze collided with shinbone. It was only because she was swearing and hobbling and bleeding and hurting all at the same time that she didn't realize, until she reached the door, that whatever talents these clever Egyptian moggies might possess, rattling handles isn't one of them.

'*What?*' She unlocked the door and flung it open.

The man in the doorway was staring at her. 'I . . . I . . .'

His mouth hung open, and either he had a speech impediment or – as she very much suspected – he was stinking drunk. For good measure he produced another guttural gargle and lurched forward.

'Get away from me, you revolting little dung-beetle!'

He really was the most unprepossessing creature she'd ever had the misfortune to lay eyes on.

The dung-beetle's mouth opened and closed. 'I . . .'

Claudia put out her left hand to push him away while the other tried to slam the door in his face, but the dung-beetle was too fast. He dived towards her. Using both hands, Claudia pushed against his chest, but his arms had closed round her shoulders.

'Wrong room, buster.'

She daren't risk connecting her knee with his groin for fear of unbalancing herself – and the prospect of this horny sod on top of her didn't bear thinking about! Along the atrium, still bright with night-torches, a blonde slave emerged from the kitchens with a wide, steaming bowl. Good. Between the two of them, they might be able to prise this animal off! She tried to call out, but the pressure of his body against hers was threatening to squeeze the life right out of her. Mercifully the girl looked up . . . and, incredibly, began to scream.

Silly bitch, Claudia thought, nearly buckling under the weight of the lecherous, gargling dung-beetle, but at least it's brought help. Doors were opening left, right and centre.

Almost rhythmically, Claudia and the drunk danced in the doorway. He pushed, she pushed, he pushed back, but all the time she was growing weaker and weaker. Surely someone has the sense to yank him off?

Inexplicably everyone seemed to be yelling, and it was only when Claudia finally lost the battle with the dung-beetle and they toppled sideways together, she began to understand why.

The dung-beetle wasn't drunk. The dung-beetle wasn't gargling.

The dung-beetle had a bloody great knife in his belly.

II

'I honestly don't know what the fuss is about.'

Claudia had changed out of the blood-soaked shift and was silently tapping her toe on the floor. The dining room faced east, where the first rays of sunshine had punched through the mist to give a rich, buttery quality to the landscape beyond and bejewelled the narrow stream that bounced down the hillside to make the valley so rich and so fertile. An early orange-tip butterfly made its wispy flight past the window to investigate the white clouds of arabis that tumbled over the rocks beside the water, and a wagtail bobbed up and down in delight.

'It's not as though I killed him.'

The only other occupant of the room glanced up from the pear he was peeling. 'Darling girl, he's not breathing and his pulse has stopped. I can't see *him* dancing the fandango again.'

'I'm well aware of his condition, Pallas.' Round the walls, Ganymede was being swept from his flocks by a giant eagle and on the floor, boozy Bacchus frolicked among maenads. 'The point I'm making', Claudia ground her heel in Bacchus' eye, 'is that it wasn't *me* who killed him.'

In fact, the whole thing was a mystery. Amid doors flying open and a positively prodigal amount of shouting and squawking, and despite Claudia's obvious shock and revulsion, she had been conscious of immense confusion within the household. Perhaps it was not entirely surprising that Sergius recovered first. Propelling her gently away from the carnage (and unwittingly straight into his sister's predatory arms!), he could not apologize enough. The shame of it, having a guest subjected to violence. Was she hurt? Was she frightened? She mustn't be put off by this, please don't think badly of us, I hope you'll feel safe still. Tulola, look after her, will you? Hot, honeyed wine, please, to put colour in her cheeks.

Pallas carefully cut away a blemish. 'Didn't winter very well,' he said, chopping the pear in half and sniffing intently. 'But then neither did the apples. Damp in the fruit store, presumably.'

Outdoors, the five monotonous notes from the wood pigeon perched on the bath-house roof added a curiously sleepy dimension to the proceedings.

'Claudia, Claudia, what a terrible experience! How you must be feeling!' Alis fluttered into the breakfast room, pale as ever. 'Was it – ? Oh, I say! What a wonderful tunic! So vibrant. Wherever did you find it?'

'It's Tulola's.' That, if nothing else, would teach her not to travel so light in future! Bright orange cotton with a blue band round the neck and a large blue flounce? It might suit Egyptian hairstyles and heavily painted eyes, but on a sophisticated city girl, it was as out of place as a corpse at a wedding. Corpse? Bad joke, Claudia.

'It suits you. I mean, *really* suits you.'

'It makes me look like a common tart!'

Claudia hadn't realized she'd spoken aloud until Pallas said drily, 'Definitely Tulola's, then.'

Alis' eyes widened in shock. 'Pallas!'

'Dear child, you are quite right and I take it back.' He laid down his chicken wing and swivelled his eyes towards Claudia. 'My cousin's morals do not aspire to such heights.'

Colour flooded Alis' white cheeks. 'Sssh!'

Pallas began to dissect a quail. 'I think you'll find Tulola is aware of my sentiments.'

Claudia bit her lip. 'Forget Tulola, what about – '

'Oh dear, were you two in the middle of a conversation?' Alis clicked her tongue. 'Well, don't mind me.' She unlocked one of the carved chests and examined a green glass jug. 'Carry on as though I'm not here.'

It was wellnigh impossible, but Claudia made a gallant effort. 'Why', she leaned over the breakfast table, 'has Sergius sent for the military?'

Why not handle it himself? Come on, jurisprudence isn't reserved for patricians! We merchant classes are equally entitled to administer justice among our own, it's one of the perks.

'Pallas, are you listening? I'm trying to work out – '

'Why Sergius sent for the Prefect; I heard you.' He searched around for a finger bowl. 'I presume you've asked him?'

Claudia pushed across a bronze bowl filled with warm, scented water. 'He felt, and I quote, it was essential for the officials to get to the bottom of the matter.' She refrained from mentioning the crispness in his tone which brooked no argument.

'There you are then.' He shook the drips from his pudgy fingers. 'Try a dried cornel and stop worrying. They're simply divine and – '

'I'm not worrying, I – '

'Claudia, which do you think will look best centre-stage at dinner tonight?' Alis weighed a green bowl in one hand, a yellow bowl in the other.

' – I repeat, I'm not worrying, but it's not every day a man's life-blood drains itself out on your nightshift.' Claudia smiled a beguiling smile. 'Couldn't you have a word with him?' There were enough skeletons in her closet to keep a pack of hungry jackals happy for a year. The last thing she needed was Officialdom picking over the bones.

'Ah!' The big man's nose wrinkled ominously. 'Unfortunately my stock is not that high with the man of the house – ' He let his voice trail off.

'But you're related?'

'The connection is not as close as you might imagine.' Pallas put a slice of pear in his mouth and chomped away for a while. 'And I'm afraid Sergius leans to the impression that I have outstayed my welcome.'

'Why? How long have you been here?'

He shot her a glance from the corner of his eye. 'Two years.'

Laughing aloud is not generally prescribed to heal bruised ribs, but Claudia couldn't help herself. I'm beginning to like you, she thought. I'm beginning to like you very much.

Across the room Alis clearly felt some decision ought to be made about the bowls, but before she could determine the verdict for herself, the green jug took the matter into its own handles and crashed to the floor.

'Everyone ignore me,' she quivered and Everyone

obeyed – Claudia by letting a slave through to brush up the slivers, Pallas by cracking a snail shell.

'Have you seen Tulola's harem?' He impaled the unfortunate mollusc on the point of his knife.

'That ragbag collection of animals? Not yet.'

'Darling girl, the beasts are Sergius'.' His chins shook in amusement. 'I'm talking about the *men*.'

Alis took advantage of the shocked pause. 'Oh dear, I did so want to get a matching set for dinner. Why couldn't it have been the yellow bowl?'

'For gods' sake, woman, a man's been murdered! Claudia and I are trying to converse!'

'I'm sorry, Pallas. Sorry.' She twisted her face in a girlish gesture which had the unfortunate effect of making her look closer to thirty-eight than twenty-eight. 'Pretend I'm not here.'

He did his best. 'Not that her odalisques stay long, you understand. Our dear cousin bores easily.'

Claudia felt her pulse quicken. 'Are you saying the dung-beetle was one of them?'

'Wander round the west wing some time, it's quite an experience, but as much as our Tulola goes for the rough trade, she hasn't sunk that low.'

'By rough trade, you mean . . .?'

'Britons, Iberians, Germans. The ruff-tuff hairy types – whereas me' – he peered down the neck of his tunic and pulled a face – 'I'm simply a martyr to depilation.'

Claudia flung herself on the couch opposite him. 'What about the Negroes?' Who could forget the sight of their sweat-drenched bodies harnessed to Tulola's chariot?

'She goes through, how shall I put it, phases.' Pallas

swallowed the remainder of a sausage before elaborating. 'Last year, for instance, she was into tattoos. Kept a whole string of Scythians, and you know how partial they are to body art. The black boys, I'm afraid, she picked up at auction.'

To use as toys, the bitch. 'So if he wasn't one of Tulola's conquests, who was the man in my bedroom?'

Pallas let out a soft belch and refilled his long-stemmed glass. 'How should I know, darling? Never seen him before in my life.'

How odd. Claudia helped herself to wine, but it was the strong stuff and she merely sipped, although her mind was working faster than a goldbeater's hammer. 'Sergius has asked me to stay for the Prefect's questions, and', not that she'd hang about once Drusilla turned up, 'I was wondering how long it would take him to get here.'

'Macer?' The fat man picked up a pickled onion and began to eat it like an apple. 'His barracks are in Tarsulae – '

Her ears pricked up. Tarsulae was the town where they'd spent the night before last, Claudia, Junius and the driver. She'd never forget that dump so long as she lived! In fact, her legs still bore a cluster of itchy red lumps from the damned bedding!

' – which, as you know, is the only town for miles since the new road was built.'

'I don't suppose anyone could give me a hand with these crocks, could they?' wailed Alis.

'Looks good on his record, a manor that size,' Pallas continued. 'Even though the population is somewhat disproportionate.'

Tell me about it! In the fifteen years since the Emperor

diverted the Via Flaminia, most of the locals had uprooted themselves and their families in order to be in at the start of the new prosperity. And, make no mistake, prosperous it was. Since Augustus had brought an end to three generations of civil war, trade had virtually doubled and whether you were a butcher or a banker, a midwife or a marble merchant, you could be assured of one thing: a damned good living on the far side of those mountains.

What sort of crimes would the military *this* side of the range be used to dealing with, Claudia wondered. Fiddling weights and measures, petty pilfering, adultery? No, no, those were civil cases. Patrolling the roads? Fat chance. To call those goat tracks roads would be like calling an ulcer a beauty spot, and as for the Old Road, well! She hadn't seen many patrols yesterday!

Lazily she tossed a hazelnut from hand to hand. Such a simple matter, this, and more than likely the culprit would be some grudge-bearing slave, so why, why, why this compulsion for the military? Surely Sergius could sort it out himself? She didn't know their purpose, but she'd seen his private security measures – big buggers who probably munched ears for breakfast, washed down with the blood of babes. Not so much slaves as mercenaries, twenty or thirty of them, and men like these weren't cheap to run.

Indeed, you couldn't hold your own in this neglected backwater without some degree of commercial nous, much less flourish – and precious little was required in the way of mathematics to deduce that one diverted road plus fifteen years of mass migration ought by rights to equal a decrease in fortune. Yet, she tapped her knuckle on the arm of the couch – this is solid bronze – and as for the upholstery – surely this particular shade of violet is unique to certain aloes? A strain that will grow only on the Isle of Socotra? Which happens to lie smack bang in the Indian Ocean?

The sudden realization as to why Sergius had called in the army sent a thousand spiders abseiling down Claudia's backbone.

She remembered the glance she had caught of her handsome host as she followed Tulola to change her bloodstained nightshift. Although fleeting, she had interpreted the expression as that of a man mining for lead and finding a thick, strong vein of gold in its place. Now she was not so sure.

For all his outward signs of hospitality, Sergius believes he's harbouring a murderess! No wonder he was so solicitous. Be kind to the nice lady and she won't stab you . . .

The hazelnut clattered on to the floor and came to rest on a maenad's nose. Why Claudia's hand was shaking, she had no idea. Good grief, I've nothing to fear, it's not as though I stabbed the wretched dung-beetle . . . The little filbert splintered under Claudia's dainty tooled sandal as she recalled the law concerning murder. It was quite straightforward. No ifs and ands and buts and maybes. In fact, there's a children's rhyme that covers it nicely. Confession is death, denial is trial. And by Jupiter, Claudia Seferius was most definitely contesting the charge!

Pallas was too busy with his boiled bacon to notice her slip away, Alis too heavily entrenched with her fripperies. *Minerva's magic, what have I got myself into?*

Her bodyguard, a bandage round his head and his left eye a splendid magenta, was waiting in the atrium and his shoes squeaked on the marble floor as he approached.

'Are you all right, madam?' His face was pinched with worry. 'There's talk in the slave quarters – '

Claudia cut him short with a flick of the wrist. 'Never listen to gossip, Junius.' I do, but you shouldn't.

'But a man was killed in front of you?'

'Some trivial misunderstanding.' Try as she might to address his good eye, there was something magnetic about the shiny, swollen, purple thing on the other side of his nose. 'The authorities will iron things out.'

'You mean – ?' His square jaw dropped. 'By the gods, madam! They're not accusing *you* of the murder, are they?'

'Temporarily. Now hop along and stick a steak on that shiner, there's a good boy.'

A whirl of orange cotton, she swept down the colonnade towards the far end of the atrium where condensation from the roof tiles dripped into the pool and where a shaggy-haired slave in check pantaloons carried a loaded salver towards the west wing. Claudia snatched it out of his hands and marched to her room, kicking the door open with her toe. Juno be praised, the blood had been mopped up, there was not so much as a single stain to show the dung-beetle had ever been there, let alone expired on the spot.

For several long minutes her young bodyguard remained motionless in the shadows, his stern blue eyes fixed on Claudia's door, and when he did finally leave, it was not towards the slaves' barracks that his footsteps were directed, but to the back exit leading to the thickly wooded Umbrian hills. Within seconds, he was swallowed up by the swirling mist.

No way!

No way is Claudia Seferius going to trial!

Claudia Seferius has enough on her plate as it is – and for heaven's sake! what sort of a man is this Sergius Pictor, thinking she has nothing better to do than to go round sticking knives into people? You'll pay for this, so help me, you will! I'll take every copper quadran you own.

It was here, in the central courtyard redolent with hyssop, wormwood and borage, which reinforced the notion that Sergius was having no problems with his investment portfolio. And it was here, in the gardens, with the mist fast dissipating, that Claudia made her resolution.

Don't get mad. Get one up.

I will sue you to Hades and back for what you're putting me through. I will take your fountains which sing and dance and make rainbows in the sunshine. I will take your parrots which perform antics with such insouciant charm. I will even take their topiaried counterparts which spread box and laurel wings to shelter white marbled busts and mythic bronze beasts. Which, of course, will also be mine.

She poked her tongue into the corner of her mouth. How *did* Sergius make his money? Bruised and bleeding as she was yesterday, and long before she saw the pens of exotic animals, Claudia was aware that there were neither vines nor olives to suggest traditional rural income. One thing, though. Sergius sure was a man to maximize his potential. None of the outbuildings (and there were scores of them) encroached on this narrow, precious fertile finger, but where herds of cattle might walk, gazelle grazed. Where sweeps of wheat might grow, row upon sprouting row of lupin and vetch, clover, bracken and spelt flourished as animal fodder. What, she wondered, waggling her finger through the bars of the parrot's cage, is going on here?

Her gaze fell beyond the archway to the wild, untamed hills beyond. Thanks to the fog, this was her first real view of them, and what a contrast to the broad skies and rolling terraces of her Etruscan vines. Well aware that Umbria oozed streams galore and was positively bursting with natural springs, woodland floors carpeted with hellebores and spurges, anemones and violets were not for Claudia. She felt her shoulders slump. How long, Drusilla, before I can leave this godforsaken wilderness? Come to think of it, what on earth possessed her to leave Rome? Bloody Rollo! He was her bailiff, for gods' sake, he was paid to sort things out!

'I ask you!' She addressed the parrot. 'What's the point of employing a chap if he can't handle the odd spot of arson?'

'Erk?' The feathers on the bird's crest perked up.

'You heard. Arson.' Except I thought we'd got that bugger taped.

When the first news of the arson attacks filtered through, Claudia had blithely dismissed the whole sordid business out of hand. You'd be surprised at the number of people who get a thrill from sending flaming arrows into a fully stocked barn or tipping a pot of blazing naphtha over a neighbour's thatched roof. Hence some pea-brained moron torching olive groves was by no means noteworthy. Until he started in on vineyards. Not any old vineyards, either. These, if you please, stood adjacent to her own.

Now arson isn't difficult. Not with barns, not with roofs and especially not with olives. That lovely oily bark flares up in next to no time, and if you synchronize your blaze with a nice strong wind, you've got a fireball whipping through the groves like breath from a dragon. But vines?

'That, my little lovebird, is where matey came a cropper.'

The bird stretched out a shiny black wing and tipped its head on one side.

'Arson in a vineyard is a labour-intensive exercise. It takes time to hack through the thick thorn hedge, time to smear oil on the newly pruned vines and even more time to stop and fire each one individually.'

In consequence, although he hadn't been caught, a good description of the arsonist was circulating. So what was Rollo's problem? What was behind that scribbled, secretive note, *'Urgent, come at once'*?

With April fast approaching, a month almost entirely devoted to games and festivals, Claudia had been loath to leave, but Rollo was not a man to cry wolf. However, if this *was* purely a request for personal approval to prune a few vines – in other words, if I've been run off the road by a gang of rowdies, had my bones battered, my flesh pulverized, my cat scared to death and a corpse thrown at me, all in the name of administration – then you can kiss your giblets goodbye, Rollo, and that's just for starters!

'Ouch!'

She snatched her finger back and sucked at the point where the beak had nipped, but the parrot merely winked in a particularly coarse manner then bobbed up and down on its perch.

'I'll have you know, you red-beaked budgie, it's not easy being a widow.'

Good life in Illyria, she hadn't married Gaius Seferius for his looks! He was old, he was a ball of blubber and the state of his dental work left a lot to be desired, but the wine merchant had one massive thing in his favour. He was rich. Filthy, stinking, rolling-in-it rich and when he'd done the decent thing and shuffled off his mortal coil rather earlier than expected, Gaius had then done something to exceed even Claudia's happy expectations. He'd bypassed his whinging relatives and willed the entire estate to his twenty-four-year-old widow.

Really, she thought, she had been very fond of Gaius.

Bless him, he'd left her enough money to last her a lifetime, provided, at the rate she was spending it, she did not expect to see thirty! Unfortunately, even that inheritance would come to naught unless she extricated herself from this trial fiasco. Dear Diana, so many problems had piled up in the seven months since Gaius had popped off; they were multiplying faster than rabbits in warm weather and she was hanging on by her fingernails as it was. She certainly had no intention of watching the business go under simply because some turnip got himself knifed on her doorstep.

'You enjoy my breakfast, yes?'

The voice in her ear made her jump. It belonged, she saw now, to the same man with long shaggy hair and check pantaloons she'd mistaken earlier for a servant.

'I am Taranis.' Vertical crevices appeared in his wide cheeks, which one had to assume was a smile. 'I am Celt.'

'About your breakfast . . . I thought – '

'Ach.' He dismissed it with a slicing motion of his hand. 'You think I am slave? I let you into secret, you are not the first.'

No, she thought, probably not. Slaves would be forced either to shave or to grow a proper beard, whereas she had a feeling this stubble was a regular feature. Also, slaves would be steered towards the bath house now and again.

'You no recognize me from murder scene? I understand. Dead man come as shock. Me, I am friend of Tulola. You?' Black eyes loitered on the fullness of her breasts, made more prominent since the borrowed tunic was a tad tight across the bosom and therefore tended to emphasize the curves.

'Just passing through.'

His eyebrows met in the middle. 'You are lost?'

Claudia explained about her clash with the thugs.

'Savages!' He spat in the dust. 'They rape you, yes?'

'They rape me, not on their bloody lives!'

'Oh.' The gleam went out of the Celt's eyes. 'I need to piss.' He made a cross between a bow and a hop, no doubt the sort of gesture that had evolved in those Barbarian climes to imply courtesy but which, in reality, was probably just another means to keep warm.

Since the parrot was now engrossed in preening its

mate, Claudia moved across to the fishpond, where graceful filaments of algae floated in the margins. Minerva's orchestrating this, she thought wryly. Yesterday was her festival and while artisans and doctors, scribes and schoolmasters left votive offerings up on the Capitol, and while white-robed priests led young heifers to the sacrificial blade by their gilded and beribboned horns, forceful, striding Minerva was playing practical jokes on those who'd displeased her. Claudia dabbled her fingers in the fishpond and decided that, if not top of the goddess's hit list, she probably ran a close second.

The ripples that nibbled the surface were suddenly reminiscent of the ones that lapped Genua harbour in the days when she used to dance for a living. Days when a tunic of this quality, regardless of colour, would have been an object to die for. Kill for, even. The sort of tunic that, had one come into her possession, she could have sold for her keep for a month. A whole month without leers and jeers, sticky hands and mouthed obscenities . . . She shuddered involuntarily. Thank the gods, those days were way, way behind her. A spot of forgery here, a new identity there, topped by marriage to a fat and unsuspecting wine merchant – what could go wrong? Claudia rested her chin in her hands. Marcus Cornelius Orbilio, that's what! What is it with life, she thought. You map it all out, bury your past so deep that, in comparison, the Emperor's Spanish silver mines are mere scratches on the surface . . . then along *he* comes. High in the Security Police and with a nose like a truffle-hog, that damned patrician (born rich, born respectable, what does he know about life in the gutter?) comes snooping and discovered that dancing wasn't the only way she'd earned her living.

A squad of blue tits descended to search the burgeoning leaves for grubs as Claudia's deliberations projected themselves into the future. Should this Macer fellow prove unequal to the task of investigating violent deaths, it's not beyond the realms of possibility that he invites the Security Police to help – and I can do without it being made common knowledge, thank you very much, that there were certain other services on offer in Genua, apart from the dancing! Oh yes, she thought, as the tiny birds twittered and quarrelled and performed their acrobatics, the very last thing I need in my well-ordered life is the intrusion of some wavy-haired aristocrat with a twinkle in his eye who thinks that if he covers his mouth with the back of his hand, no one notices he's laughing. Not that Claudia remembered what he looked like, of course. Good gracious, no, it was just that . . .

A shadow fell across the fishpond and a second reflection appeared in the water. Dark, sultry, her heavy breasts heaving, the girl who'd hung around the atrium yesterday leaned low over the sweet-smelling flags. The ripples on the water could take no blame for the contortions in her face.

'I know what you're up to,' she hissed. 'But you won't get away with it.'

Pretending to study the irises, Claudia watched the scowling reflection for several seconds. Presumably another sister – nine, ten years younger than Tulola? – but, in true Pictor style, no one had bothered to introduce them and any reluctance on this madam's part wasn't down to shyness.

'You just watch me,' she replied evenly.

Sulkyboots was unfazed. 'No,' she rasped. 'You watch *me*.' She kicked a pebble into the fishpond and both reflections disintegrated.

Then suddenly the girl's breath was hot on Claudia's cheek and she smelled sweet aniseed from her mouth.

'Interfere and I'll kill you.'

A small obsidian blade was suddenly thrust in front of Claudia's eyes.'

'I mean it,' she spat. 'Fuck with me and I'll kill you.'

III

Balbilla squeezed past the counter and peered up the main street for the umpteenth time. That fog had lifted, you could see a long way, but there was still no sign of Fronto. She chewed her lip and frowned.

'What's wrong, love?'

'Nothing, Dad.' Umpteen times they'd had that exchange, too.

High noon and market day at that, the street was as busy as it ever got. Word was, once you could hardly move through the crush, leastways, not without getting your bum pinched, but Balbilla had been spared that indignity. When the Princeps diverted the road, she was just eight years old and it had been left to her father to explain why folk didn't travel this way no more. And, later, why her family and friends had moved away.

'We won't have to move, will we, Dad?'

Her mam had died giving birth to her brother, so it had been just the three of them, Balbilla and her Dad and the baby, and even he'd died before he turned three. She didn't want to have to move on.

''Course not, Bill.' She remembered the way her father had ruffled her hair. 'We're Tarsulani, we don't go no place.'

And so they hadn't, but the trade from his shop had

dwindled. Once, long ago, he ran a profitable clothes dealership. Then he moved into the second-hand market. And five years ago, around the time she met Fronto, he'd been reduced to selling rags.

Her nose wrinkled as she squinted into the sun. All around Tarsulae the same daily scenes were being enacted. Kiddies playing, dogs grubbing, spits turning, gossips embroidering the meagre news. There were mingling smells of over-used cooking oil, badly tanned hides, temple incense and yeasty bread. By the Mausoleum Gate, the little beggar girl who'd been blinded by her mother so she could earn more rattled her bowl, and opposite the Temple of Vulcan, the brickmaker was bad-mouthing his pregnant wife, taking out on her the fact that he had no livelihood left in this ramshackle town. Sneaking out from the basilica was the advocate's bow-legged secretary, off to tup his boss's wife while the lawyer was engaged with a client, and down by the tavern was that new Prefect, she'd forgotten his name, adjusting his chinstrap before clambering into the saddle. But no Fronto.

'Dad, I've got to nip home, all right?'

It was one of his bad days, she felt awful at leaving him, but she just had to know. Besides. There was something she had to tell Fronto. Something important.

'Want me to close up?'

Her father shook his grey face vigorously. In all his life, he'd never shut during the day and he wouldn't start now, sick or not.

'Well, I'll be back soon as I can.'

Chances were, no customers would call to bother him, and if they did he wouldn't notice. He spent a lot of time sleeping now she'd got him that draught from the herbalist.

'Why don't the old sod give up like any normal bloke?' Fronto had been most indignant when she'd told him she intended to help out in the shop. 'Croesus, I've offered him dosh enough to see his days out, he don't need to work.'

'It's charity, love, and you know how Dad feels about hand-outs.' Stubborn was too kind a word! Many's the time she'd begged him to move in with them. (Well, she could clear it with Fronto later, couldn't she?)

'You've got a nice place, Bill, and don't think I don't appreciate the offer, but this here's my home. Was my father's before me, and his father's before that.'

Balbilla sighed. Four generations had slogged to build up the business and a whim of the Emperor's knocked it flat. Just like that.

Not that Fronto let the matter rest. 'What'll it look like, Billi, my wife working in a dump like that? Jupiter alone knows where half those rags have come from, and you know what tongues are round here. Look at Fronto, they'll say. Can't keep his young wife satisfied.'

Balbilla giggled. 'Well, I know better, don't I!'

The age gap never bothered her, even with him being nearly as old as her Dad. The only thing that made her self-conscious was him having a position and all. She paused at the gate. Even if she weren't quite sure what that position was . . . All the same, she thought, hurrying on, this was her father they were talking about.

'I can't leave him in the lurch.'

'Of course you can, you soft dollop.' Whenever Fronto scooped her into his arms, she felt six years old, loved and protected. 'I've worked my balls off to give you the best, Billi. Tell him to sling his bloody hook.'

How could she, though? She'd stood by while his family, his town, his business and now finally his health had trickled away. She owed her father that much.

Dad's right, though, Balbilla thought, stepping into the cool of the colonnade. It *is* a nice house. Grander than anything I ever expected, but then Fronto was in the army twenty years, he was bound to have a stash put by, stands to reason. Each time she looked around she felt the same tingle of excitement. A garden of her own! Servants, fancy linens, rings for every finger. Even a wet-nurse for the twins! And you wouldn't have thought it of Fronto, not to look at him.

Yet for all the gilded stucco and pretty mosaics, the house was nothing without her husband. Balbilla swallowed hard. It was dead important, too, what she had to tell him. She searched around for a rough edge of her nibbled nails to chew. He's never gone off without saying nothing before. Idolizes them babies, he does, always tucks them up when he can – or at least said so when he can't. She thought back to yesterday. What was it he'd said? There was work a bit north, that's right. Nothing much, and he'd be back by supper time. She remembered that last bit. Back by supper time. Because he liked his food, did Fronto, and she always tried to give him a good meal to go to bed on.

When he was home, that is. Since the army he didn't really have a job – not what Dad called a proper job, any road. Private commissions Fronto calls them. Nothing regular, but he always treats his Billikins to a new tunic or a silver bangle when he comes home, and adds a bit to the house – a bust or a frieze or something – so it pays handsome. Whatever it is.

Well, I suppose I'll have to wait before giving him me message. Balbilla shrugged her shoulders, kissed her sleeping infants then trudged back up the hill towards her father's shop. I expect he's got held up, she thought as she passed the flushed face of the advocate's secretary sneaking back into the law courts, and we'll have a good old laugh when I tell him how worried I was.

'You daft pudden,' he'll say. 'You know I gets called out all hours.'

Oh, he was a popular man was her Fronto. She just wished she knew why he hadn't come home last night.

Watched pots never boil, this is a fact. They simmer gently for hours and hours, then the instant you turn your back, over they go, leaving a godawful mess for some poor sod to mop up. So staring into space with your fingers crossed is unlikely to improve a cat's navigational facilities; neither, Claudia acknowledged ruefully, is self-imposed starvation. While the midday meal had come and gone, who knows, there might be scraps in the dining room?

Well, there was a scrap. Of sorts. On the couch beneath the window a knot of squirming limbs and tangled linen writhed like serpents, and a man's doughy buttocks rose and fell in the grip of long, hennaed talons. Claudia spun on her heel, but a woman's voice restrained her.

'Don't rush off, sweetie. I've been meaning to catch you.'

Claudia's fingers remained gripped round the door latch as she considered Tulola's definition of the verb 'catch'. 'Gooseberries were never my favourite fruit,' she said to the woodwork. 'You can join me in the garden when you're not quite so . . . busy.'

'Who's busy?' Tulola disentangled herself and stretched sensuously. The Egyptian hairstyle was quite unruffled apart from the fringe. 'You recognize Timoleon, don't you?'

'Not from that angle.'

Claudia studied the Ganymede frescos as the hunk adjusted his tunic and then, to her surprise, he began swaggering, as though he was waiting for something. God knows what. Did he expect her to go all-of-a-flutter at his magnificent physique, his jewels, his finery? Because, if so, he was in for something of a shock. Far from handsome, his face was battle-scarred, his body musclebound and while, yes, the clothes and gewgaws were expensive, they were ostentatious and gaudy. In fact, the air he gave off was of a man going rapidly to seed, and for a chap on the good side of thirty, it did not bode well.

Tulola ran her finger down his cheek. 'You'll know him best as Scrap Iron.'

Now she recognized him. It was the hair that fooled her, he'd grown it long and dyed it yellow, and in the year since the gladiator had retired, he'd laid down more fat than was good for him. 'A true son of Rome.'

Immune to sarcasm, the cocky sod puffed up even further. 'That's me right enough. Fifty-seven crowns in me eight years. Show me another bugger who's done that!'

'An impressive record.' Claudia felt a pang of conscience. For all his trumpery, you couldn't fault his talents in the arena and it wasn't Timoleon's fault she was about to be handed over to the army. Then she remembered his reputation. He was an arrogant son of a bitch, a trouble-maker on and off the sand.

'Cold steel and no quarter, that's my motto.'

I know, Timoleon, I know. You earned your laurels by sparing no one. Which included the life of a fighter who'd once spared you at the point of his sword.

'Did you see me pitched against Strongarm?' He jumped up and began to demonstrate. 'Billed as the best in the business, he was.'

'Oh, you're the best, sweetie,' purred Tulola, but the gladiator was back in the arena.

'Typical sodding Samnite, hiding behind that great shield of his and trying to whack me with just that one arm exposed. Strongarm, geddit? But I'm quick, me. Nips behind – '

Claudia had switched off long ago, intrigued with the harem's relationship with one another. Talk about claustrophobic. Did they know they were in competition? Was it the competition that kept it hot? Or had, as Tulola's remark intimated, each one been led to believe he was special?

' – cuts his leg straps and spears him where he lay! Strongarm, my arse! Tripped by his own leg greaves, silly sod.'

'Fascinating.'

'Then there was that time I – '

'Time?' Claudia jumped on the word. 'Glad you reminded me, I'm meeting – ' think, think ' – Sergius.'

Who? Claudia, can't you, for once, think before you open your stupid mouth?

'Lord, yes. I'd forgotten all about the show, as well.'

Show? What show? Tulola had finally detached herself from the gladiator. 'We'll lead the way, it's quite difficult otherwise.'

What is?

'Huh! You won't catch Scrap Iron ankle-deep in elk shit.' Timoleon seemed to think he'd made a joke and bellowed with laughter. 'But hurry back, we've got un-finished business.' He emphasized his point with a lewd gesture, which somehow managed to encompass Claudia in the motion.

Tulola blew him a kiss. 'Quite something, isn't he?' she said in her low, husky drawl, and Claudia forced herself to be objective about it.

Once, maybe, she acknowledged. By definition, the retarii had to be fast, because theirs was the most dangerous role of all. Bareheaded and armourless, they had only net, trident and dagger to protect themselves, and once they were cornered they stood no chance. Claudia had watched Scrap Iron in action – indeed, had backed him in many a fight. A real daredevil, provoking his lumbering, but superior, opponents by a courageous exhibition of darting and diving, slashing and thrusting until the weight of their armour eventually exhausted them. A true professional, he made it look easy, but Claudia knew Timoleon would have spent hour after agonizing hour practising the moves that had made him famous – and that had also saved his life. She gave a non-committal grunt in reply as they passed from the cool of the atrium into the warmth of the courtyard, as

37

her mind tried to evaluate what type of woman blatantly manipulates several men at a time, pitting one against the other in her sexual politics. Did Tulola, in her arrogance, ever stop to consider the danger?

By the fountain, Taranis sat slumped with an old felt hat shading his head. Tulola nudged him with her foot as they passed. 'Wake up, my little blue warrior.' She turned to Claudia. 'Sometimes, if I ask nicely, he'll paint himself with woad in bed. Quite a turn on. Hey!' She raised her voice to the Celt. 'It's time for Sergius' show.'

'Ach.' The battered hat shook from side to side. 'You go. Tell me about it after.'

'Honestly.' Tulola linked her arm through her companion's as she led the way to the orchard. 'For a man who's supposed to be supplying bears for next season, you can't get him near the zoo. Anyway, sweetie, what I wanted to ask you is, how much will you take for your henchman?'

Claudia passed her faltering step as a trip over a paving slab. 'The driver's hired help, I'm afraid.'

'Not that ugly lug, I'm talking about your Gaul.'

I know.

'Forty gold pieces? He's very handsome and, ooh, those muscles!'

Bumble-bees searched the last of the pale pink blossoms, and a kitchen slave with a baby on her hip gathered basil and purslane and mint.

'I'm afraid', Claudia spoke in a confidential whisper, 'I can't sell him.'

'Aha! The stallion services your own stables.'

'No, no. I *can't* sell him. He's – how can I put this?'

– she glanced up at the unfurling leaves for inspiration '– incomplete, poor boy.'

Tulola's arm recoiled like a striking snake. 'A eunuch? That's no bloody use!'

Claudia nodded sympathetically. 'Tragic, isn't it?'

As they climbed the steps of the terrace, she calculated that it would cost her two gold pieces to keep his trap shut, possibly three since pride was involved. Men! They get het up over such trifles, don't they? Not that it was Junius who concerned Claudia at this moment.

'Earlier, down by the fishpond, your baby sister showed me one of her charming little keepsakes.'

'I don't have a sister – oh, do you mean Euphemia?'

'The sort who causes more ructions than a dozen earthquakes?'

Tulola laughed. 'That's her and she belongs to Alis, not me.'

Um. 'Belongs?'

'Euphemia's her sister.'

Good life in Illyria, what a turn-up for the books! Where Alis was pale, Euphemia was dusky; where Alis was high-breasted, Euphemia was voluptuous, and where Alis was respectability personified, Euphemia had temptress written all over her.

'Half-sister, really,' Tulola explained, steering her guest through the labyrinth of pens and sheds, barns and outhouses. 'Alis' father divorced her mother on grounds of adultery. Apparently it was only a matter of days from the mother marrying her lover that Euphemia was spared the stigma of bastardy.'

I'm not sure the moody baggage entirely escaped, thought Claudia, with the pungent smell of animals and ordure hitting her full blast as they turned the corner into an open yard. Say what you like about Timoleon, he had a fair point. Dainty leather sandals with open toes would not have been Claudia's first choice of footwear.

'Whatever she said, sweetie, just ignore the silly cow, she's – '

'Ladies!' The ancestry of the man who greeted them with an extravagant flourish of his hands was beyond question. Only a true Etruscan stood that tall, moved with such grace but, like all Etruscans, his looks were marred by the distinctive double bump on the bridge of his nose.

'Our trainer, Corbulo,' purred Tulola. 'Scrumptious, isn't he?'

No, but unlike the other two there was at least an intriguing quality about him, enhanced by the contrast between high cheekbones, which would sit well on a prince, and the horny hands of what was unquestionably a son of the soil. Because for all the splendour of his spangled costume, when he performed that theatrical gesture, the calluses were plain for all to see.

'You are here to witness the performance to end all performances, is that it?' Appreciative grey eyes twinkled at Claudia.

'Wouldn't miss it for the world.' Miss Euphemia Sulkyboots would have to wait.

'This way, then.'

They followed him past a penned rhinoceros, two caged lions and an enclosure packed with beady-eyed ostriches, their sharp beaks barely out of pecking range. Corbulo fell into step with Claudia and grinned.

'Not afraid of those Mauritanian chickens, are you?'

'Let's say the prospect of them being turned into fans perks me up no end.'

They were passing a particularly ugly warthog when Tulola stopped abruptly. 'Hey! Barea!' On the far side of the ostrich compound, a skinny individual in a yellow tunic and slicked-back hair was leading a black stallion in a circle by a rope. 'Come and watch!'

The horse-breaker signalled acknowledgement, handed the rope to a bald man and cleared the fence like a trained athlete. Oh, for gods' sake! thought Claudia. How many of them are there? What goes through Barea's head when he smells Timoleon's unguent on his lover, or are his brains as sparse as his flesh? Does he care? Or was the way she drapes a proprietorial arm around his neck reward enough? Corbulo, busily inspecting a line between two sets of blocks, seemed oblivious. To his left and below them, a palisade enclosed a group of snoozing crocodiles and to his right a curious giraffe poked its head through a special opening in the roof.

'Hello, lover, who's your friend?' Claudia placed the accent as coming from the Iberian peninsular, but couldn't pin it closer than that.

'Don't pretend you don't know,' admonished Tulola, playfully biting the young man's ear. 'You were there this morning when Claudia had that dreadful encounter with the dead man. You heard the screams.'

Barea's eyes glistened with curiosity and, like the Celt before him, he seemed to find the prospect of violence exciting. His hands began to caress Tulola's hips. 'I trust the experience hasn't scarred you?' he asked, not waiting for an answer before his tongue danced with Tulola's.

Sweet Janus! I thought I was disturbing Tulola in the

dining room earlier, but clearly it's Tulola who's disturbed! In the valley below, gazelle bounded gracefully and smoke from a charcoal kiln rose high into the air; few cross-eyed cats slunk along the waysides.

'Feeling better, now?' Sergius emerged from one of the sheds and made his way down the steps to join Claudia as a gang of labourers lugged an oversized couch into the yard.

'No.'

'That's the spirit.' The grin he gave was sincerity itself and, despite her circumstances, Claudia laughed inwardly. *Smile at the nice lady and she won't stick a knife in you.* Oh, Sergius, Sergius. I wonder what your face will look like once I've slapped out my lawsuit.

Tulola jemmied herself free of the horse-breaker and sauntered over to join her brother and his guest. 'Barea can't stay. Some trouble with the gelding.'

Claudia glanced over her shoulder. Trouble was an understatement. The rope had caught and the bald man was being pulled round the ring on his stomach as the black stallion reared and bucked in a cloud of dust. Poor sod. If he didn't get trampled, he'd probably choke to death.

The couch was set down in the middle of the courtyard and a table placed beside it. When this had been piled high with fruit and cakes, Sergius brought his arm down as a signal to start. Ears flapping, a brightly costumed elephant lumbered towards the line Corbulo had been inspecting, which, to Claudia's astonishment, was no drawing after all, but an enormously sturdy rope. When the trainer swished his baton – up, across and back – Claudia drew in her breath. She was, she realized with a tingle of excitement, about to witness something far in excess of ordinary.

Slowly, very slowly, with the gems on his coat glittering in the afternoon sun, the elephant obeyed Corbulo's commands. Clambering up the blocks and without so much as changing pace, he marched across the tightrope, down the blocks the other side and made for the table. Then, like the good Roman that he was, he rolled on to the couch and proceeded to help himself from the goodies spread before him. Stunned by the performance, Claudia nevertheless drew the line at petting the wrinkly lump, which Tulola and her brother had rushed to do, until gradually she became conscious of the grey eyes of the trainer concentrated upon her.

'Impressed by my Abyssinian cow?'

Who wouldn't be? 'Your team is riding into history, my friend.'

'My – ? Oh, the labourers were just drafted in to help with the exhibition.' He tossed his baton into the air and caught it as it fell. 'I always work alone.' The elephant was revelling in the praise, his button eyes twinkling as he demolished bun after bun. 'Can't stand interruptions, it interferes with the training, the concentration, mucks everything up.'

'Then your talents will make you one very rich man, Corbulo.'

Irritation clouded his face. 'This isn't about money,' he snapped, then nodded towards the surrounding sheds. 'You know, I've trained monkeys to ride chariots, leopards to sleep with hares and when Barea's finished with it, I'll have that Spanish spitfire dancing to the flute.'

'And is your passion purely confined to animals?' She was only partly teasing.

'Oh no.' A fire lit his tundra-dark eyes. 'Since you ask – '

The flirtation got no further. The little blonde slave girl, the one who'd screamed her bloody head off this morning, came running up. She shot Claudia a nervous glance, gave her a wide berth and ground to a halt in front of Sergius.

'Please, sir, it's the Prefect,' she said breathlessly, darting another furtive glance in Claudia's direction. 'He's here.'

IV

Marcus Cornelius Orbilio was woken by the sound of hammering. In Rome, the city that never sleeps and refuses to let anyone else sleep either, hammering was not unusual, night being the only time goods traffic was permitted through the streets. In consequence, much of the Emperor's massive restoration programme had to be undertaken by torchlight, and if you add on the constant throb of axles being whacked, wheels bumped, sacks thumped, you're in for a fun-packed show.

This hammering, however, was altogether different. It seemed to come from within the walls of his own house. Struggling to sit up, Orbilio realized the pounding was closer than he thought. Mighty Mars! It was inside his skull!

He flopped back on the bed and groaned. His mouth was furred up, his eyeballs tender, and the same instinct that told him it was a long haul to daybreak scoffed at his chances of getting back to sleep. Mother of Tarquin, every joint, every bone ached to the marrow; his skin was dry and his gut felt like someone had plaited his intestines. Putting tentative fingertips to pounding temples, Orbilio was forced to face facts. There was no remedy known to medical science for the condition that racked his youthful body and he cursed silently.

Surely, in this golden age of peace and prosperity, a cure for hangover could not be that difficult?

A chill breath of wind brushed his cheeks and he noticed he hadn't closed the shutters. His blurred vision could just about determine a reddish tinge to the sky and his mouth turned down. Another oaf, clumsy with his tallow and, whoosh!, up goes another tenement, killing as many occupants when the building collapses as are killed in the fire itself, the poor sods trapped by the same heavy safety chains they needed for their doors in the first place. Did the landlords care? Did they hell! A few new timbers, a bit of plaster and, hey presto, here's a brand new tenement; we can charge double the rent.

Regardless of what he professes, Augustus doesn't give a shit. He makes the odd sop, like limiting storeys to six, but what good's that when tenants sleep four to a bed, there's just one toilet on the ground floor and water has to be hauled from the street? What would it take to form a fire corps, eh? Remus, a million people are crammed in this city. Fires break out four, five, six times a day! If the Emperor truly cared about his people, he'd forget lavishing the spoils of war on stone and marble and organize cohorts to man pumps and form chains –

Orbilio stopped short. *Jupiter in heaven, this is treason!*

Worse, he suddenly became aware of a figure buried under the covers beside him. He felt a trickle of sweat run down his forehead. Suppose – oh, Janus! Suppose he'd been thinking aloud? Soft snores reassured him she was sleeping deeply, before a second question formed on his lips.

Who the hell was she?

He would not, he swore, touch another drop. Not one more drop. He pinched the bridge of his nose. Croesus, he thought he had his drinking under control, but there were times lately when chunks of his life disappeared without trace. Small chunks, but they were missing none the less. Like tonight . . .

The intensity of the blaze changed the oblong of light in the wall from red to yellow, then a splintering crash told him the army had been called in and were doing what they normally did. They grabbed long poles and tore the building down. Far quicker. Far easier. And it wasn't their fault, was it, if families were trapped inside?

He sighed with envy. In an ideal world, it would be nice to close one's mind to life's less appealing aspects, but Orbilio had discovered long ago that his conscience was a shrew, nagging him like a fishwife, prodding him with her bony finger whenever he wanted to be idle. He could feel her now – prod, prod, prod – and she wouldn't stop until she got what she wanted.

The most cursory glance assured him his bedmate wasn't Attica – even bombed, he wouldn't be that stupid. Without doubt he'd enjoyed their brief dalliance, teaching her things her pretty little head had never dreamed of even though she was married herself, until it slipped out who her husband was.

Gisco. The charioteer. Gisco, whose jealous nature and volatile temperament were legendary. In fact, the last man who'd forced Gisco to wear the cuckold's horns had been found in a back alley, bound and gagged, with his balls tied round his neck . . .

When he'd learned that, he'd bundled Attica into her

clothes and out the side door in one single motion, but for Marcus Cornelius Orbilio, twenty-five years old and so healthy he was verging on immortality, the flame of Venus burned strong.

Thus – lying beside a total stranger, as the tenement fire snuffed out a dozen lives and wrecked scores more – he was able to run his hands abstractedly through his hair and tell his conscience to piss off. He was young and single and had no dependants, why shouldn't he sow his wild oats? Then he felt it again. Prod, prod, prod. The fishwife had picked up the word 'single' and was throwing it back at him.

'You're an aristocrat, Marcus, whose ambition burns as fiercely as that inferno in the valley below. To pass through those ivory-inlaid doors of the Senate, my boy, you need a wife to your name.'

Mother of Tarquin, he needed the reminder like he needed the hammering in his head, but one thing was certain. Never again would he make the mistake of letting his family contract a political alliance. Divorced, thankfully, from a profligate wife who ran off to Lusitania with a sea captain, he resolved that the next time he married, it would be for love.

Orbilio rolled over on to his stomach. In a bid to circumvent the rules, he had cultivated the acquaintance of one Paulus Vibius Corvinus, ex-tribune, ex-prefect, ex-consul. Corvinus was not the most affable of men and sucking up to people was not Orbilio's strong point, but if it meant smoothing a primrose path to the Senate House, so be it, and only last night the ex-tribune, ex-prefect, ex-consul had confirmed to him personally that, in his eyes, merit was paramount and Orbilio need have no further qualms.

It was on the strength of those wheels being oiled that Orbilio had got so comprehensively oiled himself. No, sir. He would not be coerced into marriage again, not even by his own uncle, and especially not to that Aemelia creature his uncle was pushing at him. The girl was fourteen years old, for gods' sake! He rolled on to his back again. The appeal of pubescence was lost on Orbilio. He wanted a companion, a friend, a lover. A woman to laugh with, cry with, grow a wrinkled old rind with, not a mechanical producer of sons. With Attica he'd enjoyed vigorous sex flavoured with the fun of conniving and the spice of forbidden fruit, but what he needed, what he desperately missed (and it sounded corny but there you are), what he needed was the love of a good woman.

Or, in Orbilio's case, the love of a bad woman.

A woman, for instance, whose untamed locks had a shine you could shave in, whose spicy perfume sent shockwaves down a man's spine, whose very image haunted him from sun-up to sun-down – after which, the pain increased tenfold.

When he took a woman like that into his arms, there would be none of the hurried thrusts and quick gratification he'd sought with Attica. He would light lamps, thousands of them, on every level and every ledge, every surface and every sill and, in the flickering heat, he would kiss her eyelashes and drown in the dip of her collarbone. He would explore every inch of her skin until his tongue tingled with the taste of her sweat, then let his nose wallow in the scent of her curls – long damp tendrils that clung to her breasts, short damp tendrils that led down to heaven.

The moon would rise and the moon would fall before he was through, and there would be no question of forgetting her name as he sometimes had with Attica.

He would whisper it, over and over again. Claudia Seferius. Claudia Seferius. He would run his tongue gently round her ear, feel the flutter of her breasts. Claudia Seferius. Claudia Seferius. The featherlight touch of his fingertips would part her thighs, pulsing, pulsing, the drumbeat of their hearts setting the tempo. Claudia Seferius. Claudia Seferius. Faster and faster their bodies would sway until finally in unison . . .

The knock made him jump. 'Sorry to disturb you, sir. There is a messenger outside who says he cannot wait until morning.'

Shit! 'No matter, Tingi, I wasn't asleep.' Now wasn't that the truth?

Grateful to the darkness which hid the throbbing thickness between his legs, Orbilio opened the door to his Libyan steward.

'The young man is also in rather a distressed state, sir.'

He recognized him the second he set eyes on him. Standing in the shadows, that muscular form was unmistakable, despite the bandage round his head, and Orbilio felt his heart lurch.

He was never sure of the relationship between them –

Claudia called him a boy, but here stood a man, barely younger than himself, the slave whose eyes never wavered from his mistress and who hung closer than her own shadow. Jealousy alone, though, had not rearranged

Orbilio's heartbeat. The injuries Junius had sustained might well be mirrored on Claudia.

Drawing himself up to his not inconsiderable height and throwing a towel round his waist, Orbilio listened to the words tumbling out of the exhausted Gaul. Pinch me, I am dreaming.

'Mistress Seferius, you say, is accused of murder?'

Junius nodded sullenly.

'Of a complete stranger?'

He nodded again, and Orbilio was no fool. The slave liked him as much as he, himself, liked the Gaul. How it must stick in his craw, this visit!

'And she doesn't know you've sent for me?'

'No. Sir.' The sir was either an afterthought, forgivable under the circumstances, or it was added as an insult.

Orbilio met the stare head on and gave no quarter in his own. 'Give me the address again.'

It was with a satisfying sense of mischief that he despatched the weary bodyguard to saddle up, then nudged the sleeping beauty in his bed.

Nothing, not a moan, not a groan, not a twitch. Dammit, where did he get her from? Vaguely he remembered doing the rounds of several taverns, but surely he'd not lowered himself to picking up a common whore? Praise the gods, the quality of the garments on the floor set his mind at rest. At least he'd had the sense to pick up a courtesan! Catching his reflection in the glass, unshaven, sunken-eyed, with his head coming off at the hinges, it was a miracle he'd been any use to her, except those scattered clothes spoke volumes . . .

'Up you get.'

He gave her bottom a gentle kick and realized he hadn't paid her. Remus! He drew on a fresh woollen tunic. What was the going rate? Tavern whores charge eight asses, but a high-class hooker? Think, man, think!

Sluicing water over his face and wincing as the cold water dribbled down his arm to his elbow, Orbilio heard himself humming. Claudia Seferius! In trouble up to her beautiful, kissable lips and who's the chap to pull her out of the mire? The humming turned into a whistle. Murder isn't necessarily a job for the Security Police and the Security Police isn't necessarily confined to murder cases, but it *was* what Orbilio did best. He towelled himself dry and decided the stubble on his chin could wait. With his widespread network of informants and spies, he'd solve it in no time – then let's see how many of my letters she returns!

Lacing his boot, he recalled the last time he saw her, the wind whipping her curls about as she stood on the deck in Sicily. Wherever she walked, that woman, trouble walked beside her, and that day had been no exception. Barely one hour before she had escaped death by a cat's whisker, yet to see her in the prow of that freighter, proud eyes flashing, her back as straight as any arrowshaft, it was almost impossible to believe the evidence. A man thought only of the liquid swish of her skirts, the molten folds of cotton over her breasts.

Scheduled to sail with her, Orbilio had instead been called away at the last moment on the Governor's orders. What had happened during that voyage from Sicily? What had caused her to return his letters? Dammit, the air sizzled whenever they were in the same room together, what had –

'Dammit, you! Up!' Harshly he pulled the bedclothes off the slumbering form. The chill night air would wake her more surely than his voice.

The woman in his bed began to groan like an ungreased axle, clawing at the bedclothes, but his grip was the stronger. 'You're out of here,' he snapped, 'and I mean now!'

He shook bronze into his hand. 'Ten sesterces should see you right.'

The moaning stopped. 'Did you say ... *ten sesterces*?'

Orbilio rolled his eyes. There was no time to argue. 'Twenty, then, you money-grabbing bitch!'

More coins showered the bed.

'But get one thing straight. Don't sniff round me again, because no one rips Marcus Cornelius off twice. Besides,' he got hold of the bed frame and tilted, 'you're a bloody poor lay.'

The woman tumbled out with an ignominious bump as the bedframe clattered back down.

'Any whore worth her salt leaves a man with a memory of his night gymnastics, but you – '

He stopped abruptly. Sitting bolt upright on the tessellated floor, outrage bulging her forty-year-old eyes, was the heavy-hipped wife of Paulus Vibius Corvinus, ex-tribune, ex-prefect, ex-consul.

Orbilio produced his most disarming grin while his mind turned somersaults. 'Honoria, love – '

Quite how he'd ended up with his patron's wife in his bed remained a total blank, but it was fairly certain that by calling her a whore and a money-grabbing bitch, his prospects weren't as hot as he'd hoped.

Especially when she seemed intent on spitting

obscenities at him, interspersed with 'don't-you-think-you-can-treat-me-like-this-and-get-away-with-it' and 'you-haven't-heard-the-last-of-me-not-by-a-long-chalk'.

Shit.

He thought he caught other threats, including one that seemed to imply that those ivory-inlaid doors would be slammed in his face assuming he was ever foolish enough to contemplate such a move, but on the whole her tirade was drowned by his feeble (but insistent) protestations.

'Joke, you say?'

The vindictive bitch was deaf to his excuses as she snapped on her sandals.

'Well, if you fancy a joke, Marcus Cornelius Gigolo, how about the one that goes: You'll pay so dearly for what you called me, you scheming bastard, you won't have those twenty sesterces left to rub together by the time I've finished with you!'

With that, she slammed the door and he could hear her clip-clopping over the tiles like some old billy goat, which – having seen her by lamplight, chins sagging and her make-up streaked – she more than closely resembled.

His hands were shaking as he gathered together the rest of his possessions, grateful more than words could express for the long ride ahead. Bacchus, old boy, you are out of my life. Forever. Henceforth it's milk for Marcus. Goat's milk, cow's milk, camel's milk, dandelion bloody milk, just keep me away from the wine. He adjusted his belt and pulled tight his cloak just as Tingi knocked at the door.

Yet it was not via the door that Marcus Cornelius Orbilio finally made his exit.

It was through the open window, with Tingi's words still ringing in his ears as he legged it towards the stables.

'There's a Master Gisco in the atrium. Shall I show him in?'

V

Prefect Macer might not have been the highest star in the military firmament, but, by Jupiter, he was the brightest. From the elaborate embroidery on his scarlet tunic to the eye-watering shine on his hammered breastplate, the good soldier eliminated any doubts the good citizens of Umbria might harbour as to their place in society once he had entered the scene.

It was clear he also felt his star was in the ascendant.

For the short term, his bearing announced, I might be posted to the back of beyond, but don't get used to my face.

Basking in this new-found importance, he'd mustered the entire Pictor household in the banqueting hall first thing after breakfast and was now intent on establishing identities. Barea came from Lusitania, did he? Whereabouts? Which tribe did you say you belong to, Taranis? The Atrebates? Never heard of 'em. Negotiating for bears, eh? Is it true Caledonian beasts fight better? Well, I never – Scrap Iron, isn't it? What an honour! I must have seen you fight a dozen times . . .

Claudia found her gaze wandering towards the window. Perfect spring day, no trace of fog. She could make out patches of beans, cabbages, leeks and onions, pens of pigs and goats. Yellow blossoms of the cornelian cherries attracted bees. A reaping machine rusted happily against a buckthorn hedge. Chickens were scratching, oxen were being yoked, field workers were trekking off, hoes slung over their shoulders.

Cats, however, were still thin on the ground, especially Egyptian ones.

Claudia swallowed the lump in her throat, but another filled up the gap. Two days and two nights. Could it, after all, be more than the preponderance of foreign scents that had impeded her built-in tracking device? Could it . . . I mean, suppose . . . What if Drusilla really was . . . It was one hell of a bounce down the hill. Claudia had time to jump clear, but Drusilla? Back in January, one of her kittens worked its wobbly way on to the roof but, before Junius could rescue it, it had slipped. The feel of that tiny, twisted piece of velvet in Claudia's hands was agony beyond words . . . And even if Drusilla hadn't been hurt in the accident, there were the wolves . . .

Macer had moved on to the traditional where-were-you-when-the-lights-went-out sort of questions, but Timoleon was reluctant to relinquish centre stage. Good. Let the lump of gristle talk all he wants.

Unfortunately for Claudia, there had been no chance for that quiet word in Macer's ear, no chance to slip him a bung to ease her passage through these troubled waters. Upon arrival, he thrust his splendidly plumed helmet into the hands of a waiting lackey (his sideways expression, incidentally, making it abundantly clear that his opinion of Claudia's orange tunic ran along parallel lines to her own) and demanded to examine the corpse forthwith.

'I shall need complete access to the premises and after

that I have one or two primary investigations to make before I can begin the business of taking statements. I presume you can accommodate my officers overnight?'

He'd been addressing the head of the household, but it was Pallas who'd whispered 'Tulola can' under his breath.

Now, with the early-morning sunshine bouncing off his breastplate, the Prefect wriggled the hilt of his sword in its scabbard. 'Salvian, round up who's missing, we don't have all bloody day.'

A boy with the same thin nose and baby-fine hair, either a son or a nephew, stepped forward uncertainly. Like children's clothes, his armour seemed designed for him to grow into; it seemed impossible he could be a junior tribune already. He had barely taken two paces when the sound of male laughter barrelled round the lofty marbled banqueting hall.

'Then Barea said, "Er what?" To which I replied, "Since you're riding that stallion without a saddle, you err on the side of caution!" '

The voice was Corbulo's, but the exuberance on the faces of both him and Sergius was instantly subdued by Macer's frown. The trainer pulled up a stool to Claudia's left. Sergius took a stand between Alis and her ever-scowling sister.

'Is that everyone?' The Prefect fingered his gold medallions. 'Right, let's get down to – Croesus, where's Tulola? Salvian, lad, you had orders to fetch her, now jump to it!'

The coughs and the shuffles began. Pallas began instructing Barea on the seventeen ways to cook sucking-pig, Timoleon and the Celt stared each other out, Sergius laid his hand on his wife's shoulder. The look she gave him was of utter adoration and this, to Claudia's astonishment, was mirrored in his own. Euphemia glowered at the ceiling and pulled at her lower lip. What I wouldn't give to know what's going through your little noodle, thought Claudia. Or do you pull a knife on every visitor? Across the room, half hidden behind a pink marble column, the driver of the gig huddled among the slaves and servants fidgeting nervously. It was the first time she'd seen him since the accident, and his arm was in a sling.

Macer yawned and plucked a hair from his tunic. 'May I enquire why you keep the menagerie, sir?'

A flame of excitement flushed Sergius' face. 'Just as Augustus has brought peace and stability, you'll find audiences will tire of watching the same old animals trotting round the arena.' His eyes were dancing with animation and he leaned forward to emphasize his point. 'I intend to revolutionize all that, Macer. I shall be the talk of all Rome, there'll be nothing like it in the whole of the Empire!'

Claudia felt equally fired with enthusiasm, although not necessarily for the same reason. Her accuser's radical aims put him on the edge of a veritable fortune and the richer he was, the harder she could sue . . .

Stealing a glance at his wife, clearly hanging on his every word, she wondered what had attracted him to Alis. It was easy to see why Alis had fallen for those saturnine looks, but Sergius? Am I that cynical, Claudia wondered, that I can't accept he married her for her personality?

'S-s-sorry, s-sir, I can't f-find her anywhere.' The

junior tribune clanked across the room to make his report.

'She hasn't disappeared into thin air, boy. Look harder!'

Red-faced, Salvian clattered back out and Macer did what he should have done long ago, so they could catch up on their backlog of chores – he began to eliminate the slaves. Forty sloped off straight away, the slavemaster swearing on his mother's grave they'd been asleep in their barracks and no one could possibly have passed without his notice. Nonsense, thought Claudia. At least half of them sneak past every other night, either to steal from the kitchens or visit the women. But that's Macer for you. Educated, aristocratic, and without an inkling about human behaviour.

Pallas was explaining to Barea that the best way to stuff a porcupine was with dormice and oysters seasoned heavily with rue when the door was flung wide.

'I do hope you haven't started without me.' Emerald green shimmered across the floor, her Egyptian hairstyle all the more pronounced by a dozen gold leaves woven into it.

The colour drained from the Prefect's face. 'Mother of Hades! What's that?'

His weren't the only eyes on stalks. Claudia's could have brushed cobwebs off the ceiling, because attached to Tulola's wrist by a heavy leash padded a long, liquid feline. Its head seemed strangely small for so powerful a body, its ears deceptively flattened, its eyes surely too high-set? Two black teardrops ran from the corner of each eye, and its pelt was ferociously spotted black.

The cheetah treated the assemblage to a show of

awesome fangs as it yawned, then looked into the middle distance in disdain. Tulola patted its head and, in that second, Claudia realized it was no mere sentiment which attracted Tulola to the cheetah. It was the same predatory instinct in both.

'Don't mind her,' Tulola drawled. 'She's quite harmless.'

The cheetah's expression changed to suggest that, actually, a nice joint of Prefect was just what she fancied. Look how the black tip of my lovely long tail twitches in anticipation!

Macer, struggling to regain his composure, barked, 'There's no one else, I presume? We're not waiting for a husband or something?'

Tulola smiled coyly. 'Married? Me?'

'Don't be so modest, cousin.' Pallas leaned back in his basketweave chair and crossed his arms. 'Tell the Prefect about your dear old spouse.'

If looks could kill, Pallas would have been impaled by a thousand spears. 'That marriage', Tulola spoke through clenched teeth, 'was over years ago.'

'We're wasting time,' Sergius said dismissively. 'Oughtn't we to move on to the peeping Tom?'

'Peeping Tom, sir?'

If Macer was confused, it was nothing compared to what Claudia was feeling. What was he talking about? Had she missed something?

'The dead man, of course.' Sergius' impatience was ill-concealed. 'I want to find out who he is and let his family know what sort of scum he was.'

Macer pulled a loose thread of embroidery from his tunic. 'May I ask what leads you to this conclusion, sir?'

It was Tulola who answered. 'Me. Several times lately I've seen a face at my window.'

'And you recognized this person as the deceased?'

'By the time I reached the window, he'd vanished,' Tulola replied.

'That's why I sent for you,' Sergius explained. 'I'd been increasingly concerned for my sister's safety – you know how these perverts operate. Starts off with spying and escalates from there.' He turned to Claudia and spread his hands apologetically. 'In retrospect I should have brought the army in sooner, I didn't realize how far things had gone. I really appreciate your staying on to give evidence.'

The room swam. *Staying on? To give evidence?* Gods-dammit, Sergius Pictor, you are one selfish, devious son-of-a-bitch! You stood by and let me think . . . 'The pleasure is all mine, Sergius,' she assured him through a mouth full of honey.

She realized, now, what he was up to. Those big beefy guards weren't here to protect property. Their job was to ensure the performing animals remained a secret. Once someone had breached that security, and clearly the dung-beetle had, what better way to ensure Master Pictor wasn't pipped to the post by poor imitations than broadcasting your copyright via the might of the Roman legions? No wonder you can afford marble on this scale!

Macer was holding up a restraining hand. 'One moment. You've lost me, sir.' He beckoned forward the little blonde girl. 'Coronis, you're on record as saying you saw – you actually witnessed – Mistress Seferius stab the deceased.'

'Well . . . yeah. That's what it looked like.' Coronis stared vigorously at her feet. 'At the time.'

The Prefect put an exploratory finger in his ear and examined the result. 'Are you now retracting your statement?'

'Re – ?'

'Disclaiming. Disowning. Withdrawing.' Macer tutted impatiently. 'You did not see the actual knife thrust?'

Corbulo leaned closer to whisper in Claudia's ear, but she was too intent on Coronis' testimony to hear what was said.

The girl had clenched her thumbs in her fists. 'Well, I saw Miss Claudie and the dead bloke, I saw the knife sticking out' – a glance flickered across in Claudia's direction – 'and since there weren't no one else, what was I supposed to think?'

Frankly, Claudia couldn't care what conclusions the silly cow had drawn. A weight had been lifted from her shoulders and she was happily planning revenge on Sergius Pictor. Should that involve regular consignments of Seferius wine, so much the better; sales were abysmal since Gaius had died.

'Prefect, we're getting off the track.' Sergius waved his hand from side to side. 'It's obvious this pervert had taken his filthy game one step further and either it was an accident, the door slamming on to him, or else, caught red-handed, he took the coward's way out.'

Possibly. I mean if you were intending to rape a helpless victim at knife point, you *would* be carrying the weapon with the blade pointed towards you, wouldn't you? Still, if Macer didn't pick it up, Claudia had no intention of drawing his attention to the anomaly. He was still addressing the slave girl.

'Who else was sleeping in the guest wing apart from Mistress Seferius?'

'Only me, I'm afraid.' Pallas saved her the bother of answering. 'And I plead not guilty.'

'That's right,' Sergius said. 'We all heard screams and came running.'

'Hmm.' Macer tapped his lip thoughtfully. 'Mistress Seferius, in your own words, how would you describe the deceased?'

'A sleazeball.'

'You knew him?'

'I know his type.'

Macer considered carefully before laying himself open twice. 'I was rather hoping you could give us a physical description. You see, most of the group gathered this morning haven't seen the body. Your description might trigger a memory.'

In a word, seedy. 'Medium height, heavy, balding, spongy nose, pouches under his eyes, yellow teeth. Oh, I nearly forgot. He also had a very large belly with a knife in it.'

The Prefect nearly laughed with the rest of them. 'That's a pretty detailed description.'

'We shared a pretty intimate embrace.'

'Distressing, I'm sure.' His gaze swept round the room. 'Your bodyguard. Where is he?'

Junius? Dear Diana, she hadn't even noticed he was missing! Come to think of it, she hadn't seen him since yesterday morning . . . 'He's running an errand.'

'Oh?'

Think! Think! 'I asked him to return to the gig and search for my ear-ring. Present from my late husband. Sentimental value. Very precious.' Wasn't it warm in here?

'You appear to be wearing two at the moment.'

'Silly me.' Claudia patted one of the studs. 'I had it all along.' Junius, you low-down son-of-a-snake, I'll roast your gizzard for this.

Sergius' eyes narrowed. 'Prefect, you will be investigating Claudia's accident, won't you?'

'Naturally.' Macer seemed less than pleased with the insinuation. 'Perhaps you can tell us exactly what happened, Mistress Seferius?'

Claudia's blood turned to steam just thinking about it. 'We were', she pointed south, 'about two and a half hours out of Tarsulae. The fog was thick, but with the road deserted, we were still making reasonable time when half-a-dozen riders came up, blasting on trumpets and banging drums. The mares bolted and – '

'Talking of mares, Barea reports one missing from the stables. Do you know anything about that?'

Try Pallas, he probably ate it. 'Are you accusing me of kidnapping a horse, Prefect?'

A titter ran round the room.

'No, no, I think we'd have noticed. Are you able to describe your attackers?'

Am I! 'One was bug-eyed, another had a birthmark on his face about here,' she indicated her right cheek-bone, 'and a third had ginger hair.'

'I congratulate your memory for faces, Mistress Seferius. You, sir, can you add anything to those descriptions?'

'Me?' The driver looked up sharply. 'I didn't hardly see them, not to speak of. Me mares was bucking like crazy and I could barely see the frigging road as it was.'

'You're not the lady's regular driver?'

'No, sir. I'm new at the stand.'

Macer tweaked the lace of his leather corselet. 'Was there much damage to your rig?'

'Complete write-off! One of me mares was killed outright, the other broke her neck and Master Pictor here helped me cut her throat, she – '

'Didn't anybody stop to render assistance?'

'Like milady says, it's only local traffic, innit? We didn't see no one.'

'Yet it was Mistress Seferius here – a noblewoman, no less – who set off alone to fetch help. Why didn't her bodyguard go? Why, for that matter, didn't you?'

The driver shuffled from one foot to the other. 'Well, young Junius was out cold, see, and – '

'Yes?'

'Well – '

'*Yes?*'

'Milady said – '

'For pity's sake, man, what did milady say?'

'Well, as I remember it were,' he coughed and fixed his gaze on the painted satyrs high on the ceiling, ' "For gods' sake, driver, where do you think you're sneaking off to? Can't you see there's a crisis?" ' He looked anxiously at the Prefect. 'It were her sandal, see?'

Macer blinked. 'I beg your pardon?'

'The red one. It fell off when me gig turned over. She said it were valuable and – well, that I should stay behind and look for it.'

'Is that right, Mistress Seferius?' The incredulity in the Prefect's voice was insulting to the point of malice. 'You insisted the driver hunt for your sandal while you went off barefoot to fetch help?'

Don't be ridiculous. I always carry a spare pair. 'The man's arm was broken, the chances are he'd have passed out long before he'd climbed the slope. I don't see where this is leading.'

Macer ignored the edge to her voice. 'I am simply curious as to why a woman of substance should choose to travel an abandoned road with no servants and no luggage, and why she should pick my home town for her overnight stop.'

It is not your home town, though, is it? You'd no sooner live in Tarsulae than I would. Claudia delved into her wardrobe of smiles and came up with a particularly dazzling model. 'It's very simple,' she said. 'Why follow the Via Flaminia on its newer, but longer route, when you can take the old road, then cross country on a local path?'

She'd reckoned without the fog, though, and she'd reckoned without the hooligans, but most of all Claudia had reckoned without the resilience of the locals. They had none. Like rats on the proverbial sinking ship, they'd left in their droves! Once-thriving settlements were reduced to ghost towns, their shops crumbling to dust, their inns providing hospitality only to vermin and spiders. Even the private huts which dotted the roadside – cabins where patricians and their friends would hole up for the night – were dilapidated, with what doors that remained swinging in the wind on ungreased hinges.

Which explained why a group of drunken oiks could

indulge in their antics and get away with it. (Or thought they could.)

'Tarsulae was simply a question of expediency and, as for servants, I'd sent them ahead by ox cart.'

'What exactly was the reason for your urgency? Family illness, perhaps? Or maybe – ' he paused – 'problems with an arsonist?'

'Good heavens, is there one on the loose?' How the hell did he know about that?

'Might that have been what your bailiff, Rollo, meant by urgent?'

'I've no idea.' None that I'm telling you, anyway.

'Prefect, unless this is relevant,' Pallas said lazily, 'I think we all have better things to do.'

Thank you, Pallas. Thank you, thank you, thank you.

'Yes, indeed.' Sergius threw his two quadrans' worth into the ring. 'My wife is distressed enough as it is.'

Two bright spots of colour had appeared in Alis' cheeks, but how long they'd been there, Claudia couldn't tell.

'Well, she would be, wouldn't she?' Euphemia cut in suddenly. 'Isodorus was another one who met with sudden death under this roof.'

The Prefect looked baffled. 'I'm sorry?'

'My first brother-in-law.' The way she stressed the word 'first' was singularly unattractive. 'His name was Isodorus.'

'Euphemia, please – ' There was a quaver in Alis' voice.

'My wife is a widow,' Sergius explained, giving her shoulder a reassuring pat. 'And Isodorus was a sick man.'

'He was only twenty-two when he died.'

'Euphemia, that's enough!' snapped Sergius. Alis pleated her gown between her fingers. 'Prefect, could I ask you to deal with this a little faster so my wife can have a lie-down? She's feeling faint.'

'Really, Sergius.' Alis' embarrassment was painful to watch. 'There's nothing wrong with me.' Her eyes remained riveted on the folds in her hands. 'I'm fine.'

Macer burnished his chestplate with the inside of his wrist. 'Mistress Pictor, I am proceeding with all haste.' She might not have spoken. 'Bear with me a few moments longer. Mistress Seferius.' He smiled ingratiatingly. 'Claudia. Am I right in believing you are negotiating to purchase a parcel of land adjacent to your vineyard?'

Claudia felt a shot of liquid fire hurtle through her veins. He was up to something. This fussy, pompous, humourless so-and-so was up to something.

'You are indeed,' she replied silkily, with no attempt to elaborate. If he has dice hidden up his sleeve, he'll have to bloody well play them.

'Well, correct me if I'm wrong,' Macer smiled a reptilian smile, 'but wasn't some of the land you are after recently targeted by an arsonist?'

You slimy bastard! Claudia took a good, long, deep breath before answering. 'The operative word there, Prefect, is "some".' She would give him no quarter.

'I see.' And he wasn't giving her any, either. 'But as a result of the damage, wasn't this land offered for sale at a greatly reduced price?'

Damn right. 'I have no idea. I leave the monetary side to my banker.'

For some time she had been trying to outwit a certain Senator Quintilian on various land deals. This was the third such occasion, but how come Macer knows about it? Shit. She'd forgotten how Quintilian boasted of his villa on Falcon Mountain – just up the bloody road from here! Smack bang in the middle of Macer's patch, and of course the local aristocracy get together from time to time! Bugger, bugger, bugger.

Macer had pulled out a handkerchief and was buffing his fingernails in silence. The atmosphere was so heavy you could have cut it into slices and fried it in olive oil, but no one dared break it, not even Claudia. What, her mind raced, was this little maggot driving at?

Time seemed to stand on its head and do nothing. The field workers were returning for their midday meal, a donkey brayed in the distance. Pungent smells of roasting goat and cabbage, chestnut bread and sprats wafted round the banqueting room. Pallas' stomach began to growl. Finally the Prefect put away his handkerchief and turned to face Claudia. The tip of his thin nose was quite pink.

'Tell me, Claudia. Why did you kill him?'

A hush settled over the room.

The breath caught in Claudia's thoat. 'Quintilian? Is he dead?'

Macer's eyes narrowed. 'Not to my knowledge, no. I was referring to your friend in your doorway.'

It was Corbulo, sitting beside her, who sprang to her rescue. 'This is outrageous! We've already established the man's a complete stranger – '

'I beg to contradict.' Macer was calm to the point of disinterest. 'We have done nothing of the sort. As a matter of fact, the deceased was a local man named Fronto and he is well known to me.'

'Remus!' Sergius, who had turned as pale as his wife, pushed Alis aside and slumped on to the stool. 'What – ? I mean, if you knew about his activities, why didn't you lock this pervert away?'

'Fronto might be many things, sir, but he was no sexual deviant. In fact, until very recently, he was employed on my staff.'

Macer silenced the buzz of excitement with his hand.

'Quiet, please. Moreover,' he continued, 'the description of the arsonist laying waste those lands so close to your own, my dear Claudia, matches your description of Fronto to a T.'

Claudia jumped to her feet. 'For gods' sake, man! Do I look the sort of woman who goes around stabbing total strangers?'

The Prefect studied her for a full five seconds before a slow grin spread across his face. 'No, Mistress Seferius, you do not.' He bared shiny, white teeth. 'Which is precisely why you thought you could get away with it.'

VI

The imbecile! The half-wit! The absolute bloody cheek of it! Claudia stomped out of the room and slammed the door into next week. Behind her swarmed a sea of faces, some slack-jawed, some shouting, some still digesting the evidence, though none made an effort to stop her. Let them try, she thought. Just let them bloody try! The opulence of the atrium flashed past unnoticed. Pyrenean marble. Friezes. Frescos. Gold lampstands. Lavender stalks and elecampane burned unheeded in silver braziers, a fountain splashed in vain. Garlands of daphne draped round the columns might have been invisible.

What was he thinking of, Macer, fixing the trial for next Wednesday? She was overtaking a bronze bust of somebody's pug-nosed ancestor and imagining a scene, not too far in the future, in which Macer lay prostrate at the Emperor's feet, begging to be spared the disgrace of patrolling the Dacian frontier for the remainder of his career, when she stopped dead.

I'm seeing things! By the gods, that moron has made me hallucinate!

At the far end of the atrium, however, clouds of dust bellying out from the cloak he was shaking, that tall, strong figure of a man was most definitely of the flesh. Patrician stock, you could tell by the length of the tunic and the high purple boots. Military background, you could tell by the set of the shoulders, the dead straight line of the backbone. Totally unwelcome, you could tell by the mop of wavy hair and a hand that would be used any minute to cover his mouth and stifle a laugh.

'Well, beat me on the bottom with a bun!'

In fact the aristocrat made no effort to conceal his grin. 'I'll have you know, madam, I've not ridden ten hours solid just to satisfy your strange sexual fantasies.' He agitated his hair with his hands. 'At least, not until I shake the dust off.'

How strange. No matter how many times she'd tried to stamp on his memory, his features were exactly as she remembered them. Right down to the rich baritone. She wanted to move, but found someone had glued her soles to the floor.

'So!' With a practised swirl, Marcus Cornelius Orbilio folded his cloak and handed it to the porter, who closed the vestibule doors behind him. 'Since when have you taken to disguising yourself as a marigold?'

'I did it to pass the thyme. Is this visit coincidence?'

'Not entirely. I thought I'd give you the chance to explain why you sent my letters back.'

The sour smell of powdered soil and horse sweat tickled the back of her throat, and yet it was a citrusy scent that lodged in her nostrils and refused to budge. Can't imagine where that came from. 'Letters?'

'Not only my beautifully scripted scrolls – if I recall, last time you returned the entire messenger.'

Poor bugger was spotted trotting along the Via Sacra with *'Not known at this address'* unwittingly pinned to the back of his cloak. Orbilio had been the laughing stock of the Esquiline for weeks.

Would I? Claudia's eyes implored.

You bet your sweet buttercups, his replied.

She smiled.

'Poor you. Saddlesores for nothing.' She walked to the vestibule and opened the front doors wide.

'Forget the explanation, then.' Orbilio stamped his boots. 'I'll hang around, anyway.'

Dammit, I don't need this. 'Despite riding all this way for a case of mistaken identity?'

'Oh, no one mistakes you for another woman, Claudia.'

'You did. You mistook me for someone who', she snapped her fingers, 'cares this for beautifully scripted scrolls or their author.'

By the time she reached the colonnade, he'd just about caught up with her. His expression was unchanged, she noticed, but the light in his eyes seemed to have hardened. Good. He might just leave her life in peace now.

'I hear you're in a spot of bother,' he said indifferently.

How? Godsdammit, it was Junius who stole that bloody horse, Junius who sent for . . . Her eyes narrowed to slits. I'll have the skin off your back, you abject little toad. No one betrays Claudia Seferius' secrets, especially not to this ferreting son-of-a-bitch. Come the next slave auction, my boy, I'll turn you into silver.

'Nothing's wrong, Orbilio. Get your ears tested.'

'In my profession, ears are always in tip-top working

order.' He paused. 'How else can we listen under windows?'

Nightmare! Deep inside her ribcage, Claudia's vital organs threatened to crush each other to death.

'Then you'll appreciate Macer is after glory,' she said levelly. 'Unfortunately, he has the wits of a woodlouse and appears to be on the wrong treadmill with his investigation.'

So help me, I'll squeeze that Prefect till his pips squeak. Day after day, the little lowlife will wake and ask himself, when will my torment end? And I shall say to him, ah, but that's the thing, Macer. It will never end. Not so long as I breathe – and even afterwards, I wouldn't count on it.

But that was small beer in the overall scheme of things and in the meantime it prickled (really prickled) finding curly-haired investigators nosing around all over the place. Last time he dug up her past. Croesus only knows what he'll unearth this time!

'The evidence is stacked in the Prefect's favour.' Orbilio crossed to the central pool, splashed his face with water, then settled himself on the tiled rim, one leg thrown casually over the other. 'Tell me about you and Quintilian and the land devalued by mysterious fires.'

'There's nothing to add,' she lied.

'This isn't your first run-in with him, is it?'

Isn't it? You couldn't have picked that up by eavesdropping. I wonder what else you know, my fine patrician friend? 'Senators aren't above the law,' she snapped. 'Why doesn't Macer pick on him?'

'Perhaps for the simple expediency that Quintilian

wasn't found with the arsonist dangling on the end of his blade.'

'Orbilio, if I wanted to dispose of dung-beetles, I'd use more style than a common kitchen knife.'

He looked up to the opening in the roof where sunlight poured into the atrium, flooding it with light. 'Claudia,' he said eventually, 'these are very serious accusations. Macer's convinced he's dealing with a simple case of thieves falling out, that you connived to meet Fronto at the Villa Pictor – '

Claudia threw her arms into the air. 'I argue with my fellow conspirator right here in the hallway, is that it? I lose my temper, stick a knife in him (which I just happen to have handy) and then what? Drag the body under the bed and hope no one will notice till summer? What sort of an idiot are you, Orbilio?'

The best in Rome, Claudia. The best in Rome. 'I'm merely repeating the Prefect's case and reminding you that it's more than sufficient for him to take to trial. Especially,' he calmly rinsed his hands in the cool, clear water of the pool and shook the drips on to the marble floor, 'as Macer believes it was no accident, that you deliberately plotted to kill Fronto.'

Shit! Claudia marched up the length of the colonnade, then marched back down, stopping short at a statue of Minerva.

'Someone let him in,' Orbilio reminded her. 'By one means or another, Fronto sneaked past thirty security guards into a house which is locked, barred and bolted.'

This is your doing, she told the goddess. You've always had it in for me! With a hefty shove, she toppled Minerva from her podium.

'This whole wretched affair has spiralled right out of proportion,' she snapped. 'I am not a violent person, I did not kill the dung-beetle, and when I've finished with Macer,' the libation jug from the family shrine crashed against a painting of the Minotaur, 'there will not be one inch left of his skin that he recognizes.'

Orbilio watched as her hand swept a bowl of dried rose petals on to the floor. Mother of Tarquin, this woman's amazing! Accused of premeditated murder, does she crumple? Does she hell! Claudia Seferius throbs with the very essence of life, spitting, cursing, hurling china as fast as insults.

It was, he decided, deftly ducking a potted fern, a highly powerful aphrodisiac.

'You can take that smug look off your face, too!' A scarlet cushion whizzed past his left ear and bobbed upon the water. 'It's not your damned cat that's gone missing!'

'Drusilla?' His eyebrows rose by a fraction.

'If it hadn't been for her' – an oak-carved Pegasus clattered off an incense burner – 'none of this would have happened.'

'But she's here.'

A sandal remained poised in Claudia's hand. 'Say that again?'

'That's right, this is my second encounter with a – ' He let his voice trail off. Perhaps this wasn't the time to mention words like spitting, snarling, hissing – or, indeed, cat. 'Outside,' he said instead. 'About an hour ago.'

'Are you sure it was Drusilla?'

He rolled up his sleeve and showed her the claw marks.

Men! Who needs 'em? One keeps you here under

false pretences. One rates the shine on his breastplate higher than justice. One sells your secrets and one . . . One turns up when you least want to see him and then he doesn't even have the decency to end your misery over images of small furry carcases ravaged by jackals! Claudia pushed hard against Orbilio's chest.

'Hey!'

It was, she decided, a thoroughly gratifying yelp that rang to the rafters. Before the splash drowned it out.

Say, twenty-four hours earlier, a friend or colleague had asked Marcus Cornelius Orbilio to define the word dignity, he would have had no problem. His answer would have mingled breeding with demeanour, propriety with self-possession, solemnity with honour. In short, he would have said, it is nobility of bearing – and said friend or colleague would have taken one look at Marcus Cornelius Orbilio and understood implicitly.

Then came the incident with Gisco the charioteer, calling at his house in the dead of night and (he imagined) flashing a short, sharp gelding knife into the bargain. As a result, half his ride along the Via Flaminia was preoccupied with the question of how dignified was it, a patrician of rank and seniority, legging it out of his own bedroom window like a common thief. He had reached Narni, where the Bridge of Augustus strides east across the valley and leaves the old road behind, before he felt close to redeeming himself. This, he told himself as his stallion's hoofs crunched the weeds underfoot, is an emergency. It would not have helped Claudia's cause, had he stayed to reason it out with Gisco. Thus it was, sporting a full set of dignities, that Orbilio had arrived at the Villa Pictor.

With great personal regret he observed the same thing could not be said at the moment.

And even now, when he thought decorum had reached its lowest ebb at the point where Sergius lent a sceptic arm to pull a waterlogged stranger out of his atrium pool, Orbilio discovered he had miscalculated.

His boot slipped on the sodden, sunken cushion and he crashed back into the water.

Taking his host in with him.

Oddly, it was not the loss of his dignity that concerned him, rather the emancipation of an almost illegal sense of jubilation. Orbilio had physically to force himself to stop grinning like a lunatic before Sergius mistook him for one and ejected him from the premises, while at the same time the flood of elation that swept through every artery was so great, he was in danger of paying tax on it.

So she hasn't found someone else, then? She still feels the same.

Admittedly it would be difficult to explain to an outsider that being shoved backwards into a pool of cold water was Claudia's way of showing affection, but Orbilio had no man to account to except himself.

And himself was more than satisfied with progress.

To the uninitiated, it might not be immediately obvious how a sleeping cat can bristle with indignation, but bristling Drusilla most certainly was.

The turned back, the stiff spiky coat, the refusal to

open a single eyelid, those signs were plain enough, but the disdain with which she treated Claudia's bolster, still bearing the impression of her head – now that was the clincher.

'Think you can treat me like this, do you?' the embattled form blazed. 'Throw me down hillsides, pelt me with stones, disguise the trail with rhino and tiger dung, then expect me to hunt for my suppers? Well, fine. Fine. Just don't expect portable pillows from me as well!'

Emphasizing her point, Drusilla butted even tighter against the foot of her bed, curling herself inwards like a dormouse and pointedly anchored her tail with her paw. The drawbridge was up.

Claudia focused on the ceiling. For a moment it was as though yesterday's fog had swept back in to blind her, and when she tried to speak Drusilla's name, a frog slipped out instead. In the far corner, paint from a cherub's cheek was beginning to crack, twisting an inno-cent grin into a leer. Of course, the cat's tantrum might have carried more weight, she reflected, had the dish of veal and flatfish not been licked spotless.

Behind her, in the atrium, a commotion started up and one ear flicked backwards.

'Nothing to concern you, poppet.' Claudia patted Drusilla's crenellated backbone and felt a certain give in the spikes. 'You stay there and unwind; I'll let you know if there's anything worth waking up for.'

She prised her bedroom door open and peeped through the crack. Not only Marcus, Sergius was also soaked to the skin – and as Orbilio confirmed his identity courtesy of his personal ring-seal, Euphemia was wringing the hem of Sergius' tunic as though it was the neck of a chicken. The only other person in the atrium was Tulola.

'Tell me, policeman,' she drawled. 'Do you like – ' She paused to run her index finger down Orbilio's breast-bone. 'Cuddles?'

Orbilio was goggling. 'I . . . beg your pardon?'

Tulola's eyes flashed like the sunlight on the atrium pool. 'My pet, sweetie. She's called Cuddles.'

I should have guessed, thought Claudia, as the cheetah fixed Orbilio with the sort of stare it probably bestowed on the average gazelle. Drusilla's nose suddenly twitched and her ears pricked forward as she caught the scent of her spotted cousin and Claudia clicked the door quietly to. Satisfied there was no threat of invasion, Drusilla settled back down and Claudia left her to drift back into her pretend slumber. Clearly finding yourself navigationally dysfunctional kicks a real dent in a cat's pride!

Leaning her back against the flat of the door, Claudia considered her impending trial. In eight days' time, Macer intended to bring her before a specially convened court consisting of one judge and some seventy-five professional jurists. Since women were strictly forbidden to plead in court, even for their own case, she would have to hire an advocate who was skilled in both rhetoric and law, yet who wouldn't be above turning a blind eye to the succession of witnesses for the defence she intended to bribe in her favour. A local man was out of the question, she'd need one from Rome – and that gave her precious little time to recruit him. Damn you, Macer. Damn you to hell. It'll be virtually impossible to keep this quiet now.

She wondered whether he could be right about

Fronto being the mysterious arsonist. Surely, she mused as she paced the floor, no self-respecting arsonist would trek half a day north. Why contend with the swirling Tiber, which is in full spate at the moment, when you have literally thousands of vines on your doorstep? Good grief, Falcon Mountain's just up the road and that's smothered with grapes. No, Macer had to be wrong about Fronto, just as he was wrong about everything else. If there's one thing a firebug takes pleasure in, it's admiring his craftsmanship at close quarters.

With a subdued squeak, Drusilla curled tight into a ball, covering her eyes with her paw.

'Admit it, you're just blinded by this tarty tunic.'

A faint purr was offered in lieu of a handy olive branch.

Claudia leaned over the bed and tickled the cat under its unresisting chin. 'Think this is bad? Wait till you meet the owner!' Talk about loud taste.

'Prrr.' Drusilla allowed herself to be stroked into a deep and sprawling sleep, which somehow contrived with her being nestled in a lovely deep dent in the bolster which smelled of her mistress's hair.

'In her clothes, in her men, even her personal habits.'

'Fffff.'

Strangely enough, it was difficult to fathom exactly where sex fitted in. Sure, it was rammed at you from all angles, but judging from Tulola's calm reaction when Claudia interrupted her frolics with Timoleon, the enjoyment was entirely on the gladiator's part. No puffing, no panting, not even a telltale blush on cheek or neck or bosom from Tulola, and even the moans were not genuine. Why, Claudia wondered, peeling off the flame-coloured tunic, would Tulola fake it? She held the garment at arm's length. Orange and blue, what a ghastly combination! Yet Tulola was the one person who *could* carry it off.

Nymphomaniacs I understand. They equate sex with affection.

Prostitutes I understand. They need the money.

But promiscuity, just to manipulate? I don't get it.

And what about that irritating gleam in her eye? Hardly a warm, inviting twinkle, and when you boil it right down, there's nothing inviting about Tulola at all. Strikingly beautiful, maybe, but Claudia had known dozens of plain women, often dumpy with it, whose zest for life made them ripe fruits for red-blooded men to pluck, both parties reaping enormous pleasure from even the most casual of couplings. Surely the harem doesn't consist solely of lazy men, who can't be bothered to court a woman and therefore enjoy being 'picked' when the fancy takes her? Timoleon might fit the bill, possibly the Celt and the horse-breaker, too, but Corbulo? He struck Claudia as very much his own man, did Corbulo. And why did Tulola try to give the impression she was bisexual?

The Negroes, Claudia suspected, were the key. Them and the cheetah, she owned both and Tulola was about power. Power over men. Power to shock. That, she believed, gave her power over women, because, in her eyes, the more outrageous the behaviour, the more superior she became. Why couldn't she see the system didn't work? Pallas hit the button when he said the men don't last long. Casual, competitive sex has a time limit, and it's they who move on, rather than Tulola pushing them. To revenge herself on what she would see as perfidy, she opts for different characteristics next time round, and the cycle is perpetuated.

'Silly bitch has it all wrong,' Claudia confided to the comatose cat. 'You see, Drusilla, men are rather like mosaics. Lay 'em right, and you can walk all over them for the rest of your life.'

Very carefully Claudia upended her wine jug over the orange tunic.

VII

As a statesman, Quintilian did not feel he set much of
an example. As a picture of misery and decrepitude, he
was brilliant. Shoulders bent, he plodded up the Capitol,
succoured by the knowledge that the Senate was in recess
until the end of next month. Ample time to peruse laws
and initiatives at leisure and concentrate on private
business.

Stopping by the Temple of Jupiter, not so much to
admire the view as to let the jarring subside, Quintilian
looked down on the Theatre of Marcellus in all its traver-
tine glory, then beyond, to the island that divided the
Tiber's strong current. Had he been lower-born, he could
have crossed that stone bridge and spent the night in the
temple. Rumour had it, Aesculapius himself came to sick
pilgrims in the form of a snake and cured them while
they slept. Senators, alas, were required to find more
dignified alternatives.

He groaned, remembering the time when he just had
the toothache!

Gingerly he moved his tongue round his mouth until
it found a hole where a walnut could fit comfortably and
where the teeth either side felt like wagon wheels. So
badly had the abscess nagged him that, when the dentist
said the tooth had to be pulled, Quintilian jumped at the

chance for relief. Only when he was strapped in that bloodstained chair did he begin to have misgivings. It is not a pleasant experience, he reflected miserably, to have an ulcerated gum scraped away from a tooth, which then gets shaken until it's loose enough for the forceps. He had never known such pain! And the blood!

'Don't worry, old chap,' the dentist had said, cheerfully pocketing his five sesterces. 'The swelling will go down in a day or two, and the bruising should fade in a week.'

'Ung.'

'What's that? Worried the bone underneath broke?'

'Ung, ung.' It never occurred to him!

'Well, if you like, we can pop the old probe in,' the dentist flexed some ghastly bronze apparatus between his reddened fingers, 'see what's where,' he swabbed his patient's bleeding mouth with a towel, 'and fish any loose bits out with this.'

At the sight of the second instrument, long and thin and pronged and grooved, Quintilian was out of the shop and up the street faster than you could say here's-your-change – and now the pain was even more excruciating.

'Ridiculous, going out in your state,' his wife had barked. 'What are you trying to prove?'

Since Faustina was always calling his abilities into question, he pretended not to hear.

'Well, don't come crawling to me when infection sets in,' she shouted after him. 'Oh, and the Consul's coming to dinner.'

Next to the Emperor, consuls were Rome's most influential citizens and Faustina lived for the day Quintilian stepped into office, except disappointment was to be her destiny. He didn't want a bloody consulship! He was lucky, he supposed, gazing across the Tiber to where another great granary was going up, that women can't vote or she'd be lobbying direct. He grunted with satisfaction at the granary's progress, it was one of his pet projects. At the last count, twelve million bushels of wheat were being shipped in each summer, and the figure was set to rise.

Leaving Jupiter to his immortal chores, Quintilian pressed on to do what he came for, to make his devotions at the shrines of Honour and Virtue and Fidelity as he had done every year since his first wife had died. It wasn't the most successful of marriages, but at least she wasn't a harridan. Or a snob. Owing to Faustina's obsession with status, Quintilian's fortune was dwindling fast, he'd be bankrupt by the time he reached sixty unless urgent steps were taken.

'We *must* bring the villa up to scratch,' Faustina had argued. 'Only then can we hope to entertain the Princeps!'

Silly, vain cow. Augustus was a family man, who rejoiced in simplicity and spurned affectation. Pausing in the shade of the Public Record Office, Quintilian watched a white-robed priest bless an offering from a well-known goldsmith who lived on the Esquiline. Assuming he would ever accept such an invitation to Umbria, the Princeps would find greater solace watching the swallows dip over the lake – the lake that he, incidentally, was draining to provide more land for wheat – and discussing administration. Should the treasury fund more of Drusus' thrust into Germany? Should an extra legion be despatched now Pannonia was annexed? Where should the next aqueduct run, since the Virgo, Agrippa's underground masterpiece, was already proving inadequate for the increased consumption?

Too late! Faustina had already ordered marble and stone and magnificent statues, organized work gangs, architects, gardeners. The watercourses alone cost 100,000 sesterces!

Puffed from his descent of the Capitol, he leaned against the side of the Rostra and thought of the great men who had addressed the populace from here. This was where the murdered corpse of the Divine Julius was shown to the people, where the hands of Cicero had been nailed by Mark Antony. Never before had Quintilian felt so distant from his illustrious senatorial predecessors. The bones in his face throbbed and throbbed. His cheek, his jaw, even his eye sockets, and the skin were stiff from the swelling. Sweat ran down his neck in rivulets to soak into his toga, making it even heavier than usual. He stumbled, scuffing the toe of his black senatorial boot, and when he tried to stand upright again, it was as though he was carrying a dead cow on his shoulders. Bloody quacks!

Being the third day of the Festival of Mars, the Forum was packed to capacity. Butchers' cleavers splintered their blocks, mongrels plundered the scrap bins. Shouts of 'stop thief' or 'make way for the chariot' mingled with smells of pies and poultry, pickles and pancakes. A spice-seller skidded on a fishhead, and a thousand exotic scents exploded into the air. Cinnamon and nutmeg and cumin clung to Quintilian as he bumbled his way through the shoppers and the charlatans. You could buy anything here today, from pastry-cutters to ivory plaques, cucumbers to scribes.

And the sun beat mercilessly on it all, pounding his head like a pestle.

Had it not been for that bloody wife of mine, he thought bitterly, I could be tucked up in bed with a poppy draught. And all for a paltry plot in Etruria. Yet the thought of the Seferius woman lifted his spirits and strangely the aches receded. By Jupiter, she could warm a man's bedsheets, she could! Sly little bitch, mind – but he'd got her! This time he'd bloody well got her! Third time lucky, but lucky was just how Quintilian felt.

Maybe when the dust has settled and you realize women and business don't mix, we could come to a different arrangement, eh? The Princeps was firm on the subject of single women. Within two years of bereavement they must wed again. Quintilian had never been sure about the legislation, although he saw no personal gain in opposing it, but, as with most laws, there was a loophole. Suppose a respected aristocrat (him for instance) became this woman's guardian?

Despite his swollen face and raging jawache, he felt a stirring in his loins. Here? In the middle of the Forum? So outrageous was it, that his desire, so to speak, swelled and the prospect of making Claudia Seferius his mistress became even more attractive. No woman had ever had such a dramatic effect on him, not even in his youth, and Venus knows how active he was in the old days! Edging his way past a shoemaker, bent double under a roll of hides, he began to fantasize about love trysts whereby she would be waiting, naked, oiled, eager to show her gratitude at being spared a loveless marriage . . .

It was the loveless marriage bit that brought Quintilian back from the Elysian Fields. Thanks to Faustina, his vines and his olives had been ripped out and replaced with bloody watercourses. The former had made him a fortune, the latter had cost him one.

He treated himself to a goblet of chilled wine from a street vendor. In theory senators were not allowed to dabble in trade, having to content themselves with their magisterial posts and, if that proved too dull, their estates. Few, though, walked within those lines and a blind eye was turned to surplus sold for profit, to the odd quarry managed through a middleman, to property bought and sold through an agent. He didn't know what all the fuss was about. She'd run up debts and, to pay for her gambling, she'd put one of Seferius' tenements on the market. Quintilian had bought it fair and square, yet the silly bitch went ape.

It was a hovel, for gods' sake! He'd told her straight. Much better to throw the scum out, do the place up, give it a bit of *class*. You should know about class, m'dear, you've got it coming out of your ears.

My word, did you ever hear such language from a prettier mouth? Class my arse, she'd said, all you wanted was an income the size of your fat belly. He'd humoured her, reminding her that if she was such a philanthropist, why sell the building in the first place, but all the while she was shouting and wagging her finger (such a suggestive little finger, too!), he could think about nothing else but straddling her. Perhaps, if he asked nicely, she'd use language like that in his bed?

Since Faustina had buggered up his Umbrian estate, he'd had to find land further afield and what started out as a straightforward deal escalated into a game of move and counter-move as once again he found himself pitted against the formidable Claudia Seferius. Could she have done what she did out of spite? Gazumped him to teach him a lesson? Who knows, but no sooner had she bought that bloody piece in Campania, she sold it again – and made a sodding great profit. That was the point when Quintilian decided to take action. The Campania Campaign might have been simple retaliation, but he could not afford to take chances.

He acquired himself a spy under her immaculately tiled roof.

Quintilian's original intention was to discredit her. Remus, the very notion of women in trade was repellent enough, not only to himself but to every decent-minded merchant in Rome, but far from indulging in wild orgies or torrid lesbian affairs (as he'd *very* much hoped), her sole vice appeared to be gambling. In less than a week, she'd squandered the whole of the Campanian profit.

Several students were clotted round the golden milestone, virtually obliterating it in their efforts to hear their master's rhetoric, even though this wasn't a school day. That's because the master was Pera, and Quintilian intended that his sons, when they were old enough, should also learn from Pera. He was truly inspirational, that man.

Unfortunately, although gambling wasn't strictly legal, the senator was not prepared to pee in waters where his own friends swam. He had waited, patiently paying his spy and biding his time. When not at the races or the games, Claudia Seferius had spent a very dull winter poring over her accounts and when, divinely inspired, he put in an offer for the whole wine business (via a middleman, of course!) he was incensed to his gills that she rejected it out of hand.

I'll teach you, you arrogant, long-legged bitch, not to dabble in matters outside your sphere!

To that end he had sacrificed a pig to Mercury, well renowned for his chicanery in the world of commerce, and, exactly ten days later, Quintilian's spy reported Claudia Seferius intended extending her estates in Etruria.

Hundreds of other plots were going begging up and down the country, but masculine pride was at stake. Quintilian could not afford to lose this round, and he made his enquiries. With the Seferius bint, it boiled down to a straight choice between Hunter's Grove and Vixen Hill, both neglected by their peasant owners for reasons stretching back to the civil wars, when conscription took men away for months at a time. With permanent peace came the disbanding of a staggering 60 per cent of the army, leaving Augustus acutely vulnerable over his responsibility to his veterans, which he also had to balance against a huge number of prisoners-of-war and the problem of feeding an ever-swelling populace. Not for nothing was this man called a genius!

Many peasants, too poor, too weary, too battle-scarred to start over from scratch, leapt at his Land Purchase Scheme and happily upped sticks to Rome, where they could be housed and fed by the State and where someone else's back broke under the plough. For others, like the owners of Hunter's Grove and Vixen Hill, it was more of a gravitational pull, but the Land Purchase Scheme kept on rolling, the answers to everybody's prayers. So what if the rich got richer? So what if estates grew to obscene proportions? We've got slaves from the wars, haven't we? Let them work my lands, I've deserved this break.

Ripe for selling, trilled the agents. Ripe for commission, thought Quintilian. Few were beyond a spot of doctoring – transplanting olive trees, piling the outhouses with grain and veg. and jars of wine – when in reality the olives would be dead by the time you arrived, the borrowed stores returned to their rightful owners. A good surveyor – correction, an experienced and *honest* surveyor – could name his own price in cases like this, and this is where the Seferius chit came in.

Quintilian turned down a side street, then turned left again to where the buildings closed in.

Claudia had hired such a man to assess the two sites and make his expert recommendation. To the senator's astonishment and admiration, she had done so with great secrecy, and it was only because of his spy that he found out.

The door that he stopped at abutted the aqueduct and was bolted.

'Who is it?' The voice was a boy's in the process of breaking.

'Ung.'

'Eh? Oh, it's you.'

Quintilian sidled through the small gap that appeared and followed the lad up the wooden steps to an attic stinking of tallow, cabbages and cat pee. In a corner, a short, squat cove with dirty fingernails and chapped lips prised himself off his pallet. Quintilian thought he saw something black scuttle under the bolster and turned his head.

'Ung!'

An imperial flick of the fingers dismissed the boy and he waited until his footsteps had rattled down the stairs.

'Nasty swelling you have there, master.'

Quintilian made an impatient gesture and pointed towards a pile of scrolls on a chest beside the doorway. 'Ung-ung?'

'No, master. No problems at all. My lad here, he slipped in while our friend was asleep, as we agreed he would, then sneaked back before our friend woke.' He gave an unctuous smile. 'Although I will have to charge you extra for the seal.'

The price agreed had been all-inclusive, but this odious individual had him by the balls and the longer he hung around this cesspit, the stronger his chances of the wound infecting.

'One extra denarius, master, if you please.'

Quintilian pointedly counted six pieces of silver from his purse and flipped them on the chest.

'Seven, didn't we agree?' The man's eyes glinted horribly. 'One for the boy, no?' Realizing he'd pushed too far, he began an oily apology. 'Quite, quite, I am thinking of another client.' He clasped his hands together. 'Always a pleasure to do business with – '

But his visitor, along with the sixth denarius, had vanished.

Later, in the comfort of his own home, tucked up in bed with a poppy draught inside him and a turnip poultice warm against his cheek, Quintilian chuckled quietly. You should not play with the boys, Claudia. I warned you once before you were out of your depth.

Slowly, Quintilian drifted off to sleep, imagining himself moulding Claudia's firm breasts between his fingers and teaching her, as he turned her on to all fours, that there are dozens of suitable positions for women – and none of 'em in trade.

VIII

One hundred and twenty miles away, with the sun painting the villa walls a deep clover pink and the stench of ordure oppressive in the narrow valley, a young man followed his shadow between the peach trees and the pears towards the seal enclosure. The half-dozen or so show animals whose domain this was had been fed and were settling down for the night, grunting, shuffling, twitching their whiskers and scratching. A late heron flapped silently overhead, and a frog croaked in the reeds. Yet it wasn't the seals that held Orbilio's attention, but the back of a young woman resting her elbows on the gate, the sunset turning her hair to molten copper, gold and bronze. Hardly surprising that since Gaius had died, proposals of marriage had come flooding in.

The sun had all but disappeared before he stepped forward. 'I have some good news,' he said quietly.

Claudia spun round. If that was good news, heaven help doom. 'You always did excel at creeping.'

'I've perfected the art of silent approach, as well.' He swept his arm in the direction of the pool. 'Now, before I come any closer, will you promise not to throw me in?'

I don't want you any closer, Orbilio. I can smell the wine on your breath, the rosemary on your tunic, sandalwood oil on your skin. I can see your eyes dark with longing and your fists clenched with tension, and there's a pulse that beats in your neck. Oh, no, Orbilio. I don't want you to come any closer.

'Promises are for schoolgirls, but if it sets your mind at rest, I'm saving my strength.'

'For tomorrow's trip to the sulphur pools?'

I should coco. 'I presume you've spoken to that imbecile Prefect?' Distance. That's what she needed. Distance. 'Since he appears to have slithered silently back into the hole he crawled out from.'

'That's what I came to talk to you about.'

Bingo! If there's one thing about Supersnoop you can rely on, it's the fact that, first and foremost, he's a policeman. Umbria might be out of his jurisdiction, but professional pride would ensure he'd smooth things over with Macer (small wonder the little insect scuttled back to Tarsulae). That same sense of rectitude would also keep him here until Fronto's killer was unearthed. By which time, she'd be long gone.

'I take it you kept my bodyguard in Rome?'

As for Rollo – well, I'm sorry to tell you this, old chap, but you can take your urgent summons and stick it in your bathwater. Claudia Seferius is going home. Home, I say! Where I should never have left in the first place!

'As a matter of fact, I sent him on to your villa.'

Why would you do that, I ask myself? 'Now that's a pity, because I'm heading for Rome at first light.' To find me an advocate I can rely on. And could be I know just the fellow . . .

'Yes. Well.' His face had that haunted look, again.

Either that, or a twinge of indigestion just hit him. 'What I'm trying to say is – '

I know what you're trying to say. You rode all this way because you thought I was in trouble and, believe it or not, Marcus Cornelius, I am grateful. No one else could have got me off the hook so quickly. But I know men like you – respectable, respected aristocrats. Now I'm not saying I don't find you attractive, there is a certain animal magnetism, I grant you, and I realize it's been a long, long, long, long time since a good-looking man stoked my furnace, but you're not my type, Orbilio. No way. And besides, Claudia Seferius is her own mistress, not a man's.

'You're staying on.'

'Yes.' He sounded surprised. 'In fact, the messenger taking my explanation to Callisunus has just left. Callisunus being – '

' – your boss. Thank you, we are all familiar with the head of the Security Police.'

'Hmm.' A different expression flitted across his face. 'I suppose there are worse places to pass time, don't you think? The scenery's beautiful – '

What bloody scenery? 'Unsurpassed.'

Nothing but mountains and woods, and what use are woods, for heaven's sake? They go green, they go yellow, and then they go twiggy. Fine if you're a huntsman, but Claudia was no Diana-of-the-Forests, rushing hither and thither with a pack of hounds at her side and a quiver on her back. Claudia belonged to the city. And that, by Jupiter, was where she was heading after breakfast.

He said mildly, 'So you won't mind staying on, then?'

With care, she'd be home to catch the final throes of

the Festival of Mars, with the Dance of the Salii and processions through the streets. There'd be music in every house, singing in every . . .

'What did you say?'

Orbilio was studiously stripping young leaves off a willow. 'Sergius is a good host, he'll make us very comfortable.'

'He can make you as comfortable as he likes, mate. I'm out of here.'

'We're only talking about a day or two. Until this thing blows over.'

'As far as I'm concerned, it's blown over, and if you think this tacky little ruse is all it takes to separate me from my underwear, think again. And since you asked why I returned your letters, I'll tell you.'

He looked up sharply. 'Oh?'

'You want me in your bed, Orbilio. I know it and you know it. But I have a past, remember? And the thing about men like you is that you never let me forget – Ow!'

His hands had closed round her upper arms and he was shaking her like a woollen doll.

'Let go of me, you bastard!'

'What's that supposed to mean?' His face shone white in the darkness. '*Men like me!*'

He released her as roughly as he'd grabbed hold of her.

Claudia rubbed her arms. With luck, there would be horrid purple weals in the morning to gnaw at his conscience.

'This isn't about your precious underwear, Claudia, this is about murder. Yes, I had a long talk with the Prefect, and he's not carting you off to the lock-up – '

'Bloody right! I'd have his balls in a pie – '

'For gods' sake, woman! Haven't you got it through your thick noodle yet? Macer doesn't believe *you*, he doesn't believe *me*, and if Junius returns, he won't believe *him*, either.' He combed his hands through his hair several times and when he spoke, his voice was level. 'As far as the law is concerned, you are guilty of cold-blooded, premeditated murder for which you were caught in the act.'

'Oh really? So why aren't I in chains?'

I might have no jurisdiction out here, Claudia, but I do have influence. High overhead, clouds began to roll in. 'That's the good news,' he said quietly. 'You're under house arrest instead.'

With the spring equinox almost upon them and thus as many hours of daylight as dark, Marcus Cornelius Orbilio, despite his ride, was far from sleepy; and since Sergius ran his estate along the same lines as any other working farm, what better time to get a feel for the place, now Macer had trooped off to Tarsulae with the corpse? The Prefect had not taken kindly to outside intervention, reminding Orbilio bluntly that his boundaries lay within the walls of Rome and not poring over the remains of the deceased.

'Unless', he stressed nastily, 'I ask for assistance.'

During the long pause that followed, neither man willing to drop his gaze, Orbilio began to sense that Macer was finding his sudden appearance somewhat suspicious, but only when he was forced to confess his was a private investigation, did he begin to grasp the full picture.

As far as the Prefect was concerned, Security Police or not, Marcus Cornelius Orbilio was a suspect. Possibly even an accomplice.

He might not have got far with his examination of Fronto's corpse, but since Macer daren't openly accuse him, Orbilio was free to make other investigations. Having already spoken to the Pictors, each the very essence of co-operation, what he wanted now was a good poke around.

The layout was standard – four blocks round a rectangular courtyard with the south wing for guests and the east being the family's preserve, bedrooms, office, and so on. The west wing had been converted from store rooms into Tulola's private quarters, with only the kitchens remaining, while terraced barracks walked up the hillside from the north wing to house the displaced servants and stores. Fanning out beyond were the more traditional farm buildings and workshops – all of which would be deserted this time of night. Apart from the security guards, the only person on the loose was young Salvian, and that solely because Macer had taken the rest of his entourage with him to Tarsulae, seconding his nephew to watch the prisoner.

Which was on a par with leaving a newborn infant in charge of a troop of baboons, thought Orbilio. Without even knowing it, she'd given him the slip, heaven help the boy when she put her mind to it.

It was always the same, he reflected cheerfully as he made his way round the crocodile enclosure, a myriad of torches lighting his path. Every encounter with Claudia

Seferius spelled trouble with a capital T and sent the blood thundering through his veins like spring torrents. What would life be like without her? His limbs acquired an unaccustomed weightlessness as he pondered whether Vulcan's own forge could produce as many sparks as that woman!

From the other side of the palisade, a black shape, as long as a man, slid silently into the water.

Orbilio had not expected an effusive wringing of his hand at the announcement of her house arrest, and could thus hardly claim disappointment. Reward came in the tearing of her hair, the release of a thousand trembling curls, and the flashing of her eyes.

There was a second bonus, too. 'Men like you,' she had hissed. Initially her words had sent his temper spinning out of control – until a flash of understanding got the better of him.

Spitting, snarling, snapping? This was part and parcel of Claudia's defence mechanism.

Deep inside she was scared shitless . . .

To that inner sanctum, unassailable and unapproachable, Marcus Cornelius Orbilio had made a small but significant dent. Winning her trust, however, was going to be a tougher, longer and more complicated business than he reckoned, but I'll get there, he thought. I'll get there.

'Glutton for punishment, aren't you?' he said conversationally to the figure coming towards him on the path.

The Etruscan dropped the bale of hay he was carrying and looked up. 'It's that time of year,' he replied, wiping his brow with his sleeve. 'Another week, maybe two, and a new batch of animals docks from Africa. We need to make room for them.'

For a moment Orbilio forgot the problems that lay ahead with that spitfire Claudia. He had, in the course of his cursory surveillance, seen the wide range of animals in Sergius' menagerie, had heard about the tricks they could turn. The elephant who stands nonchalantly cross-legged. Seals that balance inflated pigs' bladders on their noses. Ponies that curtsy. Monkeys strutting round in miniature army uniforms, even with their own monkey standard bearer. What he wouldn't give to see a show like that! Striped horses, someone said, and leopards that lick hares. Mighty Mars, Pictor was teetering on the brink of a fortune – and so, although you wouldn't guess from his face, it always looked serious, was the trainer.

'I thought Sergius was shipping this lot to Rome for the Games?' he said.

Corbulo grinned ruefully. 'I don't know whether he thought leopards would be like horses to train, but the message is starting to filter through.' He heaved the bundle back on to his shoulder. 'He's resigned to missing April, but I've told him till I'm simple. You can't hurry a project like this.' He set off down the steps whistling under his breath. 'Nature takes its own course.'

It certainly does around here. Orbilio was skirting the outhouses when strange grunts emanated from the ox stalls and he moved stealthily round to investigate. Was, he wondered, shaking his head in amusement, Tulola double-jointed or did that foot belong to the chap she was with, whose hair looked as though it had been cut with a ploughshare?

As he turned to leave them to it, he thought that, in

the faint, flickering light of a lantern at the far end of the barn, he detected movement. There it was again. Darting. Furtive. Twice more the shadow quivered and he edged silently round the haybales. He was barely halfway along before loud cries told him Tulola and her lover had climaxed. He heard a shuffle amongst the straw. Picking up the lantern, he raised it slowly. An ass blinked mournfully back.

'Hey! Who's down there?'

The Celtish accent was less than welcoming, and Orbilio turned the lamp to his own face. 'Marcus,' he shouted back. 'I thought I heard noises.'

He heard Tulola's deep chuckle in the darkness and felt, rather than saw, her pick up her tunic and walk naked back to the house.

'Ach! Is nothing,' Taranis yelled back, tucking his shirt into his pantaloons. 'I just checking the stables.' He slammed the door behind him and Orbilio heard footsteps running to catch up with Tulola.

With the barn to himself, he lifted the bar of the donkey's stall. Someone had been here – the straw had been trampled where the watcher had waited. Why? Trapped and too embarrassed to excuse themselves? Orbilio crouched to search for clues. Or was there a more sinister purpose? Had the straw been crushed in an effort to crane a head over the barrier?

His mind busy on the peeping Tom, Orbilio stepped back and felt his boot slide on the slippery, shiny straw. Windmilling wildly, one arm knocked the pole as his other cannoned through the stall divider, knocking the lantern from its niche. The dry fodder caught instantly. Scratched and bleeding, Orbilio smothered the flames with his cloak, but it was not fast enough. Eyes rolling, the donkey bucked against the woodwork, terrified by the splintering and the smoke and the blood.

As he lunged to restrain the animal, his foot slipped sideways in something soft and he fell forwards just as the ass bolted out of its stall.

Prostrate on the barn floor, Orbilio stared at its galloping rear end, looked round at the demolition, looked at the sole of his boot and thought, 'Shit.'

IX

Sulphur pools! The very thought conjures up visions of burning yellow treacle and the smell of eggs that have not fared well in the sunshine, of vulnerable invalids being purged by rich and zealous doctors. From parasites to paralysis, dropsy to dysentery, sufferers have been led like white bulls to the sacrificial altar to stew in the sweat baths and guzzle down jug after jug of crystalline emulsion, coming away relieved not of their symptoms but of several sesterces, but swearing until copper quadrans covered their eyes that they'd never felt fitter in their lives.

Claudia couldn't wait.

Today, being a public holiday, humankind of every shape and variety had been drawn to this phenomenon of nature, whinging, laughing, splashing, grousing, and every damned one of them putting his heart and soul into it. You could almost sniff the roistering from the top of the hill, and it was as close to heaven as you could get away from Rome. Far from noxious, the air smelled fresh, like the sea, and even the rushing waters were blue, except where they swirled in the channels and over the rocks and thrashed white like the waves in the ocean.

An ox cart had set off at first light taking the women, the food and the servants while the men, apart from

Pallas, enjoyed a hearty breakfast of pancakes before saddling up and racing each other like schoolboys. Claudia, who believed the only thing you should put on a horse was a bet, also declined Tulola's offer to accompany her in her chariot, and opted for a good couple of hours' gossip with Pallas and his considerable picnic breakfast in a fast, two-wheeled car.

'Did you hear that Timoleon?' He fanned away the dust kicked up by the hoofs. ' "*We Corinthians are born riders*"? Croesus, that man must have a brass neck as well as brass balls.'

'Oh?'

'Well, look at him! He's no more Greek than the Emperor.' Pallas peered at his reflection in a silver serving dish propped against the buckboard.

'You don't like him, do you?'

'Darling girl, I don't like any of them,' he replied cheerfully, smoothing his eyebrows into shape.

'Excellent.' Claudia snuggled up beside him. 'Because if you can't find a good word to say about these people, you'd better pass me a honeycake and tell me all about it!'

As a result, the journey whizzed along. Timoleon, he hold her, was a local boy, born near Tarsulae to farming stock. When the Emperor had diverted the road, his family had merely broadened their horizons and taken up banditry. It was only due to his age that the youngest brigand escaped execution and served five years in gladiator school instead, where he obviously worked hard to suppress his Umbrian accent and where he adopted the name Timoleon. After his sentence was up, he opted for a further three years in which he earned himself the name

Scrap Iron as well as the immeasurable riches that went with the crowns.

Interesting, she thought, because not all his opponents would have been skilled fighters. The vast majority were common criminals sentenced to die in the arena. Like his own family, for instance.

Salvian, fearing conspiracy among the giggles, rode his horse closer to the car, the tuneless clanking of his ill-fitting armour drowning the boundary calls of the flycatchers, the courting coos of the turtle doves.

'You never fancied joining up, then?' He couldn't always have been fat, and in his youth Pallas would have stood head and shoulders above the average legionary.

'Me?' He took a bite of black pudding and patted his ample girth. 'You'll not catch me with steel in my belly, better the surfeit than the sword.'

She thought long and hard about the next question. 'And you never married?'

'Oh, I married, I married. In fact, come to think of it,' he grimaced theatrically, 'I'm still married.'

Claudia's affection for the fat man was growing stronger by the minute. 'What went wrong?'

Pallas laughed, his chins shaking, and he wagged his pudgy finger. 'You don't want to know, you really, really don't.'

With a whoop and a cheer, they overtook the plodding ox cart, resisting the urge to pull faces at Alis and Euphemia, and it was there, on the brow of the hill, that Claudia got her first glimpse of the sulphur pools. You could tell the channel that fed them by a straight line of wild cane stretching back to infinity but which terminated in a crashing, splashing waterfall the height of a cottage. Below these falls, a series of smaller cascades had been carved by the blue torrent to leave a score of shallow saucer-shaped pools, some no wider than a wine press, others the width of a bedroom, before the warm waters became lost in the river they tumbled into.

The same river where, stripped to his loincloth and plastered with grey-black mud, stood the man she most wanted to avoid. Silly cow, she told herself. Still can't tell the difference between passion and compassion, can you? His eyes weren't dark with lust last night, he was apologizing because he hadn't cleared your name.

'You made good progress.' He rinsed the health-giving slime off his skin and bounded on to the bank.

'I have just two words to say to you, Orbilio. One rhymes with pod, the other with toff.'

The gracious bow and twinkling eyes implied he hadn't heard, but Claudia knew better. To her left, a small cave had been hollowed into the rock, its mouth covered by deerskins and guarded by a dragon, where freeborn women could rent bathing shifts. Claudia tipped the crone and marched inside.

'Oi! Where d'you think you're going?' An aged claw snapped over Salvian's wrist.

'I'm ac-c-companying my prisoner.'

'Not in 'ere, you ain't. Not unless you're a girlie.' To the delight of the crowd, her hand whipped up his tunic and a raucous cackle confirmed her suspicions. 'Nope.'

As women shrieked and men hooted, Claudia took advantage to duck round the drapes and up the steps of a tiny stone building with just two columns and a weath-ered old portico. Mingling with the throng, she became as anonymous as the next woman – unlike certain young men in full military uniform who stuck out like sore thumbs. Very, very sore thumbs.

The shrine, it seemed, served both Metaneira, the nymph who lived in the river, and Thoas, the sulphur god who plunged into her, and was suitably revered by men and women seeking improvements in their own love lives. And not all of them married to one another, to judge from the inscriptions on the lead sheets which had been so tenderly consigned to the sacred pool.

A pinched-nosed priestess dripping with gold filigree stood on call to aid the lovers, selling simple cyclamen at five times its value. Powder the root and he's yours for ever, madam. Roving eye, dearie? My magic potion will cure that. Claudia sniffed the proffered flagon and detected only vervain. No wonder the old bag stooped with the weight of the gold!

Predictably the friezes were also of a suggestive nature, and you could hardly move for children sniggering and whispering as their grubby fingers traced the rudest of the paintings. Claudia kissed a coin and tossed it in the fountain for Metaneira, who, even if she possessed Tulola's incredible stamina, must be heartily sick of Thoas' attentions by now.

Outside, in what was now a Salvian-free zone, the place was buzzing. Theoretically, on public holidays you weren't supposed to engage in trade or commercial activities, but try telling that to the people! Fortune-tellers predicted cures beyond the expectations of even the most optimistic of quacks and a group of lepers, fenced off from the healthy, clamoured to buy holy water for their wretched mutilations. Brown grasshoppers, as long as your little finger, bounded and chirruped and got crushed underfoot. From the pools there came squeals of delight, groans of relief, cries of encouragement as tetchy babies were coaxed into the shallows. Grown men squabbled over places in the pools, small boys held weeing contests under the waterfall.

Claudia clambered up steps hewn from the rock with the aid of a rope handrail, and inhaled. The smell of oceans and open spaces, of travel and adventure all rolled into one! Without warning the age-old feeling of restlessness welled up inside her. It was her craving for adventure that had got her into this mess and that selfsame drive would probably bring about an early demise – but heaven knows it would be worth it. The thrill of the unknown! The excitement of each new, unfolding challenge!

I will always live life on the edge, she thought contentedly, gazing down on the saucers below. I cannot help it.

Here, at the top, the channel was narrow and surprisingly deep. Two portly gentlemen discussed oil prices as the blue-green waters gushed over their chests, and upstream Tulola's Negroes laughed and joked and chased each other like elvers.

'I've changed my mind about your henchman.'

'Tulola! For gods' sake, you nearly gave me heart failure!'

One carefully painted eyebrow rose provocatively. 'Then I'd follow through with mouth-to-mouth.'

Dear Diana, was there no stopping this woman?

'I've decided I want your delicious young Gaul after all.'

Even standard-issue shifts could not escape the Tulola treatment. She'd chosen a size too small to ensure her breasts and her hipbones stood out, leaving no one in any doubt that it wasn't only her fingernails that had been hennaed. Her nipples looked like poppies through the thin, white cotton.

'Despite his deficiencies?'

'Because of them, sweetie!' She brushed away a troublesome fly. 'I rather like the idea of making him watch while I perform with a *real* man.' A furrow appeared in her lovely brow. 'Where is he, by the way?'

'Around,' Claudia replied airily, and counted to six before adding, 'You recognized Fronto as the peeper, didn't you?'

Tulola unleashed her throaty laugh. 'My, my, you catch on quick, so I'll let you into a secret.' She lowered her voice. 'I did recognize the face at my window but it wasn't Fronto.'

'Then who – '

'Claudia! Claudia, for gods' sake, is it true?' Sergius came racing up the steps, wet hair plastered over his forehead. Salvian followed hot on his heels. Alis brought up the rear.

'Is what true?'

Naked apart from a loincloth, Pictor's physique was that of an athlete. Who could blame Alis for staying close? Far too many feminine eyelashes fluttered as he passed – and one or two masculine ones besides. Was that it? Was marriage to Alis a cover for his true orientation, good old Greek love?

'This idiot says you're under house arrest, he's to watch you day and night.'

'I have no idea what his instructions are, but I rather

think following me into the changing rooms goes beyond the call of duty.'

The boy's eyes bulged in alarm. 'I didn't kn-kn-know it was for w-women,' he protested, his face once again matching his tunic. 'Honestly Claudia!'

But when they looked round, she had vanished.

Launching herself into the cascade was one of the most exhilarating experiences of her life. The force of the torrent coupled with the utter helplessness was one of the most powerful feelings on earth! All too quickly it deposited her in a deep, warm pool that tasted faintly of mint and whose currents pummelled and massaged every inch of your skin. Breathless, she surged upwards out of the foaming waters and felt the spray dance on her face.

'Good of you to drop in.'

On a rock at the edge of the waterfall, his legs swinging nonchalantly, sat the most infuriating policeman she had ever had the misfortune to meet. Dogged was not the word. In future she would need to trail aniseed.

'You have the adhesive qualities of a leech, Orbilio, and only two-thirds of the charm.'

As fast as an otter she dived back down, but there was nowhere to go. As he well knew, because when she surfaced for air he hadn't moved so much as one well-developed muscle.

'Do you like children?' he asked, his eyes fixed on a small boy, naked as nature intended, holding his sister's head in an armlock as he tried to kick her legs from under her.

'Too chewy,' Claudia snapped.

'How many should we have, do you think? Three? Four?'

Godsdammit, he was doing it again. Using sex appeal as a decoy! Except last night, what she'd mistaken for lust had been nothing more than a tweak of guilt at leaving her under a shadow. How could she have been so stupid?

'Orbilio, do me a favour. Hold your head underwater till nightfall, will you?'

'Come on, admit it. Admit that you love me! Admit you didn't mean what you said last night! I didn't.'

'About me being accused of murder?'

'No. About you keeping hold of your precious underwear.'

After splashing around like a demented tadpole for ten minutes, she realized there was no alternative but to accept the offer of that irritating outstretched hand. *Slooop!* She was out of the water like a cork from an oil jar.

'You know, it could have been Junius,' he said, passing her a towel.

I like a thrill, Orbilio, but I don't employ homicidal maniacs simply to avoid the odd spot of boredom. Claudia rubbed her wet curls vigorously. 'Yes, I heard it was a hobby of his, carving up strangers with a kitchen knife.'

'He could have killed Fronto to protect you.'

Claudia lifted the cloth and peered underneath. 'His job, my clever investigative friend, is to protect me. If he felt I was being threatened, I rather think he'd have mentioned it.'

Orbilio's toes splashed in the water. 'Not if the motivations weren't entirely straightforward.'

Slowly Claudia lowered the towel. 'Meaning?'

'Let's suppose, for the sake of argument, there was a green-eyed monster prowling around at the same time.'

'*Junius?* Grow a brain, Orbilio. The boy's a slave.'

'He's not a boy, and as for slavery, I recall he was offered his freedom and refused. Unusual behaviour, wouldn't you say?'

Downright peculiar, now you come to mention it. 'That was ages ago. He helped me out of a jam and in return my husband offered him a straight choice between money and freedom. Under Seferius rules, you only get one bite at the pomegranate.'

Orbilio's gaze continued to rest on the children. Three more bare-bottomed tiddlers had come to join them, and they were chasing each other round the saucer rims, squealing and squeaking, last one standing the winner. Their mothers might fuss and fret and turn grey with worry, but when you're eight years old, there is no such thing as danger and the slippery, slidy basins were just one more piece on the board.

'It never occurred to you why he might have taken the money?'

'Why does anyone take the money?' Claudia didn't bother to hide the exasperation in her voice. 'Look, we're doing the same thing as those kids down there, going round and round in circles. Junius serves as my personal bodyguard because he's trustworthy and he's loyal. I haven't forgiven him for running off to you, but I'm damned sure he didn't do it because his conscience was at risk.'

'Why not? He sees Fronto, a complete stranger, knocking at your door and suddenly he thinks, why him? Why not me? So – '

'That's a damned good question, Orbilio. Why *would* I invite Fronto into my bedroom an hour before dawn?'

' – racked with jealousy, Junius runs off to the kitchens – which, incidentally, are in close proximity to your bedroom – grabs a knife and wallop. How's he supposed to know you would fall under suspicion?'

'I repeat, why should Fronto come to my room? Do I look desperate?'

'Claudia Seferius, you know full well what Fronto was doing there.'

She slapped her hand against her forehead. 'Does nobody listen to me? I have never – never, ever, ever – seen the dung-beetle before in my life!'

His eyes homed in on hers. Is that the truth, they signalled.

Shame on you for asking, hers flashed back.

Then I can safely assume it's all a pack of lies, his replied, dancing with laughter.

Claudia snapped her gaze away. Down on the river-bank, a group of musicians was setting up to entertain the hordes and overhead a kestrel was being run out of town by a flock of starlings. The urge to run with it was overwhelming, but he would only follow. Boy tribunes were easy to shake off – create a diversion and go – but Orbilio was no Salvian.

'Isn't it beautiful?' he said suddenly. 'Green and lush, throbbing with vitality. It's as though Venus herself came down and scattered scallop shells under the waterfall.'

Claudia felt her muscles tense. Dammit, he had no

right to do this! 'Don't tell me, the water is as liquid larkspur, the air as pure as – '

'There's no poetry in your soul, you know that? Well, if you want to talk business, that's fine by me. Let's discuss your previous run-in with Quintilian, shall we?'

She picked a violet and began to pluck its petals off. 'I haven't a clue what you're waffling on about.'

'Let me refresh your memory. Firstly there was the tenement deal, then you diddled him out of his land in Campania – '

How the hell did he find out about that? 'Rubbish! It was up for sale and my bid was the best. I rather fancy a villa in the suburbs – '

'It wasn't on the open market, though, was it? The Senator already had a gentleman's agreement with the agent.'

Of course. Cleverclogs has a whole network of spies, and like the threads of a fungus, they are deceptively widespread!

'Can I help it if the seller got greedy? Besides, there are times when a purchaser has a moral responsibility towards certain lands. I personally feel that in this particular case he was right to sell to the person most sympathetic to the existing landscape and the established way of life. What's so funny?'

'Nothing. It's just that, for a second there, I thought you were referring to yourself! Ow!'

Since a backflip from her towel did nothing to eliminate the maddening sparkle in his eyes, Claudia concentrated on footholds as she made a direct ascent up the rockface. Free from Salvian, free from Supersnoop, free from the ragbag Pictor family, she could throw herself into the holiday spirit and get blissfully lost in the throng. Phrygian melodies hung in the air – harp and pipes and tambourine. There was probably dancing going on, as well.

The climb was stiffer than it looked, but these were man-made crevices and, dammit, she would not be beaten. Not with Supersleuth watching her progress! Nearly there. Nearly . . . Her hand slipped and, flailing out, she grabbed the nearest solid object, an upright leather pole, and levered herself over the ledge. It was only when she'd rolled both knees safely on to turf that Claudia began to wonder what a leather-covered pole was doing up there in the first place.

'I've b-been looking everywhere f-for you!'

Pole? Claudia had both hands round a leather-clad military ankle. She released Salvian's boot and glued a very broad smile into place. 'Now there's a coincidence,' she said brightly. 'Because I've been searching all over for you, too.'

And it could have been the rush of the waters, but she thought she caught a rich baritone laugh float up from below.

X

Metaneira's health-giving mud and Thoas' restorative sulphur were, between them, having a powerful effect on the appetites of the nobility. Portable ovens churned out anything from rissoles to hazel hens and such was the atmosphere among the aching backs and muscle pains that interchange of food was commonplace, oysters swapped for ostrich tongues, porcupine for pike, with Pallas' gourmet experience ensuring the Pictors' popularity remained stable. But Claudia preferred informality.

'This way.'

She led a bewildered Salvian to the top of the waterfall, passing Euphemia at the bend in the steps. For one person, at least, the sulphur pools were giving their money's worth because, incredibly, she shot them not only a smile but one that was almost pleasant – suggestive, in fact, of Drusilla among a flock of slow-witted sparrows.

It was not that the division between classes meant that poorer people were unwelcome in the shallows; they simply didn't feel comfortable around conversations revolving round which Senate initiatives had been taken into protocol and filed, or whose sons were shining lights in the Emperor's Youth Movement. Not when their own sons were street porters or butchers' boys, and babies had to be left on the middens because another mouth was too much to feed.

Besides, outings like these were far too precious to waste. Protracted holidays might be the norm for the rich, but public holidays were few and far between. Among their own, the fires were open and flames crackled and spat as fat and meat juices dripped from the spits. The bronze cauldrons might have been patched and patched again, but their thick broths of bacon and beans, salt fish and broccoli were as wholesome as they come.

Here men and women, freeborn and slave, subdivided yet further, this time by race, to gossip, to reminisce, to sing songs in the mother tongue. Big, brawny Germans, hook-nosed Parthians, they chewed on chestnut bread and pickled trotters as they trod the foaming waters, cheered themselves on absinthe and honeyed wine.

Claudia selected scallops and veal, skewered and basted with garlic and basil; the young Tribune gnawed on a shoulder of mutton, taking quite for granted the fact that his food came free. She did not think he understood why.

'How old are you, Salvian?'

'S-s-s –'

'Sweet sixteen and never been kissed?' The down on his cheeks gave off a soft sheen in the sunshine.

'Seventeen,' he said firmly. 'And I'm m-married.'

'Are you, indeed!'

A trickle of grease ran unnoticed from the corner of his mouth. 'We wed last June and Regina's expecting our first child any day.'

You didn't waste much time! 'So this freebie peep-show isn't much interest to you?'

'P-p-peep show?'

Claudia licked the garlic from her fingers. Bless him, he hadn't even noticed. 'The girls, Salvian. Transparent shifts clinging to round, ripe bosoms. Wet, linen-clad thighs. Nubile young hips.'

He buried his flaming cheeks behind a cloth and pretended to wipe his face. 'Oh. I see. I mean, no! No, I hadn't seen – '

Claudia pushed a bowl of warm elderberries in honey and ginger under his nose. 'Lighten up,' she said gently. 'Take your uniform off and do what the others are doing.'

'Huh?'

'Have fun!'

'Well, I – '

She tried another tack. 'Salvian, let me ask you a question. Do you think I killed Fronto?'

'My uncle says – '

'I know what your uncle thinks. I'm asking you. Put it another way, do you think I am a dangerous criminal who's likely to go berserk with a knife amongst these happy people?'

He gave a sheepish laugh. 'No. Of course not.'

'And you agree I could have stolen a horse and run away at any point this morning after I gave you the slip?'

'I suppose so. But my orders – '

'Oh, sod your orders.' She stuffed a beaker of wine into his hand. 'Let your hair down!'

She was helping him unbuckle his breastplate when familiar voices floated up. 'Sssh!'

'What is it?' The bronze piece fell on to the rock with a crash.

'*Ssssh!*'

Much of the exchange was drowned by the crashing torrent, but by swimming across the channel and snaking down the rocks between the wild cane plants, Claudia caught the final snatch.

' – I don't have to take that from you, you fat faggot.' Timoleon's strident tones were unmistakable.

'Choose your words with care, dear boy.' As were Pallas'. 'Else I'll think you're soliciting.'

The gladiator turned purple. 'How . . . How – ' he spluttered.

'Much?' Pallas asked mildly. 'Well, I'm not willing but there's a tender young boy in the stables who charges ten asses. Or would you prefer just the asses?'

There was an explosion as Timoleon lunged, and suddenly the Pictor party was there to restrain him. It took three of them – Barea, Corbulo and Sergius – to hold him, although Pallas, interestingly, hadn't so much as flinched.

'Gentlemen, gentlemen!' Sergius chided softly. 'Let's be civilized, shall we?'

'I'll get you, you fat bastard.' Timoleon huffed himself free and jabbed an accusing finger at Pallas. 'Never turn your back on me – '

Pallas held up both hands. 'Perish the thought!'

The colour flooded back into Timoleon's face and he swung a punch that would undoubtedly have broken Pallas' nose had Corbulo's arm not deflected it into thin air.

'What was all that about?' whispered Salvian.

'Search me.' With the swirling torrent between them and the others, there was no need for secrecy, but Claudia sensed he was enjoying this cloak-and-dagger lark. 'Tulola's name cropped up a few times,' she whispered back, 'but as for the rest! I caught the word Macedonia, and something about marriage.'

'I've got it! Timoleon has a wife in Macedonia and Pallas is threatening to unmask him as an adulterer!'

Poor Salvian. Innocent as the sky at night. 'Could be,' she said, just to keep him happy. 'Now let's move, I'm getting cramp.'

'Wow! I didn't realize the water was so warm,' he said, pedalling noisily across the current, 'or so deep.' Reluctantly he pulled himself out, then chewed his lip for a while as though wrestling with a momentous problem. 'If I stay up here,' his eyes were goggling between Tulola's painted nipples and what her hand was doing inside Taranis' pantaloons, 'I'm still carrying out my orders, aren't I?'

'Absolutely.'

People were starting to notice. They began frowning, nudging, covering their children's eyes at Tulola's blatant antics and although the set of her face suggested she was unaware of their reaction, the gleam in her eyes told a different tale. Instinctively Claudia knew this was the first time she had dared be so bold in such a public place, that today she was testing her boundaries – and the sad fact was she had misjudged them. Disgust had never figured in her shocking scenario. She could not recognize it, poor cow, because even when someone hissed 'Slag!' she laughed at what she thought was a joke. Small wonder she'd picked on Taranis, a foreigner with no preconceived notions on Roman morals, as her start point.

'Providing you don't leave without telling me, Macer shouldn't mind, should he?' asked Salvian.

'He'd be the first to approve,' Claudia assured him, crossing her fingers behind her back.

'Great!' Like a ten-year-old, he ripped off his tunic and, pinching his nose, jumped feet first into one of the deeper basins, oblivious to the fact that two elderly matrons were drenched in the process.

Down in the lower cascades, the mood was no less lively. Rope dancers had bridged Metaneira's sluggish stream and were performing acrobatic feats before a crowd just itching for them to tumble into the mud. Bent-backed laundresses rinsed scores of white shifts and hung them in the willows to dry, maids struggled to unknot their mistresses' hair without breaking the teeth of their combs. Enterprising urchins trawled the pools for lost property and came up with everything from brooches to buckles, fans to false teeth. The boatman, Claudia noticed, was doing a brisk trade conveying courting couples to the privacy of the lower reaches.

With a blissful sigh, she slipped into one of Thoas' small saucers (who'd call them scallop shells?) overhung by broom. With her arms outstretched against the rim and her legs buoyed by the eddy, Claudia tipped her head back and closed her eyes. Sunshine and spray stroked her face like velvet as the gurgling force strove to heal the scabs and bruises that were the legacy of the gig turning somersaults. Slowly the fresh, salty smell of the sulphur began to prevail over the smoking, dying ovens and an occasional hiss told of tong-loads of charcoal being cooled in the torrent. A red kite hovered and mewed over the hilltops beyond.

'Now we've established you have no link with Fronto, you'd better tell me who has a grudge against you.'

Funny thing about broom. It has no discernible scent and yet bees flock to it.

'I know you're not asleep so you might as well answer.'

She could hear them, buzzing, backwards and forwards, closer and fainter . . .

'Claudia, I asked you a question.'

One eye opened and swivelled in his direction. 'I know.' Then the long lashes closed together once more.

Orbilio stretched out in the shallows, crossed his legs at the ankles and folded his hands behind his head. 'This is the ticket,' he said breezily. 'I could lie here for hours marvelling at the way the minerals have built up over the years. Just like marble, really. Or quartz. Dozens of differing blues, greens and greys – '

'No one.'

'I beg your pardon?'

You heard. 'I said no one has a grudge against me, the idea is preposterous.'

'You mean, everybody loves you, it's not just me?'

'Sorry? Are you still here?'

'Just call me Limpet.'

Marcus the Mollusc. I like that. It has a ring to it. 'It seems to me, my little sucker, that I am what you policemen call a pasty. The wrong place at the wrong time.' She sat up and massaged her neck. 'Macer will twig on soon enough.'

Orbilio shielded his eyes against the dazzling sun. 'I wouldn't put money on it. He sees only the bright lights of Rome and a glittering career serving the Emperor. You'll be lucky to escape with exile. And I think you mean patsy.'

Claudia slipped back into the waters. 'You're so full of wind, Orbilio, I suggest you try putting it up someone else. You don't frighten me.'

'Then you're a fool,' he said savagely, sitting up and swiping the hair out of his eyes. 'Someone at the Villa Pictor hates you enough to set you up for murder. Think about that for a minute.'

Thoas' waters seemed to run damned cold all of a sudden. Claudia waited a full half-minute before flipping on to her stomach and leaning her arms casually on the rim. 'Tripe,' she mumbled, more to convince herself rather than him.

Orbilio turned to lie beside her. 'Something stinks here, Claudia, and it sure ain't sulphur. Look at them. Look carefully. They're all down there. Are you sure – absolutely sure – you don't recognize anyone?'

She wanted to stand up, toss her head and stalk off back to the changing cave. Only her knees wouldn't let her. Claudia took a deep breath and concentrated.

On the riverbank, Timoleon displayed his scars to a gaggle of children, cutting the air with an imaginary trident, casting an illusory net. He was the only one she knew (if that was the word), and then only from the arena. Surely pitted against superior armour and weaponry, a retarius didn't have the luxury of examining his audience in return?

What about Pallas, buckling his belt as he emerged

from the latrines? She tried to picture him thin, and failed.

Or Sergius, playing knucklebones with his sister? Would those tight curls and saturnine good looks pass unremembered? And tall, slinky Tulola, even with a traditional Roman hairstyle, would surely have made an impact?

What of Taranis, cheering them on? The only person present today who hadn't ventured into the water? Or Corbulo and Barea, wrestling on the rocks? Two foreigners. One Etruscan. Three strangers.

That left Alis. Yes, Alis. She was too flowery, too insipid, too middle-aged even at twenty-eight, to make a lasting impression . . . unless, of course, the whole thing was an act, in which case – Good grief, Claudia, pull yourself together. Where's the poor girl's motive? Godsdammit, where were any of the motives?

Wisely or not, Claudia told Marcus about Euphemia's threats and his breath came out in a whistle. 'Little peach, isn't she?'

Watching her as Coronis fixed lapis-lazuli studs in her ear, her heavy breasts straining against the flimsy shift as she chewed the obligatory lock of hair, the fruit that came uppermost in Claudia's mind was in fact a pear.

'Dearly as I would love to lay the blame at Princess Sulky's door, I doubt she has the intelligence to plan a complicated crime. Assuming,' she added pointedly, 'there was anything to plan.'

Orbilio rolled over and rested his head on the mottled rim to allow the spray from the waterfall to tickle his face. 'Pulling a knife implies hot passions,' he said. 'This is cold. Very, very cold.'

The horror of being set up was starting to diminish. Goosepimples had flattened themselves, the hairs on her neck had also long since relaxed. 'I hate to disappoint you, Limpet, my friend, but in my humble opinion you are as far off base as Macer – '

'That's another thing. Doesn't it strike you as strange that Fronto happened to be working for him until recently?'

Macer's on the take, I'm sure of it. The merest shadow of a plumed helmet and food and drink is thrust upon you as though it's going out of fashion. Not to mention the whores, although Salvian's ignorance was quite touching.

'It's a tad far-fetched, Macer going to the trouble of killing Fronto in order to frame me in order to get to Rome in order to further his career.'

'Maybe, maybe not.' Orbilio stood up. 'I'm getting out before I turn into a prune. Coming?'

'For all I know, it could have been Fronto himself, committing suicide to make it look like murder to get himself noticed for once in his miserable, unprepossessing life.'

'Don't even joke about it! Until we've exhausted every other avenue, it's – '

'We?'

'Why not?' He threw her a towel. 'We could work cheek by jowl on this one.'

'Put your stubbly jowl within a mile of my dainty cheek and you'll be tasting the finest footwear in the whole Roman Empire,' she replied, but there was no sting in her voice. 'Besides, you'll soon see I'm right.'

'The wrong place at the wrong time, eh?'

'Horseplay from a few rowdies still drunk from their binge? Happens three times a night in Rome, remember?'

The flippancy in her voice was deceptive. I'll give you harmless bloody fun. Let's see what it's worth when the skin's being flailed from your backs. I'll bet there's a yellow streak as long as my arm down the middle!

'I grant you something fishy's going on,' she continued, 'but my arrival in the Vale of Adonis is pure coincidence, I'm afraid.'

Orbilio wrapped his towel round his neck. 'Policemen don't believe in fairies, demons or coincidence, we – Hold on, I've just had a thought.'

'No wonder you look different.'

'Early this morning, roughly the same hour Fronto was murdered on Sunday, I walked the same route I'm sure he would have taken – and guess what?'

'Thrill me.'

'Later, darling, later. In the meantime, listen to this.' He paused significantly. 'I needed an oil lamp for my reconnaissance.'

'So?'

His eyes were shining. 'When Fronto knocked at your door, you said – '

Claudia felt a thrill of excitement prickle her skin. 'All the torches were burning!' Not just the couple of night lights you'd normally expect.

'Tell me again what Coronis was doing?'

'Carrying a tray. Right!' For once, Orbilio, I'm with you!

'Cheek by jowl, Claudia. Together we'll nail this son-of-a-bitch, but right now let's get hold of Blondie and ask her exactly what she was doing at a time when the rest of the household was abed yet the hall was lit like a Vestal Virgins' vigil.'

How did he get his teeth round that? Claudia tried and got a Vestal Virgil's wigeon. She hauled herself up the rockface with the aid of the rope handrail. Vested Virgin's widget. She scoured the groups of slaves and freeborns in search of a familiar blond head. Vesper Virgin's strigil. Oh, sod it! Let him show off if he likes.

Blast. 'There she is.' Claudia pointed to one of the smaller bowls down by the river, where Coronis was stretched out the way Claudia had been, resting her chin on her hands and taking a well-earned siesta. It would have saved a whole load of physical exertion if they'd just turned round and looked behind them in the first place.

'Two-pronged attack?' Orbilio suggested, running back down the steps.

'I'll take the left,' she wheezed. It was closer.

All the same, this boy's-own stuff was quite enjoyable once you got used to it.

Simultaneously they slipped into the saucer either side of the sleeping slave and sat staring upstream until they got their breath back. It's a pity they don't have something like this in Rome, she thought. Individual hot tubs, constantly recycled by the warm waters of a river god striving relentlessly to impregnate his water nymph. I could get used to this.

'I hate to disturb you,' Orbilio said eventually, 'but we need you to answer a few questions.'

Claudia drew her knees up to her chin. This should be interesting.

'Coronis?' The change in his tone alerted her. 'Coronis?'

Claudia sat bolt upright. Pushing aside the blond hair waving in the water, her hand froze. 'Marcus.'

He leaned over. 'Shit!'

Automatically he reached for the pulse in her neck, although both of them knew it was useless. One look at the girl's half-opened eyes and protuberant tongue was more than enough.

'Shit!' he said again. 'Her neck's broken.' He glanced round to where bathers and invalids splashed and groaned and laughed and fidgeted. 'It had to be damn quick for no one to notice what happened.'

Claudia hugged herself tight and rocked back and forth in the water. Coronis looked so peaceful . . .

For a long, long time they sat in the torrent, flanking the dead girl like book-ends, as divers launched themselves into the waterfall, winesellers emptied jug after jug and herbalists touted their foul-smelling unguents. Tonight these people would trek home to their mansions or tenements, or they'd gravitate to the village on the hill for board and lodging and the ministrations of whores. But whichever they chose, they would gossip and grouch, quibble and quip, and whether rich or poor, sick or healthy, it was bed they looked forward to tonight. Not a funeral bier. And the kite still circled and mewed.

Finally it was Orbilio who broke the spell. 'Now do you believe me?' he asked thickly, his face twisted with emotion. 'Now will you believe you've been framed?'

XI

In Rome, the crowds jostled Callisunus as they made their rowdy way towards the exit. Not for nothing was it called the vomitorium, because quite literally it spewed spectators out of the amphitheatre and into the streets at a truly awesome speed. Since space inside was limited, the people leaving were, for the most part, those who had queued all night – although for such sacrifice they demanded the very best in entertainment. Today, on the fourth day of the Holiday of Mars, they had not been disappointed. Bulls had been provoked with whips and prods and given straw dummies to toss before the bestiarii, clad only in white loincloths, were even admitted. After the break, four lions had been roused to a fury, first by flaming arrows fired into the sand then by a pack of baying hounds, before another team of bestiarii had been set against them. But the highlight of the festivities, and the reason people had queued all night, was the leopard hunt.

The bulls, the lions, that was just a game, the warm-up if you like, in much the same way as the chorus belts out cheerful songs before a comedy begins. Ducking and diving, leaping and lunging, a great deal of skill had been involved this morning, but generally speaking both beast and bestiarii lived to see another day. The leopard hunt was entirely different, and Callisunus was lucky that his position as Head of the Security Police secured him a decent seat. For a start, the stage was transformed into a miniature but quite authentic forest. Trees, rocks, shrubs were wheeled in, then half-a-dozen hungry, angry leopards were smoked out of their cages, snarling at the half-thrilled, half-terrified audience. Finally a roll of drums, and out ran the hunters, or venators as they were called. Despite fancy tunics in greens, blues and mauves and despite the fact that they were considerably better armed than their less-glamorous colleagues, the bestiarii, these men had but one thought in their minds.

Kill or be killed.

It was astonishing, thought Callisunus, shoving his way up the steps towards the exit, how quickly a large leopard disappears among the branches, its spots mimicking the shade of the leaves to perfection. It was equally amazing how a hush had settled over the whole amphitheatre, leaving just man pitted against beast, the way it always had been and always would be. The leopards might be outnumbered two to one, but they had been starved inside their cages; they could not afford to be reckless. Then, as leopards always do, they began to stalk their victims with an eerie calm. By the end of the hunt, three venators lay dead after giant fangs had punctured their skulls, and four of the cats had gone down for skinning. The remaining leopards were rewarded with live giraffe to bring down, while the venators, two of them badly mauled, received crowns and accolades and were cheered to the rafters.

Overall it was agreed that honour had been satisfied on both sides, time now for a bite to eat.

Callisunus mopped his brow with his handkerchief. Spring had arrived with a vengeance today, and a heavy woollen toga combined with the heat from twelve thousand bodies made it uncomfortable in the extreme. Yet the heat he could take. That wasn't what was making him sweat.

'There you are, old boy!' Callisunus felt his cousin's hand on his shoulder. 'Not coming back to dine with us?'

'No,' he growled. 'I've got work to do.' Castor and Pollux, when he got hold of that Marcus Orbilio, he'd hang him on a line to dry, so help him, he would.

'Fair enough.' His cousin seemed quite happy about the reply, but then the bastard would. 'See you at the procession tomorrow, then,' and with that he disappeared into the crush.

Tomorrow was the final day of the Holiday of Mars, and in many respects the most important day of the month. Once, and long before the Divine Julius had made this final revision to the calendar, the first day of March had the honour, since it heralded the start of a brand-new year, but now, while many of the sacred rites were still practised, the full veneration of Mars himself was not felt until the 23rd. Tomorrow.

For the Head of the Security Police, the day held particular significance. In the morning came the Purification of the Trumpets up on the Aventine, where holy water was sprinkled over military instruments to symbolize lustration of the whole Roman army. Callisunus, naturally, would be at the fore, and despite his equestrian, as opposed to patrician, background and his lack of military training (he had bought his way to the top, a common practice among magistrates), this was one of those rare chances to be seen, by the populace, rubbing shoulders with the high and the mighty.

Moreover, his brother was one of the two dozen carefully selected priests who would make the third and final Salian War Dance in the afternoon. Unfortunately, although they were twins, his brother was a baboon, and sure as eggs were eggs, he'd cock up. It had cost Callisunus a small fortune to wangle his brother into this élite band, and almost half as much again to teach the twit his steps. Jupiter's balls, it wasn't choreography, for gods' sake! All he had to do was beat his fucking shield with his fucking sword and leap about a bit at set points along the way, but could he do it? Could he hell! Twice already the Salian Priests had peformed their ritual dance, and twice the silly bugger had fucked up. If he dropped his sacred shield just one more time, Callisunus would wring his fucking neck!

With the sweat pouring down his neck, he called for his litter.

'Where to, sir?'

'Home,' he barked.

The whole fucking city's out revelling, even my fucking wife, and I'm stuck indoors writing fucking letters! He threw off his toga and called for his secretary.

'I'm sorry, sir,' his steward explained. 'It's a public holiday, he's out celebrating.'

'I know it's a public holiday, you arsehole. Just fetch him.'

What is it with Orbilio? I'm dumped with a fraud case, where thousands of sesterces of public money have gone missing with none of the suspects living the life of

Riley, which means someone's salting it away, and at a crucial stage of the investigation, what happens? My undercover man buggers off to Umbria! Well, I don't have too much choice about that. His family has clout in this city, the name means something, and if the Princeps doesn't mind him following some tart round the country, why should I bother?

'Assign the case to someone else,' Augustus had said mildly, when Callisunus made his weekly report. 'I've heard interesting stories about the Seferius woman, and young Marcus has potential, don't you think? So unless there's an emergency, why don't we give him his head?'

Because it's set the fraud back several weeks, you silly arse, and when the suspect buggers off with a trunk full of public money, it's my balls you're going to fry, that's why!

'Umbria's out of his jurisdiction, sir.'

'I'm sure he knows that.' The Emperor never invited Callisunus to sit. 'It'll be another learning experience for the boy.'

'As you wish, then.'

'I do, Callisunus, I do wish,' Augustus had replied. 'But I still want a result on this fraud, and fast. If word gets round that one man steals from the Empire, others will jump on the bandwagon. Do I make myself plain? I want this bastard nailed quickly, and if you aren't up to the task, others are.'

Great! The Princeps takes away my best man, leaving me with a god-almighty chasm and, when I try spanning it, he promptly burns every bridge! Callisunus already knew the Emperor didn't like him, but until then he didn't realize how deep it went. However, there was more than one way to skin a coney, and rumour had it Augustus was thinking about reintroducing the old post of Priest of Jupiter after a gap of some seventy-five years. Now if Callisunus could just get his brother ordained . . .

'Where the fuck's my secretary?' Everything hinged on how well his twin performed tomorrow afternoon.

'We're still trying to locate him,' replied the steward. 'Shouldn't be long now.'

'It's been too bloody long already,' he snarled. 'Put a bit of steam under it, will you? No bugger drowns in his own sweat!'

Least of all you, thought the steward, backing silently out of the door.

Callisunus cleared the top of his desk with the sweep of his hand. Stuff it. He'd put Metellus on the fraud, and if the case went down, Metellus could bloody go with it. He paused, to kick a scroll into touch. Naturally if the money was recovered – well, Callisunus would deliver it personally to the Emperor up on the Palatine. His toe was playing with the upended inkwell when the door burst open.

'You wanted me, master?' The secretary, red-faced and stinking of cheap wine, rolled through the doorway with his pen and parchment.

'Write!' he ordered.

But the secretary misheard. He thought his boss said 'right', and Callisunus had to pinch the man's belly twice before the idiot had sobered up sufficiently to pay attention.

'Get this down,' he barked. 'To Marcus Cornelius Orbilio, at the Villa Pictor in the Vale of Adonis – What? Yes, of course, I bloody want a messenger going off with it this afternoon! Yes, of course, I know it's a public fucking holiday, now quit yapping and write.'

The letter, when he eventually read it over, was concise and to the point. Callisunus liked that.

It would also make one cocky young aristocrat very hot under his collar. And Callisunus liked that even more.

Dusk, swamping the Vale of Adonis with its sepia tints, had been thwarted by a hundred flickering torches, but the darkness inside Orbilio's head refused to go away. His mouth was dry, he needed a drink, and the need brought him out in a sweat. Dammit, he should have spoken to Coronis earlier! Frustration tightened an invisible band beneath his ribcage. Again and again he saw the coronet of blond hair swirling in the cloudy current and again and again he asked himself, could he have saved her? When Orbilio ran his hands over his face, to his shame he realized they were shaking.

With the basins at the sulphur pools worn so shiny and smooth, it was relatively simple to pass the girl's death off as an accident, a tragic end to an otherwise perfect day, thereby allowing the killer to think they'd got away with it. Because, for the moment, there was nothing to be gained from showing his hand. Cynically Orbilio had wondered how many other murderers had 'got away with it' over the years, their inconvenient spouses slipping and, oh dear, breaking their necks? Uncomfortable with the answer, he'd concentrated on his search of the girl's meagre quarters.

'How can you be sure it *wasn't* an accident?' Claudia

had asked, and his answer flowed without need for concentration.

'I'm willing to put my job on the line that our Coronis was paid to take that early morning walk,' he'd replied, 'and that the bowl she carried was a mere prop.' The subsequent discovery of two shiny gold pieces sewn inside the girl's moth-eaten bolster sealed the matter.

The murderer needed a witness.

With hindsight, it explained Coronis' nervousness, which was in the face of interrogation, rather than authority – not to mention her inability to look Claudia in the eye. Her best friend, a fat girl with rabbit's teeth, swore black was white through gulping sobs that Coronis couldn't – wouldn't – have taken money to lie, that she was a hard and honest worker who wouldn't say boo to a goose, but her final statement brought everything into focus. All she ever wanted, the friend had said, was to go back to Greece. While two gold pieces wasn't enough to buy Coronis her freedom, Orbilio reflected as he made his way towards the fodder store, it was one hell of a good start.

So many times he had witnessed violent death – on the battlefield, on the streets, it was part of his job – yet he could not recall one single instance when the sight of the corpse had not moved him. Relentlessly and without fail, death diminished every last one. They were smaller, slighter. Even Fronto, whom he hadn't even known. Diminished and cheapened. Perhaps that's what happens when the soul departs? The shell is simply devalued?

Inside the fodder store, Coronis rested on a rude, wooden handcart, one stiffening arm over the side where it had fallen unchecked, small bronze coins for her eyes.

Not for Coronis oak wreaths or laurels, sacred myrrh or cinnamon. She would be burned on a pyre at night – this night – her unmarked, unmourned ashes buried in a field. No feasts, no mourning, no elaborate purification ceremony. Marcus Cornelius Orbilio slipped a silver denarius under her tongue to speed the oars of the ferryman and hasten her soul to Hades. There was no other way to tell her how sorry he was, how ashamed.

He heard the steward strike the gong for dinner and bowed reverently in the dusty barn.

On the other hand, he told her ghost, it was still within his powers to avenge her.

The deep reverberations of the dinner gong had not yet died in the air before Timoleon was out of his room and striding towards the dining hall, rubbing his hands together and whistling. Claudia watched him through the hole in her bedroom door that she'd made by wheedling a knot out of the woodwork, and when she was sure the atrium was empty she flitted across to his room.

Praise be to Juno and to hell with the cost, he'd left three good-sized lamps burning, the place was lit like a carnival. When she'd searched Barea's quarters, all she'd had was one measly candle to work by and had broken two nails in the process. Here, it was a different problem. You could hardly find the bed for clutter, but the most striking aspect of the room was the portrait of the great man himself, a recent one to judge by the yellow hair, set against a backdrop of Corinth. Claudia supposed that was to remind him as much as anyone else of his sup-posed antecedents.

But where Barea had almost nothing – no personal possessions, no keepsakes, no mementoes to speak of – Timoleon more than made up for it. A set of silver cutlery with the initials 'S.I.' (Scrap Iron?) engraved on it. Combs of ivory, knives with bone handles carved in the likenesses of ducks' heads, Mercury the messenger, snakes and seahorses. He had tunics of every damned colour of the rainbow, ranging from complex twills to embroidered cottons, one even woven with a fine gold thread. There were travelling cloaks with hoods and travelling cloaks without them, boots, shoes, sandals. She wondered, as she rifled through his five sets of underclothes, whether Barea felt envious of his colleague's comprehensive wardrobe and decided probably not. He was an easy-going soul, Barea, who travelled light both physically and spiritually. Three serviceable tunics, one heavy cloak and his well-earned Cap of Freedom, proudly hung on a hook above the bed, that was all he had need for.

Not that Barea couldn't afford more. In a small wooden chest under his bed he had a fair pile of coins stashed away, as well as a promissory note from Sergius for payment at the end of his contract. Interestingly, the casket also contained a sprig of what looked like dried heather, a small silver bell – the sort tied round the neck of a sacrificial lamb – and a ring set with a stone of green glass. For a man with few possessions, these few trinkets must be treasures indeed. But of what?

Whereas Barea's chest had been locked (a small complication for Claudia's hairpin), Timoleon felt no need for secrecy. Had he been able, she suspected he'd have slapped his finery over the walls to show off, and from the crumpled appearance of most of the clothing, it seemed they were often taken out and admired. She moved on to the untidy row of onyx, glass and alabaster pots which contained a variety of precious oils. Poo! What's *that*? Claudia sniffed again and chuckled. Dates mixed with castor oil mixed with carobs meant just one thing. Poor old Scrap Iron's got piles!

She was replacing the lid and turning to his jewellery box when she heard voices outside. One deep, masculine and heavily accented. The other, unfortunately, pitched too low to identify.

'I tell you again, is not necessary.'

She daren't risk opening the shutter. With so many lanterns, even the smallest crack would light up the yard and Claudia had a feeling this was a conversation that was meant to be secret. Why else hold it outside what should have been an empty room on the wing opposite the dining hall? Cocking her ear to the embrasure, she strained for the reply and heard only an indistinct muttering which could have been male or female, young or old. Claudia wished they'd move closer to the building.

'Has been enough trouble as it is. Suppose someone see you?'

Mumble, mumble, mumble. Dammit, I wish I could see you! Just a shadow, a silhouette, to show me who you are.

'Look, is late. Dinner already under way, people start to wonder. We talk later, yes?' Taranis put a bit more coaxing into his voice. 'Yes?' Which obviously paid off. 'Good.'

Claudia realized she had two choices. She could either abandon her search of the gladiator's room, knowing it was unlikely she'd get a better chance. Or she could finish her task and risk Taranis' suspicions.

The decision had to be made fast if she was to beat the Celt to the dining couch . . .

Zigzagging between the chests of finery, she paused. Either way, she thought, meeting the painted eyes of the portrait on the wall, she had a horrid feeling she had been watched.

XII

In the opulence of Sergius Pictor's dining room, where vivid paintings of Ganymede, cup-bearer to the gods, covered the walls and Bacchanalian revels patterned the floor, the death of one slave girl, Marcus Cornelius Orbilio reflected sadly, had left no appreciable impact on the diners. Only Claudia, he noticed, avoided his – and indeed anyone else's – eye, picking at her baked eggs and slipping a partridge into her napkin when she thought nobody was looking. The others, predictably hyped up from the outing, were drinking heavily and laughing loudly. Except one.

'For pity's sake,' Tulola chided. 'Cheer up.'

'What's up, sunshine?' asked Timoleon. 'You've got a face as long as an elephant's dongler.'

'A yellow one,' put in Taranis, without bothering to empty his mouth.

Sergius' petulant expression deepened. 'The Megalesian Games kick off in a fortnight, what's to be cheerful about?'

'Uh-oh.' Corbulo took a deep draught of wine. 'I feel a nag coming on.'

'Hands off,' mocked Barea. 'Horses are my job.'

Everyone laughed, the slaves topped up the glasses and even Sergius was tempted to smile.

'I hear Agrippa's come home sick.' Provocatively Tulola licked mustard sauce from a spear of asparagus. 'Isn't that right, policeman?'

'The prognosis does not look good, I'm afraid.' Orbilio was relieved the conversation had moved to more general topics. 'He bypassed Rome and headed straight for his house in Campania. That tells you how serious it is.'

The Emperor's most trusted general, his closest friend, his dearest ally so weak he can't even face the city?

'If I'd spent all winter freezing my bollocks off,' Timoleon snapped, 'I'd want to defrost them, too.'

'Oh? Where he been, then?' Taranis wiped his nose with the back of his hand.

Tulola ruffled his shaggy mophead. 'That's what I like about you, my little barbarian. You're so blissfully, utterly ignorant.'

Taranis stiffened. 'I am foreigner. I no understand Roman politics.'

'Pannonia.' Orbilio was too weary to sit through Tulola's explanation and the indignation that would inevitably follow. 'The Danube campaign's not fully resolved, hence Tiberius – '

'You don't understand!' Sergius thumped the table and the glassware rattled. 'The Megalesian Games are without parallel.'

'Give it a rest, old son,' Barea interjected, but Sergius was unstoppable.

'There's a full week of spectacles I've missed, and two days after they wind up, the Ceres Games begin, and that's *another* eight days I could be exhibiting.'

Corbulo assumed a mock-serious expression. 'It takes time to – '

'Bollocks! You've had six months and more to knock those bloody beasts into shape.'

This time the trainer's solemnity was not forced. 'Those Syrian lions had been caged for three months by the time they reached me,' he said, his eyes narrowing. 'They weren't very amenable to being asked to play parlour games, not with half their fur rubbed off on the bars.'

'I've told you it won't happen again, but there's no reason why the elephants and the leopards – '

' – and the bears and the giraffe and the horses. What about them?' When the Etruscan thumped the table, not only the glasses but the plates and the pots and the serving trays danced. 'Or the camels, the warthogs and the rhino? And let's not forget the ostriches and the seals and the monkeys, either. Janus, man, what do you think I do all bloody day? Play hoops and throw javelins?'

'You've done well, Corbulo, but surely – '

The trainer hurled a silver platter across the room. 'If you don't fucking like what I've done, then fucking sack me!'

'Sit down,' pleaded Alis. 'Sergius doesn't mean it, he's tired – '

'He's drunk.' Pallas, as usual, took the shortcut. 'So I suggest the rest of us catch up. All right by you, my friend?'

Corbulo shrugged irritably but settled back down on the couch nevertheless.

'I'm not bloody drunk,' Sergius protested.

'Well, you look like shit,' said Euphemia, 'and if you're going to throw up, you want to do it outside.'

'Euphemia!' Alis had about as much control over her sister as Salvian had over his prisoner.

'I do feel groggy,' Sergius admitted. 'Maybe I'll just – ' His knees buckled as he tried to stand.

'Bedtime,' Timoleon intoned musically, slinging his yellow-faced host over his shoulder as though he were a roll of cloth. 'But no rumpy-pumpy for you tonight, Alis!' He guffawed at the high spots of colour that appeared in her cheeks. 'He's too far gone.'

'She doesn't get it, no matter what he's like,' Euphemia said spitefully. 'What is it you practise, sister? The Emperor's strategy?' She turned to Orbilio. 'You know what that is, don't you?'

'Well, um, Augustus has several strategies.' Somehow he'd lost the thread here.

'Sergius hates his darling wife to talk about it, but hadn't you wondered about the lack of brats? He wants his precious circus first – '

'Euphemia, please!' Alis wailed.

'Hence the Emperor's strategy. Abstinence! Can you believe that?'

Frankly, no, thought Orbilio. Augustus might cart his wife with him round the provinces, but his infidelities were legendary! Who, he wondered, thought that one up?

'You'll have to excuse me.' He yawned noisily. 'Long day.'

He was enjoying the quiet of the garden, with the cicadas rasping and moths dicing with death round the torches, when the messenger arrived from Rome. The letter bore the seal of the heron and Orbilio swore under his breath. He tipped the rider, and made two full, slow circuits of the colonnade before he even thought about reading it.

Callisunus was an oily bastard, who'd weaselled his way to the top, surrounding himself with high-calibre officers whose consistent results compensated for his own shortcomings. When they did well, Callisunus did well. When they failed – huh! talk about a man with sloping shoulders! A foul-mouthed so-and-so at the best of times, Jupiter alone knows what he had to say to an officer who'd abandoned a complex fraud case in the middle of the night to investigate a murder that was not even in his jurisdiction.

Orbilio found a marble bench and broke open the seal.

Callisunus, as ever, was to the point.

'What the fuck's going on?' the letter began, 'The Princeps is shouting down my throat and I've had to transfer Metellus to your case – not because you're arsing about in the country, but because a certain Paulus Vibius Corvinus (who you might recall is an ex-tribune, an ex-prefect as well as an ex-consul) claims you raped his bloody wife.'

The bitch! Orbilio rubbed his forehead. The absolute bitch!

'If that's not enough, now I get a complaint from Gisco to say you're shagging his wife, too. What is it with you, Orbilio? Too much red meat? Is that what makes you ride every filly within reach?'

He put it down. He couldn't read, the parchment was shaking so badly it was making him cross-eyed.

Mother of Tarquin, I've really cocked up this time. He leaned back and closed his eyes, waiting for the nausea to subside before picking up where he left off.

'The rape charge I've thrown out' – did he know Honoria's reputation? – 'but get this. Under no circumstances can I allow an officer of mine to be responsible for any further outbreaks of cuckolding, least of all amongst our most prominent citizens. A few weeks of "night starvation" ought to bring you to your senses, so until I say so, you will not set foot within these city walls. Do I make myself clear?'

Underneath, and written in Callisunus's own handwriting, as opposed to that of his scribe, was a postscript.

'So you know I mean business. I've told Gisco where to find you.'

For a cheap inn down the squalid end of town, it was doing a roaring trade by the time Froggy elbowed his way through the guffaws of laughter, the maudlin tales, the off-key shanties. The rest of his gang, he noticed with a tinge of rancour as he thumped down his goblet, had already dipped deep into one pitcher of wine and were calling for a second before he'd taken so much as a swill of the first.

'You're late tonight, Froggy,' chimed Pansa, tipping a set of knucklebones out of a dog-eared leather bag before stacking up an assortment of coins. 'Much longer and we'd have started without you.'

Froggy said nothing. He drained his goblet then pulled up a stool in the space the others had made for him, secure in the knowledge that they wouldn't pee without checking with him first.

'Put the bones away,' he ordered.

'No one's watching,' Ginger protested amiably. 'You can't see what goes on in this corner.'

'I know that,' Froggy replied irritably. It was why they always sat here on a market-day evening. Gambling, even in this dive, was still illegal. 'I want to talk.'

A collective groan rippled round the table, but the coins disappeared back into their respective purses. Froggy had been their leader since they could remember and they knew when they were beaten – Ginger, imaginatively named after his thatch of red hair; Pansa, who walked with his hand shielding the birthmark on his cheek; the two brothers Lefty and Restio; plus Festus, the shield-maker's son. Reluctantly Pansa scooped up the knucklebones.

Glancing about, Froggy satisfied himself the other revellers weren't listening. Right now their attention was fixed on a couple of newcomers making passes at the serving girls, and the innkeeper, who was having none of that, was pointing out a brothel over the way if they wanted, and of course they did. This was Narni. The Via Flaminia passed through it, so did the river Nera, and so did a constant procession of soldiers, bargees, porters and stevedores. The wealthier types – the merchants and their agents – lodged in more salubrious establishments, but there remained a whole host of clerks and labourers left to fend for themselves until their masters' business was done. The whores of Narni, like those of many a staging town, offered a bright spot of comfort in an otherwise bleak and ragged existence.

Froggy turned back to his friends. 'You know that job we did recently?'

'The burglary up by the – '

'The other one,' corrected Froggy, brushing his hair as a spider – or worse – fell from the rafters. Whatever the creature, he crushed it under his fist on the table. 'Sunday morning.' He wiped the remains of the insect down the seam of his tunic. 'When we ran that rig off the road.'

Easy money, that. He paused as plates piled high with boiled bacon and lentils were plumped in front of them, another part of the market-day ritual. A dish of grits completed the feast.

'What about it?' asked Ginger, blowing on his spoon. 'Something go wrong?'

'Not exactly.' Froggy was idly twirling his knife round his plate. 'But that's what made me late. Apparently some widow was on board, and now she's been charged with murder.'

Restio whistled. 'What a psycho!'

'Not half,' echoed Pansa. 'Count ourselves lucky she didn't do for one of us, eh, Froggy?'

A drunk bumbled over, a bargee – Froggy could tell by the smell of oxen which clung to him no matter how clean the poor sod's clothes. 'Piss-house is over there, mate,' he said, jerking his thumb towards the far corner. The drunk belched gratefully and lumbered towards the door.

'The trial', he continued, taking care not to raise his voice beyond the reach of the table, 'takes place here, in Narni, on Wednesday. You know what that means, don't you?'

'Narni?' asked Ginger, through a mouthful of veg. 'Why not Tarsulae?'

'Where', Froggy scoffed, 'could they scrape up four-score jurists in that shithole? No, the show's coming here, so you see the significance? Everyone, and I mean *everyone* at the Villa Pictor will be called as a witness.'

'Wow!' said Restio, because although he hadn't a clue what Froggy was driving at, he sensed it was important enough to warrant reverence.

Froggy leaned forward. 'It seems to me, lads, that here's our chance to make a bit of dosh – '

'We got paid well for that,' Pansa put in, but Froggy ploughed on.

'Now, as I see it, we have two choices. According to my contact at the courts, this old bag's supposed to have arranged to meet with the bloke who got killed – '

'But she couldn't have,' Restio protested. 'Because we run her off the road and according to that innkeeper in Tarsulae, she was headed north.'

'Thank you, witness for the defence, you may step down now,' said Froggy, topping up his wooden goblet. 'Now if you'll let me get on, as I said, we have two choices. Either we approach the widow's lawyer, tell him what we know – oh, we can say it was an accident, didn't realize anyone had been hurt, how sorry we were – but there's no mileage in that.'

In all probability the widow was old, she certainly wasn't well off or she'd have been travelling the main road for a start, and she'd have had a retinue of slaves and baggage. Frankly Froggy couldn't see the old girl heaping rewards upon his head for coming forward – not on the scale he fancied, any road.

'Which leaves us with our second option. You see, boys, I don't think our client will want it bandied about that we were paid to run that rig off the road. Do you?' In fact, I think we're on to a nice little earner with this one.

XIII

'Is going to rain.'

Good, thought Claudia, taking half a step back from the Celt. You might be tempted to stand out in it.

'And Sergius, he not look so good.' Taranis fell into step along the colonnade, his long hair flicking up at the ends as he walked. A stranger to the strigil, it was difficult to see what Tulola saw in him. Ruff-tuff hairy types Pallas had said, and from that aspect Taranis certainly fitted the bill. Self-respecting Romans shave their body hair; they don't have whopping great tufts of it sticking out the neck of their tunics and the hems of their sleeves like horsehair stuffing from an old couch. Idly she wondered how Tulola came by so many oddballs.

'You visit west wing later, heh? We play fours, you go with Barea and I do Tulola?'

'I'd sooner drink hemlock.'

'Ah!' Two paws latched over her breasts. 'You want Taranis to yourself – *eeeeeeeeh*.'

Claudia squeezed his testicles tighter. 'Listen to me, lizardbreath! Lay so much as one black fingernail on me again, and I shall twist these right off and stuff them up your nostrils. Do I make myself plain?'

She took the tears in his eyes as affirmative and stalked off to her bedroom for a wrap. Drusilla, her ancestry bestowing magnanimity despite the string of indignities, was balanced on the windowsill studiously washing behind her ears. So the barbarian was right? It was going to rain.

'Brrp.' The cat bounded down. 'Brrip, brrip.'

'I know, poppet, but it won't be for much longer.' She raked her fingers along Drusilla's arched spine. 'Only we have a slight problem here.'

'Mrra.' The cat stretched up on tippytoes, her eyes squeezed tight in ecstasy.

'The Prefect, you see, is a moron.' Although he has yet to appreciate this particular aspect of his character.

'Mrrap, mrrap.' Drusilla's stiffened tail received the fingernail treatment right up to its tip.

'Are you getting dandruff? Oh no, it's only flaky plaster. Anyway, what I was saying was: to avoid the idiocy of a trial, it is up to us to show Macer the error of his ways, is it not?'

'Prrr.'

'Prrrcisely. And in order to do this we must unveil the killer ourselves.' One murder is undesirable. Two murders smacks of self-indulgence. 'Do you have any suggestions where to begin?'

'Brrrp.'

'Neither do I.'

Drusilla lifted her wedge-shaped head. 'Mrrow.'

'Me? Framed? You're getting as bad as Supersnoop.' The wrong place at the wrong time, Orbilio. You'll see. 'But we have a nose for sniffing out murderers, don't we, poppet? We'll get him – or her, it could be a her, I suppose – and that'll put paid to this ridiculous talk about exile. Ah! I have a treat for you.'

A cold partridge plopped on to the mosaic and the cat sniffed it carefully from all angles. You might call flabby poultry a treat, her manner seemed to imply, but you forget, my lady, that I'm used to dining on food I've hunted myself. Even as we speak, there's a fresh mouse outside with my name on it. Catch you later.

With a smile at her lips, Claudia covered her shoulders with her palla.

'I wouldn't venture far, if I were you.' The voice of the trainer in the courtyard made her jump. She'd forgotten how light he was on his feet.

'Oh?' Was this a warning?

The Etruscan quickly closed the distance between them. 'There's a storm brewing.'

Claudia's breath came out in a hiss from where she'd been holding it. 'I need the fresh air.' Fresh? With that number of wild beasts? 'What about you? Do you always work this late?'

He held the gate open for her. 'Work? Oh, you're thinking about that scene back there with Sergius.'

I wasn't, but go on.

'We do that, him and me. I throw pots, he throws insults, then it's forgotten.' A big cat snarled as they passed its shed. 'Quiet, Sheba!' He paused by the ostrich pen. 'May I walk with you a way?'

Intense grey eyes bored into hers. For a man who works all day with animals, she thought, you always manage to smell of citron and woodsmoke.

'Why not?'

In silence they passed along a line of clipped laurels, the imminence of the storm intensifying the scent of the leaves. A flash of lightning silhouetted a rhino against the sky and a bear growled.

'You have a farm in my homeland, I gather?'

'Vineyards,' she corrected. 'Across the Tiber then half-a-day's hard ride. Is that close to your stomping ground?'

'No,' he said. 'I'm from the coast, but like most other Etruscans you'll meet, I was uprooted without a great deal of ceremony.'

She picked up on the sour note. 'The Emperor's Land Purchase Scheme strikes again, eh?'

'Worse than that. I lived in Carrera before Augustus turned it into a marble quarry.'

'Well, if it's any consolation, Corbulo, you shifted for a good cause. When you do take those show beasts to Rome, you'll see half your motherland slapped over the temples.' The Oil Market is positively dazzling.

'Don't start on about the Games, Claudia,' he said, but this time there was a jocular tone to his words. 'I'm getting enough of an earful from Sergius. He expects bloody miracles.'

Was it the distant rumble of thunder that made the air electric? Or the proximity of the Etruscan?

'From what I saw of the elephant, you've delivered bloody miracles! Is he really as ill as Taranis says?'

'Nothing's ever like Taranis says. I think you'll find Sergius has miscalculated on the amount of wine an empty stomach can cope with.'

'They say things come in threes,' she replied carefully. 'Fronto, then Coronis. It makes me wonder who's next.'

The trainer's face creased into a grin. 'Well, stop,' he said. 'Accidents happen all the time.'

'Fronto was no accident, and Macer has me pegged for a murderess, remember?'

'Macer has straw for brains. None of us think you killed Fronto, and Sergius intends to draft a complaint to the Emperor himself when he's feeling a bit more chipper. Now let's turn back, those clouds look ugly.'

Claudia couldn't decide whether the deafening noise was thunder or the thumping of her heart. It wasn't that she was drawn to him physically – he did not, after all, have the desperate magnetism that, say for instance, Marcus Cornelius possessed by the boatload (as of course did hundreds of others whose names would no doubt come to her later) – but the intensity of those tundra eyes was incredibly flattering, and who doesn't respond to that? Moreover, he was strong and he really wasn't bad looking once you got past the double bump that proclaimed his heritage. Most of all, Corbulo looks the type who takes his time – and aeons had passed since Claudia Seferius had felt the slow touch of a man's hand . . .

Plus which. Unlike an affair with a certain security policeman, there would be no repercussions afterwards! It was certainly something to think about.

'I'll venture another hundred paces,' she said, hoping the rumbles would drown the hoarseness of her voice. What did he see in Tulola – apart from the obvious? 'Alone, if you don't mind.'

You don't associate Corbulo with a role in the harem.

'I can't leave you out here!'

He was as far removed from the likes of Timoleon as Neptune from a wood nymph.

'I can look after myself,' she assured him. Always have. Always will. 'Goodnight.'

'Very well, then.' He reached for her hand and kissed the back of it. 'If you insist.'

Surprisingly he did not retrace his steps, but turned to the right instead. 'It's you who needs help,' she quipped. 'The house is straight on.'

He hesitated. 'I don't sleep in the house,' he called back. 'My quarters back on to the elephant house.' There was a moment's silence before he added, 'If you should ever want to call on me.'

She walked on up the hill, her thoughts chasing each other like puppies in hay. It made sense – in retrospect! She'd never seen Corbulo with Tulola, simply made an assumption. Which changed everything!

A bolt of white lightning shattered the night, its jagged veins scarring the sky. Claudia shivered. There was a primeval quality to storms without rain. Flashes of whitehot fire. Crashes of Jupiter's thundersticks. She pulled her wrap tight and watched the night tear itself apart. In their sheds in the valley, the wild beasts roared and bucked and faced down the elements. Up here, familiar shapes contorted into sinister strangers. Mundane branches of gnarled oak became the twisted limbs of fiends. The perky stream that gave the Pictors their water turned into a menacing river of blood.

It's getting to me, she thought. The strain is beginning to tell.

The wind began to howl through the trees. Time to turn back. She wished now she'd brought a brand to light her way. Perhaps she should follow the brook? Dammit, she'd forgotten the hedge that fenced in the gazelles. Her palla snagged on the thorns. Damn!

The path. Where was it?

A barn owl, white and silent, swooped for the safety of the canopy.

Uneasy now, Claudia stumbled through the undergrowth, tripping on a stone, stubbing her toe on a fallen branch . . .

Far below, the house shone in a blaze of light. It was just a question of reaching it . . .

A wild-eyed doe crashed through the brambles and Claudia cried out. She could taste juniper in the air, and sickly sweet manna. Bats! There's a bat in my hair! But it was just a briar, which drew blood when she pulled free. High above, the wind conducted a malevolent orchestra. Poplars whistled, chestnuts wailed and there was a tuneless flute in the pines. Then, suddenly, the path showed clear in a flare of white.

Dear Diana. I thought I'd never find you!

Blindly she raced down the hill, heedless of rocks that trip and roots that trap, and only when she was well clear of the woods did she begin to slow down. Claudia Seferius, pull yourself together. This is foolish. She brushed away cobs of blood where the briar had scratched. Extremely foolish!

Yet the sense of evil was all-pervasive . . .

What utter tosh! Fancy letting yourself be frightened by a storm! Now get a grip. It won't do, walking through the atrium with every goddamned bone rattling!

Resisting the urge to belt the rest of the way, Claudia decided to beat the demons by singing. That, and the rumpus from the menagerie, should put the wind up even the Minotaur! She was passing the monkey house and was well into the second verse of a bawdy winehouse ballad when her scalp began to prickle. Half of her, the educated half, said this is silly, slow down, you're on edge. But the other half, the half that remembered growing up in the slums, said stand by your instincts and remember that in situations like this, only one word applies.

Runlikehell.

But she could not run fast enough.

Out of the blackness a hand lashed out and caught at her wrap. She shrugged the palla free but the hand was prepared for that. Like a striking cobra, it lunged at her flying tunic. She heard that tear, too, but the grip was solid and she was spun helplessly round. Suddenly a sack was flung over her head, blinding her, pinning her arms. Frantically she scrabbled and clawed, but with the advantage of sight, her assailant twisted and dodged, and none of the kicks found their target. The cloth muffled her screams. An arm clamped round her waist like a band round a barrel. She heard thunderclaps and bellows and terrified roars from the pens. The rhino charged its shed wall, the elephant trumpeted. Yelling and fighting, she was dragged backwards into the bushes. Another rip, as her hem caught on holly.

Rape! The bastard intended to rape her!

A second vice locked round her neck, forcing her head back. The sacking rasped against her cheek, clogged her mouth, blocked her nostrils. She could hear herself gagging on the dust. Desperately she tried to break free, but the armlock tightened and she began to choke.

Progress was faster now her resistance was gone. Frenziedly fighting for breath, Claudia tried to get her bearings. He was dragging her up the hill, hardly surprising . . . No! Not a hill. That's terraced. This was more an embankment. Why didn't he throw her to the ground here and now? No one could see, no one could hear. What was he waiting for?

Then something hard collided with the small of her back. Wood. Sharp. Pointed, surely? A fence? Without warning, he let go her neck, grabbed her ankles and tipped her backwards.

Oh, no. Sweet Jupiter, no!

As the reverberations of the fall crushed the breath out of her, the full horror became clear. This wasn't rape. *He intended to kill her!* Because there was only one palisade on Sergius' estate. It enclosed the crocodiles . . .

Hacking, choking, Claudia twisted her foot and found a toehold between the posts. Not much, just enough to give her purchase so she could jerk free of the sack. She heard a thud as he vaulted the fence, and too late she was back in a headlock. Claudia heard him (her?) grunt with the effort. Man or woman, it needed precious little brute force, a crime like this, based on the mechanics of haulage. Her ankle wrenched under the strain and she tasted blood where she bit through her lip with the pain. At her back, the sack was twisted round and round, tighter and tighter for leverage. Dear Juno, if there is any mercy in your breast, give him heart failure. Right here on the spot.

Utterly helpless, she was wrenched from the palisade. Tears rolled down her cheeks. Don't let me die, she prayed. Don't let me die in a grainsack. Not a grainsack. Not gagged and trussed and –

Wait a minute! Claudia gulped at the hope that dangled in front of her. He could have suffocated or strangled her at any point and he hadn't. Why not?

Because her death must appear accidental, that's why not. Dark night. Storm. Terrified beasts who might rampage any second. Poor Claudia. Took fright and ran. Didn't know where she was going. Until it was too late.

Very soon, then, he would have to remove the evidence. But how? Pulling off the sack would free her to fight back, unless... of course! She'd have to be unconscious.

Bugger that for a game of knucklebones!

As the attacker fought to heave his struggling bundle over the peak of the earthworks, she let out a short moan and fell limp. Heaven knows there were enough rocks about; any one could have knocked her cold. But would he fall for it?

Several scary minutes passed and nothing happened. Was this a test? Would a boot ram into her ribs any second and expose her trickery? Or was he taking advantage of the lull to get his wind back?

The tension was almost as terrifying as the struggle. Then, finally, he grabbed the top of the sack and yanked, and she prayed that in tipping a dead weight out in the dark, he wouldn't be concentrating on where her hand went.

It closed over a rock.

Seizing hold of her ankles, he began to lug her over the brow. Above the storm and the growls and the trumpeting, she could hear him wheezing with the effort.

Sinister splashes came from the water below and she felt her heart lurch. Timing was crucial...

When he leaned forward to push his unconscious victim down the bank, Claudia lashed out. There was a sickening squelch as stone drove into flesh, and his mouth formed a wide O as the cry was drowned by a clap of thunder. Stunned only momentarily, his face twisted in fury and he swung towards her. With reflexes dulled by the fight, she just had time to brace herself as strong hands closed round her throat. The night, low and heavy, obscured her attacker's face. Who are you? Why are you doing this? Thumbs pressed into her neck, deeper and deeper, then suddenly one hand released her and they both stumbled.

Blinded by the blood in his eyes, her assailant had lost his balance. As he looked round for a foothold, the rock she still clutched in her fist caught him on the nose, and this time she made no mistake in the force she should use. His nose exploded under the impact, his hands flew up to protect himself and, in that split second, he realized he had lost. A second cry rent the air as he stumbled backwards, his feet scrabbling furiously on the bank, his hands clawing gouges in the mud as the momentum carried him down the bank towards the snapping jaws of hell.

Then, in a flash of silver lightning, Claudia saw for the first time the face of the person who was trying to kill her.

XIV

'Janus!'

For a split second the shock was so great that she couldn't breathe, let alone move, and when she did recover, it came as a bigger shock still to find her instinct was to pull, rather than push.

Using one of the larger rocks as leverage, Claudia flung herself flat and stretched out her arm. 'Take it!' she yelled. 'Take my hand!'

The face below was white with terror, panic barely a short gasp away.

You could see the dilemma. The loose earth had slipped far enough, and like a burr on a blanket, her attacker was stuck on the side of the embankment. To move would court disaster.

The words 'Fetch help' were mouthed to her, but it was too late. The rains had already begun.

'No time,' she yelled back, as the look of bewilderment on her assailant's face deepened. 'Take my hand!'

They started with just a few large drops, yet within seconds a cataract was falling from the sky, beating the parched earth like a drum, the overflow gushing down gulleys.

'Quick!'

There was no time to dither! Any second now and

the packed earthworks would turn to slippery mud. In the waters below, stippled with raindrops, larger shapes twisted and dived.

Claudia strained forward, her hair plastered flat to her face. 'It's your only chance!'

Like most opportunities, this came but the once. With a hiss, the side of the bank began to slip forward, the gap between them widening with obscene slowness. For several seconds, inhuman scrabbling kept the burr on the blanket, but the torrents had turned the earth to slime.

There was only one direction left.

Claudia felt her own weight slide and she lurched at the rock with both hands, throwing herself on top of it. The angle she landed and the desperation she needed to cling on gave her no choice but to watch.

And listen. Above the howling of the wind and the battering of the rain, unearthly screeches rent the air. Then, mercifully, the sky began to go dark, yet she could still hear the frantic thrashings, the snapping of jaws, the crushing of bone even as the blackness closed in . . .

'Claudia! Claudia, wake up!'

Someone was hitting her. Godsdammit, someone was slapping her face.

'It's all right, you're safe. It's over.'

Now someone was holding her wrists.

'Dammit, Claudia, stop kicking me!'

'Marcus?' Where was she? Why were security policemen holding her down? 'Marcus?'

'I like it when you call me Marcus. Makes you sound sweet and pliable, warm-hearted and understanding.'

'Clog off.'

'That's better! Thought for a minute you were losing your touch.'

Claudia sat up. 'What happened to my head?'

'You've had a knock,' Orbilio replied, supporting her shoulders, 'but I reckon you'll live.'

Claudia looked round. She was lying in the lee of one of the animal sheds, camels by the sound of it, where he must have carried her. The rain was hammering down on the roof. 'There's a lump on my temple the size of an ostrich egg.'

'Quail's egg,' he corrected, wiping her hair off her face and wrapping his cloak round her shoulders. 'So stop trawling for sympathy. Can you stand?' He helped her gently to her feet.

'How did you find me?'

'Your wrap. I found it lying on the path, ripped to shreds.'

'Oh.' She wanted to thank him, but didn't know how. 'What are all those lights?'

'Once I got you to safety, I sent for help. They're searching for the body. Er – I'm presuming there *is* a body to find?'

Claudia nodded numbly. She wanted to tell him what had happened, but for some reason her teeth wouldn't stop chattering and her hands seemed to be shaking like an old man with palsy.

He shouted for one of the slaves to come over. 'Help Mistress Seferius to the house, will you? Give her a sleeping draught and – '

'No.' If her mouth wouldn't work properly, at least he'd understand the violent shaking of her head. 'I'm coming with you.'

'No, you're not!'

She tried to say, try and stop me, but it came out like a death rattle. Instead, she pushed him aside and set off in the lashing rain towards the embankment, her torn tunic flapping and her calves caked with mud. She had to see this through to the finish. Barely a dozen paces later, her knees turned traitor.

'Silly bitch,' he said, grinning at her from ear to ear. 'Come along.'

Scooping her into his arms, he carried her to the top of the bank and set her down on a wide, flat rock well clear of any landslips. 'Stay!' he ordered, as though addressing a dog.

Hell, she couldn't move if she tried, but it was a good vantage point. A hundred torches had been lit, guttering in the deluge but still managing to survive; ladders and ropes had been brought along for safety, since dusty paths had turned to quagmires, irrigation channels to flash floods. Gingerly she rubbed the lump on her forehead and huddled deep under Orbilio's weatherproof cloak.

None of the amphibians resisted the lasso round their tails. Now I'm full, they seemed to say, I'll let you play tag if you like. Even so, the search was not easy, and it was lucky one of the party hailed from Egypt and was able to throw light on these primordial creatures' habits.

As the search party trod the murky waters, Claudia felt an overwhelming relief that, finally, the nightmare was over. It made no sense, but this was the person who had watched Claudia Seferius leave the villa, had lain in ambush for her return, planning long and hard that her murder should look like an accident, the same way Coronis' murder was designed to look like an accident.

This, then, was the person who'd stabbed Fronto – but what had Claudia seen, or was imagined to have seen, that turned her into such a liability?

Probably – regrettably – she would never know.

Suddenly a cry went up as the bloody trophy was ferried back and the crowd began to concentrate itself on one small part of the shore. They were all here, she realized. Storm or no storm, master and slave alike, the whole household would have assembled for the climax.

The corpse, when it was finally hauled on to the slippery bank, was a total mess. One leg had been taken off completely, the other severed above the knee, and an arm was missing. Claudia began to retch.

'All right?'

Orbilio held her while she was sick, wiped her mouth with his handkerchief. She could do no more than nod.

'Just the reaction,' she explained, although the words didn't actually make it past her larynx.

Later, in the shelter of the house, with mulled wine on the inside and dry clothes on the outside and Claudia Seferius out cold from a hyoscine draught, everyone was agreed that they had never, in their lives, seen such a sickening spectacle as that mangled body.

Equally they were unanimous in that they had no clue as to who the dead man might be.

XV

Old age might bring maturity and wisdom, experience and nous, and it might well conceal a chicanery all of its own, but it is no substitute for the zeal and fire of youth. Or the fact that youth brings about a speed of recovery verging on the indestructible.

Claudia yawned, stretched and tickled Drusilla's ears. 'Time, young lady, for you to pack up your mouse bones, your furballs and any other souvenirs you might have acquired from the Villa Pictor.'

Only this time, please, let's leave the fleas behind!

Claudia reached for the goblet beside her bed and sniffed. 'Ugh! Henbane!' No wonder she'd slept so well. A good twelve hours at a guess, although there was no sun to pinpoint it further. The rains might have gone, but the clouds hung like hammocks, low and heavy, the sky bark-grey and cheerless.

'Mrrrr.' Drusilla wriggled in pleasure and rolled on to her side.

Whoever had come into her room to open the shutters had also been thoughtful enough to leave a tray. Claudia slapped a chunk of pecorino cheese, her favourite, on to a still-warm roll flavoured with parsley and chives as Drusilla helped herself to a prawn.

'Thank heavens there's no red meat on this tray, we

had quite enough of that last night, thank you very much!'

Claudia quickly skimmed over the lump of humanity mashed to a squelch by the crocodiles and moved on to the question of why that total stranger should want to kill her in the first place. Very odd. But then the whole place was very odd.

'I suppose it was *me* he was after?' Who else could he have mistaken me for? Not a man. Tulola? Too tall. Euphemia? Too fat. 'Alis?' she said aloud.

Drusilla, chomping on another prawn, didn't turn so much as a whisker.

'I know you can hear me, you little fraud.' Judging by the debris all over this counterpane, you've been stuffing yourself since the moment my breakfast arrived. 'I said, could anyone mistake me for Alis?'

'Brip.'

'I don't *know* why, poppet, I was simply asking whether it was possible. Not that it matters. We're heading back to Rome.'

'Mrrip.'

'House arrest? Forget that.' Not even Macer, with his unique propensity for putting two and two together and coming up with twenty-two, could lay this latest attack at Claudia's door. 'No, very soon we'll be home again, life will be back to normal before you know it.'

Normal? What was normal? Between being born in the south and her dancing days in Genua, life had been anything but predictable, and since marrying Gaius . . .? Put it this way. If Claudia Seferius had been a knife, she'd never have gone rusty.

Realizing Drusilla was not going to be sidetracked so

long as one pink prawn remained standing, she eased the cat to one side and slid out of bed.

'First your mistress needs a long, hot soak' – for all youth's advantages, it couldn't heal injuries like hers overnight – 'and then we'll set off. How's that?'

A lump of fish fell from Drusilla's mouth. Her body arched and her hackles were fully erect before Claudia's ears picked up the whistle.

'Junius!' One of the first things she'd taught him was that three-note signal. 'What brings you to darkest Umbria?'

The Gaul's jaw dropped. 'By the gods, madam! Are you all right?'

In the course of four days I've been run off the road, bounced down a hillside, had a dying dung-beetle thrust upon me; I've seen the sharp point of Euphemia's knife, been accused of murder, discovered Coronis, been beaten then half throttled by a total stranger *and you ask, am I all right?*

'Bubbling with health.' To prove it she shot him her healthiest, heartiest, halest of smiles. 'Now, answer the question.'

'Three reasons.' Junius, unconvinced, produced a scroll from the belt of his tunic and passed it through the open window. 'First, this was waiting for you up at the villa.'

Claudia recognized the seal. It was the report from her surveyor.

'I think it could have waited,' the young Gaul continued, 'but while I was there, one of Macer's officers called to see Rollo.'

'So?' It sounded terribly routine to a girl for whom a deep soak in steaming hot water beckoned very loudly.

'I'd briefed him on most of what had happened, I just hadn't had a chance to tell him about the servants.'

'What servants?'

'You told Macer you'd sent them ahead by ox cart, when, of course, we never took any with us.'

'Water under the Milvian Bridge, Junius. Last night some homicidal maniac damned near killed me, so I don't think anyone's going to lose sleep over one titchy-witchy fib, do you?'

'There's something else, too.'

Claudia waved an airy hand. 'Don't care, don't want to know. I appreciate your efforts, but my advice is go to the kitchens then see if you can grab forty winks. In an hour or two, we set sail for Rome.'

'But, madam – '

'Butts are where archery is practised, Junius.' To emphasize her point, she snapped the shutters to.

She heard a finely rounded oath of Gallic origin then, when silence prevailed (or what passed for silence, when you're billeted next door to a hundred yowling beasts), she flung back the shutters and studied the sky. Was that a break in the clouds she detected?

'With luck, poppet,' she picked up Drusilla and swung her several times round in the air, 'we should be home for the equinox.'

Always a good excuse for a knees-up, and heaven knows she needed one after this. Umbria? You can keep it! It'll take a lot to prise me away from Rome in the future, and then if I travel, I stick to main roads!

'Bbbrow!'

That's the trouble with Egyptian cats. The effect of twirling them isn't immediately obvious, they're boss-eyed to start with.

The bath was tempting but . . . 'Let's just see how that report reads, shall we?'

Claudia threw herself face-down on the bed. Drusilla dived through the open window without so much as a backward glance.

'Ingrate!' Bet you won't be so proud when it comes to a piece of bacon at lunchtime.

Claudia broke the seal and flipped open the letter.

'Madam,' it read, 'I am pleased to report that I have assessed the two Etruscan sites and my conclusions are as follows. With reference to the damage by fire, this is entirely superficial and has no real bearing on the plans you have for either property . . .' blah, blah, blah ' . . . and in conclusion, I would say this. Hunter's Grove would be a suitable proposition for the growing of vines since the soil, though light, has excellent water-retention properties and is devoid of both chalk and tufa. White grapes will grow best here, and I strongly recommend the Thrasian variety to optimize soil conditions.'

Thrasian grapes, eh? He was smarter than she thought, this surveyor chappie.

'As for Vixen Hill, although the site is superficially appealing, being south-facing and fed by a small brook, it is my recommendation that you steer clear of this property, since the land is not, as has been made to appear, in a state of neglect. The soil is exhausted and totally unsuitable for wine production, or indeed any other agricultural project. Should you require any further . . .' etc, etc, etc.

She let the scroll drop on to the floor and rested her chin on the bolster. The auction is on Saturday, the same day as the spring equinox. Do I bid in person or do I send an agent? No matter. There are far more pressing issues. Such as, which of Tulola's brightly coloured tunics could I borrow next? And can I be certain the bath house operates a segregation policy?

The last thing Claudia wanted at the moment was to find herself naked and alone with Timoleon or Barea barging in, but at least the Celt wouldn't be a problem. The fastest way to get Taranis out of a bath is to open the taps.

The changing-room steward assured her there was no chance of men barging in on her ablutions and left her in the capable hands of a large Cappadocian woman with characteristically curled hair and a laugh that rattled the finials on the roof.

'Hot room? Wouldn't if I was you, ducks.' Not madam. Ducks. 'You want them cuts to seal over, don't yer? Well, steam 'em and clean 'em, that's old Cinna's motto. Right now, luvvie, into the buskins. Don't want them pretty feet burned on the tiles, do we?'

Which just about set the pattern for the next half-hour. To a backdrop of life in the Cappadocian Uplands, which this woman could only ever have heard second-hand, Claudia's flesh surrendered itself to be oiled and scraped, steamed and massaged. Truly heaven on earth!

'Them weals round your ankles looks worse than they are, but old Cinna's camomile compress'll fix 'em in a jiffy. By tomorrow they won't even show.'

Between the harmonious scrape of the strigil, the lilt of the woman's voice and the impenetrable swirling steam, aches eased and bruises were banished. Bastard! she thought. She didn't even know the man, why should he pick on her? Still, he was dead now – and it was a death Claudia wouldn't have wished on her worst enemy. Except, hang on, he *was* her worst enemy! He was the one who'd deliberately planned to feed her to the crocodiles! Hell, yes – and I tried to save the bugger, too.

'My word, you have been in the wars. Rub my balsam salve on them bumps and cuts, luvvie, and they'll be gone before you look in the mirror. Oh, hello, duck. Which do you want, the hot room or the steam?'

Tulola ungirdled her gown. Like all her tunics, this was also designed to slide away in one piece and she wore neither breast band nor thong underneath.

'Steam's fine,' she purred, her eyes raking Claudia's naked back. 'Is that your famous rose oil I can smell?'

'That you can, my luv, and I expect you'll be wanting a rub over with it, too. Let me give you a hand with them buskins – '

'No rub today, Cinna. Why don't you go and check the plunge pool?'

'I'm not half finished with my first darling, yet.'

'I told you, Cinna, you check the plunge pool.' She laid one stiffened finger on Claudia's bare shoulder and began to trace a pattern. 'I'll finish the massage.'

Claudia slithered off the bench. 'Don't trouble yourself, I'm off to soak in the hot room.'

She knew Tulola would follow, but at least you could see where you were and pre-empt the strike. 'How's your brother?' she asked, easing herself into the water. 'Fully recovered from last night's little episode?'

'Funny you should ask,' Tulola replied, a frown

furrowing her usually unlined forehead. 'I'm rather worried about him, as a matter of fact.'

The change in Tulola startled her. 'Why?'

'He's such a ghastly yellow, and he feels bilious all the time.'

Claudia, who knew nothing about nursing, suggested that if he was too ill to ride into Tarsulae, why not let the horse doctor take a look at him?

'I suggested that,' Tulola said earnestly, 'but he wouldn't have it. Insists there's nothing wrong, apart from a spot of food poisoning.'

'He could be right, you know.'

'Nonsense, sweetie. He'd have been as sick as a dog if it was something he ate.'

'What does Alis think?'

Tulola snorted. 'Alis! If my brother told her blue was yellow and she was a grasshopper, she'd believe him. "Anything my husband says goes" is all you get from that pompous little cow.' She kicked violently at the water.

'Sergius is a grown man, I dare say he knows what he's doing.' Claudia bobbed right under to wash the caked mud out of her hair.

'That's what that sulky bitch Euphemia said.' Tulola began to chew her nail. 'No one seems bothered about him except me. Even Scrap Iron thinks it'll pass, and he's well used to death and injury.'

'But not illness, remember. Look, it was a long day yesterday, one way and another, perhaps the others are right. Maybe you're worrying unduly? Now, if you'll excuse me, I'm finished here.'

There was an argument raging in the atrium, she

could hear it from outside. Timoleon, who had taken to fighting with words in lieu of net and trident, had this time picked on the Celt. Claudia positioned herself behind a pillar.

'Who you call coward, you dirty motherfucker? I leave because there are too many dead men.'

'Frightened of ghosts, Taranis?'

'Who knows who is next to have knife in his back, heh?'

'The killer's dead, you saw him – or at least what was left of him.' Timoleon's taunts were having little effect, so he moved up a gear. 'Unless you set him up and you're the murderer?'

'You crazy, you know that? Killer need motive, I have no motive.'

Timoleon picked up the Celt's ragged pack, upended the contents over the tiles and sneered. 'Psychopaths kill for pleasure.'

'Like you, yes? Like you kill in the arena? Well, maybe you kill this Fronto? Maybe you kill me when my back is turned?'

'You'd call me a backstabber? You little turd, I'll – '

Pity. Just when it gets interesting, Macer makes his entrance.

'What's going on?' He held out an imperious foot for a slave to clean his boot. 'More trouble?'

For all his faults, he had a perfect sense of balance, did the heavily armoured Prefect. Not so much as a wobble as the servant scraped off the mud.

'No trouble, Macer,' Timoleon replied, deliberately crushing one of Taranis' cloakpins underfoot. 'One big, happy family, us.'

And I'm a Vestal Virgin, thought Claudia from behind the column.

Glimpsing his buckled brooch, the barbarian turned puce. 'You bastard!'

'Did you hear that, Salvian? One big, happy family.' Macer held out his other foot. 'Yet I don't recall your father and I throttling each other as boys. Separate them, will you, lad?'

That was another thing. Normally you had to be eighteen to qualify as a junior tribune, and the days of favoured sons being given soft commissions went out with Augustus' shake-up. Interesting.

Salvian, however, wasn't as daft as he looked. Rank might hold in the forces, you could see him thinking, but it wouldn't separate two strong civilians. Whereas a bucket of water from the atrium pool would.

'Now we have that sorted out,' Macer unstrapped his helmet and brushed the red plumes into shape, 'perhaps someone can brief me on the events of last – And just where might you be going, sir?'

Taranis, his grimy face streaked with the water, hefted his pack on his shoulders. 'I . . . I go to homeland, to Atrebates. Is not safe here.'

'I think you'll be perfectly safe here, sir, while my officers and I are stationed on the premises. So until I get to the root of this nasty business, no one leaves, and I mean no one. Is that clear?'

A low grumble emanated from the Celt's throat, which could have been construed either way.

'In fact, until I say to the contrary – ' not only a good sense of balance, Macer, he had a nice way with words, too – 'you don't even fart without my permission. Pass the word round.'

Hidden behind the pillar, Claudia waited until the atrium emptied. She watched Macer clap his arm round his nephew's shoulder as the two of them disappeared into the courtyard. She watched the legionaries file out of the main entrance and head towards the slaves' barracks. She watched Timoleon wring the water out of his yellow hair as he chuckled his way to his room.

And she watched Taranis throw a murderous glance at what she first thought was the the gladiator's retreating back, and then was not so sure that Timoleon was the intended target.

Unfortunately the marble column prevented her seeing who was.

XVI

The last place you'd expect to find an oasis of peace and tranquillity in this madhouse was at its centre, but that's life for you. One surprise after the other. In consequence, while the Prefect and his entourage jangled off to inspect mutilated corpses and snack-happy crocodiles, and while an army of slaves waged war on cobwebs and dirt with an arsenal of sponges on poles and ostrich-feather dusters, Claudia twiddled the rings on her fingers and examined the marble statuary dotted between the topiaries.

The impending trial aside, to say she was at a crossroads in her life was to elevate understatement to an art form. Augustus' sweeping reforms were not confined to the army or the land, public buildings or public works, far from it. Since poor health had effectively grounded him twelve years previously, he sought greater and nobler causes to advance, with morals topping his agenda. Other people's morals, that is. He meant well, she'd give him that. On the whole he was a decent, honest and well-meaning bloke whose infidelities were no more than light relief at a time when the weight of the Empire was enormous, and for so elevated a position he lived humbly and he lived frugally, the days when he prostituted himself to a consul for financial advancement or became Caesar's catamite as the price for adoption almost forgotten.

But only almost. Doubtless it was his past that shaped her present – that and the fact that the number of actual citizens, as opposed to prisoners-of-war who had become slaves, was dwindling fast. In an effort to stabilize marriage and encourage larger families, Augustus' moral reforms discouraged birth control, made divorce difficult and adultery a criminal offence (at least as far as women were concerned). More pertinently, widows had two years in which either to mourn or to rejoice before re-marriage became mandatory.

Already one-quarter of Claudia's freedom had slipped past. . . .

She paused between the laurels and looked up. Jupiter's storm clouds were gathering again, there would be another tempest tonight. Beside her, the winged dragon that had carried Medea to Corinth bared its sharp bronze teeth.

When she first heard Gaius had left her the whole lot – his house, his vineyards, his investment properties – her immediate thought had been 'sell them'. All of them. Turn them into cash and be done with. It was why she'd married him, wasn't it? And let's face it, Claudia Seferius' knowledge of wine was strictly limited . . . to the level of the contents of her glass! Later, though, when a reliable source suggested the business should net 10 per cent comfortably, it seemed sensible to hang on and live off the earnings.

So what went wrong? And why, after a winter spent poring over accounts that showed profits closer to 7 per cent and maybe as low as 6 per cent, had she felt a physical revulsion about selling? Quintilian wasn't the only patronizing son-of-a-bitch to put in an offer, whether for outright purchase or marriage in which, ha-ha, the Widow Seferius came as a bonus on top of their, ha-ha, shrewd investment.

She'd give them ha-bloody-ha.

Fortunately, she was, so far, the only person who knew that sales were ... not as good as forecast (that was it, not as good as forecast), but word would get out soon enough. With a shiver, Claudia left the dragon and studied a marble satyr. Clearly drunk, his outstretched goblet begged for a refill. She patted him on his goatish knee. It's true, isn't it? All roads lead to wine. One way or another.

In her own case, and with little else to occupy her during the long winter evenings, she had set out to improve her knowledge of commerce. Since, by a strange quirk of fate which had nothing whatsoever to do with her, her gambling debts had spiralled up the wall and over the ceiling, it was a gushing flow of liquid cash she needed, not a few dribbling investments. Strangely enough, the raising of hard crunchy currency had not proved too arduous a task. For a senator, Quintilian showed a distinct lack of munificence in chucking out the poor and installing the educated classes and she had rapped his knuckles for that by retaliating in the Campanian deal, but that was only part of the pleasure.

To his new tenants he leased the apartment block for 20,000 sesterces. Claudia had simply applied for tenancy herself and was now subletting the block for 35,000. (Come on, where did he think she got the money from to buy that land in Campania!)

But that wasn't the point. The point was, sales were tailing off and this was solely on account of her gender.

She looked up at the reeling satyr. The bias was unlikely to change once word got round that Gaius Seferius' widow was up for murder! As it would. In Rome, rumours spread faster than floodwater, no matter how half baked Macer's reasoning.

Like a carcass being torn by jackals, Gaius' empire was being laid open to the bone, but, and here is the difference, she thought, the quarry isn't dead, not by a long chalk. These arrogant merchants might have the smell of blood, but the hunt is a long way from over – and, as every huntsman knows, many a stag outwits the archer.

For, contrary to popular opinion, the archer is not as good as his arrow, he is only ever as good as his aim.

It was the sound of snoring, audible above the trumpeting of the elephants and the honking of the seals, that interrupted Claudia's train of thought. Sprawled on his back on a marble seat beside the fishpond, his mouth wide open, Pallas dreamed of self-shelling lobsters and an eighteenth way to cook sucking-pig. Beneath the bench, a column of ants and a cluster of flies competed for the remnants of his lunch, but the wine seemed to have been spared and it seemed a pity to let it go to waste. She was on to her second glass before the inevitable fit of coughing woke him up.

'Darling girl, what a pleasant surprise.' Pallas gulped gratefully at the glass thrust in front of him.

'Me or the wine?'

'Both,' he said chivalrously, heaving himself upright and straightening his tunic. 'Although I feel slightly disadvantaged, caught in so undignified a posture. Are you recovered from last night's shenanigans? That looks nasty.' He pointed to the marks on her throat.

'I'm still sore,' she admitted, 'but the lividity is misleading. Don't tell Macer, though. I might need to trade on his sympathy.'

'Now there, oh yes, there's a man who's sharper than he looks.' Pallas shot her a cryptic look.

'Sharp? If that imbecile has his way, I shall be standing before a judge in six days' time!'

'Ah, but have you considered the possibility our Prefect might be using you as bait? That by focusing attention on you, it leaves him free to investigate the real killer?'

Holy shit, no, it had not occurred to her! Well, well, well. But before Claudia could draw breath to follow up, the big man had launched forth again.

'I'm just pleased our man in the crocodile pond wasn't another of his long-lost troops. I had visions of a whole host of his ex-employees turning stiff on our doorstep, one after the other.'

'It's weird, don't you think, two dead strangers in three days?'

'This is Umbria, darling; anything can happen around here, you only have to look at Timoleon to see that. What the f—?'

The screeching was inhuman and it came from the far end of the courtyard.

'Jupiter, Juno and Mars!' Claudia blinked hard.

Hands up to protect himself, feet slipping wildly, Taranis had nowhere to go, his back was already to the house wall and strong as he was, he was no match for the wild creature attacking him.

'*Bastard!*'

Tulola was pummelling the Celt's chest and shoulders with her fists, screaming like a demon, the skin on her face so tight with anger that her exposed teeth looked huge and obscene.

'*Bas–tard!*'

Taranis could offer no resistance. He cringed lower and lower under the demented assault, his forearms fending most of the blows.

'That'll teach him to sneak off,' Pallas whispered, linking his arm into Claudia's and leading her back down the path. 'Although, under the circumstances, one can hardly blame even that pig-ignorant hippopotamus.'

'It tallies with my theory. Tulola likes not only to control her men, she needs to be seen to be doing it.'

Could you call that ferocious onslaught being in control? It seemed to Claudia that Tulola had fooled herself into believing she could bewitch any man she wanted and keep him in her thrall for as long as she, not he, desired, until occasionally a Taranis appeared to show her the reality. And Tulola, to judge from that little tantrum, was patently allergic to reality.

More painful still must be the realization that when you're knocking thirty, it's a very fine cloth that separates the uninhibited dominatrix from a rancid old slag.

'Her husband was the first to rebel, you know.'

'Oh?'

Pallas resumed his seat by the fishpond. 'I'm going back six, maybe seven, years, though you need the whole picture to understand. You see, their parents may have fixed the marriage, but for the young couple it was every bit a love match. Puppy love, of course. Tulola was only fourteen, but the stars were in their eyes and that was enough for them.'

He snapped his fingers to catch a slave's attention.

'Bring us more wine, will you, my good man? Only make sure it's Falernian this time, I want none of that Campanian rubbish.'

'What went wrong?'

'The concept of young marriage is not without foundation, but as you know, what lies at the core of one's character at fourteen remains the same at forty. Tulola, naturally, came a virgin to her wedding. Unfortunately, so did the bridegroom.'

'Ah!' Claudia poured the wine. 'Your cousin began to experiment?'

'Tarsulae was reduced to a small town by then, where gossip became a marketable commodity. It's good stuff, this Falernian, how does it compare with your Seferius wine? What grape do you use?'

How should I bloody know? 'What happened when he found out?'

'Now that, darling girl, is where it gets *really* interesting. Uh-oh, look who's coming! Quick! Run!'

Faster than a jackrabbit, Pallas had grabbed the jug and was lumbering back to the house, but Claudia's arm was caught in a vice.

'Ah, Mistress Seferius! How enchanting you look in cinnabar.'

Macer, you slimy little salamander, how obnoxious you look in daylight.

He released her arm. 'May I join you?'

Why don't you crawl back under your stone and wait for the moon?

'I am, you see, eager to hear your account of the terrible events of last night.'

Oh, Pallas. How wrong can you be.

With his handkerchief he brushed the marble before allowing his red embroidered tunic to make contact, but, alas, not before Claudia had tipped the remains of Pallas' lunch on to the seat.

'In case my story clashes with that of the crocodiles, Prefect?' She tossed the plate in the shrubbery and flicked an ant from her finger. With any luck, there would be a small army of the little beggars sinking their pincers into his bottom even as she forced herself to smile at him. 'Or out of concern for my personal safety?'

'I fear you are making fun of me, Mistress Seferius, but murder is a serious matter.'

'Especially when one is at the sharp end and the distinction between breathing and investigating the possibilities of an afterlife are beginning to blur.' She leaned forward so her nose was a mere hand's span away from his. 'These bruises are not fake, Prefect. Last night someone tried to kill me.'

His smile was pure reptile. 'I realize that, my dear Claudia, and one of the things I am trying to establish at the moment, apart from his identity, is a connection linking Fronto with the dead man and, *ergo*, with yourself.'

'The eternal triangle, how original. We'll see your name carved on great monuments yet.'

Actually he was more the sort who'd want a sundial

for his memorial to ensure you saw his name whenever you looked.

'Mock me all you wish, Mistress Seferius, only there is a nasty smell to this place which has less to do with the menagerie than appears on the surface.'

Do smells appear on the surface? Frankly, she was too disinterested in this little maggot to waste breath baiting him, and besides, if there was a ready answer, then he would find it as soon as he stood up. Pallas had had mullet on his plate, as well as mustard and vinegar and soft-boiled eggs.

'So while my men delve for clues, perhaps you and I could go over a few of the facts that you have already presented to me, since there appear to be one or two anomalies in your statement.'

If you've only found a couple, then I'm doing better than I hoped! 'Such as?'

'Well, for one thing, you told me you had sent your servants on ahead by ox cart, when in fact you did nothing of the sort.'

'Macer, you surprise me. You're the Prefect of a legion covering a very large territory,' which as we both know boasts a microscopic population, 'yet you find that an anomaly?'

Puncture his pride and you prick Macer's innermost soul. 'I don't' – the bluster was almost painful – 'quite follow you.'

'Come, come. Surely you must have realized that in questioning me before fifty, sixty witnesses, I was hardly going to admit, a woman of my social standing, to travelling without servants! What would people think?'

'You're saying you lied to retain your self-respect?'

'Wouldn't you? The truth, Macer, is that I have been a widow for but a short time.' She dabbed at the corner of her eye. 'This opportunity to travel unencumbered, it was like a godsend. I am not' – sniff – 'the type of person who needs a retinue of slaves to flaunt her status and naturally I keep a chest of clothes at my dear husband's farm.'

He scratched the tip of his thin nose. 'Let's recap, shall we?' Damn! It didn't work! 'You received a note from your bailiff urging you to come to Etruria at once?'

'Correct.'

'You decided this was a much-needed escape from a crowd of attentive servants and, with the exception of Junius, left them in Rome?'

'Correct.'

'You hired a gig from the stand, taking your chances with a new and untried driver?'

'Correct.'

'You left the Via Flaminia at Narni in order to take a shortcut through Umbria on the abandoned road and spent the night at Tarsulae simply because that was the only town with a half-decent inn?'

'Correct.'

'The following morning you were run off the road by person or persons unknown and stumbled upon the Villa Pictor by chance?'

'Correct.'

'You did not recognize Fronto, even though he might (note, I say might) have been the arsonist, you did not argue with him, you did not plunge a kitchen knife into his belly?'

'Correct.'

'And last night another man, who has yet to be identified, tried to kill you by throwing you alive and kicking to the crocodiles?'

'Correct.'

He breathed on one of his gold medallions and polished it with the heel of his hand.

'Suppose I put it to you, Mistress Seferius, that you are lying through your lovely white teeth? That right from the very beginning you have tried to pull the wool over my eyes?'

'I don't think the servant issue constitutes major controversy, Prefect, I've explained – '

'Servants? My dear Claudia, that's neither here nor there, just another minor incident which shows your contempt for what you undoubtedly think of us yokels. I am referring to a far more contentious matter, the crux of your defence if you prefer.'

'If I knew what a gog was, Macer, I would undoubtedly turn into one on the spot. Exactly where *does* the crux of my defence fall down?'

The Prefect stood up and flexed his shoulders. 'There are several small irregularities, insignificant in themselves, yet lumped together they do cause me considerable grief. For instance, listening to the stories which abound, you've been through Hades and back, yet I see no broken limbs, Mistress Seferius. No cracked skull, no concussion.'

'So if I was dead, you'd believe me?'

Macer's teeth bared in a smile which didn't extend to his eyes. 'Your driver sustained a broken arm and Junius was, most fortuitously, knocked out, whereas you, my dear Claudia, you've had three encounters with violence in as many days and mere superficial scratches to show for it.' He ran his finger under his collar. 'And then there's the cat.'

'Drusilla? What about her?'

'I have inspected her cage personally.' He stared up at the darkening sky. 'There is nothing wrong with that bolt.'

'I never said there was, I merely said it shot open and she went to ground. If your accusation hinges on my hiding my own cat, I can't wait to see the jurists' faces. Is that your case, Macer?'

As he turned, she was eye-level with the splattered remains of Pallas' lunch.

'Not quite. There is also the little matter of the note.'

She stared at the stain. If it came out at all, it would need bleaching several times, and that's a nasty place to have a big white mark, on your bottom.

'Note?'

A fly settled on the egg yolk and she resisted the urge to swat it.

'The message from Rollo. You see, my men have been asking questions at your villa and your bailiff seems a decent sort of chap. Honest, up-front. Quite without guile, I should say.'

A chill wind passed across the garden. 'So would I, that's why I employ him.' She hoped this change of temperature was attributable to the impending storm.

'So when Rollo tells me he didn't send you a note, I am rather tempted to believe him.'

Claudia watched the Prefect stride up the path, where her attention was no longer held by the splurge on his tunic, but by his parting words. Because for once she agreed with this smarmy, smug weevil. She, too, was inclined to believe her reliable, hard-working bailiff. If he said he sent no summons, he sent no summons.

Which meant Marcus Cleverclogs Orbilio was right.

Someone at the Villa Pictor hated Claudia Seferius enough to want either to frame her for murder, or, when that failed, kill her outright. By definition, last night's attacker must have been a hired assassin, but would the brains and the money behind it stop there?

The sky turned dark as charcoal, a rumble of thunder bellowed along the Vale of Adonis, then another, then another. But long after the heavens had opened, Claudia remained bolt upright on the smooth white marble bench as though she had been grafted there.

How long before the killer tried again? she wondered.

And what method would they employ next time round?

XVII

Like other people's lives after personal bereavement, the Villa Pictor set about its business none the wiser and certainly none the worse. As Claudia dripped across the atrium floor, two men staggered towards the kitchens, laughingly balancing an amphora of oil between them. A gap-toothed maid buffed up the bronzes. An apple-cheeked redhead tickled the corners of this splendid marble hall with her heather broom. Alis was making devotions at the family shrine, a young Syrian topped up the water-clock, the porters changed shifts in the vestibule.

Proof positive that victims don't suddenly glow in the dark to distinguish themselves from the rest of humanity.

And proof that the expression on one's face doesn't necessarily reflect the fact that one's brains are bubbling so loud you're surprised other people can't hear them.

Once inside her bedroom, however, cosy and warm thanks to the gentle heat of the charcoal brazier, a sense of balance prevailed and Claudia finally thought to peel the cold, soggy tunic away from her skin. Yeuk! She hung the gown over the back of a chair and as clouds of steam rose up from her clothing and dribbles of condensation ran down the walls, she vigorously towelled herself dry. The very action – instinctive, elementary, primordial – was sufficient to restore perspective, and she cursed herself for allowing that snide little Prefect get to her. Now had the crocodiles eaten *him*, they'd have had a belly-ache to remember! Probably turn them vegetarian!

Flipping the towel into a roll to dry her back, Claudia wondered what Sergius intended to do with those plug-ugly reptiles. They won't dance very gracefully, and somehow I can't see them jumping through hoops. Ah, now, wasn't there some talk of him employing Egyptian natives to swim amongst them?

She leaned down and rubbed between her toes. Good grief, people will hand over small fortunes to watch a gang of youths splashing around with the crocodiles! Indeed, these spectacles are going to turn established shows right on their boring old heads. What innovations, what vision this man Pictor has!

And talking of animals . . . Cat fur and rainwater is an explosive combination and by the time poor old Drusilla can leg it to shelter, she'll have a hump the size of a camel's. I really don't know where she learned swear words like that.

Today's storm, though, had an entirely different quality about it, throwing out an invigorating energy as opposed to the ill-mannered depletions of last night's tantrums. It was, Claudia thought, listening to the raindrops pitter-pat on to the broad, flat leaves of the elecampane, the difference between a play by Plautus and a torrid melodrama. One blows life – the other just sucks!

It was only when she reached for a comb to untangle her curls that she realized that, even in her own bedroom, she wasn't safe. The room had been searched. Not just cleaned. Not just heated. Not just tidied. She meant searched. By an amateur at that.

She teased open the door. 'Pssst.'

'Who? Me?' The red-headed slave looked round in confusion.

Claudia crooked her finger. 'Tell me who came into my room while I was gone and this little fellow is yours.' Her hand opened to reveal a shining silver denarius.

The girl's heather broom clattered on to the floor, but Alis seemed not to notice as she continued to pour libations at the family shrine.

'Um – '

Utterly transfixed by the coin, you could see the girl's mind working out how to spend it, which, of course, was the object of the exercise. A couple of asses would have ensured Claudia had her answer, but it would not necessarily have given her an honest one. Silver would.

'Um – '

'Um, what? Umpteen Umbrians umpiring under umber-coloured umbrellas?'

'Ever so sorry, m'm,' the redhead bobbed down and picked up her brush. 'I can't say.'

'Blackmail is a depressing concept,' Claudia reminded her. 'Let me make it quite plain that a single denarius is all that's on offer.'

'Oh, no, you've got me wrong, m'm! I mean I don't know.' Her eyes said goodbye to the silver coin. 'We've just changed shifts, see? But I could ask around, if you like.'

Good life in Illyria, anything but that! For the time being, this remains our little secret, me and the son-of-a-bitch who's been prying.

'It's not important,' she replied airily, flipping the coin towards the servant. 'And this should ensure I never asked the question. Now, fetch me a raw octopus, will you?'

'A raw – Sorry, did you say octopus?'

'Are you deaf?'

Actually, it was the only thing Claudia could think of that would reduce Drusilla's hump to a meaningful proportion. The cat could slap it about a bit, and it would make her feel she'd gone some way towards catching the horrid slimy creature for herself.

Claudia looked again at her jewellery box. Walnut, inlaid with mother-of-pearl and with a hinged lid, it was an exquisite piece of workmanship. It contained bracelets and anklets of gold and of silver, diadems set with sapphires, pendants set with pearls.

Also, until very recently, it had contained the wing feather of a wren.

In colour wrens are very similar to walnut. You place the feather on the rim of the box and then you close the lid very, very gently to keep it in place. But no matter how carefully you open it again, that feather, that microscopic, insubstantial, practically invisible feather, becomes dislodged.

Intuition told her there was no need to unlock the box to learn nothing had been stolen, but Claudia went through the motions anyway. The key, which she kept on the webbing under her mattress, had been replaced, but the searcher had not been careful enough. The key now faced east instead of west.

Claudia tapped her lip thoughtfully. Whoever it might be, the spy was not Marcus Cornelius Orbilio.

Credit where it's due, Supersleuth would have come and gone and probably taken the air he'd breathed with him to ensure he left no trace, so what was this person looking for?

A long soft whistle followed by two short ones came from the far side of her window.

What imbecile could possibly imagine Claudia either had something to hide or held incriminating evidence – and at the same time was foolish enough to leave it lying around? Someone who didn't know her very well, that's for sure.

The whistles were repeated before she realized it was her bodyguard's signal.

'Junius, did you know Rollo hadn't sent any blasted message to Rome?' Godsdamnit, she'd need to start sealing her letters.

'Yes, madam – '

'Don't you turn your face away from me!'

'But – '

'Butt is just where I'll kick you if you don't look me in the eye. Now did you or didn't you . . . For gods' sake, boy, what's the matter with you?'

Now the idiot had his hand across his forehead. Oh! Claudia bounced back from the window and grabbed her tunic off the back of the chair. It was damned hot, that cotton, because when she turned back to Junius, her cheeks were as scarlet as the tunic.

She cleared her throat. 'Yes, that letter – '

'I tried to tell you, madam, when I got back from Etruria – '

'Rubbish! I'd have remembered something as vital as

that. Anyway, what are you doing skipping around in this downpour?'

'I wanted to ask you when you thought would be the best time for me to create a diversion.'

I suspected as much. You've been drinking. 'What diversion, Junius?'

'The one which enables you to slip away from here.'

'Oh, and exactly where do you suggest I slope off to? Greece, Crete, Alexandria?' And how long till the heat dies down? A year? Two? By then, I'll have lost control of my wine business, I'll be lucky to keep a roof over my head. Unfortunately I have to ride this one out.

'No, no.' When the young Gaul shook his head, it was like a dog shaking itself. Water sprayed everywhere. 'I was only talking about Rome,' he said in a small voice.

Rome! Bless him! 'Junius, it's a kind thought, but I can't see that my doing a runner is going to help my case, so why don't you – '

'The Prefect can't touch you in Rome, can he?'

Claudia stared at the elecampane as its leathery leaves shrugged off the raindrops. By Jupiter, the boy's right! The same way Loverboy has no authority in the provinces, Macer holds no sway in the city.

'Junius, come under the eaves, you're starting to look like a water vole. That's it.' I don't want my little genius catching a cold. 'Now, one simple question. Do you want your freedom?'

'I beg your pardon?'

'Come on, yes or no? Tulola wants to buy you' – it'd go to his head if she told him how badly – 'and I need to know where your loyalties lie.'

The bodyguard's face flushed. 'Where they always

have. Madam.' The last word came as something of an afterthought. 'I didn't think you'd ever need to ask.'

Dear me, his voice sounds a bit croaky, I trust he's *not* going down with the fever.

'That's settled, then.' He probably keeps some doxy over on the Aventine, or else he goes moonlighting, that's why he sticks with me. 'Now about this diversion of yours – '

Plans are fun. For a start they are such flexible little beggars, you can tweak them, twiddle them, you even have the luxury of abandoning, postponing or advancing them, all with the underlying reassurance that, come what may, they will repay you with the immeasurable satisfaction that can only be gained from voracious mental stimulation.

Then again, it could just be down to that indescribable, delectable, mouth-watering wait.

To a girl like Claudia, for whom anticipation was a drug, the dry throat, the increased heartbeat, the constant swallowing, was unadulterated bliss, exquisitely enhanced by the knowledge that the very earliest Junius could put his proposals into action would be tomorrow, Friday.

Which left her, she calculated, skipping up the atrium, the rest of the afternoon and all of the evening to gather as much ammunition as she could possibly muster against the residents of the Vale of Adonis. Snakes, each and every one, but among them, oh yes – among them was a viper. Would she have time to find out who?

It would not be easy defending herself far removed

from the scene of the accusations, but at least in Rome there was a reservoir of lowlife willing to swear on their mothers' graves that Claudia Seferius was with them at the time of the murders.

My word, the old spondulicks comes in jolly handy at times. Of course that was valid more for equestrians, she mused, ducking behind a marble bust to avoid certain marauding security policemen, than for patricians. There would be no need for the likes of Fancypants, for instance, to dip into his coffers. Toadies cluster round the aristocracy for free. She watched him knock at a door along the east wing and waited until it swallowed him up.

Strange. That was Sergius' bedroom. Why should Orbilio decide to visit the sick? Claudia ran her finger up and down the cool, smooth upstand, absently noting the quality of the Numidian marble. It was difficult to know what to make of that man Pictor. On the face of it he was urbane and charming, and he'd extended every hospitality since her arrival, it was difficult to read anything sinister into his actions. Except, maybe . . .

'That's my father.' Alis' voice made Claudia jump.

'Handsome,' she remarked, glancing at the serene, white face set in its eternal watch over the colonnade.

'I fear the sculptor somewhat flattered him.' The enigma that was Sergius' wife let out a slight, self-deprecating laugh. 'He had the same ill-defined jaw as the rest of us.'

Providence might have pushed Alis into Claudia's path, but there was no way Providence was going to have her back again. Not until Claudia had extracted her ore.

She was on the point of commenting that Euphemia's jaw was exceptionally well defined when she remembered that the man in the statue was in no way related to her.

'How come you didn't stay with your father after he divorced your mother?'

The law was rigid. Adulteresses, by definition, lose all their rights and access to their offspring – in fact, most consider themselves lucky if they're granted an annual visit.

Tears filled Alis' eyes. 'Papa was such an honourable man, Claudia, I wish you could have met him. As a merchant who spent much of the year travelling, he believed that, at nine, I was too young to be subjected to constant upheaval.'

'You'd have preferred that?'

'Claudia, I'd have followed him through the Pillars of Hercules and searched for Atlantis if he'd so much as whistled! Instead I was stuck at home with the woman who'd cuckolded my father then laughed in his face when she was heavy with another man's child.'

Quite. 'Didn't you get on with Euphemia's father at all?'

'That man!' The keys at her girdle agitated as she shuddered. 'He was coarse, he was common and oh! the way he and my mother flaunted their bodies! If I told you what they got up to, you'd throw up.'

I doubt it. 'How did Euphemia cope?' It was probably just honest, earthy sex.

Alis' lower lip twisted and untwisted. 'To be truthful, I'd have to say she was too young to understand and, in any case, they spoiled her rotten with pets and toys –

will you think me terribly wicked when I say I was glad the plague took them?'

It makes you refreshingly human, Alis. Welcome to the human race.

'They ruined my life, marrying me off to Isodorus like that, it was a nightmare, I can't begin to describe it. Look, I have to go. It's been such a relief talking to you, would you mind awfully if I . . . if I – '

'Oh no,' Claudia replied truthfully. 'Come and have a chat any time you like, Alis.' Enlightenment is always a welcome visitor.

'Thank you! Thank you so much, but I'm late.' Alis had reverted to type, fluttering her hands and tut-tutting. 'I still haven't prepared the dining hall for dinner.'

She set off up the atrium on the run, then stopped suddenly. 'Where are my manners? I forgot to ask whether you'd like to organize the silver. Claudia? *Claudia?*'

The side room into which Claudia had dived was small and cosy and very, very comfortable. Its friezes commemorated Agamemnon, the warrior king, from his initial involvement in the Trojan War through his quarrel with Achilles to his ill-fated return to Mycenae, and, on the floor, an exquisitely tessellated Paris was dithering about who to dish that golden apple to, which, to judge from his expression, was getting a tad too hot to hang on to.

Had it not been for the fact that the room was full of Euphemias, Claudia would have liked it very much. She was slouching against the window, watching the rain hammering down on the bath-house roof as she chewed a lock of hair.

'I hate the country, don't you?'

With every fibre of my body! I've had it up to here with birds tweeting, buds opening, bees buzzing and frog-spawn clogging up the ponds. You can keep your blue swathes of Venus' Mirrors, your marsh marigolds and your aconites in the orchard. I want to watch the concentrated frown of the leather-worker as I munch on hot sausages, wince at the burned arms of the glassblower as I drink tansy wine – and forget migrating cranes honking all over the place, give me the cheeky backchat of the fruiterer's boy any day.

'How can you say that, when the fields and waysides are chequered with anemones, the bellies of hinds are heavy with fawn and baby bear cubs are gambolling their paws off after winter hibernation?'

'If Sergius makes the money he thinks he will with his shows, we're going to live in Rome, did you know that? The Esquiline's the place. Since they pulled the old stuff down, it's gone really upmarket. Is that where you live?'

The Esquiline Hill is a pocket of aristocracy, Euphemia. Old money only need apply. 'My house – '

'Is Rome fun? Is it exciting? What's it like this time of year?'

How could you explain, to someone who's never been there, that in Rome the spring equinox signals more than the end of the winter rains? Trade routes reopen, bringing gold from Asturia, cotton from the Indus, cedar from Phoenicia. Ivory from Africa will flood in to the Forum, along with porphyries and pomegranates and pitch. Seas will be open, too, and wives, glad to see the back of their drunken lazy menfolk, will be dancing in the streets as their sailor spouses swap henpeck and trivia for life on a knife-edge and jokes with the boys. How could you begin to describe that?

'Average.'

'We'll get to see all the races, the games, the gladiator fights. I'll wear Syrian linens and watch every play going, even the Greek ones. Sergius says there's entertainment laid on for every single day – '

'Not quite.'

' – and on top of that, there's jousting on the Field of Mars and rowing on the Tiber. I can watch – '

'My dear child, steady on – '

Euphemia flashed her a glance of undiluted insolence. 'I am *not* a child.'

'Indeed you are not,' Claudia smiled back. 'You're eighteen years old, and well versed with delivering messages with menaces.'

'Nineteen, actually, and the threat still stands.' Euphemia spat out the lock of hair. 'Fuck with me and I'll kill you.'

'I thought you'd already tried,' Claudia replied calmly, positioning herself the other side of the window.

Euphemia pulled a sarcastic face. 'Now why should I want to do that? As long as you don't interfere with me, I won't trouble myself over you.'

Consider me indebted!

Claudia was staring at the opposite wall, where a wounded Agamemnon was facing the prospect of the Trojans breaching his Greek defences, and wondering why Euphemia remained unmarried, because if she'd been Sergius, she'd have got rid of the moody little trollop ages ago, when she heard voices in the next room. As though eavesdropping was a social grace to be trumpeted from the rafters, Euphemia moved across to the dividing curtain and put her sulky little ear to it.

'I don't see the problem.' Tulola's voice drifted across. 'We'll get one of the carpenters to run you up a pretty pyx to take home to Thingammybob and – '

'R-R-Regina.'

'Whatever you say, sweetie, just leave me to square it with Auntie Macer.'

Claudia peeped round the edge of the curtain. Draped on a couch in the next room her tunic slit to the hip to reveal a shapely oiled thigh, Tulola dangled a bunch of black grapes in the air. Slightly wrinkled after a winter in barley, they didn't seem to deter her couch-mate in his efforts to snatch one in his teeth. The cheetah, chained to one of the couch's solid bronze feet, settled down as Salvian, plum red in the face and his hair ruffled, shifted his weight from foot to foot and looked everywhere except at Barea's hand moving around inside Tulola's tunic.

'I d-don't think I – '

'Salvian, Salvian, leave the thinking to me. Every great man marks the occasion, even Augustus, so what do you say?'

'B-B-But the Emperor was twenty-three, he had a p-proper beard to shave off.'

Claudia's face creased into a smile. To round off the Festival of Mars, which, to say the least, had been over-shadowed by events, Tulola intended to give the Tribune that well-looked-forward-to rite of passage every young man hungers for, the First Shave. Poor old Salvian! Railroaded again!

'Bollocks.' Barea spat pips into the corner. 'You're scared shitless.'

If possible, Salvian turned even pinker. 'That's n-not true! Look,' he shot a tortured glance at Tulola, 'I only f-followed you, because my uncle said to t-tell you he can't find a record of your divorce.'

'Tell him to look harder,' she snapped. Then, raising one seductive eyebrow at Salvian, she murmured, 'What it boils down to, sweetie, is whether you want to join the ranks of Real Men or whether you'd prefer to wait until your beard grows like a billy goat.'

Grudgingly Salvian nodded. 'I suppose so.'

Tulola and the horse-breaker exchanged looks. 'Come on, then!' As one, they leapt up, each grabbing an arm and dragging a totally bewildered young Tribune to his doom, laughing at the tops of their voices.

'Must see this,' cried Euphemia, racing off to join them.

Claudia pulled back the curtain, saw the cheetah's face contort into a snarl and quickly jerked it closed again. Jupiter, Juno and Mars, that animal makes Drusilla look like one of those little pink-cheeked cherubs that decorate my bedroom ceiling! Pallas assured me it only eats gazelle, but hell, I'm not going to be the one to find out Pallas makes mistakes!

She retraced her steps across the Judgement of Paris and pulled open the door to find a man leaning against the jamb, his patrician boots crossed comfortably at the ankles.

'You're sick, Orbilio, you know that?'

The policeman grinned, uncrossed his legs and advanced into the room, clicking the door quietly behind him. 'Wrong,' he said. 'Sergius is sick. What do you make of that?'

'Nothing. Would you stop blocking my exit?'

'First a marigold,' he remarked, his eyes sweeping over Claudia's tunic, 'now a pimpernel.'

'I'll have you know, Marcus Cornelius Orbilio, the Prefect says I look *enchanting* in cinnabar.'

'Well, he would, wouldn't he? It's the same colour as his military tunic – which, incidentally, appears to have been ruined by a mucky mark on the back. You don't happen to know anything about that, I suppose?'

Claudia's smile was as innocent as a babe's.

'I didn't think you would,' he said, scrutinizing Agamemnon's fight with Achilles. 'Tell me, doesn't it strike you as strange that Alis, sweet, doting, follows-him-around-like-a-puppy Alis, is not bothered by her husband's illness?'

'She's merely doing what she always does. Carrying out Sergius' wishes.'

'Tulola's pressurizing her to send for medical help.'

'She won't get anywhere. Sergius hates doctors.' And I'm with him on that. Mistakes they can bury.

'Does he really?' Orbilio's gaze wandered towards the window. 'The rain's easing. The smell of the soil after a downpour is exquisite, don't you think?'

Claudia saw no reason to reply to that. She traced her toe round Paris' golden prize.

'I just spoke with Euphemia, too,' he continued in

the same dreamy voice. 'She said Sergius Pictor was perfectly able to look after himself, he always had.'

'The trouble with many of the more serious playwrights, they will include soliloquies. So deadly boring, don't you agree?'

'I wouldn't know, I'm an Aristophanes man, myself, but one thing I'm absolutely certain of is that, whatever you might pretend, bored you are not.'

'Damned well am so, too.'

A corner of his mouth twitched and that irritating sparkle was back in his eyes. 'You can lie to yourself, but never to me, Claudia. You're enjoying this.'

She threw up her hands and pretended to look out of the window. 'I'm amazed asylum owners aren't queuing back to Narni for your patronage.'

'Come on! Action-packed adventure? It's just what you're made for! Look what it's done for you.'

She pointed to her neck, wrists and ankles. 'Oh yeah?'

'Beaten, battered, bullied or bruised, you bloom under them all. Danger becomes you, Claudia Seferius, and you damned well know it.'

'Have you been drinking?'

The merest mention of the milk he'd been swilling lately made Orbilio's stomach churn. 'You still haven't told me what you make of Sergius Pictor.'

He was right, the rain was easing. The sky was lifting, despite the onset of twilight. 'In my opinion, he's a clever, strong-minded, ambitious man who undoubtedly knows what he's doing. Now will you shift your fat carcass?'

'Certainly, milady, seeing you put it so politely.' Orbilio prised himself away from the door, but his hand remained poised on the latch. 'But I've just looked in on him, and do you know what I think?'

'No idea, but I have a feeling you're going to tell me anyway.'

'I think Sergius Pictor is being poisoned.'

XVIII

Sensationalism for its own sake had never appealed to Claudia and she was in the process of saying so when the commotion in the hallway cut her short.

'Where is he? I'll chop his balls off!'

The door to the adjoining room bounced off the wall with the force and she heard the cheetah snarl. It was followed by a sharp intake of breath and a surprisingly respectful oath.

But the change of mood didn't last.

'Come out, you coward! Face me like a man!' The door to the little room swung open. 'Where are you, you bastard?'

Claudia smiled at the wiry individual glowering in the doorway. 'Looking for someone?'

The eyes narrowed. 'Where is he?'

'Who?'

'That randy bastard, Orbilio. Where's he hiding?'

Claudia's hand swept backwards. 'He's here. No, I'm wrong. It would seem he isn't here, after all.'

The red curtain shimmered slightly, and this had nothing to do with the breeze from the open window.

'I'll cut his bloody balls off.'

'Yes, I rather gathered you were souvenir hunting. I

don't suppose you'd care to introduce yourself, would you?'

'Oh. Gisco,' he said gruffly. 'The name's Gisco.'

'The charioteer?'

The fists unclenched slightly. 'You've heard of me?'

My dear Gisco, you cannot imagine the fortunes I've gone through, believing this is the one time you'll bloody well lose, but of course you never do!

'Red faction, am I right? Well, I'm sorry, Master Gizmo, but your bird, it would appear, has flown.' Would it, she wondered, be frightfully rude to enquire why, exactly, he wanted Orbilio's groceries?

Gisco put his head round the doorway and yelled. 'He hasn't come out, then?'

'Nope,' a voice hollered back, from which Claudia deduced he'd posted a guard at next door. Wonderful! Now she could really start enjoying herself!

'I know that chickenshit's in here somewhere,' the charioteer said menacingly, lifting the lid of a large chest and prodding with the point of his dagger. 'And when I find him, I'll teach him to go rutting my wife.'

Ah! 'Master Cosmo, if Orbilio can fit into that box you're so busy emptying, he's physically incapable of even reaching your wife. Unless, of course, she's a midget.'

'Are you trying to be funny?' he growled.

Claudia held up her hands. 'Whatever gave you that idea?'

Thorough was the word that applied to Gisco. Thorough, but alas not very bright.

'Aha!' It took him a while, but eventually his eyes

hit upon the curtain. 'So that's where the craven sod's hiding!'

The triumph in his voice was short-lived as he turned on Claudia. 'You'd do well to steer clear of the likes of him, hiding behind a woman's skirts. *Bastard!*' he shouted. 'Come out, you lily-livered, yellow-bellied coward!'

He strode across the room and in his fury the curtain not only ripped from top to bottom, the whole mechanism came off in his hand. Intent on disentangling himself from fabric and pole, he failed to notice Cuddles's lithe body turn on its axis. Her furled lips revealed giant white fangs, the black teardrops were compressed to obscurity.

'Holy shit!'

Ears flat, whiskers forward, pupils down to slits, this was an animal poised and wanting to strike. Gazelles, indeed!

Swallowing a giggle, Claudia stepped into the room and spun round in a circle, the scarlet cotton flaring prettily at her ankles.

'See for yourself, Master Compo.' The cheetah's tail swished angrily, but that chain was strong and the couch was solid bronze. 'The room's quite empty.'

'So it is,' the charioteer replied thickly. 'Only – well, I could've sworn I saw him. Orbilio. Coming in here.' His anger began to boil up again. 'I'll find him, though, make no mistake. I'll find that spineless, gutless son-of-a-whore and then he won't go fucking my wife!'

Oh dear. Looks like action is called for. 'Tell me, Master Gusto, would you say I'm an attractive woman?'

Gisco checked his stride. 'What?'

'Am I, or am I not, physically attractive?'

'Well, yes. Of course, you are. I don't see what – '

'Most men find me attractive, I'm swatting them off like flies half the time. Therefore I think you can safely say that I know from experience, Marcus has not been – how did you put it? – rutting your wife.'

'Oh, yes he has, the horny bastard. Every bloody Tuesday and sometimes on a Friday.'

That often? It's a wonder he ever gets any work done. 'I assure you, Master Fatso, you are quite mistaken. That man's interests lie elsewhere. In fact,' she advanced closer to the charioteer, 'I'd say *you* were more his type. Strong and muscular, just how he likes them.'

'*What?*' Gisco was having trouble with his eyes, they were blinking nineteen to the dozen. 'Are you sure about that?'

'Why should I lie?' she asked, opening her own eyes ingenuously wide.

'Marcus Cornelius Orbilio's a . . . a fucking queen?'

'Blame his mother,' she said generously. 'She raised him as a girl, in fact he was twelve years old before he learned otherwise.'

Gisco's breath came out in a whistle. 'Marcus Cornelius, eh?' He shook his head in disbelief. 'You're absolutely certain about this?'

'I'll show you where he keeps his make-up, if you like.'

Gisco's mood darkened again. 'Faithless, bloody bitch!' he barked. 'Lying to me, sending me chasing after goddamned fairies while she dallies with her fancy man in Rome. Wait till I find him! I'll have the bugger's balls!'

His voice carried up the atrium and out of the vestibule as Claudia sucked in her cheeks. In the next room, the cheetah's attention was back to where it had been prior to Gisco yanking the curtain off the wall.

'Coast's clear, Loverboy.'

Feet first, Orbilio crawled out from the far end of the couch, his hair sticking out in every direction, his face flushed and dripping with perspiration.

'I'm not sure whether to thank you or spank you.'

'Decide quickly,' she said. 'Gisco's still within ear-shot.'

'In that case, Mistress Seferius,' he replied, going down on bended knee and holding his clenched fist to his breast, 'I beg you to accept my heartfelt gratitude.'

'Don't I just love it when you beg! Now on your feet, Hotshot, I think you've teased that cheetah long enough.'

XIX

Tarsulae in daylight was nowhere near as tacky as Claudia had envisaged, although it took a while to convince her. When she'd passed through (was it really only six days earlier?) it was late, they were tired, it was simply a case of stabling the horses and flopping into the nearest, least verminous bed before an early-morning start in that damned fog. Today, with the sky a confection of white puffs on blue, her first proper view of the town was of a jagged line of tombs, some circular, some turreted, some simple oblong boxes, stretching down a hill so steep the mules were puffing before they were halfway to the top. Undoubtedly coloured by earlier experiences, Claudia found it difficult to shake the impression that a long, dangling tongue flanked by sharp teeth reached out to suck up and devour travellers foolish enough to pass by. She closed her eyes on the approach and pretended it was to enjoy the spring sunshine on her face.

'We're here, madam,' Junius said quietly.

Claudia's eyes snapped open. 'What did I tell you?'

'Not to open my mouth between here and the Capitol or you'd have my guts for gargoyles.'

'Then do as you're told or prepare to walk back to Rome.'

The rig was entering the Mausoleum Gate, where the

grass was cropped by wild goats and robber jackdaws sought nest sites in the masonry. The face of an unnaturally mutilated blind girl lit up as she heard silver clatter into her begging bowl, and Claudia sent up a silent prayer. Merciful Apollo, please don't let her mother drink it away. The gate itself, a splendid lofty triple arch, bore an inscription that testified how the original span had been extended to honour Augustus in his victory at Actium nineteen years earlier. Graffiti qualified how, four years later, the augur who had pronounced favourable the auspices for this glorious extension had been stoned out of town, his house sacked.

Like an ageing mistress, Tarsulae seemed resigned to the inevitable and yet there was dignity in her surrender. Shutters down side streets might rot on their hinges, but the balconies that lined the main thoroughfare were dotted with pot plants and the aired bed linen that hung over the railings reflected the townswomen's rabid tournament for spotlessness.

The Villa Pictor was not the only estate isolated by the rugged contours of the Umbrian landscape, far from it, and whereas even at the best of times it would have been a lonely existence, with the trade route diverted round the mountains, the jewels within Tarsulae became more and more precious for her dwindling populace. A caller outside the Temple of Vulcan broadcast the evening procession of trumpets, a notice painted on the wall of the wheelwright reminded people of the race between schoolboys on Sunday morning. Big deal!

'Not long now, poppet,' Claudia addressed the cage in the back. 'We change animals at Tarsulae, stock up on provisions and hey-nonny-no, it's Narni by nightfall.'

And Rome, the fire that stokes the Empire's furnace, where the Tiber runs yellow with sand and mud, where the streets are so narrow you can shake your neighbour's hand from the balconies, yes, Rome will be ours by Sunday. No tame foot races there, I can tell you! Yesterday, Salian Priests in scarlet striped tunics and sacred shields would have made their elaborate leaps round the city centre and tomorrow, what a pity I'm missing it, the spring equinox will be greeted like a soldier back from the wars, with singing and dancing and feasting long into the night . . .

At the smell of water, the mules snorted, tossed their dejected heads and made a beeline for the trough, despite Junius' pull on the reins. She glanced at him out of the corner of her eye. Imbecile! Fancy starting a fire to create a diversion! Claudia would have clipped him round his Gaulish ear, had it not been for the fact that the rig was juggling her bones and she needed a firm grip on the buckboard, but she had told him in no uncertain terms that short of finding another dead body on the wrong end of a hilt, the very last thing she needed was a second charge of arson thrown against her.

'I made it look like an accident,' he had argued as the car sped away from the villa. 'A loose coal, dry straw – happens every day in the city. I made sure it was one of the new sheds being built, no harm done, but there'll be enough smoke to agitate the animals and cause a bit of panic for a three-hour start at least.'

Those were the last words he'd been allowed to speak, because, Claudia said, if he so much as opened his mouth to cough, she would choke him with his own chitterlings. However, as the mules slurped at the lichen-covered trough and a tawny comma butterfly flitted back and forth, she grudgingly admitted that Junius' getaway plan, while flawed in places, was pretty sound when you looked at it as a whole.

Checking Drusilla's cage, she accepted the groom's offer of assistance and jumped down. '*You!*'

She snatched her hand back as though it was scalded, and Marcus Cornelius Orbilio bowed gracefully. 'Your servant, ma'am,' he smiled.

'Junius, why didn't you tell me this barnacle was here?'

'You told me not to say another – '

'Oh, be quiet!' She screwed her palla into a roll, stuffed it under the seat and glanced at the mules. Impatiently tossing their manes, their ears pricked forward, she decided to give them a wide berth. You could never trust mules. Irritable buggers at the best of times, this pair looked like cannibals.

'I had a feeling you'd pull a stunt like this,' Orbilio said, matching her frantic pace up the high street.

'I've no idea what you're talking about,' she replied, snatching a bun in each hand as she swept past the pastrycook's.

'Oh, no?' Orbilio paused to settle with the irate shop-keeper and, when he looked up, Claudia Seferius was nowhere in sight. His oaths sent the pastrycook into a second cataclysm, but he was unaware of the raised fists and wild gesticulation as he bounded up the temple steps. In the temple grove, under the shade of Vulcan's sacred lotus, a young woman with her curls in disarray sat feeding the sparrows. 'How did you do that?' he asked.

'Do what?'

'Get past the priest.' Everyone knows Vulcan's inter-
mediaries guard their god like Cerberus guards Hades.
Many a deadly ritual has to be endured before entrance
to the sacred grove is permitted.

'Same way you did, I suppose.' Which they both
knew was nonsense. Orbilio would have claimed an
emergency and flashed his personal seal to get past, but
Claudia had no intention of admitting she'd promised to
cough up for the May Day sacrifice ... could she just
check the premises to ensure they were sufficiently sancti-
fied? Ple–ease?

'Then would you mind telling me what brings you to
Tarsulae this fine and sunny morning when you're supposed to be under house arrest?'

Orbilio ran the tree's leathery leaves between his
thumb and forefinger and thought of Odysseus whiling
away his days with the lotus-eaters. The comparison
with Claudia was automatic – especially when the sharp
prickles at the base of the leaves stuck into his thumb.
He sucked at the blood with amusement. No wonder
Odysseus stayed on! Pleasure and pain – you can't fully
appreciate the one without the other, can you?

'To clear my name, of course!' The temple priest gave
Claudia an oily smile as she passed by, the warden an
unctuous bow.

'I'm not convinced burning down one of Corbulo's
sheds is the best way to set about it,' he said, suspiciously
eyeing the obsequious clerics, 'but I'm prepared to bow
to superior knowledge.'

'You're wittering again,' she replied, skipping down
the steps and into the street. Abruptly, she turned left

past the law courts, where a fat, red-faced advocate was laying into his bow-legged secretary with a bullwhip.

'Humour me,' Orbilio said evenly.

Claudia stopped short and Orbilio nearly tripped over the flagstones. Oh well, better luck next time. 'What woman in my position isn't curious to know what sort of a man Fronto was, who his friends were, how he earned a crust, whether he was capable of arson?'

Actually she couldn't give a toss. All she knew was that the dung-beetle was the cause of this bloody trouble and had he not been dead already, she was quite prepared to throttle him with her own bare hands, he'd made her that mad!

'Presumably Drusilla and your luggage can assist you in your search?' he asked mildly, watching a yellow-haired whore curse the punter who'd shortchanged her. In the gutter, a dirty child screamed for its mother.

Claudia tipped her chin up and looked him straight in the eye. 'Someone searched my room,' she said defiantly, turning on her heel. 'From now on, I leave nothing to chance.'

'I can understand that,' he replied, without a hint of sarcasm, but she knew it was there. 'And now you're here, why don't we wash the dust from our throats?'

'I was intending to visit the widow,' she said.

One eyebrow rose to say like hell you were, but otherwise he chose to ignore her. 'I've something to show you. Over the street, there.' He appeared to be leading her towards some smoky dive opposite the basilica. 'Macer's watering hole,' he explained. 'Hope you don't mind roughing it.'

'I'm with you, aren't I?'

And don't think it's because of the way your hair curls over your collar, either, Marcus Cornelius Orbilio, or the way you stifle a laugh with the back of your hand. Tall, dark and handsome's six a quadran where I come from, you've only got to look round here –

'Well, maybe not.'

The words were Orbilio's and referred to the tavern.

The sentiments were Claudia's and referred to her thoughts.

Regulars? More like men with nowhere else to go. Their woollen tunics were stained with wine and stank of grease and sweat and stale urine, and if you put them together and pulled all their teeth, you'd be lucky to find a full set. Broken pots gathered dust in the straw, a desiccated crone snored beneath the benches, and a one-eared dog growled at a rat which had ventured a shade too close to his chop bone.

'See what I mean?' he asked outside.

'No,' she replied, but they both knew she was lying and that they were both wondering why fussy, pompous Macer would choose that fly-blown joint.

'I'll have what he's having,' she told the waiter in the next tavern, then seeing it was milk, sent it winging straight back. 'So our policeman has more than one vice, has he?'

Orbilio winced at the reminder of Gisco. 'Stomach ulcer,' he said, pointing to his left side. 'Just here. Very tender.'

In the wine shops in Rome you could choose between red wine or white, vintage or thin, mustard or mulled, rose wine or hyssop, the list was virtually endless. Here she opted for a potent Lagean white and discovered that not only was it watered, they probably pickled eggs in the residue. However, the unweaned kid roasting on the spit and the smoked sausage and celery casserole more than compensated.

'So, have you interviewed the widow?' Claudia pictured her, painted and flabby and dressed like a newly-wed.

'I treat my cases the way a doctor treats his,' Orbilio replied between mouthfuls. 'They require a thorough examination and a bedrock of background information before I make my diagnosis. I'll see Balbilla later.'

So that was her name. Claudia rolled it around on her tongue. Balbilla. Balbilla. The sort of name that would belch, slap you on the back and have a laugh like a horse. She almost felt sorry for Fronto.

'Did you notice the amphitheatre as we came in?' he asked.

You could hardly miss it. Behind the law courts, a splendid edifice soared to the skyline, its brickwork interspaced every cubit with a wafer-thin layer of baked clay whose purpose was purely to advertise the wealth and prosperity of the Tarsulani. Happy days.

'It made me wonder why Pictor didn't exhibit at least some of his animals there,' Orbilio added. 'Can you imagine the impact of even the tamest of shows upon the audience? The dancing bears, for instance, or the monkeys riding in saddles upon goats?'

'Sergius is going for broke with these spectacles, it's Rome or nothing, and he has no intention of getting pipped to the post by someone sniffing out what he's up to.' Sworn to secrecy, apparently the estate workers felt the bite of the lash if they so much as opened their mouths in public, because although the locals knew he kept a menagerie, they didn't know the purpose behind it.

Orbilio ordered a bowl of stuffed dates and received a plate of pastries instead. 'Fair enough, but you'd think he'd at least take the elephant to the Megalesian Games, wouldn't you?'

Claudia bit into the crumbly, cheesy pastry. 'The trouble is, Corbulo would need to go with the wrinkly beast,' she explained. 'Sergius' schedule would be set back still further, he'd then miss the games in June. Why do you ask?'

'Just curious,' he said, licking his fingers. 'It's like a mosaic, this case. I'm sure all the pieces are there, only I can't seem to make sense of them.'

Who can? 'Who cares?'

You do, his eyes said, but she refused to listen to them.

'A man who, until recently, worked for the newly appointed Prefect of Police is lured to the Villa Pictor and stabbed in order to make you appear a murderess,' Orbilio said, 'and the girl bribed as a witness has her neck broken in order to silence her.'

'But in apparent and utterly confusing contradiction, I am almost a victim myself, by an unknown assassin at that – '

' – and it is distinctly possible the head of the household is being poisoned.'

Claudia had seen Sergius, eyes rolling, legs dragging, supported by slaves on his way to the bath house as she was making her getaway this morning. The colour of his skin was neither yellow nor grey, but like catkins on a pussy willow, it was a combination of the two.

'I have a fair knowledge of herbs,' she said – in fact it was better than average but that was none of his business – 'and I've never encountered symptoms like Pictor's – and besides, who'd want to kill him?' She helped herself to the last little pastry on the plate and wished the wine had been as good as the food. 'Not Alis, that's for sure.'

That little mouse wouldn't have the guts to kill her own husband, especially while there was a Prefect, a senior representative of the Security Police, a junior tribune plus a whole host of uniformed officers prancing round the house. That wouldn't be gall, that would be outright stupidity.

'Unless she's desperate for money,' she added as an afterthought.

Orbilio leaned back and put his feet on the table. 'How do you mean? What would she gain by killing Sergius?'

Claudia wetted her finger and collected several cheesy crumbs on the tip. 'The estate must be worth a tidy sum, especially with the performing beasts.'

'But – ' Orbilio frowned. 'You obviously don't know.'

'Know what?' She licked the crumbs off her finger.

'The estate is hers already. She inherited it from Isodorus when he died.'

Claudia felt her eyeballs bulge. 'You mean it's *Alis* who's rich and not Sergius?' Now that put the wolf among the nannygoats! She ran back over events in her mind, but while it might change the perspective, the basic picture remained unaltered.

Shame.

The fire crackled amid sounds of laughter, clanking

goblets, the clatter of plates. Watching him at ease in his chair, boots on the table, running his finger round the rim of his glass, there was an inexplicable tightness around her solar plexus. Damned indigestion! Wouldn't you just know it?

Orbilio tapped his finger against his chin. 'You know, I have a feeling that if we can just crack open the shell of this case, the whole nut will come tumbling out.'

That, thought Claudia, is the crunch, isn't it? Knowing where to begin.

And praying that, before the killer is unveiled, more souls won't be ferried across the river Styx.

XX

Outside the tavern, Claudia ground her heel into a weed growing up through the flagstones and wished it was Orbilio's nose.

'I suppose you'll be sticking to me like a tick from now on?' she had asked ten minutes earlier, smoothing out the creases in her scarlet gown as he sorted the bill and thinking, now *that* will have set me up for the journey.

'Front or back, which would you prefer?'

The look she gave him could have turned grapes to raisins, but Marcus Cornelius seemed to be adjusting the purse on his wrist with immense detail.

'I was referring to the element of trust. You see, when it comes to me, yours appears filigree thin.' That's it, shame him into leaving you alone, that way you can slip away while his back's turned.

'I can't imagine where you got that idea from.' Orbilio was nonchalantly tossing a key in the air.

Claudia looked round in mock agitation.

'What's up?' he asked.

'I'm looking for the rat I can smell.' Not for nothing had that key materialized out of nowhere.

'You'll thank me in the end,' he said, taking care to

keep his eye on the metal object flipping into his hand. 'I've been doing you a favour.'

Like hell! 'Like what?'

'Like . . . keeping Drusilla out of the midday sun.' The key had disappeared deep into the folds of his tunic. 'Like . . . knowing how frightened she'd be without Junius to keep her company – '

His voice trailed off into the gutter where it belonged, and much to Claudia's disappointment, this aristocratic prig did not break out in the mass of suppurating sores that she prayed so violently for. He simply winked and strode off.

Now, as Claudia ground another weed into juice, there was a bubbling sound in her ears as her blood reached boiling point. Godsdamnit, Orbilio, this is not your manor. You can't go locking up people's cats willy-nilly, or banging up their bodyguards whenever the whim is upon you!

But no matter how intense her fury, no matter how numerous the curses she visited upon him and his family, his house, his job, indeed anyone who'd ever spoken to him in their entire lives, the fact remained.

Claudia Seferius was grounded.

So just what does a girl do when she's stuck in this dead-end town for the rest of the afternoon? She digs out the grubs who ran her off the road, that's what. Before she takes the skin off their backs to hang on her walls for her to paint pictures on!

Across the street a young mother, a child at her hip and another clinging to her skirts, helped her one-legged husband up the steps of the public baths. An old man, as thin as Barea, hobbled to the barber's for a long overdue shave and outside the fuller's yard a frizzy-haired washerwoman made sheep's eyes at the temple warden when any fool could see she was wasting her time, it was boys he was interested in. A random slice of Tarsulae life, Claudia thought, which succinctly sums up this town. It shows the two very separate divisions, those who have little option but to stay on, to eke a living where otherwise they could find none and whose only alternative was the Emperor's dole. And those who make a living from these proud, possibly stubborn, survivors.

She clapped her hands to cleave a path through a gaggle of pecking hens and feared not only for the future of the townspeople, but for the soul of the town itself. Tarsulae was degenerating fast. And as she began her search for the yobs, she pondered which of the two categories Fronto had fitted into.

'How old yer say?' The hunchback clipping his donkey with a pair of iron shears shook his head. 'Nah! No young men left nowadays, they've all found work in Hispellum or Narni.' Which is rather what Claudia had concluded, but it didn't hurt to double check.

'Don't know of no one with a birthmark like that.' Ankle deep in sawdust, the wizened carpenter worked on smoothing a yoke. 'Couldn't have made a mistake, could you, lass?'

After a while, Claudia began to think well, yes, maybe she had. Maybe that ginger thatch had been dyed, maybe that birthmark was no more than paint. Then she remembered the third boy.

'Eyes like a frog?' The bone-worker shook his head. 'Not from round here. Fancy them dice, do you? All four for a brass sesterce?'

As the shadows made their inexorable progress across the forum, Claudia sat on the steps of a bronze mounted hero and tried to come up with a feasible alternative to the monstrous thought that kept swelling and swelling inside her head. Any minute, and I'll explode like an overripe pumpkin, because it can't be true, it can't, it can't. Those boys have to be local. What other explanation could there be? She dare not admit, even privately, that they might have been hired in Narni or Hispellum. Or that the prospect of returning to the Villa Pictor, to share her roof with a murderer, was more than she could cope with . . .

There are, of course, ways to combat fear and the swell of nausea that comes with it. You tense all your muscles, then release them. You take little breaths, and sigh them away very slowly. And you do this while reciting an epic poem backwards, preferably one of Virgil's. Claudia was halfway through the sack of Troy before she felt able to attack the practicalities of her situation.

She moved round the statue to follow the shade. Firstly, since the chances of another getaway seemed unlikely, the hiring of a lawyer became paramount. The man she wanted – correction, the man she intended should represent her – was middle-aged, lived on the Esquiline and took an equal interest in horseflesh and beekeeping. His name was Symmachus, he won seven cases out of ten, charged exorbitant fees for his services, and, somewhat predictably, was fully booked for months in advance.

But Symmachus would come to Narni on Wednesday. In an effort to conceal her vast gambling debts from her husband while he was alive, Claudia had taken to offering certain services to men rich enough to pay for such exclusivity. How well she remembered Symmachus' love of horses. In fact, the number of times he'd whinny and neigh while she led him around by a bridle beggared belief. Oh yes, the advocate would be here on Wednesday, it was just a question of phrasing the letter . . .

Then there was the question of the land sale in Etruria. With the auction just two days away, she had no intention of allowing Quintilian to win this round by default. Best write to her agent, telling him . . .

Having rooted out a scribe shifty enough to ask no questions and having entrusted her scrolls to a multi-scarred army veteran whose appearance was forbidding enough to deter even a hardened thief, Claudia drew a deep and satisfied breath then rapped at Fronto's iron-studded door. The house was an impressive affair of gilded stucco and far too many servants, but why oh why, she wondered, wasn't she surprised to find Marcus Cornelius Orbilio waiting in the atrium, one leg flung over the other, his hands folded behind his head, as he leaned his chair against the gaily painted wall?

'Great minds think alike,' he remarked to the room in general, and Claudia stuck her tongue out just at the point Fronto's major-domo arrived, flanked by two of the ugliest infants you could hope to find in a freak show. The lady of the house was not home, he apologized, and again Claudia was not surprised. Had she been married to the dung-beetle, she, too, would have been out celebrating. The steward, however, suggested the widow might be found at her father's clothes shop on Pear Street, he would be happy to furnish the guests with directions.

Orbilio had been busy, he told Claudia, linking his step to hers as they hiked up the hill. At the time Macer took over the prefecture, Fronto had been working in what some called civilian and others a mercenary capacity, though whether Macer decided external help was unnecessary or whether it was a straightforward personality clash, no one could say for certain. But one thing was sure. Fronto was off Macer's payroll faster than a comet through the night sky. Moreover, Fronto was not only celebrated for taking backhanders in the army; since retiring he'd acquired the reputation of a Master Fixit among certain unsavoury orders of the Tarsulani – in other words, Orbilio said, if anyone had been able to arrange for a group of hooligans to run Claudia off the road, that man was Fronto.

'I think what I'm saying', Marcus Cornelius said wearily, as they turned left at the Shrine of Ceres, 'is that every goddamned person on Pictor's estate could know about this scumbag's activities.'

After that, they walked to Pear Street in silence.

Clothes, Claudia discovered, was something of a euphemism.

'Be charitable,' Orbilio whispered. 'The old man sees plenty of life in those rags yet.'

'I know,' she hissed back. 'I just saw one jump.'

Balbilla's father had the sweet breath of the terminally ill, although one didn't need to get that close to see how it was with him. 'Good riddance to bad rubbish,' was all he managed to get out before their voices brought an overweight, spotty creature in ill-fitting mourning clothes clambering down the rickety steps from the garret.

'What is it you're looking for?' The lump wiped her tear-swollen face and began to pick over the rags.

She obviously thought nothing of two well-heeled strangers standing at the dilapidated counter, but then you rather got the impression she didn't have the necessary equipment to think with.

'Balbilla?' Claudia hoped her blank look passed unnoticed, because whatever she had expected, it wasn't this.

Something about the visitors seemed to click. 'Are you here about Fronto?' She sniffed noisily. 'They say he were in bed with some rich bitch and she stabbed him, but it's not true,' she gulped. 'He adored me and them babies, did Fronto. He'd never do nothing like that.'

'I'm sure he wouldn't,' Orbilio said smoothly, as Claudia intently examined some blue cloth that wasn't even fit for dusters.

'There'll be better men than him along for our Bill,' the old man put in, his palsied hand patting hers. 'She'll find one, you'll see.'

Balbilla, as you'd expect of the recently bereaved, did not share her father's opinions and expounded at such length on her husband's generosity, his devotion to work, to his family, to his Emperor, that Claudia doubted she had the faintest inkling of how Fronto earned his living.

'I had such important news for him, and all,' she wailed, repeating it over and over as she rocked back and forth. 'Dead important, it were.'

Claudia's pulse leapt.

'Can you tell us?' Orbilio urged.

'Now he'll never know.'

'Know what?'

'She's expecting again,' her father explained, his grey face contorting with pain, and then his features softened slightly and he managed a smile. 'When the leaves begin to fall, I'll be holding another grandchild.'

A shiver ran down Claudia's arms. Before the leaves began even to turn, Balbilla would have watched another pyre burn . . .

With nothing to be gained from prolonging the meeting, Claudia and Orbilio walked silently back along the main street. They were just passing the baths when a horseman came hurtling through the Julian Gate, his mount steaming, foam streaking its flanks. Curiosity had ceased to be a characteristic of the Tarsulani, but it had not dimmed in Claudia. Without appearing to hurry unduly, she followed the rider to the back of the law-courts, her stride outstripped by a certain policeman.

'What's happening?' she asked. Something was seriously amiss, you could tell by the horseman's pinched expression.

'No idea,' Orbilio replied, taking her elbow and leading her round the corner. 'But we should be able to find out from here.'

His police training had done him proud. On the other side of the wall, she could hear the rider as clearly as if he was addressing them personally.

'Agrippa's dead! Marcus Vispanius Agrippa is dead!'

Wide-eyed, Claudia and Orbilio stared at each other. Agrippa was the Emperor's right-hand man, they were closer even than brothers! Sweet Jupiter, you couldn't count the years they'd been together, the gentle aristocrat and the low-born man of action, the battles they'd fought, the victories they'd won, and the peace that was proving even harder to keep.

'Now what?' she said.

Despite being the same age, Agrippa was also the Emperor's son-in-law, Augustus having married his friend to his silly, capricious daughter to tie up the loose ends of his complex administration. By adopting the result of their union as his heir and effectively making Agrippa Regent, Augustus thought he'd succeeded. But now, with his general dead and his grandson barely eight years old, what would happen if Augustus died?

More than at any time since the end of the Republic, the Empire had been plunged into a state of crisis.

Anything could happen.

Anything at all.

XXI

'You sure this is the right place?'

Pansa took a step backwards and grimaced at the ramshackle building, its door bowed, its fallen shutters overtaken by fungi and woodlice. This was an old patrician hut, one of the lodging stops for those too rich and fastidious to pass their nights in taverns with the commoners. They preferred their own private domiciles, wooden affairs of sufficient dimensions to afford a modicum of comfort during the nomadic course of their aristocratic duties. But fifteen years of neglect, of merciless summer suns, pitiless winter rains and a relentless stream of pillaging had taken a heavy toll on these rudimentary constructions. Several had collapsed, many more lolled drunkenly, needing only the next spring gale to finish the job.

'Yep!' Confidently Froggy screwed up the parchment detailing directions to the cabin and tossed it into a bed of wild liquorice. Startled, a black-eyed rat scurried away. 'Oi, Ginge! Still having problems back there?'

'Just about cracked it.' A mop of red hair poked round the back of the hut. 'Two more minutes should see me right.'

'Good.' Froggy nodded wisely, because the instructions were clear. The sum of money requested would be paid, but on the strict understanding it was to be a one-off remittance and that it should be made in absolute secrecy. To that end, the Client (as Froggy insisted all marks should be called from now on) had chosen the time and the venue.

As Ginger returned to the tricky business of hiding the horses from view now that the stables had disintegrated and as Pansa tested his weight on the second step leading to the shack, the first already fallen to woodworm, Froggy looked at the lengthening shadows and rubbed his hands with satisfaction. The sum he'd requested was high, though not beyond the Client's reach – and should the old widow be found guilty of murder, he was equally certain the Client, regardless of what was written in that note, would not be averse to handing over similar sums in the future to ensure their silence on this rather ticklish subject.

'What's it like inside?' he asked Pansa, squinting up the highway. Once, this was nose to tail with wagons and riders, the air filled with the exotic scents of the Orient, the din of livestock, of crated peacocks, hazel hens, squealing sucking pigs. Nowadays the same smells, the same sounds headed eastwards from Narni, and the only movement on this stretch of road was likely to come from the Client.

'About what you'd expect,' Pansa called back. 'Damp. Gaping great holes in the roof, floorboards rotten. No furniture left except one cruddy table and a couple of stools.' Which looked in surprisingly good nick.

'How about the back door?'

'No problem.' It was Ginger who answered his question. 'The way I've fixed it, hitching the horses to the back wall, anyone coming in that way will have to push his way through the animals. No chance of sneaking up.'

'Besides,' the muffled voice of Pansa added from deep inside the cabin, 'the bleeding thing's jammed, innit?' Looks like someone nailed it up at some stage. Funny. You'd have thought those nails would have gone rusty long ago.

'Then we're in business,' said Froggy.

He wasn't stupid. He understood enough of human nature to know that people don't always mean what they say and that if they can slit a throat to avoid a payment, it doesn't always hang heavy on their conscience. Which is why he'd brought Ginger and Pansa along. As back-up. You don't tangle with three armed, able-bodied men. If the Client tried any funny business, he, Froggy, was ready for it.

'Bang on time,' he said, observing a lone figure on horseback appearing over the brow of the hill. 'You know what to do, don't you, lads?'

Pansa, swiping the cobwebs off his sleeve, nodded vigorously. Ginger, following Froggy up the steps, also gave a resounding 'Yes!' because they'd rehearsed it twenty times by now, although his eyes had caught two large bolts on the outside of the door.

'What do you reckon those are for, Froggy?'

The young man with the protuberant eyes paid no heed. 'If questioned, it's not that we don't trust the Client, we're brothers, see? You two came for the ride. Now, inside. Let's look relaxed about the whole thing. Pansa, pull up them stools. Ginger – that crate over there, sit on that. Casual, like.' The coolness that he thought he projected was betrayed by the tumbling of his words.

'Daggers on the table. Don't clutch them, we're not threatening, just make sure they're handy – '

A shadow in the doorway made them look round. Ginger and Pansa exchanged glances. Froggy had told them about the Client, but they were still taken aback.

Outside, a horse snickered.

'I wish to make it quite clear, if it is not already so,' the Client swung straight in to take the initiative, 'that this', a heavy leather sack plonked on the table top, 'is purely a one-off payment to ensure you boys will not be in Narni, or indeed anywhere near it, next Wednesday.'

'No problem,' Froggy said confidently.

'Miles away,' echoed Pansa.

'Good, because I take a dim view of blackmailers. This matter between me and the widow, call it a joke if you like, a practical joke, there is nothing – shall we say, sinister – behind it.' The Client leaned forward. 'For that reason, you have my assurance that should you approach me again for money, I shall not hesitate in laying the matter before the judiciary.'

Froggy bit his bottom lip to stop it curling into a grin. Nothing sinister? Some poor cow's up for murder, you want us well shot of the city – and then you expect us to believe that bullshit about the judiciary?

'And you have my word,' he said solemnly, 'plus that of my brothers here, that you won't hear from us ever again after today.'

His gaze fell on one of the bright shafts of sunlight which penetrated the gloom. Well, not until the next time, eh?

'I'm greatly relieved to hear you say that.' The Client,

seeming to relax, drew a drawstring bag from the sack, which chinked comfortingly. 'Count it, if you will.'

Froggy teased open the string and saw his friends' eyes bulge at the coins twinkling inside. 'I trust you,' he said amiably. Growing up in a busy tavern, he was more than familiar with the weight of silver.

The Client made to leave, then paused. 'I would just like to say, before we go our separate ways, that I was very impressed with the job you did last Sunday. It was timed to perfection and quite without overkill.'

'Well, we – ' Froggy didn't know what to say. Praise had not visited him often in his eighteen years. 'I – '

'And considering we all have a long ride home, what say you we share this before setting off?' A flagon of wine appeared from the copious depths of the leather sack.

The boys licked their lips. It *was* a long ride back to Narni . . .

Three cheap cups also materialized and the Client filled each to the brim. 'Since we are a mug short, you will perhaps pardon my manners if I sip from the jug. Do you wish to propose a toast?'

Froggy could smell the wine. It was good stuff, Campanian, or maybe even Falernian. 'Why drink to anything special?' he said, eager to sample that which had previously been beyond the scope of his pockets. 'Straight down the hatch, that's what I say!'

He did not notice the Client's slanting smile. 'I could not agree more. Straight down the hatch!'

As their heads tilted back, the boys were only vaguely aware of the Client lowering the jug and backing towards the door.

'*What the fuck?*' Froggy's hand flew first to his throat, then to his dagger, but he was too slow. The coins had gone, the door was closed, he could hear two heavy bolts being shot.

'I told you – ' began Ginger, and then the pain hit him. The searing, burning, tearing pain as the acid reached his stomach. Writhing and hissing, he gouged at the decaying wood.

'The back way!' cried Froggy. His eyes were on fire, and his mouth, his belly. When he gasped for breath, a stream of dark vomit shot across the room.

Pansa, convulsing violently, began to make hideous screeching noises.

Froggy thought he heard 'Nails', but it made no sense to him.

And looking upwards through the hole in the roof, he wondered why the sky had suddenly turned red.

XXII

After a long day in Tarsulae, Marcus Cornelius Orbilio knew how Atlas must have felt when, having lost the argument with Perseus, the gorgon-slayer turned his grisly trophy upon the giant. His bones solidified, his shoulderblades turned to granite as the weight of the heavens was thrust upon him for all eternity.

The loss of Agrippa was every bit as personal to Orbilio as the death of an uncle or a boyhood friend, and his only consolation came in the satisfaction that the great man's works – the aqueducts, the Pantheon, even the Tiber's anti-flood defences – would stand the test of time so that for centuries to come, Romans would know that here lived a man of vision whose love for his people showed in the bridges he built for them, the basilicas, the warehouses, the porticoes, the museums.

That Orbilio had been able to confide his sentiments to Claudia had been of great comfort to him, and had little to do with Agrippa's death. Inside she was nowhere near as brittle as she liked to make out, and intimate moments such as this allowed him a glimpse of the small, frightened child locked in the labyrinth of this complex woman's emotions – and they aroused every masculine trait, from the instinct of challenge to the instinct to protect.

She had listened in silence while he talked (rambled?) about his personal encounters with Agrippa, asked intelligent questions as to the impact of his death. Would Augustus not have to make Tiberius his heir now? How could he, he'd countered. The young man who'd shown his military and administrative qualities in the provinces and who'd proved himself a respected and, above all, loyal general, was no blood relation. Ah, but neither was Augustus to the Divine Julius, she reminded him, and look how that turned out. Couldn't he just put the adoption of his wife's son to the Senate and see how they vote? The complication there, Orbilio had explained, was that Tiberius was married to Agrippa's daughter, who just happened to be several months pregnant. No matter how strong the Emperor's feelings, the Roman people won't countenance lack of purple blood. Interesting, she mused; because had Tiberius been free to marry Agrippa's flibbertigibbet widow, the Empire would be in very safe hands indeed . . .

Orbilio had enjoyed computing the odds with Claudia, almost as much as he'd delighted in the way her curls bounced in time with the wheels on the journey home, the way she tipped her head back when she laughed. Minerva's magic, the sun in her hair was like a celestial forge working all the metals of the Empire, copper, brass, bronze, gold, and he'd wanted to sink his hands in that thrilling furnace, bury his head in the flames and nuzzle the sparks. Every movement she made was electric, energizing him, quickening his emotions, his wits and his loins, and now that he was parted from her, even for the short while that she soaked her bones in Sergius Pictor's bath house, he was forced to face facts.

Life without Agrippa's influence would be the poorer. Life without Claudia Seferius would be barren indeed.

The last thing Marcus Cornelius Orbilio desired at that particular moment was company, but a policeman investigating three cold-blooded murders cannot afford the luxury of solitude and when a man slaps you on the back and says, 'Come and test my latest stallion', you have very little option. Especially when he qualifies the invitation by adding, 'Assuming you're up to it.'

Three hours spent steering a pair of cantankerous mules on a derelict road with a cat yowling all the way puts considerable strain on the biceps, the wrists and the patience, and when it comes on top of hearing of the death of Rome's second most beloved citizen, all underpinned by the presence of the woman you (careful, Marcus, careful!) . . . underpinned by Claudia Seferius, then the last thing a man fancies is a ride round the ring with a temperamental stallion. However, with a decent chunk of daylight remaining, Orbilio was in no position to refuse a challenge thrown down by a man who was still very much a suspect in the case.

'Great!' He'd told bigger lies in his time, though none, he reflected, with quite such conviction.

'This is the last,' Barea explained, stroking the horse's nose as the groom saddled up, 'and the best. Corbulo thinks he can teach him to dance, he's that good. What do you think?'

After a canter then a gallop then a couple of difficult jumps, Orbilio was inclined to agree. The horse was the best he'd ever ridden. 'The new animals arrive soon, don't they?'

'Who cares?' the horse-breaker shrugged. 'For me, it's time to move on.'

Orbilio dismounted. 'You've formed no attachments here?'

Barea wrapped his bony arm round Orbilio's shoulders in a conspiratorial gesture. 'You might be a high-flying policeman and I might be the poor son of a Lusitanian peasant, but we both work our bollocks off, and when the sun begins to sink, you and I want what men everywhere want.'

'Marriage?' he asked innocently.

'Knock it off, my son.' Barea chuckled as he scratched at his jaw. 'Take that girl in the kitchen, the one with the dimples. She'll give you the same as Tulola – only with her, she expects a bloke to listen to her tittle-tattle for an hour while he strokes her hair and tells her how pretty she is and then afterwards he's got to hang around and tell her he don't even look at another pair of tits, not while he's got her.'

'You're not exactly into heavy relationships, then?'

Barea closed the stable door behind him and tested the lock. 'Whores'll do me, mate, except with Tulola I even get that for free.'

'It'll be hard to give up those perks,' Orbilio ventured.

'Freedom's my perk, mate.' Barea wiped his hands down the length of his tunic. 'Who is it you Romans pray to? Fortune? Well, I reckon I owe her one, because if she hadn't stepped in, I'd be stuck in that poxy mining village watching convicts and captives slog their guts out for the same nation which put me and my people under the yoke, while our women, our beautiful, virtuous, virginal women, spread their legs for the nearest legionary.'

A small nugget of understanding found its way into Orbilio's possession. He saw a small Lusitanian town swamped by men with silver in their purses to lavish on dark-eyed girls whose menfolk were unable to compete. No wonder Barea's opinion of women was so low, with resentment on that scale seething beneath the surface.

'How did you break away?' he asked.

'Easy as a poke in the eye. Rounded up three mares and a stallion for the Praetor, broke 'em in, and then found out he was shipping nags to some posh chariot school in Rome.'

Orbilio thought of Gisco and felt several conflicting emotions caper through his body at once. 'Not the red faction?'

'Yeah.' Barea vaulted the fence. 'Now you mention it, I think it might have been. Anyway, two years later the Praetor moves on and I'm in the queue for me cap of freedom. Farewell Lusitania, hello world.'

As Orbilio climbed the fence rung by rung, the sun dropping fast and the crickets starting their evening chorus in competition with the caged beasts, he studied the thin, tanned face of the horse-breaker. Older than he looked, in all probability he'd have been a free man for five, maybe six summers. A 'V' of geese made their untidy way across the orange sky, and the tips of the clouds turned black. In the sheds to the north, a buzz of activity signalled the end of the day for the field workers, and the little stream that fed the Vale of Adonis gurgled contentedly.

'You're not going to Rome with the Pictors?'

'Rome sounds good.' The horse-breaker bent to pick

up a stone and rolled it around in his fingers. 'But not with Sergius.'

He aimed the pebble and lobbed it into the seal pool, receiving a disapproving honk for his pains. 'There's been nothing for a bloke to spend his dosh on here. I've got enough of a wad put by to go independent – learn more about them chariots, you know?'

It made sense. At a certain age, every man needs to anchor his career and Orbilio could picture Barea studying the racehorses, then offering his services to a leading stud farm.

'Will you keep in touch with Tulola?' he asked.

'If I can't afford tarts, who knows? But I wouldn't mind a crack at the other one.'

'Euphemia?'

'*Claudia*. Very tasty! Got your leg over yet?'

'It's getting late, I think I'll – '

'What! Smart, intelligent aristo like you and she gave you the elbow?'

'Time's pressing, I need to spruce myself up for dinner – '

Barea's laughter drowned the chatter from the monkey house. 'Don't take it personal, my old son, she probably prefers a bit of rough, them types do, know what I mean?' He tapped the side of his nose knowingly.

Orbilio feigned a sudden interest in ostriches as they passed the compound.

'In fact,' the horse-breaker ran his bony fingers over his blue-black, slicked-back hair, 'I wouldn't be surprised if she's dancing the four-legged limbo with me before long.' With a confident wink, he turned on his heel and marched off.

Orbilio's mouth twisted into a grin. You can try, Barea, you can try.

He began to laugh aloud. I just pray Claudia doesn't hurt you too badly in the process.

While Barea slipped round the door of Tulola's heavily scented bedroom and Orbilio slipped beneath the steaming waters of the hot-room bath, Claudia Seferius, subject of their recent conversation, cradled a jug of mulled wine and the knowledge that, by rights, she ought at this moment to be rubbing shoulders with merchants and porters, astrologers and ferrymen in the bustling town of Narni. She should not, as she was now, be sitting alone in Sergius Pictor's courtyard; she should be surrounded by hordes of late-night carousers gathered together on the banks of the Nera where in daylight the barges sail past, with their high sterns and curved bows, laden with everything from marble to saltfish to slaves.

But no.

Fancypants has to stick his nose where it doesn't belong. Never mind that it was tantamount to throwing her to the wolves, duty is duty, isn't it, Marcus? What does it matter if innocent people suffer, so long as Truth is the victor?

Irritably she got up and flounced round the topiaries. Dammit, he gets under my skin almost as badly as the dust from the journey and heaven knows, that was awful enough. Yesterday's rain and today's sunshine meant the gunge kicked up from those mules stuck like porridge, clogging her pores and making her queasy by the time they got back to the Vale of Adonis.

It had to be that? What other explanation could there be?

Not Agrippa. His death was shocking and, yes, desperately disturbing. He was such a *fit* man, a genuine hero of the people – heavens above, we *rely* on men like him!

Who suggested the nausea was connected with Loverboy? No, no, no. With the inevitable unrest in Rome, Callisunus would recall him immediately, because when the Empire moved, it did so with astonishing pace, and Orbilio was an ambitious sod. He'd be off to Gaul, probably before the month was out, and that's what she wanted, wasn't it? Him out of her hair once and for all? Well, of course it was, what a damned silly question.

It's that baby goat I ate at lunchtime. More milk than blood in its body, no wonder I felt queer.

Claudia inhaled the steaming vapours from her goblet – honey, saffron, cinnamon and, oh, was that a hint of pepper in there? Before she could identify the other ingredients, Pallas burst out of the south wing in a stream of light.

'There you are, there you are!'

Good old Pallas, nearly wetting himself to tell her that when a certain fire broke out this morning, Macer's finger of suspicion pointed directly her way – only someone, Pallas added gleefully, his brows lifting just as high as they could go, had given her an alibi.

'Who?' He spread his hands apologetically. 'Darling girl, how should *I* know that, I'm simply repeating what I heard.'

Reading the message emblazoned in his eyebrows,

Claudia pressed further. 'But you could, no doubt, hazard a small guess?'

'We–ell,' he began, then, as he glanced over her shoulder, his tone changed abruptly. 'Of course, it was difficult to keep track of anyone today.'

Claudia spun round. Perhaps it was merely a trick of the light that suggested a door to the north wing had swung shut?

'Because of Macer,' Pallas qualified. A born bureaucrat, it appeared the temper of his Imperial Majesty's illustrious Prefect had not been mitigated when he learned the grease patch on his scarlet tunic would not come out and that the acid used to remove it had, dear oh dear, burned a nasty hole in the wool. Therefore, Pallas related cheerfully, it was in good old civilian white that Macer had his minions pacing the distance between kitchen and bedroom, footpath and palisade, crocodiles and bedroom, measuring this, measuring that, heights, depths, breadths, then he'd made them do it again to double check. Disrupting just about every schedule on the estate, he'd taken statements, querying, quantifying, qualifying and generally making a balls-up wherever he poked his skinny pink nose. 'As a consequence,' the big man added casually, 'no one was where they should have been this afternoon, no one at all.'

As he disappeared through the door of the east wing, Claudia was left with a distinct feeling that Pallas had been trying to tell her something, although for the life of her she didn't know what. However, there was one thing she *could* be sure of. If Pallas knew she was off the premises, it would be common knowledge among the rest of the family! Luckily, such would be the impact of

Agrippa's death that Macer would have no time to divert his energies into proving his preposterous case against Claudia Seferius.

Civil unrest was a possibility.

Military unrest was a real threat.

Even before he'd buried his friend, Augustus would have been battening down every corner of the Empire, moving his generals like men in a game of Twelve Lines, appeasing, reassuring, castigating if necessary. Without doubt the Prefect intended to play a full part in the crisis for which, joy of joys, he'd have to do without full dress uniform! Claudia heard disembodied humming and discovered it was hers.

Pallas claimed he had no idea who provided her alibi – indeed, with his sense of mischief, it could well have been the fat man himself – but more perplexing than who, was the why. Because by protecting Claudia, someone had very cleverly covered themselves . . .

A flurry of activity along the colonnade caught her eye. A messenger. Then Macer. Then much urgent mumbling. The two men disappeared indoors, leaving other sounds to tell the story. Hobnail boots as the legionaries were rounded up. Jangling harnesses as horses were saddled.

'What happening, you know?' Taranis, appearing from nowhere, scratched at his stubble as the hoofbeats echoed into the twilight.

Since it was not in Claudia's interests to enlighten him – or anyone else for that matter – she shrugged and examined a broken nail.

The Celt failed to take the hint. 'You and me, we go see, yes? Er – ' His itch seemed to spread to his uncombed thatch. Either that or he was puzzled about something. 'You – all right?'

The furrow in his brow was so deep his eyebrows met in the middle. Taranis was confused. Here is Roman noblewoman pinching thumb and first finger and making circles over her head. Is not normal.

'Perfectly,' Claudia replied, replacing her non-existent money-spider among the borage leaves and was not surprised, upon straightening up, to find herself alone once more with her thoughts. The sun had set, yet the sky retained the same fiery quality that you feel yourself when you embark on a brand-new venture. Around her, the circus animals had pretty well settled down – an occasional howl, the odd bark – it was as quiet as it ever gets down this end of the valley, and even the vultures, constantly scrounging offal and carrion, had flown back to their roosts for the night. Slaves lit the torches, and a smell of fresh apple cakes wafted from the ovens.

Claudia leaned back and thought of the tart her mother used to bake, filled with spinach and smoked cheese and pine nuts. Used to! Ha! She made it just the once, on one of the rare occasions she'd been sober, because Claudia's father was due home from campaign. He was only an orderly and the glory never rubbed off on the likes of him, so Claudia had suggested the pie as a treat. She never knew what happened to that tart, because within minutes of his walking through the door, her parents were at it hammer and tongs, rowing like he'd never been away, and Claudia had stuffed rags in her ears and hidden behind the woodpile until her father slammed the door and her mother passed out in an alcoholic haze.

'Taken with my chimera, are you?'

'I beg your pardon?'

Alis was standing behind her, clutching a set of
bronze scoops in one hand and a ceramic jar in another.
It was difficult to imagine her in Rome, where domestic
chores were assigned to lackeys. Silly cow would probably take up spinning.

'My statue. I thought you were admiring it.'

Good grief, no. Beastly thing! Quite unintentionally,
Claudia's eyes had been fixed on a fire-breathing marble
monster across the courtyard, part lion, part dragon, part
goat. 'Oh yes, I was,' she smiled, patting the seat in polite
invitation.

'It was a present from Sergius, you know.' To Claudia's immense irritation, Alis settled down next to her.

'Really?' Unlike the other mythical creations dotted
between the topiaries, this did not stand tall and still on
its pedestal, it writhed and twisted so its head was at the
same level as its cloven hoofs. 'Hardly your average token
of love,' Claudia murmured.

'Oh, not a personal gift,' explained Alis. 'It was for
Isodorus and myself to commemorate our fourth
wedding anniversary.'

'You knew Sergius before you were widowed?' The
revelations about this diffident creature grew more and
more complex.

'Oh – ' Alis blushed and burnished the ring on her
wedding finger. 'Sergius was a friend of my stepfather's,'
she twittered. 'The only good thing to come out of that
awful alliance, really.'

'I see.' And she was beginning to.

Alis darted a sideways glance. 'Claudia, you'll think

me a strumpet, but I fell in love with Sergius long before Isodorus died. Oh, not that we *did* anything. Not – not, you know, *sexually*. But my husband, Isodorus I mean, had been in poor health all his life. Sergius', the blush deepened, 'Sergius was the one who escorted me to the theatre, taught me to play softball and darts and the lyre.' Her eyelashes fluttered as she twisted her wedding band. 'It was Sergius who ran in the foot races with my favours pinned to his tunic.'

Oh, was it now! Heady stuff indeed, when a man-about-town shows a shy, country girl a good time. Somebody fell hook, line and sinker – but was that person Alis? I take it back about the spinning.

'Alis, my dear, I think you'll enjoy living in Rome.'

'Rome?' Alis laughed quizzically. 'Why should I want to live in a dirty old city? This valley's far too beautiful to leave.'

'But the animals . . .? Alis, this is hot news! Your husband is about to take Rome by storm, he'll be fêted, a celebrity.'

'We'll stay a week, two maybe,' she said dismissively, 'but then he can hand over to an agent while he trains the next batch. Have you seen Sergius lately?' Her pale face creased into a broad beam. 'He's a hundred per cent again, fit as a fiddle.'

'That was quick.' This morning he looked on his last legs.

'He was right, too, about not needing a doctor.' Alis stood up and gathered her scoops and pot. 'But that's Sergius for you. Always knows what he's doing.'

The keys at her belt jangled as she walked towards the east wing.

'Alis,' Claudia called after her, 'just as a matter of interest, how did Isodorus die?'

Flickering torchlight reflected gold on the rippling waters of the fishpond and turned the artemesias round the statuary into tiny molten shrubs. Bats squeaked and dived for insects on the wing. A peaceful scene, which would have been all the more restful had Alis not answered in much the same voice you'd use when choosing between soft, scrambled or hard-boiled eggs.

'Snakebite,' she said. 'Right where you're sitting.'

And suddenly everything in the garden was not lovely any more.

XXIII

The pale blue gown that Claudia stepped into was one of three she'd picked up in Tarsulae. The style might be a little old-fashioned, the linen neither Syrian or Alexandrian, but the colour was perfect – reminiscent of seaspray breaking against rocks. Tulola would not look twice at such subtlety – indeed, when Claudia was returning to her room, it was the woman's brassy robes embroidered with scarlet that caught her eye long before she noticed the rest of the family grouped around the atrium pool.

Familiar with Tulola's plans to celebrate the equinox tonight, Claudia had paid scant attention to them. Her own plans had been galloping a somewhat different course, because by the time Tulola's frolics began, Claudia intended to be tucked up in Narni before her final push to Rome. Damn, damn and double damn! Still, a party is a party, the boys would be in fancy dress, various entertainments were lined up – wrestling, knucklebones and board games, all worthy of a bet or two – and then there's the feast itself. Why not?

A hennaed talon beckoned her over to the pool. 'We have so few diversions compared to you capital-dwellers, sweetie, it amuses me to play another little game tonight.'

I'll bet it does. Except Claudia's interest lay in her host, rather than his sister. Alis was right, she thought,

Sergius Pictor is health personified. A muscle tugged at the side of her mouth. Marcus Cleverclogs Orbilio's conclusions about poison were way off target. She must remind herself to tell him so.

Tulola stroked her long neck. 'I think I'll introduce a note of – how can I put it?'

'Discord?' interjected Pallas.

Playfully Tulola bared her teeth at him. 'Forfeit. Tonight I'll forgo my perfume; Euphemia, you can forfeit your jewellery' – there was a sharp movement in Miss Moody's eyes which Claudia could not interpret, but the girl remained silent – 'while you, Alis, what shall we omit for you?'

The cunning bitch actually pretended to consider the problem. 'I know! Cosmetics!'

Awkward, flustery Alis could not be considered plain exactly, but even she knew that, with a pallid complexion, carmine and antimony were her best friends. She opened her mouth to protest.

'Excellent!' In clapping his hands, Sergius very effectively silenced his wife. 'Tulola, my dear, I don't know where you get your ideas from. Claudia, what will you do?'

Claudia had smiled sweetly. 'I, Sergius, will think about it.'

Now, girdling her gown with a single, dark blue ribbon, she watched the dolphins leaping round her bedroom walls, the prickly sea urchins, the squid, the lobster, the writhing sea serpent. Ah, yes. Isodorus. Claudia adjusted the folds of her tunic. The invalid who, curiously, died of snakebite, not his ailments. As though reading her mind, Junius whistled his secret signal.

'Well?'

Prudence was not a quality one immediately associated with Claudia Seferius, but on this occasion she had deemed it of sufficient importance to find out what she could about the manner of Isodorus' death and this is where slave gossip became invaluable. She listened, and wasn't sure she was hearing right.

'Excuse me?'

Far from a long dissertation on violent death, the imbecile appeared to be babbling about slipping away. *Again!*

'Junius, do you have bubbles for brains? As it is, my hipbones are clashing together like cymbals.' Really! Sergius ought to check out the suspension on his vehicles occasionally instead of spending every waking hour with his silly striped horses!

'There's no better time,' he urged. 'With the Prefect gone, it's dark, we could easily – '

Dear Diana, give me strength! 'Did you ask around about Isodorus?'

'Well, yes, but – '

'Then dish the dirt, or the party will be over before I arrive.'

The Gaul had done well, she'd give him that. He'd pieced together how Alis was married off to Isodorus, whose wealth could not compensate for his congenital ill-health and who, as a result, had had great difficulty in securing a wife. The general consensus, Junius said, was that although the marriage had been consummated, it was hardly a regular occurrence, and that when the boy's faint spark finally extinguished itself, few expressed surprise.

'Although there was some irony about his death,' he added. 'The snake was curled up inside the mouth of one of the marble monsters in the courtyard.'

Claudia felt herself sway. 'Don't tell me. The chimera?'

'How did you know that?' he asked. 'Anyway, I can have another car rigged in ten minutes flat – '

'Junius, do you seriously believe I can go swanning off to Rome' – snap! – 'just like that?'

'You wouldn't be enjoying yourself, would you, madam?' he'd replied with what she could only describe as a sly smile.

Teeth began to grind. 'I'll forgive you for that, because I can see from your colour that you sat out in the sun, it's obviously coddled your brains, but tread gently, young Gaul.'

'Or is it because *he*'s still here?' he jerked his head along the guest wing. 'The copper?'

Dammit, that breached the pale! As of now, Claudia informed Junius with chilling clarity, he no longer headed her bodyguard, and if he wished to avoid standing on the blocks at the next slave auction, the best way to set about it was to get out of her sight. Now, forthwith, and immediately. *Scoot!*

In the looking-glass, Claudia noticed that her lips were pursed white as she snapped a faience pendant round her neck. How dare he, she thought! She drummed her fingers on the table at a speed that would have made any self-respecting woodpecker envious. In fact, she decided, with the full light of reason shining on the issue, if Tulola wanted the boy, she could bloody well have him.

With an hour before the festivities started, she called for a jug of white wine. Chilled, because, by Jupiter, it was warm tonight. This year, she calculated, the equinox coincides with the first quarter of the moon, meaning the first of April, Juno's sacred Kalends, will fall when it's silver, shiny and full. A rare occasion and cause for much celebration; Juno's powers will be great indeed after the sacrifices and rejoicing in her honour. Blowing out all but one lantern, Claudia looked up at the millions of stars twinkling bright above her. Your places will be different by the time I return, she thought, in fact, knowing Tulola, you mightn't even be around! She was clipping on a gold anklet set with Sicilian agates when she heard a knock at her door. If that was Junius, he can damned well slither under it – and then she remembered the wine she had ordered.

'You won't find better service anywhere in the Empire.'

'Wasn't that the basis of Gisco's complaint?' She snatched the jug out of the waiter's hands. 'However, I do feel that even our red charioteer, limited though his deductive powers may be, could rumble that cunning disguise.'

'Tulola said fancy dress,' Orbilio explained, stepping into her room. 'What's wrong with coming as a slave?' For some reason, his eyes were sweeping every flat surface, including under the bed. Ah!

'Drusilla's out.' Such exquisite pleasure, the minute and a half before she put him out of his misery. 'Tried to pounce on a flock of pecking doves, but they cooed and flew off, so – '

' – on the basis that if you can't eat 'em, join 'em – '

' – she was last seen scavenging in the kitchens. Exactly.' What is it about Supersnoop? Every time you open a chest, you half expect him to come popping out. I'm wondering if he's attached to my skirt hem by string.

'Good!' Orbilio flung himself lengthways on Claudia's bed, bounced a few times then folded his hands behind his head. 'Hey, this couch is comfortable.'

'Make yourself at home,' she muttered, tipping half a glass of wine down her throat. Dammit, I'll be glad when you're posted to that distant corner of the Narbonensis or wherever it is you have your beady eye on.

'I've been thinking about your shortcut.'

Hope the barracks are swampy and the bedbugs have rabies. 'Was this while you skinned rabbits as part of your undercover work?'

'Which reminds me. Oughtn't you to tip the waiter?'

'Only off my bed.'

'I'd rather you didn't, it's far comfier than mine.' He prodded the bolster, pinched the mattress. 'Who knew you were taking the old road? That's what's been bothering me.'

'Couldn't it have bothered you in your own room?'

'It wasn't luck, snatching part of a conversation from your overnight stop in Tarsulae. No, this took planning – and you know what I think?'

'You're squashing my slipper.'

'Not a lumpy mattress, then? Mine's riddled with them.' He pummelled the leather back into shape. 'I reckon that at some stage in the dim and distant past, this route was suggested to you. Think back – maybe you were at dinner, in the baths, meeting with clients?'

Sore point, Orbilio. Dinner, perhaps. Baths, perhaps.

But the meetings with clients have been pitifully few and far between.

'It's possible,' she admitted slowly. A faint bell was beginning to ring.

He sat up and swung his legs over the side of the bed. Generally encased in long patrician tunics, a girl doesn't expect a sudden plethora of thighs all over her bedroom. Especially firm, bronzed, muscular ones. Not when there's just one small light flickering in the darkness. And definitely not when the room you're in seems to shrink and shrink to the size of a closet. Claudia drained her glass in one swallow.

'You were wrong about Sergius.' That should put Hotshot in his place. 'He told me he gets these bouts from time to time – Are you listening to me?'

'What do you know about Tulola's husband?'

Obviously not. 'Only that he walked out on her eons back and she still gets uppity.' It would be truer to say that the merest mention of the subject and Tulola goes ape.

'Do you know why?'

'She was shaking her tail feathers beyond the confines of the nuptial couch, behaviour which apparently failed to coincide with her husband's views on love, loyalty, marriage and fidelity.'

'No, I meant do you know why she won't have his name so much as mentioned?'

Tulola is not a girl who takes lightly to being dumped. 'I can guess.' She seeks revenge on all men.

'I'd bet you a quail to a quadran you'd be wrong.' He stood up and stretched his arms upwards towards the ceiling. 'Suppose I tell you the husband comes home one night, discovers Tulola's been playing around, they have an almighty row and he walks out?'

Claudia felt the tension pull in her neck and in her shoulders as she wondered where this was leading.

'Then suppose I tell you that he's never heard of again? That she takes his clothes, his books, his lyre, dumps them in a pile and makes a bonfire? What would you say to that?'

What indeed! 'You're suggesting it was an excuse for a funeral pyre?'

'Not necessarily, I was merely canvassing your opinion, but it's interesting how we both arrived at similar scenarios.'

He wandered across to the table, rattled the dice cup and tipped out the contents. 'Full house,' he chuckled. 'Would you believe it?'

Claudia quickly scooped up the dice and tucked them into the folds of her pale blue gown. Of course they'd turn up a different face. They were weighted to!

'Then there's Pallas,' he continued, pouring the thin, white wine into the gaming cup. 'Where does he fit in?'

'Not many of his tunics, that's for sure.'

Orbilio refilled Claudia's glass and passed it across. 'By his own admission he's been here two years, almost as long as the newlyweds. I trust there aren't three on *our* honeymoon.'

I shall ignore that. 'Four, actually. You're forgetting Tulola.'

'Five, then. We're both forgetting Euphemia.'

For several moments they stood together by the open window watching the moon bleach the treetops and turn the clouds to silver, and the silence grew. It took on a life force all of its own. It began to condense, heat, pulsate. There was too much of him, she decided, the short tunic, the smell of sandalwood, that one bare shoulder with a little scar just to the left of . . .

'One thing struck me as odd.' Why the hell did she blurt that out? 'Sergius was bloody quick off the mark when it came to summoning Macer.'

'Meaning that finding his house guest stab a stranger in the dead of night is *not*?'

'Don't be obtuse, Orbilio, it's beneath you.'

'After the names you've called me lately, I thought nothing would fit!' It was the moonlight, of course, that looked as though his eyes were sparkling. 'So, what's worrying you?' he asked. 'You think Sergius set you up?'

'Uh-uh. He went white as a sheet when Macer made his accusation, but I have a feeling he knows more than he's letting on.' She tapped one finger thoughtfully on the windowsill. 'Maybe Fronto stumbled on to the training programme and asked too high a price for his silence?'

'Why send for the might of the military? Sergius would more likely want it hushed up.'

'Full circle,' she replied, 'and that's what's so damned peculiar.' A vixen screamed across the valley, tightening the screw of tension. Blood throbbed in Claudia's ear. 'If Sergius is on the level, he could have dealt with the matter himself, and if he's not, why play cat and mouse with the Prefect? Why aren't you drinking your wine?'

'Uh – stomach ulcer.' He patted his rough, hessian belt. 'Right here. Very tender.'

'I thought it was the other side?'

'Eh? Oh, the pain moves about. Wicked. What do you know about arson?'

The nearness of his profile began to irritate her. 'It wasn't me.' She could see every line, every goddamned crevice. 'Subject closed.' Bloody moonlight.

'Wrong words to use to a policeman who is both tenacious and uncompromising.' Today's dust was still lodged in his throat, why else was his voice even deeper and huskier?

'Born under the sign of the Bull, were we?' Any second now, the ceiling would come brushing her head and the walls smash together like the Clashing Rocks off Sicily.

He shot her a suspicious glance. 'What makes you ask?'

'You give out so much of it, it was an obvious conclusion.' Someone was already sucking the oxygen out of the room.

'I think it's time to join the party.' She turned to face the open window, resisting the impulse to gulp the fresh air. 'Sounds like they've started without us.'

'We don't have to join them,' he spoke so quietly she could barely make out the words. 'Not if you don't want to.'

What I *want*, Marcus Cornelius, is for you to take me in your arms, to feel you pressed against me so tight I can hear both our hearts beating at once. 'Of course I bloody want to.' It's a party, right?

She heard a loud exhalation, smelled the sweetness of rosemary on his breath. 'I see.' There was a terrible long pause. 'Well, for gods' sake, be careful, will you? Three people are dead before their time, one attempt has already been made on your life – '

'These points didn't seem to trouble you when you followed me to Tarsulae.'

'Pre-empted,' he said stiffly. 'Running away won't help one iota.' He leaned forward, and now she could smell sandalwood and juniper as well. 'I'll protect you as much as I can – '

'I don't need a bloody nursemaid,' she snapped. And I don't need your dark eyes under my nose reminding me how bloody handsome you are, and I don't need that damned sandalwood stinking my wine . . .

'Oh, yes, you do!' he barked back. 'Stop pretending, Claudia. You thrive on risk! You get high on the odds, that desperate thrill of uncertainty, those heart-stopping near misses – '

Her eyes flashed in the lamplight. 'How dare you preach at me!' she hissed.

'Preach? You think my job's different? Compulsion, addiction, obsession, call it what you like, Claudia, it drives me the same as it drives you, only with me there's a difference.'

'Damn right. I'm free to go where I choose, with whoever I choose and whenever I choose, and you know what, Orbilio? I've had just about enough of you.' This room's not big enough to take both of us. 'Now get out!'

'Dammit, woman – '

'*Out!*'

'Listen for a minute! I'm on equal footing with the villains, I know their game and the rules they play by, but out there is another player,' he jabbed his thumb towards the banqueting hall, 'with a very different set of rules.'

Claudia wanted to scream, Don't you think I don't

know that? Don't you think I'm not starting at shadows every time I leave the sanctuary of these four walls? That every time I see Alis or Corbulo or Barea I wonder are they going to turn on me and slit my throat?

She gave a short, hollow laugh. How can you get through to an over-rich, over-confident, overpowering sexual magnet like Supersnoop? You can tell him you're frightened, he'd understand that, and sure, he'll be happy to comfort you . . . for the night! But try telling him how deep it *really* goes. That with danger comes a fire in your belly you never want extinguished. That unless you feel the cold thrill of horror you don't feel truly alive. How can you explain the passion, the craving, the hunger for this prodigal life force to Marcus Know-it-all Orbilio?

On the other hand, survival was high on Claudia's agenda and extra security (no matter what tall, dark, handsome form it came packaged in) was not to be sniffed at. Sergius' guards had done bugger all when she nearly fed the crocodiles – and, as for the army, Macer had laughed in her face. Fed up with house arrest, was she? Well, he had a nice warm lock-up available if she preferred, all mod. cons, and he knew what she meant by cons, didn't she?

And Cleverclogs had a point. The attack could come from anywhere . . . Since there was no obvious suspect, the whole family fell under suspicion. Claudia parted her lips and hoped it resembled a suitably abject smile. 'Let's call a truce.'

It seemed to take a fair bit of adjustment on his part, but Orbilio went for it eventually. He lifted his gaming cup, still full of wine. 'To you,' he said.

'To peace,' she corrected. Why was it from this angle

the moon lit exactly one half of his face and that one paltry little flame managed to light the other?

Orbilio kissed the lip of the dice cup to the lip of her glass. 'What about to friendship?'

She felt her heart thumping against her ribcage, and when she nodded, albeit reluctantly, a curl fell over her eye. 'To friendship.' Dammit, where did that stupid little quiver in her voice come from?

'What about to', his own pitch had dropped to a gruff rasp, 'to more than friendship?'

A pulse was beating at the base of his throat, and Claudia watched the light of the lantern flicker in the shine of his unruly mop, saw it reflect dark hairs on the back of his hand.

So much from one little flame, how hard it has to work in the cloying blackness.

Too much.

'Too soon,' she said, and the faience pendant round her neck threatened to choke her.

'Too bad.' Orbilio's face broke into a sad, lopsided grin and, taking Claudia's nose between his thumb and his index finger, he gave it a gentle tweak. 'That really is too bloody bad,' he said quietly.

XXIV

The party was in full swing by the time Marcus Cornelius Orbilio had composed himself. On the pretext of checking the security of the courtyard, the animal sheds, the barns and the outhouses, his feet had covered some considerable distance and it was only now, standing barefoot on the marble floor of the atrium, that he fully appreciated the benefits of his own handmade patrician boots. Making his inspection, Orbilio had been only too glad of the cheap woollen tunic which itched and the rough leather sandals which flipped and flopped and chafed and blistered. They took his mind off a woman with wild curls and wilder eyes who kindled a white-hot passion inside him.

For the past hour or more he had breathed nothing but the acid stench of animal ordure, yet he could taste only the heavy, heady spice of her perfume. Was he being fanciful in thinking, in that distinctive mix of rare aromatics, there was a faint hint of the Indus Valley, the subtle fragrance of Babylonian lilies? He had been to Babylonia, spent long, hot nights under her stars as long-haired men in embroidered robes played thin and haunting melodies for the dancing girls, and he still remembered how those same girls jangled as they swayed in time to the music and the graceful way they arched under his love-making.

He wanted to take Claudia to Babylon, to Nineveh, now, this minute. He wanted to show her the wide, open skies, the rich, fertile plains, feel the baking sun of the desert, the sluggish pull of the Euphrates. He wanted to sail with her down the Tigris, show her ancient sites and magical rites, mysteries and pyramids and strange symbols etched on the walls. But most of all, by the gods yes, most of all he'd wanted to pull her into his arms and claim her as his own.

There on her bed, which was soft and springy and smelled of nothing but her, he had wanted to kiss and caress her, slowly, tenderly, nibbling and nuzzling until the crowing of the cock when the first motes of dust danced in shafts of early-morning sunshine and then – and then –

Orbilio rammed his feet back into his penitent sandals and winced at the blisters with an emotion close to pleasure. He was so close, dammit, so close! Spearing his fingers through his hair, he remembered the rise and fall of her breasts in that slinky blue tunic, the one wayward curl which caught in her eyelashes, the way her tongue darted over her lips to cover the tremor in her voice.

He could have pursued it.

Then and there, she was ripe for the taking, he knew it, she knew it. One hair's breadth, that's how close he was. A hair's breadth from heaven and, Orbilio swallowed hard, equally a hair's breadth from hell. To seduce her there, while she was vulnerable, and he would have lost her for ever. Janus, though; how he had burned for her. Still burned for her –

He steadied one hand against a column and thought how a man should make love to Claudia Seferius. Of the hundred lamps on every windowsill, chest, table and chair. Of a night full of laughter and longing, passion and pain. He imagined the lingering build-up, the tantalizing and the teasing, the stopping and the starting. Mother of Tarquin, the knowledge that he'd have to wait weeks, maybe months, wrenched at his gut, but to put a halter on Claudia Seferius would, at this moment, be like trying to bottle moonlight. At the Pictor family shrine, Marcus Cornelius poured a libation.

I cannot promise celibacy, he offered silently, *there will be women, I cannot live without them, but so you accept my libation, hear also my vow. Such liaisons will mean nothing to me, for in my own way I pledge, henceforth, fidelity to Claudia Seferius.*

Through the heavy oak doors of the banqueting hall, he could hear the babble of pitilessly cheerful chatter, relentless shrieks of laughter, and among it all, the distinctive cadences of a tempestuous widow with wicked curls and sinful eyes who marched to the beat of her personal drum and woe betide the man who interferes with the tempo! Orbilio silently saluted her. Far from perfect, that vow was the best he could offer; he would continue to seek physical gratification from other women, but when he made love, when he truly gave of himself, it would be to one woman and one woman only.

The timing he would leave up to her.

Inching open the door, he was greeted by a scene that might well have come from a Bacchanalian orgy. Tables and couches had been pushed back to accommodate a race, now in full throttle, where the mounts were men and the riders the women, their skirts hitched high to gain adequate purchase. The subject of his pledge was clinging like a limpet to a red-faced Pallas, Alis rather daintily to Corbulo, Tulola to Barea and Euphemia's lusty thighs were clamped round Sergius, whose recovery was (Claudia was right) more than adequate. In the van, however, and leading by a considerable margin, strong sturdy Timoleon barely tottered under the weight of the junior tribune, throwing himself wholeheartedly into the party spirit by pretending to whip his horse along the straights. Taranis, the only man without a partner (and that presumably down to Orbilio), acted as umpire and marked each lap of the columns with a pitcher of wine.

Unseen, Orbilio quietly closed the door and decided there was only one way he could possibly make his entrance at this late stage.

The question is, where, at this time of night, could he find someone capable of harnessing a camel?

The bloody thing spat and shat all over the shop and stank worse than a midden in summer, but you couldn't have scripted a better comedy had you won the myrtle crown as a playwright. Accustomed to the shifting sands of its Libyan home, the reflective marble of the banqueting hall came as a right nasty shock to old Humpy, who promptly showed his dissatisfaction by attempting to ditch his rider at full gallop.

Amazed by the speed it could reach from a standing

start, bets were immediately placed on how much longer the valiant rider could hang on.

Barea clapped Salvian on the back and espoused the benefits of army training, although everyone else seemed of the opinion that it was Orbilio's grip, rather than his jousting experience, that saved the day.

Four times the shimmering surface rose up to grab him, but you don't have a pedigree stretching back to Apollo without some adhesive qualities and by the time poor Humpy had come to terms with this slippery, slidy flooring, Marcus Cornelius Orbilio was being greeted with raucous approval and generally hailed as a hero, even though his body appeared to be doing another circuit without the aid of the camel. By the time Orbilio's eyes had stopped rolling, a heated debate was in progress, since the camp was now firmly divided between whether Humpy surrendered on the eighth or the ninth lap and what do you mean, you can't help, you were riding the stupid thing, weren't you?

When the general consensus had more or less settled on nine, Taranis pointed out that the animal appeared to be backing into Tulola's cheetah, who would have got quite a decent fanghold had Corbulo not jerked Humpy out of range at the last moment, a debt it repaid by doing its damnedest to bite him until it was hauled away, honking and urinating, so that by the time a cohort of slaves had mopped up with sawdust and perfumed the room with incense and juniper, there was not a dry eye in the house and brave was the man (or woman) who could stand up straight after that.

Wisely Tulola calmed things down by calling for the

roasts, because, as Pallas said, 'A man's gotta chew what a man's gotta chew.'

It was wellnigh impossible, thought Claudia, rubbing the stitch in her side, to picture one of these people as a cold-blooded murderer.

Indeed, thinking about it logically, why should they be?

Supersleuth was a policeman, whose job revolved round intricate cases of treason, corruption, forgery and extortion – crimes that had two facets in common. One, they were all committed against the State, and two, by their very nature they had to be complex. More often than not murder ran hand in hand with such activities, usually in an effort to kick over the traces, and as a result his investigations would necessitate plunging deep. (How else could he have uncovered her own past?) Simple solutions were rare animals as far as the Security Police were concerned, and the case he'd made about Claudia being framed had, at the time, made sense.

In retrospect, though, wasn't he reading too much into this miserable affair? Assuming Fronto and Crocodile Man had been in cahoots (for reasons she'd probably never know and didn't really care about), surely it was safe to conclude the whole nasty business was now over and done with? That, whatever Fronto was up to, the scam had died with his accomplice? In the space of ninety hours, three people had met with violent death, but over the past two days it had been exceptionally quiet without a single attempt on her life – or anyone else's for that matter. Suppose, like poor deluded Macer, Crocodile Man also laid the blame for his partner's death at Claudia's door. What was wrong with exacting his revenge?

In short, what was *wrong* with a simple solution? Why couldn't the revenge plan have backfired? Why couldn't Coronis have slipped on the shiny surface and broken her neck?

More than satisfied that none of the partygoers could possibly be a killer, Claudia jostled to take her place for the roast and, in doing so, found herself brushing against a rough, woollen workshirt. The sensation was electric. Damn you, Marcus. Damn you to hell.

Wedging herself between Barea, in a long Phoenician tunic, and Corbulo the Camel Tamer, she deliberately set out to flirt. 'Is that what they mean by painting the town red?' she quipped. 'Or are you a genuine redneck?'

'Ritual ochre,' he laughed, taking a great draught of wine. 'Tonight,' he made an elaborate flourish with his hands, 'I am an Etruscan king.'

Tonight I could believe it. In white kilt and traditional gold torque, Corbulo strutted like a peacock, a prince among men, a pearl among pebbles. And had the double bump on his nose not screamed his heritage, then the way he'd looped and bound his hair did. She glanced across to where Orbilio was settling himself on the couch. Was it accident or was it contrived, that the hero of the hour just happened to be directly opposite? Who cares, she thought. Not me. I've decided there's something horribly claustrophobic about the atmosphere in bedrooms where the lights are low and the moon is swelling. Nevertheless, as Corbulo's tundra eyes bored deep into hers, Claudia felt a strange stirring inside.

'That's the trouble where you come from.' She forced herself to listen to Timoleon baiting the Celt. 'Men are men, but by Janus, your women are ugly.'

'Huh!' Taranis wiped his hands down the length of his pantaloons, his only concession to fancy dress being to twine his hair. 'I have job to do, selling bears. When I make money, then maybe I take wife.'

'Betcha bed the grizzly by mistake,' the gladiator muttered under his breath.

'You laugh,' the Celt rejoined, 'but you no marry.'

'Damn right. Women are fine for one purpose, but who the hell wants to spend time with them? Bore me rigid, they do.'

'I'll drink to that,' threw in Barea, flashing a contradictory wink at Claudia as he wrestled with the unaccustomed volume of linen.

'Drink to what?' asked Tulola. 'Marcus, is that *milk*? Darling, how gross. Oh, look everybody!' Even the cheetah glanced up from its lump of gazelle. 'My masterpiece!'

Four slaves staggered into the hall carrying a whole roasted boar. On its head it wore a miniature cap of freedom, from its tusks dangled woven baskets bulging with dried dates and walnuts, and attached to its teats as though suckling sat a little bread piglet.

Salvian, who'd come dressed as a Spaniard, put his fingers in his mouth and whistled loudly. His face was a map of cuts and scabs from its first scrape of the iron blade, but behind the redness and the rashes, a chrysalis was beginning to emerge. Like shaving a pomegranate, yesterday's razor had been totally unnecessary, yet psychologically the ceremony had boosted his confidence and Tulola rose in Claudia's estimation. Salvian, she mused, as the hams and the hares and the ducks were wheeled in, is finally growing into his armour.

'I don't half feel a tit,' mumbled Barea, his heel tangling in the long hem. 'How them poor sods managed, I don't know. They're seafarers, right? Yet they traipse around in woman's robes!'

Just up Tulola's street, that egg-yolk yellow. 'At least,' Claudia quipped, 'Phoenicians don't miss one another in the dark.'

'Here, Pallas,' bawled Timoleon, palming a glazed figpecker as the tray went past. 'How come you didn't wear your long frock tonight?'

'What? And fight you off all ruddy night? No fear.'

Timoleon's vulgar gesture played right into Pallas' hands.

'Darling boy, your roots are showing! And I don't mean your hair.'

The gladiator lunged, but Sergius put out an arm to restrain him.

'Yes, sit down, Muscles, he's just winding you up.' With a thigh-revealing swirl of her skirts, Tulola stepped over her couch and began stropping the carving knife as Pallas pretended to pout. 'Will this make it better, sweetie?' She tossed Pallas a boned pheasant stuffed with onions and asparagus and sensuously licked the sauce off her fingers.

'Of course it won't,' the gladiator sneered. 'The fat slob can eat a whole farmyard at a single sitting.'

Yes, thought Claudia, whereas Tulola devours the farmer.

'Gourmet food is an art, my boy,' Pallas replied, sinking his teeth into the dripping fowl. 'In its pursuit, I have squandered fortunes and – '

' – not one your own.'

'That's enough,' the keeper of the harem chided Timoleon. 'I won't have you keep taunting my house guest.' Tulola ruffled the fat man's hair. 'I'm very fond of Pallas, aren't I, Lover?'

'Positively attached,' he replied drily, eyeing up the remnants of the fish course. 'Pass those oysters, will you? Criminal to see them wasted.'

As the conversation turned to which were tastier, oysters from the Lucrine rocks or those from Tarentum, Claudia was acutely aware that throughout this charged interchange, the gaze of Marcus Cornelius Orbilio had been in one direction and one direction only. As her wine was topped up, she tried not to think of the way he had chinked his gaming cup against the lip of her glass in the close confines of her bedroom.

'Now before my poor boar starts shivering with cold, let's move on to the business of carving,' purred Tulola, and as the beast was sliced open to reveal a whole goose, which in turn was stuffed with a pullet stuffed with a thrush, Claudia ensured her eyes went anywhere except opposite.

'I wish I'd been fit for the chase,' growled Sergius. 'I do enjoy a good hunt.'

You're not the only one, thought Claudia. I know policemen who use sex the way hunters use spears.

'That's the trouble with these Umbrian pimples,' Corbulo mumbled, heaping her plate with carrots and broccoli and celery. 'They're only fit for bloody hunting.'

Well, this time, my fine patrician friend, your weapon has missed its target.

'Where's the scope to cultivate the soil?' Corbulo

seemed to be talking to himself. 'And yet isn't land the most important thing for us all?'

'What? Oh. Oh, yes.' And that business about the ulcer! I've seen you, Marcus Cornelius. Every time the wine jug comes round, your hand closes over your glass, which means you, sir, are on the wagon.

'Don't you love it, Claudia? The living, breathing soil?'

'Absolutely.' But I can see why Gisco's wife succumbed. Sleek, witty, urbane? Tinged with danger round the edges? Just the ticket for a woman tired of the marriage bed and seeking outside adventures.

'The way it changes with the seasons, filling the barns and the vats and the cellars?'

'I'll say.' How many more women have you strung along who'd grieve for the tragic waste should the charioteer make you sing castrato?

'It nurtures us while we live, hugs us when we die.'

'My dear Corbulo, I couldn't have put it better myself.' What's wrong with me tonight? Every time I look up, my cheeks start to burn! Dammit, I should never have called for that jug of white wine earlier. Red and white never mix.

'Claudia,' the Etruscan's painted hand closed over her own, 'would you say we get on well?'

From under her lashes she was aware of a certain twinkle coming from the star of the show and hotly turned to face the man beside her. 'Damned right we do.'

A short while ago that arrogant son-of-a-bitch over there was sincerity personified, a girl could have been fooled into thinking she meant more to him than a quick tumble, but now look at him. One camel later and he's absorbing adulation the same way he'd take medallions of honour to hang round his belt.

'That's what I thought.'

Trophies, that's what he's after. Well, I have news for you, Marcus Cornelius, I have been a trophy wife, and it's rewarded me with a grand house, my independence, a business empire and a pile of glittery gold pieces.

'You know Sergius is winding up the first stage of his operation?'

'Mmm?' You get sod all for being a trophy mistress.

'I'll be moving on after that.'

With a truculent toss of her head, she smiled at Corbulo. 'What? I mean, what . . . what about the new shipment of animals? Won't you stay on to train them?'

Grey eyes searched hers. 'I could, if I wanted, but you know how I yearn for Etruria. What do you say I work your land with you when my contract's up?'

'Corbulo!' Just how silvery can a laugh get? She hoped it carried. 'Are you drunk?'

'Steaming,' he admitted, taking a tighter grip. 'How else do you think I'd pluck up the courage to ask?'

Across the hall Orbilio had stopped eating. 'Do you know how to pinch vines?' she asked. There was no way Smartypants could make out the words, though!

'Well, no – '

'Or which cycle of the moon is right for racking?' From that distance it's body language that counts, and accordingly Claudia covered the trainer's callused hand with her own. To one side, a group of musicians filed in and began to play.

'You know full well I don't, but,' he beckoned the slave to top up his goblet, 'you're extending, aren't you?

Sergius has made me a rich, rich man, Claudia. Together, you and I, we could afford both plots, not just the one. What say we raise cattle?'

Shit! She stared into her glass for several seconds, pretending to listen to the music. He wasn't the first man to want to follow Claudia Seferius to the ends of the earth, washing her feet with his sweat, but . . . Shit, shit, shit.

'Keep training the beasts, Corbulo.' Gently she removed her hands from his and stood up. 'You have a natural affinity with animals, the land would stifle you.'

'There's good profit margin in hides and beef – '

A furtive glance showed a man opposite, propped nonchalantly on one elbow. Dammit, hasn't he got anything better to do than watch me?

'Not as high as with wine,' she explained softly, 'and I can't afford to diversify.'

'You can. *We* can! It decreases any risk of losing the vintage because a late storm rots the grapes where they hang – '

'I will not have cows on my land!' She concentrated on the click of the castanets.

'Cabbages, then. Or bees and wheat. Claudia, we could keep chickens and goats – '

'And what? Train them to pull carts reined by monkeys? Corbulo, I'm a wine merchant,' she said, searching with her toe for her second sandal. 'Vines are my business and as much as I appreciate the offer – and believe me I do – I need to work alone.'

An ochred hand closed over her wrist and pulled her gently towards him. 'You want to talk about needs?' he asked huskily.

Claudia felt the tingle of citron and woodsmoke in her nostrils, red dust on her skin.

'Corbulo, Corbulo,' she said, tugging softly at the loops of his hair. Marcus Cornelius Orbilio was sideways on now. She remembered his profile lit first by moonlight, then by lamplight. She tasted sandalwood and juniper in her mouth. 'I can't alter my plans.'

Citron versus sandalwood. Grey eyes versus charcoal. Braided loops versus wavy mop. Prince and pauper, pauper and prince. She heard cymbals and drums banging inside her head, as though the musicians themselves had moved in.

Then, suddenly, it stopped and everything fell into place.

'Leastways,' she added quietly, 'not in the way that you mean.'

For in that instant, in the fraction of a second between the end of the music and the applause starting up, Claudia Seferius had made a decision.

XXV

Milk, it has to be said, does not fan the flames of passion quite like a good, old-fashioned Falernian wine. In fact, it gets to a point when the very thought of another mouthful makes a man not so much rampant as downright bilious. After an energetic bout of hoop trundling, Orbilio felt a pounding in his head and a shaking in his hands that owed nothing to his camel ride.

'Try this, sweetie.' Tulola thrust a goblet of fragrant, pink liquid under his nose. 'It's my special-recipe sherbet.' She pushed the milk aside and pulled a face. 'That's fit only for pigswill,' she said.

Orbilio sniffed the frothy concoction. 'What's in it?' he asked. They drank it in the Orient and they drank it in Arabia, but he'd never considered it a Man's Drink exactly. Wine, definitely. Beer? Well, the Egyptians survived on it, but it would never catch on, and as for those foul, fermented brews – no wonder the men who drank it were barbarians!

'Pomegranates, catmint, saffron and carob pods,' she laughed. 'Satisfied?' She leaned low to whisper in his ear. 'Because if not, I can arrange that, too.'

She clapped her hands and two girls in transparent tunics began to dance to their own lyre strains as figs, sorbs and medlars were passed round.

'You can have either of those girls. Both, if you wish.'

'Another time, perhaps.' She knew damned well he wasn't interested. 'Great sherbet, though.'

'Great party, too, don't you think?'

'I do,' he said graciously, although few seemed to be enjoying it as much as Tulola. Corbulo was drinking himself under the table, Timoleon was boring Sergius and Euphemia with his exploits, Alis was comparing with Pallas the virtues of braising versus a good fricassee and Taranis had grown positively maudlin. Across the room, his complexion dark against the brilliant yellow, Barea cringed under a heavy lashing from Claudia's tongue. Under the circumstances, Marcus thought, the Lusitanian had got off rather lightly.

Orbilio smiled to himself. Rarely did he go undercover, but when he did, the art of lipreading came into its own, and he had been thoroughly entertained by her performance with Corbulo. Up to the point where the Etruscan's hand closed over her wrist and drew her slowly towards him! Orbilio's gut twisted. She had not resisted. The conversation became not only secret but intimate, but it was only when Claudia began tugging on Corbulo's looped braids and whispering so earnestly, that he realized how serious a rival the trainer really was.

He refused the figs and the sorbs and the medlars, and tried to quench the burning in his heart with the sherbet.

'What', Tulola purred in his ear, 'do you think of my library?'

'I haven't been in there.' Yet he thought he'd searched all the rooms . . .

'Which would you prefer? Philosophy? Travelogues?

Eulogies?' She waved her arm to indicate her six Negroes who, while his thoughts were turned inwards, had arranged themselves in a circle facing outwards. 'We have them all.'

Holy Mars. 'You don't mean – '

Tulola rolled on to her back and let out a throaty laugh. 'Of course, I do. Wonderful, aren't they?' She spun back on to her stomach and clicked her fingers. 'I think the occasion calls for poetry, don't you?'

Orbilio nodded dumbly. Croesus above, were there no depths Tulola could not plumb? Weren't these men degraded enough, pulling her chariot, without being turned into a human library?

'Can you imagine how difficult it is,' she drawled, tracing a sinuous tongue round her lips, 'finding handsome specimens able to recite?'

He should not have been surprised when the poetry turned out to be explicit erotica, but he was, and this time he couldn't lay the nausea entirely at the door of his milk. Orbilio gulped at the sherbet and to hell with its potency. It was cool and refreshing, with the sweet, fizzy tang of pomegranate and in three swallows the goblet was empty. In front of the couch, the cheetah yawned.

What was he doing, for gods' sake, playing this bloody charade? He could put paid to it this instant, by announcing Agrippa's death. Why didn't he?

Tulola clapped her hands again and two waiters brought in a giant phallus dripping with figs and apricots, plums and cherries, which had been preserved in honey over winter. Orbilio felt the room begin to swim.

Why had he held back? The reason lay in this very

hall, a vision of loveliness in pastel blue, her curls tumbling over her faience necklace as she laughed and made jokes with young Salvian. Janus, Croesus, what did she see in the trainer?

When Tulola topped up the sherbet, Orbilio swigged the lot as he pictured lighting the lanterns in his bedroom – hundreds, no thousands of them – one at a time. The heat would be cloying, heady; bay leaves and alecost would burn in the braziers; oil of cade would be splashed over orange blossoms strewn white on the floor. Compared to Claudia's sensuality, Tulola's raw sex grated – the dirty verses, the fruit phallus, the demeaning spectacle of men trained like animals. Even to imagine making love to Claudia at this moment would be to defile the very act, but he couldn't help thinking that when it was over . . . when it was finally over and there was no breath left in either of them and the couch was damp with sweat and the air heavy with the scent of their fusion . . . he knew then he would be home.

'Master Orbilio.'

Home – and never want to leave.

'Master Orbilio.'

A gentle tug on his tunic broke the spell, and he realized he was alone in the banqueting hall, that the fruit course was long finished.

'Where are the others?' His mouth was furred, he must have fallen asleep.

The young girl who was trying to attract his attention seemed confused. 'It's the darts match, sir.'

'Right, I'm on my way.'

'Oh, no, sir. I'm not here to get you, I'm to tell you

to go straight to your room. Lady wants you, says that it's urgent.'

He stumbled to his feet. They felt weighted. 'Which lady?' he asked, but the room was empty again and the ceiling was spinning. Bloody camel, he thought, crunching his way across the debris of snail shells and cherry stones, grape pips and lobster claws. Well, they say riding one makes a man seasick, serves you bloody well right.

Brighter than daylight thanks to the scores of torches, the atrium was deserted as Orbilio fumbled his way across the wide open space. This was how it must have looked the night Fronto was murdered, he realized, skirting the pool, but that was as far as his thoughts went, because when he turned right, the torches, the columns, the marble busts all multiplied a dozen times. Goddammit, that ugly, humped son-of-a-bitch has given me concussion as well.

What was wrong, he wondered, as he stumbled towards his bedroom? What was so urgent, so private, that whoever it was had to see him now, this minute, in his own guest room?

'Hello?' The shutters were closed, the room was in darkness. He nudged the open door with his toe. 'Hello?'

Janus, it's a trap!

Too late the door slammed behind him, smothering him in blackness, and then the blast hit him. Judean balsam. The sultry heat of the Indus. Babylonian lilies . . .

'I might have known!' he began, but two hands shot out of the void and pulled his head fiercely towards her. When his lips touched hers, the full force of Vulcan's fire shot through his body and he jerked like a snapped twig.

It was like being at the centre of a whirlwind. Marcus Cornelius Orbilio was sucked out of the Empire, out of Umbria, out of the house, out of this room. There was nothing else in the universe but himself and a passionate, sensuous woman, burning, hungering, devouring each other in the vortex. Curls tumbled and fell round his fingers.

He heard the rip of wool as she tore at his costume, felt the cold of plaster against the heat of his flesh. In a single wave, linen cascaded to the floor and he could see the faience necklace shimmering against her skin in the dark.

He did not know who moaned, him or her, when he reached out and ran his hands down the curves of her body. With a frightening intensity, she trembled under his touch, her kisses more and more frantic as her breastband unknotted in his palm. Eager nipples were thrusting against his tongue and he could feel her shuddering as his fingers explored the wetness of her thong.

Together they spun along the wall, tearing at each other in hungry fury, a ferocious explosion of lust, love, passion. A trickle of hot blood ran down his back where her nails raked, and when he blinked away the sweat which dripped into his eye, he tasted the salt from her body, felt the furnace of her fingers on his chest. He groaned at the searing pain in his loins as her hands moved lower and lower, up and down, round and round, until he could take it no more.

He cried out. She cried out. And then they were crying out together, thrashing, throbbing, drowning in each other's furious ecstasy. When it was over, when – panting and running with sweat and with the flat of his hands supporting the weight of his body against the wall – Orbilio marvelled how this was nothing like he'd ever imagined. Far from spent, every muscle still twitched, his skin was aflame and his vision, even in the dark, remained clouded.

'Claudia,' he croaked, his throat almost closed. 'Oh, Claudia.'

The huskiness of the laugh jolted him backwards. 'I think you've made a mistake, sweetie.' The pendant clattered to the floor as Tulola's long, low stride took her across to the doorway. 'Be a love and return this, will you?'

In the oblong of light shining from the hall as she sailed out of his bedroom, a mass of dark ringlets skimmed through the air to land at his feet. And now he knew why Tulola Pictor was so desperately keen to play forfeits.

XXVI

The goddess Aurora still had one or two snores in hand
before duty bade her rise and push away the night skies,
and Claudia, flanked by her vigilant bodyguard, was
taking the opportunity to walk off the sweetmeats when
she noticed so disgusting a spectacle propped against the
lion shed that she couldn't resist the urge to examine it.

'Good grief, Orbilio, last time I saw something that
gruesome, it lay belly up in a drainage ditch.'

A muscle twitched at the side of his mouth. 'Flattery
will get you nowhere.'

She peered closer. 'Dodgy oyster, was it?'

'Let's just say it left a nasty taste. What's wrong with
the party? Not over already?'

No, but the prospect of watching a flabby has-been
wrestling an unwashed, hairy Celt, both of them buck
naked, was simply too horrible to contemplate and she
told him so, nodding her head at the same time to dismiss
her bodyguard.

Orbilio waited until the Gaul had disappeared round
the monkey shed before prising himself off the wall.
'Forget what I said earlier,' he whispered urgently. 'Pack
your things and go.'

Claudia held up her hands in mock horror. 'Marcus

Cornelius! You, of all people, incite an honest citizen to break the law? Shame on you!'

'Bugger the law, bugger Macer, this place is evil, Claudia. Evil.'

'Too much milk,' she said to the moon, 'makes a man light-headed.'

'Claudia, I'm serious. Get out of here.'

I see. Or at least, I'm beginning to. 'I suppose this wouldn't have any connection with your returning to Rome at the same time, would it?'

That's torn it! Now he'd know she'd been rifling his papers! When she'd slipped inside his room ten minutes earlier, Claudia's initial reaction had been shock. Something had clearly taken place here – tables tipped over, chairs upended, it was a right bloody mess – but the signs pointed away from some desperate search. A fight? The mosaic was slippery with oil of bay, as though someone had tried to disguise a rotten smell, so no, not a fight. Also, and even more telling, the inside of Orbilio's maplewood chest was still in immaculate order. His clothes, his comb, his purse, everything rested neatly in its allotted place. It had not been intentional, her search – at some stage this evening she'd dropped her faience necklace, and rumour said Orbilio had found it – but when faced with a couple of scrolls bearing the seal of the Head of the Security Police, who *wouldn't* have been curious? The first informed her that Orbilio had not confined his extra-marital activities to charioteers (apparently an ex-tribune, ex-prefect, ex-consul was also after his valuables), and the second, even by Callisunus' silvery-tongued standards, was terse: 'Get your fat arse back to Rome. Right now.'

Behind the lion shed, Claudia braced herself for the onslaught . . . which never came.

'I'm going nowhere,' he growled, 'until this case is solved. Go – tonight – and leave me to cover for you.'

'I don't need a man to hide behind, thank you.'

'I'm not suggesting you do.' He was rivalling the big cat for snarls. 'This is something I need to sort out myself, that's all.'

How interesting. The Empire is in crisis, yet here we have a dedicated and professional aristocrat suddenly telling us he's turning his back on duty and ambition and a shot at the Senate for the sake of . . . Of what, exactly, Marcus? A widow of lower rank and dubious past? Pleasant scenery? An obligation to see this non-crime through to its non-existent finish? Somewhere along the line, young Master Supersnoop, the arithmetic does not quite satisfy the tallyman.

'Well, you're not the only one with unfinished business,' she said airily. Adding in reply to the half-raised eyebrow, 'The day will soon dawn when the merest mention of my name will bring Macer out in warts. I want to be here when the bumps rise.'

'You'll have a bloody long wait,' he barked, 'because whoever's behind this – '

My, my, we are in a bad mood! 'There is no deadly deed, Orbilio, trust me on this.'

She might as well have saved her breath.

' – the Prefect will come out smelling of lavender. His type always do.'

'Like Callisunus, you mean?'

'Even if this turns out to be a conspiracy with

Quintilian at its heart, Macer is a supporting pillar of this dwindling community – '

'Did you say pillar or pillock?'

'For gods' sake, can't you take this seriously?'

'Take what seriously?' She pulled her wrap tighter and wasn't sure it was purely down to the chill, pre-dawn breeze. 'Two men tried a scam and it failed. Happens twice a day in Rome; that's what pays your salary.'

'Aren't you forgetting the arson attacks?'

Claudia shrugged. 'There'll be a hundred Frontos the length and breadth of Umbria. No doubt one's torching a vineyard even as we speak.'

'Your estate's in Etruria.'

'Don't split hairs, Orbilio, you're in no condition for skilled work.'

Suddenly he punched his fist into the timber shed, sending the lion into a paroxysm of roars. 'The bitch drugged my sherbet.'

'The what dragged your shirt out?' Claudia had to shout.

'Forget it.' The big cat stopped snarling and Orbilio wiped his face with his hands. They seemed to be shaking.

If that's what comes of being on the wagon, thought Claudia, I can make an excellent case for staying pickled.

The lion staged another small protest before settling down. Two sheds along, a bear considered growling out in sympathy, then decided against it. It was the fact that it arrived at its decision mid-growl that made Claudia and Orbilio exchange glances.

'Corbulo?' she called out. 'Corbulo, is that you?'

'Stay behind me,' Marcus hissed, plucking a brand from its iron bracket. Whispers of wind played with the flames.

'No fear,' she whispered back, grabbing another torch. 'You're not fit to fight a flummery.'

But that wasn't strictly true, because a dagger had appeared in his right hand and the grip was steady. Oh, well. Two can play at that game.

'Where the hell do you keep that?' he asked in amazement.

'Safe,' she replied. Although from time to time it gets a mite uncomfortable.

A dark figure flitted between the elephant shed and the giraffe house and Claudia felt the hairs on her scalp prickle. Corbulo would not behave so furtively. There it was again. Darting. Silent.

'This way,' Marcus whispered.

'No, this way.'

'Claudia, just for once, do as I say, will you?'

'Let's compromise,' she mouthed, 'and do it my way. Come on!' Without giving him a chance to argue, she ran down the path and disappeared behind the camel shed.

Orbilio groaned. Please. Anything but dromedaries! 'Listen!' he said, catching her elbow and spinning her round. 'What's that?'

The yelp from the area of the seal pool was no animal.

Together they raced in the direction of the cry, lifting their torches high to avoid tripping. The gate was still barred. Sleepy seals honked at the intrusion.

'Over there!' he cried. 'The hay store!'

As they sped across the stone slabs, they could hear gurgling sounds, a frantic tattoo.

'Remus!'

The sight that greeted her as Orbilio flung open the door would stay with Claudia the rest of her life.

'Holy shit!' In one fluid movement, Marcus had bracketed the brand and sheathed his dagger. 'I'll take the weight, you cut him down!'

For ten seconds, or ten minutes, or maybe even ten hours, Claudia stood paralysed, hoping – praying – this was a dream and she'd wake any second. Against the wall, its eyes popping, a life-sized model of an Etruscan noble thrashed and jerked and made grotesque rattles from its throat. The frenzied drumming they'd heard was its feet.

But why was the puppet's facepaint the colour of knapped flint? Why were its lips purple?

'Claudia, for gods' sake, I can't hold him much longer!'

Snapping out of her hideous reverie, she realized Orbilio was supporting Corbulo by the hips and suddenly she was leaping up the bales to saw at the rope. Janus, it was thick! She turned her head away from the black suffusion, her hands too busy with the knife to dwell on the implications. Rasp, rasp, rasp. Below her, Orbilio struggled with the strain of his burden. Rasp, rasp, rasp. In the twisting of the fibres lay the rope's strength. Come on, you bastard! Then – whoosh! Corbulo and Orbilio collapsed into the straw, the policeman wrenching at the noose to expose its livid legacy as the trainer's eyeballs rolled upwards.

'Sweet Jupiter!' Claudia jumped down. 'Is he – ?' The dusty shed seemed to have made her mouth dry.

'He's only passed out.' Orbilio shot her a quizzical look. 'He'll be fine.'

All around, the signs of a skirmish were obvious, and it was also apparent that this was no chance encounter. Even the most dedicated homicidal maniac refrains from carrying a knotted noose on his person!

The Etruscan spluttered at the water splashed on to his face.

'Sssh!' Claudia ordered. 'Don't say anything.'

'Who was it?' asked Marcus.

'Lie still,' she urged. 'Save your strength.'

'Corbulo, who did this?' Orbilio ignored the glower from beneath a tumbling mass of feminine curls.

The trainer gave a faint shake of his looped braids. 'Dunno.' The hoarse whisper was barely audible. 'Left – party.' Bloodshot eyes flickered at Claudia. 'Needed – to – sober up.'

'Did you see anyone prowling about?' Marcus persisted.

Corbulo shook his head. 'Ambush,' he croaked. 'From behind.'

'Damn!' Orbilio began to pace the barn, but on the second turn he dropped to his knees. 'Well, well, well! Recognize this?' he asked.

In the flat of his hand, a scrap of material the colour of egg yolk trembled in the same pre-dawn breeze that had chilled Claudia earlier. Only now it seemed to blow straight from the Arctic.

XXVII

Tulola's celebrations were almost spent, the guests along with them. They'd drunk too much, eaten too much, and were starting to bounce off the pain barrier. Corbulo had not been missed, neither had Claudia or Orbilio and their haggard faces, when they burst into the room, seemed little different from the others'.

'Oi, oi, hold on a minute.' The horse-breaker was amused rather than angry when Orbilio grabbed him by the scruff of the neck and shoved the scrap of fabric in his face. 'Why should I want to see Corbulo hanging like game from a meat hook?'

'Then what happened to the robe?' Orbilio released Barea the way a terrier lets go an ankle. 'You aren't wearing it.'

'Same reason, I suppose, that you're out of costume,' Barea replied. 'Glad to be shot of it. Damned women's clothes, if you ask me. Don't know why Pallas kept the bloody thing.'

'So it *was* yours!' Timoleon turned to face the fat man. 'Now why aren't I surprised.' It was an insult, rather than a question.

'That garment was presented to me by a Phoenician nobleman with more class in his little finger than you've got in your whole body, you blowsy pig-sticker.'

The mood was all wrong, Claudia thought. Mockery? Indifference? And then she realized. They were frightened. All of them. She recalled the expression on Alis' face when the news broke, it was that of a stag whose antlers had been caught in the huntsman's net. They had all felt the shockwaves, but only she had been too slow to cover up, and suddenly Claudia was reminded of a pack of lionesses, each moving as one.

She had a horrible feeling that Orbilio, however hard he searched, would never find that missing tunic, because the Pictors had closed ranks. Fear had formed a bond that friendship never could.

Claudia thought of Corbulo, refusing to be fussed and insisting that, honestly, a good night's sleep was all that he needed, he was fine. Any single person here in this room tonight, she reflected miserably, could have taken that tunic as a disguise and followed the trainer.

She looked around, and shivered. Any single person here in this room tonight could be the killer.

Oh-so-silently suspicion stalked the Villa Pictor, insinuating itself into the outbuildings, the fields, the gardens and the orchards. It masqueraded as shadows, as creaks, as gusts of wind, and coiled its way into every crevice of every mind. The clamour of the kitchens was reduced to terse whispers, plates rattled in nervous hands, field workers looked over their shoulders and Junius camped beneath his mistress's window. In the atrium the water-clock dripped with exasperating slowness, the sunshine that flooded the marble took for ever to creep across the floor. In the courtyard, grown men jumped at the lovebird's squawks and avoided the shadows of the mythical beasts. When the elephant trumpeted, a flowerpot smashed to smithereens in the gardener's hands. Three of the slaves, a man and his daughters, tried to decamp under cover of darkness, but Macer had left eight of his men as contingency, four north and four south, two on and two off.

At the same time the runaways were marched back to their barracks, Taranis also slipped quietly into his own room, unshouldered his bulging rucksack and unleashed a bitter Celtish curse.

Like the build-up to a storm, the atmosphere was oppressive, torrid. People sat with their backs to the walls and pretended they were hung over from the night before; it explained the beads of sweat on their foreheads, the gooseflesh down their arms, the nausea in the pits of their stomachs.

No one dared voice the fact that they were prisoners on the estate.

No one dared whisper trust was a thing of the past.

Only Orbilio threw caution to the wind as he went about his investigations and his attitude puzzled Claudia greatly. There was a fanaticism about him now, and instinct told her it was Marcus who had overturned his own furniture.

Somewhere along the line, she thought, this has got personal.

Meanwhile, Corbulo appeared in part to be the weathervane for the family's emotional wellbeing, for it was upon Corbulo that hopes were silently, secretly, collectively pinned. Here was the man who had brought Sergius to the pinnacle of success finding the road to recovery difficult – and it had frightened them. Always they had seen Corbulo as strong and reliable and while physically he seemed mended, his movements were wooden, his thoughts remained locked in his head. When Corbulo got better, everyone would get better. Or so they told themselves . . .

Come Saturday night, when the moon had reached half and the rest of the Empire rejoiced at the equinox in full voice, the relatives and guests of Sergius Pictor were gathered round his dining table, leaning on their elbows and playing with their food in abject silence. The little girl who strummed the lyre might just as well have not bothered.

'Look at us!' Sergius drove the point of his knife into the tabletop as the pork and stuffed marrows were cleared away virtually untouched. 'You'd think we were facing mass execution!'

He was right. No appetites, no colour, no feelings even. Just a numbness, in both body and spirit. Passing time until Something Else Happened.

More eyes were watching the blade quivering in the woodwork than the irritation which washed over Sergius' face. 'There's a madman on the loose, I can't deny it,' he snapped. 'But I'm buggered if he's going to take us down with him.'

Too late, thought Claudia. On the walls, Ganymede was swept off to his new job on Mount Olympus and he was the lucky one. He got away.

'Won't anyone answer me? Are we to sit in silence for the rest of our lives?'

'You think we sing and tell jokes, yes, while the killer pick us off one by one?' The lines in the Celt's face became trenches, and the girl on the lyre hit two duff notes in succession.

'That's why Taranis wears long pants,' Timoleon growled in something close to his normal manner. 'He's always wetting them.'

'Tch!' The Celt made a gesture that none of them had seen before but they all recognized as vulgar. The gladiator curled his lip in disdain.

But small though the squabble was, the spell had been broken. Pallas made a lunge for the prawn rissoles before they were cleared from the table, perhaps not with his usual vigour, but he hung on to them none the less.

'What exactly do you have in mind?' Orbilio asked, and Claudia was surprised that, although he addressed the question to Sergius, his eyes flashed dark on Tulola.

Sergius began to sniff victory. 'At this very moment,' he said, 'half of Rome is comprehensively pissed and the other half's well on the way. What say we forget this maniac and celebrate ourselves? Tomorrow?'

'I think that's a wonderful idea,' gushed Alis.

'Me too.' Euphemia speared a scallop with the same knife she'd drawn on Claudia. 'I'm fed up seeing your miserable faces all the time.'

Hark who's talking, thought Claudia, 'Celebrate how?' she asked.

Sergius wiggled his blade out of the tabletop and called for the fruit. 'I rather thought an outing to the springs would be nice.'

'I d-don't think we should leave – '

'Rubbish, sweetie.' Tulola waved aside the Tribune's protests. 'It's a brilliant idea. This hanging around is driving us demented, even you, Salvian, young as you are.' She leaned over and tickled him under the chin until he turned red as a turkey cock.

'M-my uncle – ' he spluttered.

But Sergius was not a man to be put off the scent. 'Come along, you lot, what do you say?'

Careful glances were exchanged, which in turn became conspiratorial glances until finally they became smug, triumphant glances.

And at least ten hands shot up.

In Rome, Senator Quintilian bade farewell to the last of his callers and settled back contentedly, running his hands over the carved boar's head that comprised the arm of his chair. This was the time of day he liked best, when the long, noisy line of clients and lobbyists had finally trickled away, leaving behind their dreary petitions, most of which he'd burn later. Dismissing his scribe, he poured himself a large glass of tansy wine and closed his eyes. Skilful time management ensured him one hour – one single, solitary, precious hour – before different calls were made upon his person, usually generated by that ambitious wife of his, but just as important, nevertheless.

Later, of course, he would take himself off to the baths for a long dip, a spot of exercise, another dip, then a massage, preferably in the company of a buxom whore, each enterprise designed to refresh him both physically and mentally. However, it was this lull before the noonday rush that nourished his spiritual needs, this Golden Hour, where time was meaningless and he could admire the marble on his walls and on his floors and of his statuary, gloat over his successes in the Senate House, brush up on his oratory.

Here, in the peace and splendour of his own office (he daren't set foot outside, or Faustina would nab him!), calmed by the aromatic wine, memories would be awake. Of the Gallic campaigns of his youth. Of the curios he'd brought back from Egypt and Noricum and Thrace. Of the political struggles over the years, triumphs and failures, good times and bad.

Surrounded by exquisite works of art, he could block his ears to the sounds of the city on the far side of the wall – the cries of the mendicants, the hammering of the restoration work, the brawls, the brays and the barks – and reminisce about his sons, the first two, strapping boys who had both died fighting alongside their Emperor, and about his first wife, fifteen years in her grave. Then he would cheer himself up thinking about the three boys Faustina had given him, because Diana, Goddess of Fertility, had blessed the Quintilian line.

Nothing but sons, he was proud of them all.

The youngest was a funny little chap, my word he was, waddling up on those fat little legs of his, chortling away. Only this morning, Quintilian had watched him in the peristyle, racing his toy chariots between the columns. Whose idea was it, anyway, to harness them to mice? Comical, I can tell you, watching the big black one . . .

'Who the hell are you?'

'Letter, sir!' The messenger saluted and closed the door behind him.

Bloody hell, who let him past? Quintilian looked at the scroll on his desk. It could wait. That idle sod of a secretary could read it aloud after luncheon. Where was

I? Ah, the racing mice! Yes, that little fellow of mine's a real chip off the . . . There was something oddly familiar about the seal on that scroll. Of course it was upside down, he couldn't see properly . . .

What the buggery . . .

Quintilian blinked and sat up straight. Damnation, that was his own seal! He ripped it open and began to read. Mars Almighty, it was from the Widow Seferius! How the hell did she do that?

'To refresh your memory, Vixen Hill was purchased yesterday on your behalf' – no salutation, straight in, he noticed – 'and I ended up with Hunter's Grove. With me so far, Senator?'

Quintilian's frame began to shake with silent laughter. I'm with you, Claudia, my love, my little doxy. But you don't listen, do you? How many times did I tell you, don't meddle in business. I'm sorry you've wasted your money on a patch of exhausted soil, but you had it coming. Oh, you women, you think you're clever, getting a surveyor to report on the land, but I'm way, way ahead of you, girlie. The report you saw was a forgery. Surprised, Claudia? Shouldn't be. For five pieces of silver that weasel who lives under the aqueduct will copy anything, it was easy to change the names of the plots. Give in gracefully, there's a good girl. So you got a bloody nose? This letter will have got it off your chest – a very beautiful chest, if I may say so, my dear, one I hope to get closer acquainted with in the not too distant future – let's call it quits, shall we? Think about my offer, it's a generous one, and besides, you can't keep the business, can you? In, what, eighteen months you'll be forced to remarry, it'll pass to your husband, so you may as well enjoy the money while you're able. Let us therefore be friends, Claudia. Don't let bitterness come between us, eh?

He picked up the scroll and read on. 'I know you don't approve of women in commerce, Quintilian, but I wasn't sure you'd stoop so low.'

Low? A spot of forgery? You should see some of the other tricks of the trade, Mistress Seferius, this is just skating the surface!

'On the other hand, it seemed sensible to take certain precautions. Such as asking the surveyor to make two reports, one verbal and one written.'

Quintilian's shoulders began to stiffen.

'Ah, I see you have guessed! For some time, I've suspected one of my secretaries of spying – documents rearranged, that sort of thing – it seemed sensible to leave nothing to chance, and that included swapping the names round. It's not entirely clear what you will be able to do with Vixen Hill, but I'm sure you'll think of something, Senator. That is a very useful little stream which runs through it.

'PS: You do realize its source begins in Hunter's Grove, don't you? I'll let you know well in advance when I plan to divert it.'

XXVIII

A world away from the Vale of Adonis, with its narrow fertile belt and dark encroaching forest, the Spring of Sarpedon surrounded itself with rich green meadows from which wooded hills rolled gently backwards, growing blue and hazy with the distance. Sacred white oxen grazed and lowed on grass heavy with anemones and dew, larks sang on the wing and peacock butterflies gorged themselves on nectar.

Unlike the sulphur pools, today was no public holiday. There were no sausage-sellers, no rope-walkers, no acrobats on Sarpedon's holy turf – and yet it was impossible for spirits to remain low amid such Arcadian beauty. The mechanics for water collection remained well out of sight, ensuring this remained a tranquil place, where bodies and differences could be aired without impediment, a place for promenading and serenading. Tall cypresses cast shade on the lakes, crack willows dangled their fingers in the water, ferns sprang up like children. Blushing maidens wore garlands of blue iris and vervain, young men showed off their prowess at rowing on the lake, the poor scattered handfuls of flour, instead of metal, as offerings.

When the wagon lurched to a halt in the temple forecourt, Sergius was still expounding about his ideas for the future and if enthusiasm was rewarded in gold, he would be richer than Midas by now, thought Claudia. It had troubled him deeply, seeing his trainer reduced to a ghost – and she realized that Corbulo had not yet told Sergius of his intentions to leave when his contract was up. Either that, or Sergius was confident of talking him round. Any fool could see there was a glittering future in these circus spectaculars. Equally, he would argue, only a fool would walk away.

Corbulo's attendance today had uplifted not only Sergius; everyone's spirits had been given a boost. That's not to say they hadn't barred their doors and windows overnight, but here, out in the open, under a wide and welcoming sky, the general consensus was that the killer could only be one of Sergius' hired henchmen and that's the price you pay for taking on transitory labour; he should have employed men from Tarsulae. Never mind there are no young men left and never mind the locals would have blabbed to all and sundry, it was his own fault, he was told, he'll know better next time.

Yet all too quickly the badinage was cut short as news about the Regent spread, and as they crossed the bridge to the island, the tone was sombre. It was Agrippa this, Agrippa that, and Taranis was confused.

'I no understand. Why unrest in Rome?' he asked, throwing his hands in the air. 'Why threat of uprising?'

'Exiles,' croaked Corbulo. It was the best he could manage since someone had tried to restring his vocal chords, but it only partly explained his reluctance to talk. The trainer had changed. Often one does, when confronted with death, but while his was a dangerous profession, there was no comparison with assault from a back-stabber. Some men, Claudia knew, were never the same after a cowardly attack. They turned inwards upon themselves, became sullen, withdrawn, and although she prayed the gentle Corbulo would pull out of it, inside she feared for him.

'How you mean, exiles?' persisted Taranis, but it was left to Sergius to explain. Behind him, rugs were being spread out on the grass.

'He means folk have short memories. Three generations of civil war are quickly forgotten, they only remember being moved away from their own land to live in the city, and for some it's an alien culture.'

'They choose to go, no? Is not forced upon them?'

'This is the next generation we're talking about. Men with time on their hands, men who see themselves at the mercy of state handouts.'

Yes, thought Claudia. It is never fathers, but sons, who grow restless.

The prospect of a fierce civil backlash did not seem to bother the Celt particularly; rather the opposite, in fact. She was watching Corbulo, red muffler round his bruised neck, carving away at a piece of wood, when Salvian appeared at her elbow and relieved her of her wrap. His face was set, and yet Claudia had a feeling this had little to do with the death of Agrippa.

'Everything all right?' she asked, with a significant nod in Tulola's direction. All morning Tulola had been skewering him with her eyes, and twice Claudia heard her hiss 'Pansy!' at him.

'She's giving me a hard time,' the Tribune confided, 'because I wouldn't come to her bed last night.' No stammer? 'Can't imagine why,' he added. 'She knows I'm married.'

Claudia's laugh nearly burst free, but she swallowed it just in time. No, no stammer. Salvian was fast becoming his own man. He'd overtake his uncle in no time, and neither Tulola nor Macer would understand why.

The clouds on his face passed away. 'I know who the killer is,' he whispered, and this time Claudia's laugh was not restrainable. Growing up he might be, but not fast enough. The expression on his face was just like a six year old's on his birthday.

'You don't believe me, do you?' he said, without animosity. 'It was something my uncle said, which put me on to it.'

Claudia made a brave stab at solemnity. 'You mean that, like Macer, you think I dunnit?'

Salvian handed back her neatly folded palla. 'Lord, no,' he said seriously. 'You have to make allowances for my uncle, Claudia, it's – well, it's understandable, I suppose. Not so long ago, he investigated a robbery, where the shopkeeper said he was raided but the injury to his head was nothing worse than a bruise. Later he confessed he'd staged the whole thing to stave off his creditors.'

'I gave you chance to escape,' he added, 'and, to be honest, I was surprised you came back.'

You? You gave me that alibi? Claudia gawped at Salvian. 'The innocent have nothing to hide,' she said smoothly. But that won't stop me pickling your uncle in vinegar!

Food was being spread on the gaily coloured

blankets. A slave chilled wine in Sarpedon's crystalline waters. Alis and Pallas chased their counters over a chequered board. Timoleon was telling an eager Barea about the preponderance of stud farms which were springing up all over southern Italy. She did not feel like joining them.

Despite the bridge having no balustrade, Claudia leaned at a perilous angle over the water. It was so clear, you could watch bubbles of air rise to the surface, hundreds of them, each sending out tightly packed ripples which ran into its neighbour, swirling the surface and giving the spring effervescence. Rooks cawed in the sycamore trees and gnats danced over the shallows. Now if we could only transfer this to Rome, she thought contentedly, life would be perfect.

In the city, of course, water was a perpetual headache. The Tiber stood no chance of meeting the needs of the people, and between them, the aqueducts pumped in a hundred million gallons a day. Yet still it wasn't enough! Not that she was affected personally, the Seferius household had its water piped in, but for the poor it was a real problem. As part of the appeasement process, she suspected that Augustus would promise more aqueducts, just as surely as he'd promise bigger and better spectacles for his citizens. Which brought her back to Sergius.

For him, the death of Agrippa could not have come at a better time. She looked round, but he was absent from the group. Oh, there he is, back at the temple. With a casual glance over each shoulder, Sergius paused by the steps, then ducked into a chasm underneath. That he was able to do so was down to the geography of the land, because what was originally a simple shrine built into the hillside to honour Sarpedon, whose holy waters seeped from the rocks there, had been extended over the centuries until it was now a fully fledged temple. So instead of a solid block of rock leading up, a stone stairway had been tacked on, and it was beneath this stairway that Sergius disappeared. Fascinated, Claudia sauntered across. A grove of Apollo's sacred bay offered her the excuse of shade, and she was ostensibly watching the priest collect the leaves when she caught sight of Euphemia darting between the cottony leaves of the poplars.

'Can I pick some bay for you, madam?' the priest asked, for the oracle would chew them to induce his trance and deliver his prophecies. This, though, he would do in the temple proper . . . not under its stairs!

In the time it took for Claudia to shake her head, Euphemia had disappeared – or had she? Claudia caught a flash of pink just before Euphemia's tunic was completely swallowed by the chasm under the stairway. Well, well, well. Who's a naughty boy, then?

She paused in the temple precincts to read the inscriptions engraved in the walls, some admirable, some sickly sweet, one or two comic. A flock of pigeons pecked among the cobbles, plump as only temple pigeons can be when they're fed on caraway to ensure they never stray, and rows of hyssop waited patiently for when it was their turn to be gathered to purify Sarpedon's altar. A fountain representing the river god sang praises in his own language, a woman wept with relief after consulting the oracle. On the surface, life was simple here, continuous and peaceful – right now, it was hard to imagine such beauty, such sanctity could be sullied by a murderer walking among its willows and its cypresses . . .

Back on the island the wine flowed freely, jokes and laughter with it. Only Marcus Cornelius and the trainer seemed impervious to the atmosphere – and one could be forgiven.

'I shall have to look you up when I'm in Rome.' Tulola directed one long finger towards Orbilio.

'Do that,' quipped Claudia. 'His residence has something no other patrician family possesses.'

'Oh, yes. What's that?' she asked.

'Fleas.'

Even Miseryguts responded to that one.

As she tucked into cold salmon, chicken legs, and antelope studded with peppercorns, Claudia's banter revealed nothing of the turmoil within. Her trial was barely three days away, now, yet she had heard nothing from Symmachus. Had the messenger delivered the letter? Would Symmachus shrug off the threat of exposure? Supposing he was ill, and couldn't travel? Claudia had no doubts of her acquittal, but the scandal would completely ruin her wine business. That she was female was sufficient to knock sales on the head; that she was a female with a penchant for cold-blooded murder was the final straw.

Sipping the chilled red wine, she refused to acknowledge defeat. A lot could happen in three days . . . you only had to look at the last week to see that! But there was work to be done if she intended to rebuild the business. Realistically, she'd need to appoint an agent, someone clients could deal with on a daily basis without feeling this preposterous sense of emasculation. In no way would this affect her control over the business, but at the party the other night, Corbulo had given her one hell of an idea.

What was wrong with a little diversification now and then? Not in the way Corbulo suggested (cattle and cabbages, indeed!), but her surveyor had sown the seed. Thrasian grapes? Why not? Gaius Seferius was renowned for his full-bodied reds; what was wrong with fruity little whites? And since we can't shift this year's plonk, why not keep it another year and flog it abroad as vintage? Some could be turned into raisin wine – now that's *really* catching on as an after-dinner tipple . . .

'You caught them, didn't you?'

She hadn't heard Pallas approach, but that wasn't surprising. He moved fast, for his bulk, and she recalled the speed with which he dashed off when he saw Macer coming. 'I'm sorry?'

'Sergius and his adulteress. You caught them *in flagrante*.'

'How did you – ?' Who was he spying on? Sergius? Or me? From the corner of her eyes she could see Pictor, his arm wrapped round his wife and with the same look of devotion plastered upon his handsome face that he always wore. Euphemia sat on a fallen tree trunk, one leg over the other, watching the boats on the lake.

'Darling girl.' Pallas reached for an artichoke. 'I know *everything* that goes on round here.'

Claudia stood up. He was tall, Pallas. She had to crane her neck to look into his eyes. 'It's you, isn't it?' she asked quietly, unable to disguise the amusement in her voice. 'You're the peeping Tom.'

Pallas tipped his head back and roared so loudly that

Timoleon and Barea had to start their arm-wrestling all over again. 'Me?' Tears rolled down his fat face. 'My dear child, Eros forsook me long ago.' For an instant, his expression hardened. 'She intimated at a certain lack of proficiency on my part.'

Eros might be many things, but Eros was not a 'she'. 'Are we', Claudia hazarded, 'talking about your wife?'

'To be accurate,' he said bitterly, 'I believe the word she used was "pathetic".' Then the old Pallas bounced back, gossiping for all he was worth. 'No, no, it's our Femi who steams up the windows. Trying to find ways of keeping her stud entertained, and who better to learn from?'

Sergius didn't know, or he'd never have called Macer. 'Honestly, Pallas, I've never been to a house with so much intrigue under one roof!' Claudia paused to nibble a handful of raisins. 'You don't believe the murderer is one of the henchmen, do you?'

'Do you?'

'Me?' She gnawed at a honey cake. 'I've no idea *what's* going on.'

Amusement filled his face. 'Haven't you, now?' he chuckled, ambling over to join Marcus by the bridge. 'Haven't you really?'

Pallas' laughter hadn't died before Tulola had taken his place. It was inevitable, Claudia thought. The girl couldn't face her own company for long.

'What was all that about?' she asked, slowly brushing an invisible crumb off Claudia's tunic.

'Sex.'

'With anyone special?' Tulola's eyes were fixed on Orbilio's rigid back.

'Pallas was telling me he'd given it up. Apparently his bitch of a wife called his manhood into question, it left a telling scar.'

Half a minute passed before Tulola answered. 'We'd . . . had a row,' she said awkwardly. 'It was the heat of the moment. Words often get said that shouldn't. I didn't expect him to take it to heart – '

Mummy Duck with seven, eight, good grief, nine fluffy ducklings paddled past and a coot honked from the margins.

'*You and Pallas are married?*'

'Were, sweetie.' Tulola's smile was clearly an effort. 'It all happened a long time ago. But I'll have you know, I'm still very fond of the old bugger.'

Claudia watched a small dog chase a squirrel up an oak tree. Round and round the bole it ran, barking, yapping, jumping up. High in the branches, the squirrel curled its tail up its back and swore. 'Chak, chak, chak, chorrrrrr. Chak, chak, chak, chorrrrrr.'

Claudia's mind was whirling as well. Chak, chak, chak, chorrrrrr. By the gods! Tulola and Pallas? Chak, chak, chak, chorrrrrr. Small wonder Sergius put up with this amiable parasite; he had little choice.

But neither, she realized, did Alis – and it was Alis who footed the bills.

XXIX

Blame it on the heat, blame it on the boogie, blame it on the chilled red wine, but by the time lunch was over, the presence of one muscular man-tracker by her side did not seem desperately intrusive. Not, for instance, the way it had been in her bedroom. Nevertheless Claudia was still not sure how she came to be sitting under a willow in the middle of the island one minute and walking round the lake with this handsome patrician the next – especially since not one word had been spoken aloud. Behind them, the Temple of Sarpedon grew smaller and smaller, and even the lake fell from view.

'A copper quadran for your thoughts,' Orbilio said at last, swishing his ankles in the long grass beside one of the many gabbling streams that drained the lake and made these meadows so green and so lush.

'Treecreepers.'

'I . . . beg your pardon?'

'If treecreepers always creep up,' she pointed to an oak across the stream, 'and nuthatches always creep down, what happens when they meet?'

There it was! That infuriating hand covering his mouth. What's *wrong* with a smile, for gods' sake? You don't pay tax on it, no one can steal it, why be stingy with it? Claudia, who had no time for misers, said, 'Tulola – '

'That bitch! She's evil, she corrupts! Everything and everybody!'

A dipper braved the gabbling waters, oxen lowed in the meadows and a dappled white butterfly came to rest on a radish. 'Relax,' Claudia breezed. (What a grouch!) 'She doesn't always get her man.'

There was a dangerous fire in his eyes. 'What do you mean?' Also something lodged in his throat, by the sounds of it.

'Salvian,' she explained. 'His loyalty to the lovely Regina triumphed over lust.'

Poor Tulola! Where will she end up? Next month she'll be thirty, with Barea, Taranis, even Timoleon moving on. Moving away. Away from her. She's no fool, she knows they've used her, and even Salvian, with his ill-fitting armour and his stammer and his blushes, can see the gold is only gilt. What, she wondered, were the chances of Tulola asking the oracle what lies ahead? Does she plan to take Rome by storm with her sensationalism? Claudia hoped not. She'd be shunned, literally, by the upper classes, who prefer to keep their vices to themselves! Or is she (radical thought) banking on getting back with Pallas? Surely she must realize that, like the others, he's just trading off her while it suits him and, worse, his respect for his 'cousin' is nil.

'But that wasn't my point.' She told him about the marriage.

'Is anyone what they seem?' he asked, tossing a stick into the stream and watching its progress round rocks and through miniature rapids.

'Timoleon never was,' she said, momentarily diverted by the flash of a kingfisher diving upstream.

Once saluting to the roar of the crowds, fifty-seven dead men notched on his belt and riches and adulation dripping off him like bathwater, Timoleon had degenerated into a flabby caricature of himself with only the past and a nickname to sustain him. Ten more years and what's left? Already pushed out by younger blades nipping at his heels, Timoleon had sought recourse in his native Umbria – only to discover he still doesn't belong. Friendless despite his massive wealth, a bandit he remains, whether the killings were legal or not. She swallowed bile. Fifty-seven lives snuffed out, and each valued at just one handful of laurel leaves . . .

'What do you make of Taranis?' Orbilio asked, leading the way back towards the spring.

What, indeed? It was the Celt who bore the brunt of Timoleon's frustrations. Not because of a certain laxity in personal hygiene. Not because he didn't shave his body hair. Eight years in the arena had sharpened Timoleon's primitive skills, because underneath the barbarian's shaggy mane and baggy pants, Scrap Iron sensed what the others had not.

A threat.

'I'm inclined to agree.' Orbilio pushed aside the willows for her as they rejoined the lake. 'But like Scrap Iron, it's only a gut feeling.'

Codswallop. Instinct is the result of years of experience, of watching, listening, fitting pieces together. Claudia always trusted her intuition, and considered all that she'd seen and heard about Taranis.

'He's no trapper, that's for sure.'

The way he backed off when wild beasts were around was amazing. So what sort of threat could he pose? Then she remembered he was always talking politics, always asking questions . . .

'Look at that!' Orbilio's voice was full of awe.

She looked to where he was pointing. In the water, a huge blue chasm gaped up at them, circular, like an eye. A bright, hideous, aquamarine eye. The eye of the river god. Claudia shuddered.

'It's only a well in the lake,' he explained. 'Watch!'

He picked up a pebble and threw it at the hole. Claudia half expected it to squint, but the stone was caught in the surge. Instead of plopping straight to infinity, it slipped and swayed and took a lifetime before gravity finally triumphed and the little pebble was swallowed by the watery abyss.

'See?'

She felt silly and foolish and hated him for seeing her that way.

'Have you ever seen such an astonishing colour,' he was saying, and she hated him for showing it to her. Which is probably why she blurted out Sergius' affair with Sulkyboots.

His breath came out in a whistle. 'Euphemia, eh? I wondered why the little sexpot hadn't married.'

'I've no idea how long it's been going on, but I'll bet one gold piece to a golliwog Alis knows nothing about it.' Like me, she'd have seen nothing wrong with Euphemia's thighs clamped round her husband's neck at the party. Keep it in the family, and all that. 'I reckon Sergius plans to install Euphemia in Rome as his mistress and keep Alis at bay here in Umbria.'

Save your breath, Claudia, Supersnoop's on a different planet. He seemed to have something stuck on his teeth, the way he was twisting his mouth this way and that, sucking his lower lip, biting it, chewing his tongue. Probably the cold duck at lunchtime, she thought, stepping over a pile of deer droppings. Glad I went for the chicken.

'It's the same old problem,' he said eventually, staring at the rippling reflections of the poplars and the willows, at the twinkling coins in the shallows. 'Motive. Find a reason and we find our murderer.'

'*Our* murderer? It's me who was nearly pickled in crocodiles,' Claudia pointed out, as bubbles of air shimmied their way to the surface.

'Oh, you can't fault the killer's versatility,' he agreed. 'Fronto is knifed, Coronis has her neck broken, Corbulo has his stretched.'

Yes, and each of them cold, calculated acts . . .

Claudia concentrated on the shouts of the rowers, the girls egging them on. It was safer. She watched a gang of children chase each other over the footbridge in a game of pirates, she felt the warmth of the sun through her dusky pink tunic.

'Here.' Orbilio delved into his purse, pulled out a silver denarius and flipped it towards her. 'Make a wish.'

Claudia scooped the spinning coin in her fist and examined it. The Emperor on one side, Venus on the other. Venus. Goddess of love. Love and sensual pleasure. Venus, protector of the month of April, which is just around the corner. Well, bugger Venus. Claudia lobbed the denarius into the deepest water she could reach and heard a soft chuckle beside her. Well, bugger him, too.

Children's footsteps reverberated on the little wooden bridge as they thundered off to kidnap the temple pigeons. With their squeals still ringing in his ears, Marcus said, 'And let's not forget what happened to Sergius.'

The Pictor party lay flat on their backs, sleeping off their lunch to the drone of the bees and the songs of the warblers. Even an attack by marauding buccaneers with sticks for swords hadn't disturbed their gentle reveries.

'That wasn't poison – ' Claudia contradicted.

Suddenly the peace was shattered. From under the cypresses came a gurgling, retching sound. They ran forward. Sergius, rolled into a ball and clawing at his stomach, was spewing his guts up, his face convulsed in agony.

Frozen, Claudia and Orbilio stared at one another.

'*That*'s poison!' they chorused in unison.

XXX

The torches guiding the party back to the Villa Pictor were as numerous as they were welcoming – not that Claudia was convinced this was the sole intention. A maniac was abroad, kindling a primordial instinct in the slaves at the house. *Light fires and banish the bogeyman.* They felt safe within their wall of flame, and quite right too, she thought. The bogeyman had travelled with us!

Jumping down from the wagon, she noticed a string of horses in the yard. Military horses, godsdammit. She pursed her lips. That Prefect was like the smell of cabbage cooking. You can never quite eradicate it . . .

She followed the stretcher carrying Sergius Pictor into the atrium. He looked a whole sight better now, thanks to Orbilio's expert ministrations – although quite what procedures he followed Claudia had no idea. She was legging it across that footbridge faster than a jackrabbit on ice. *If he's looking for a nurse, let someone else volunteer.*

'I'm fine, now,' Sergius croaked, more with optimism than conviction, she thought. 'You can set me down here.'

Claudia looked at him. Weak was an understatement; his skin was waxy, his eyes still red from the vomiting.

'Drink this, dear.' Alis held a cup of water to his lips,

but he shook his head so violently, beads of sweat sprayed through the air.

'Something the matter?' Macer swept into the atrium to the jangle of armour and the clipclop of hobnailed boots, neither of which, Claudia noticed with a thrill of delight, were his own.

'I'm damned glad you're here,' Sergius said wearily, as the legionaries snapped to attention behind their leader. 'Damned glad.' He heaved himself up on one elbow. 'I want you to arrest her.'

From the edge of his eye, Macer darted a glance towards Claudia, and she didn't much care for what she read in it. Pointedly, she began to admire the tall marble columns, the white marble busts, the garlands of white scented daphne.

'Arrest who, sir?'

'Alis.'

Macer's wasn't the only stare to freeze on the sick man. 'Your wife?' he asked incredulously.

'Oh, yes.' Sergius wiped his mouth with the palm of his hand. 'It's not the first time, but now I think – no – I am certain.'

The tip of the Prefect's nose glowed pink. 'Certain of what, sir?'

'That's Alis is trying to kill me.'

Pandemonium broke out almost at once.

Alis, her pale face turning grey, swivelled her eyes towards Sergius, then sank to the floor before a word passed her lips, and Marcus Cornelius Orbilio, for the second time that day, put on his nursing cap and set to work while the rest of the room shouted each other down in an effort to make themselves heard. Claudia stood welded to the spot. Alis? *Alis?* Orbilio had loosened the neck of her tunic and was gently slapping her face.

Then, above the commotion, one voice cut through. 'Sergius is right. I suspected it myself ages ago.'

Euphemia shouldered her way to the front and stared unblinkingly at Macer. He stared unblinkingly back. 'And why is that, might I enquire?'

Credit it where it's due, thought Claudia. He is one cool customer, our Prefect. Perhaps it was he who got under Fronto's skin, she mused, rather than the other way around. Fronto. The dung-beetle who got himself killed just over there, in my doorway. A man who nobody misses apart from Balbilla, and she'd bring out the mothering instinct in a rabid hyena.

'Lots of things.' Euphemia stood with one hand on her hip, and looked every inch the trollop she was. 'For instance, every month he'd go down with food poisoning when none of the rest of us did.'

'But he is still alive,' the Prefect observed drily, investigating something wedged between his teeth.

'He's young and he's strong,' snapped Miss Sulky-boots. 'More than her first husband was.'

Macer's dental practices were abandoned. 'Isodorus?' he asked sharply. 'Are you suggesting – '

'Why not?' said Sergius. 'Only this time, she won't get away with it. By her own admission, Alis fed me mushrooms she'd gathered herself. Let her talk her way out of that!'

Had she been conscious, it was doubtful Alis would have been capable of talking her way out of a sack of black-eye beans, but Claudia's skin had begun to prickle. He was lying. Sergius Pictor was lying through his perfectly formed teeth, and Euphemia was backing him up. Why?

Tulola and Pallas were lobbying Macer to move Sergius. He was too ill to be arguing in the middle of the atrium, they said; for gods' sake, put him in his bedroom, at least. Timoleon and Barea, Corbulo and Taranis, vociferously denied any inkling of what was going on. They'd only seen Alis drooling over her husband, why should they be suspicious?

Why, indeed, thought Claudia. Yet all the while, Sergius had been having it away with that heavy-breasted siren, then slipping his arm round Alis' shoulders as though . . .

Of course! Now she realized why Euphemia had said such spiteful things about her sister. She was jealous of her! Holy Croesus, she and Sergius were in it together! They'd planned this, the devious bastards, right from the very start! Alis had told her, hadn't she? Sergius was on the scene long before Isodorus popped his sickly clogs. It was *Euphemia* he was in love with. It was Euphemia he wanted to marry. But it was Alis who had all the money!

He gave them a gift, the writhing chimera. The snake would have been placed in position, Isodorus encouraged (dared?) to put his hand in the lion's mouth. Claudia was willing to bet that neither Sergius nor Euphemia would call that murder. Assisted accident at best, the same way they callously planned to dispose of the silly, conscientious creature Sergius couldn't even bear to sleep with.

Attempted murder by his wife? Nothing can be

proved, that was never the intention, but this was why he wanted the might of the militia. There would be more than sufficient evidence for Sergius Pictor to divorce Alis ... and guess where the money goes! Claudia thought of Sergius, putting himself through hell and back, and for what? The performing beasts would make him ten times as much money as Alis brought with her, but he got greedy. He wanted it all. The house, the farm, the circus, the girl.

Click! Claudia understood now how he'd made himself sick. Whose idea was the sulphur pools? It was the mud he was after. He'd caked himself, very thinly, in mud and sulphur, what else explained skin the colour of pussy willows? The combination clogged his pores and made him ill – Claudia had experienced much the same thing on the trip back from Tarsulae – and just like he'd poisoned himself today, the more people who witnessed his suffering, the better.

Bastard! He arranged for the yobs and for Fronto, and everything subsequent because he was getting desperate for an excuse to call in the army!

Staring up at the vaulted ceiling, she wondered whether Alis could prove any of this – or indeed whether Alis would want to. Claudia smiled to herself. This could backfire on you yet, my handsome, devious host. If Alis can question just half of your actions, bang goes your divorce, and even when the money comes rolling in, how will you get away? She'll have you by the balls, old chap; you'll be dancing to her tune like a puppet. And as for you – Claudia glanced across at Euphemia – Alis'll have you married off within a month, and I'll bet it won't be in Umbria, either. Because if you can't trust your own baby sister, who can you trust?

Orbilio was lifting the limp form of Mistress Pictor into his arms. Despite detailed investigative work by the army and the Security Police, it was unlikely even a slender case could be made against Sergius, and even if he and Euphemia fell out and accused one another, it was his word against hers. Nevertheless, Claudia felt a great weight lifted off her shoulders.

It was over.

Finally, the nightmare was over. She could return to Rome knowing she didn't have to keep her back to the wall from now on.

As Orbilio carried Alis to her room, the clamour in the atrium became, if that was possible, even louder. Macer had to bellow to make himself heard, and was trying to verify the facts with his nephew. Claudia sidled over to Taranis.

'You know she be murderess?' he marvelled.

'I know you be spy.'

His face went rigid. 'You say again, please. I no understand.'

'You understand perfectly, my primitive friend. You came to find out whether the Emperor planned to invade Britain, am I right?'

'You know damn well.' His hands dug into her upper arms as he spun her behind the pillar. 'Is why you're here, no? You and security man?'

To his amazement, she began to laugh. 'Is that what you thought? That we're here to keep an eye on you?' He should consider himself so important! 'Well, I regret to tell you this, Taranis, but my story was the gods-honest truth. I was run off the road.'

'Tch!' The Celt made a vulgar gesture with his hand, but it was aimed at himself, rather than Claudia. 'Now you turn me in, heh?'

I ought to, if only for turning my room over. 'The Divine Julius made one attempt on your barbaric coast; Augustus won't fancy tangling with you lot again, take my word for it.'

'Is good,' Taranis said, nodding sagely. 'Is good we no have war, is good you have problem in Pannonia, and is good – good for Atrebates – your general is dead. It take heat off Britain, no? We trade in peace.'

Claudia felt a faint ruffle of unease. 'How could you possibly hear about invasion plans from this wretched little backwater?'

'I try Rome, people notice me. So I take, what's the word, accomplice, yes? I take accomplice. Freeborn man, poor. Need money. I pay him to stand outside Senate instead, he tell me what is said.'

The spy has a spy, whatever next?

'I – ' he paused. 'I sorry he try to kill you.'

Claudia goggled in indignation. '*You* tried to feed me to the crocodiles?'

'Not me! Accomplice! I not know what happen.' Be fair, Taranis did look miserable. 'He come visit, to Vale of Adonis, to make report. I tell him you here, you bring security man with you, and he panic. He say to kill you, I say no need, but – ' He spread his hands apologetically and shambled away.

She thought back to the night she searched Timoleon's room, and realized now the conversation she'd overheard was Taranis talking to his accomplice. What irony! If only she'd listened more carefully, she'd never have been dragged to the compound and a man would still be alive today.

Orbilio must have thought he was walking into a cockfight, there was such a rumpus in the atrium. 'Sergius has really kicked up a storm,' he remarked in Claudia's ear, although what his next words were, she was never destined to find out, because they were drowned by a noise which by rights should have dislodged the roof tiles.

'Enough!' Macer held up an imperious hand to quieten the rabble, and gave an imperceptible nod to his trumpeter to indicate that one blast was sufficient. 'If you could all retire to your rooms, please, I'll conduct interviews in the morning, you can have your say then. Ah – not you, Mistress Seferius. A word, if you please.'

He beckoned her over with an obsequious crook of his finger. Orbilio, she noticed, took just one pace backwards, and that to rest his weight against a column.

The Prefect smoothed his bright, white, civilian tunic. 'You'll have heard about Agrippa, naturally? So you'll appreciate I have a lot on my plate at the moment?'

Claudia shot him her prettiest smile. 'Tying up the loose ends of your illegal gambling racket?'

His face turned ugly. 'Do you accuse me of improbity, Mistress Seferius?'

'Only if that fly-blown dive doubles as a brothel at weekends.'

'That patronizing smile', he hissed through his teeth, 'will soon fade, because I have you, my girl. I have you.'

'In your dreams, perhaps.' She tried to sweep past, but he stepped to the side and blocked her way.

'No, no, I have you, Mistress Seferius, bang to rights as they say.'

Claudia raised one insolent eyebrow in reply.

Macer drew himself up to his full height, and rolled his tongue round the inside of his upper lip. 'This morning,' he announced, and this time his voice carried to the rafters, 'an itinerant pedlar reported a strong and unpleasant smell coming from one of the old patrician huts. Most of them have fallen into some disrepair along this neglected stretch of the Via Flaminia. I expect you had noticed.'

'If you had a point, Macer, it's long since gone blunt.'

'Oh, apologies, if I'm boring you. But you see, Mistress Seferius, when our itinerant pedlar went to investigate this objectionable odour, what do you think he found?'

'Your wife?' she asked sweetly.

Marcus Cornelius Orbilio had turned the other way, but his frame seemed to be shaking silently.

'He found', Macer sneered, 'the bodies of three young men. One had bulging eyes, one had ginger hair and the other bore a birthmark just about', he ran his finger slowly down Claudia's cheek, 'here. Acid, it would seem, had been added to their wine.' The Prefect examined his gold cloakpin. 'It was not a pleasant death.'

Sweet Jupiter! Sergius Pictor wasn't desperate, he was sick. To kill three boys, just to silence them – it was Coronis all over again! Claudia's stomach clenched and unclenched. Surely he could have spared a few coppers to pay them off?

'Prefect,' Claudia said sadly, 'I have a whole host of alibis.' Obsessed to the point of delusion, poor chap. They'll laugh him out of court on Wednesday. 'Including your own nephew.'

Even as she spoke the words, she knew . . .

And, worse, Macer knew . . .

'Yes.' He smiled, and it was not a pretty smile. 'He told me.'

Idly, he turned to face the captain of his soldiers. 'Arrest the bitch,' he said calmly, jerking his chin towards Orbilio. 'And him too, if he tries to interfere.'

Claudia Seferius didn't think twice. Spinning on her heel, she raced across the atrium and out through the courtyard.

'After her!' yelled Macer. 'Stop her! Any way you can.'

Vaulting the rosemary, she fled past the parrots and the topiaries and leapt over the fishpond. Torches that had previously been so welcoming became her enemy. They threw her fleeing figure into stark relief and gave her a thousand shadows. She jumped at each one.

Any way you can, Macer said . . .

Oh no! The gate's locked! She rattled it, pushed it, then when it refused to budge, ran to the far gate. The soldiers were gaining. They did not have to cleave a path, negotiate obstacles. Like migrating geese, they only had to stay in her slipstream.

Damn you, Macer, damn you to hell! Because even as she was boasting of Salvian's alibi, she realized the hole she was digging for herself. Of course, the boy would tell his uncle. Trusting, idealistic – he saw no reason not to. *Any way you can.* Dead or alive. It might yet prove a grave she had dug for herself! A thousand silhouettes flickered around her. A thousand hobnailed boots echoed in her ears. Shit! This gate's locked as well! Finding a toehold in the woodwork, Claudia shinned over it, her dusky pink skirts billowing as she darted between the peach trees and the pears.

Shouts told her that the soldiers were splitting up, fanning out. Thinning out ... She glanced over her shoulder. Three only in direct pursuit.

'Fuck!' A legionary, unfamiliar with the terrain, had tripped on the steps and was rocking himself as he rubbed at his ankle – the way people do, when the sprain is severe. One down, two to go.

Croesus, she was almost upon the labyrinth of sheds. She didn't know her way well enough to tangle with them. Think, Claudia, think!

One of the soldiers had paused to check his colleague, but the third man was gaining rapidly. Merciful Juno, be praised! Claudia grabbed the hoe leaning against a walnut tree and ducked behind its ample trunk. Wallop! Right in the solar plexus! The running soldier gasped once, then pitched forward on to his face.

Two down, one to go.

At the end of the orchard, she paused under the full light of a brand burning in its bracket on the wall, as though unsure which way to turn. She glanced to the left, then to the right, then to the left, then to the right. Fat lot of use, hoping Junius might suddenly spring to her rescue. Macer would have nabbed him long ago. Taken in for questioning, he would say.

Torture was the word.

For a second time she hesitated under a light, looking in all directions and hopping indecisively on the spot. Her pursuer was close now. But so was the first of the barns. Claudia spun to her left.

Junius was a stubborn cuss, he'd die rather than lie to the Prefect.

Timing her run, she jumped and swung upwards, her skirts barely clearing the branch as the legionary turned the corner. The blood in her temples pounded like thunderclaps, but he failed to connect the significance of a shower of soft, pink petals and Claudia sent a silent prayer of gratitude to Mars for setting brawn above brains for his warriors. The soldier swore loudly and then crashed his way into the first of the sheds. Banging and thumping told her he was searching the building, and she heard him thunder out of the other door. Straddling the smooth, grey bark she thought of Junius, bound in rawhide as one of Macer's minions applied red hot irons on the soles of his feet . . .

Kill my bodyguard, she vowed, and I'll kill you personally.

'Cut her off!'

'Get her before she reaches the sheds!'

Claudia timed her fall with the shouts. For the moment they had lost her. Now was the time to turn back, because Macer would not expect something so obvious.

Crouching along the shadows of the east wing, Claudia felt her way towards the south entrance where Macer's horses were hitched to the posts. Ducking beneath Alis' window, she heard loud wailing. The wail of a widow. Or *was* that Alis' window?

Relief welled up in Claudia's chest when she saw the horses were not only tethered, they were still saddled up. Dear, sweet Juno, I owe you one!

Third from right, he's my mount. Can't be difficult, can it, riding a horse? Just swing yourself up, dig your knees into the animal's side and hey presto, the wind's in your hair before you know it. And I'll grab the reins of the others as I go, they can scatter when we're clear of the valley.

Sprinting across the yard, Claudia failed to notice another figure.

Too late she heard the crunch of a boot on the cobbles.

'Not so fast!' a voice snarled in her ear.

Then the night shattered into a thousand fragments, and everything went black.

XXXI

When Claudia came to, she realized Macer had taken no chances this time. He had tied her up like a despatch rider's satchel: five hours of joggling would still never loosen the bonds! Claudia paused for breath. Talk about tunnel vision! That pompous, fussy, on-the-take Prefect was like Agrippa's underground aqueduct – except whereas that was designed to keep litter and scrap out, the Prefect's tunnel repelled justice, logic and anything resembling an open mind. I'll have your lungs on a skewer for this!

Lying on her side in the dark, it was difficult to take stock of her surroundings, but Claudia was pretty sure, from the cidery smell, that this was the old fruit store, the one that Pallas had suspected of being damp. Like the others, it would be stone-built, devoid of windows, boast a high, pitched roof, a floor of dry, compacted earth – and just the one door.

Now then, Macer, you blockheaded, imbecilic numbskull of a nincompoop, just what have you tied me to, eh? Writhing and thrashing, twisting and squirming, Claudia could not even sit up. So what was it she was tied so securely by the arms, waist and ankles to? Well, it was heavy, but not solid – a sack? No, sacking would have chafed her back – *her back?*

For the first time, Claudia realized her tunic was missing, that she was lying in just breast band and thong. Godsdammit, Macer really was taking no chances! Using her skin as a sensor, she began to eliminate the possibilities one by one. All right, we know it's not a sack. Or (rub, rub) wood or metal or terracotta. It feels like . . . She jolted in the darkness and felt the blood freeze in her veins. It feels like flesh!

Jupiter, Juno and Mars, I'm tied to a corpse!

She felt a pulse of revulsion. Then another, and another and another. In a surge of nausea, she kicked and writhed, but the ropes held good and Claudia forced herself to subjugate the revulsion. A corpse is just a person who's stopped breathing. A corpse is just a person who's stopped breathing. She had no idea how many times she repeated it before some semblance of calm set back in and she began to pray to Fortune that the body wasn't Junius. And yet, logically, who else could it be? Not Supersnoop, he was too smart and, dare she say it, too important. She remembered her vow. *Kill my bodyguard, and I'll personally send you to hell.*

What the devil . . .? There was a noise in her ear, not unlike the squeak of a door. A . . . groan? Junius? Her heart started walloping against her ribs. At her back, she felt the first flutterings of movement as the corpse began to revive. Then it began struggling, then thrashing, then jerking so violently she was forced to tell it, in no uncertain terms, to have a care, there are others involved in this, you know.

'Claudia?'

'*Orbilio?*' I do not believe this! 'Did you do this on purpose, for a cheap thrill?'

'This doesn't come cheap,' he laughed, shaking his ankles. 'I'll be charging you twenty sesterces at least. Do you know where we are?'

'The old fruit store, and I won't pay a quadran over twelve.' Then she reminded him that, if he pleased, there were other ankles attached to his.

'Make it eight and you're on.' He gave another kick. 'The rope has a bit of slack in it, can you feel it? If we can just roll from side to side and loosen it – '

Like a landlocked hippopotamus, they wallowed and rolled, rolled and wallowed, momentum gathering all the time.

'Oooof!'

She heard the air spurt out of his lungs as she landed smack on top of him. 'Don't blame me, this was your idea.'

'Ptth.' She heard him spit out a mouthful of dirt. 'Can (wheeze) you (wheeze) wriggle your foot free?'

'I can see a rope dangling from the rafters.'

'Could you (rasp) hurry?'

'We could climb that – '

'Claudia? Ple–eeze?'

' – and escape through the roof.'

'Claudia, move your godsdamned foot!'

'Don't shout, I'm only trying to help!' Her face screwed tight in concentration. 'Yess!'

Puffing, they rolled on to their sides, Orbilio gasping for air for what she told him was a very selfish amount of time and would he please let her know when he'd finished playing with the dust in his mouth, so they could at least shuffle into a sitting position.

'If we could find a rough edge,' he said, oblivious to the verbal spillages, 'we could saw through these ropes.'

'Try using your tongue.'

He ignored that as well. 'But we'll need to stand up, so . . . on the count of three, right? One, two – are you trying?' He supposed the raspberry meant yes. 'Again. One, two – up!'

'You said on the count of three.'

'That was three.'

'It was only two.'

'All right, all right, this is no time to argue. One, two, *three*. PUSH!'

Backs together, they thrust their way to a standing position.

'First it was sherbet,' he said, 'then it was milk.'

Claudia's eyebrows furrowed. 'You took the trouble to sniff the contents of the jug before it landed on your head?'

'You were the only one who was knocked out,' he chuckled. 'Tonight, when I went to my room for my sword after Macer set up the hue and cry, I realized, somewhat belatedly, that my milk had been laced.'

'Ah, yes; that mysterious movable ulcer.'

'Please!' he protested. 'Do you know how long I've gone without a drink?'

Gently she knocked her head back against his. 'The longest I've ever seen you without liquor, Marcus Cornelius, is thirty paces. Now are you going to get us out of here or not?'

It took a complicated set of hop-skip-and-jumps, which in the dark proved often painful what with jutting shelves and unexpected crates, but eventually they found what they were looking for. At some stage in its history, a bronze cooking pot had been left on an unattended stove for a jagged hole to burn through. How thoughtful of it to wait in the store to be patched!

'How is it,' he asked, manoeuvring the vessel into position and rubbing off the thick crust of verdigris with his thumb, 'that wherever Claudia goes, trouble trots beside her?'

'Me? I'm just your average little catalyst, I'm afraid.' She heard the rope grate against the rough, serrated bronze. They all had their secrets, Tulola, Pallas, Sergius, Euphemia, even Taranis the Celt. Her stumbling into their lives merely accelerated the situation. She concentrated on the rope, rasping and scraping. Surely, yes surely she could detect a bit of give in it?

'I could get used to this,' he said languidly.

Claudia's mouth twitched at one side. Half an hour of wiggling up and down, back to bare back, loin cloth to thong? 'I'll bet you could!'

Twang! As the strands burst free, they massaged the weals, then Orbilio spotted a tallow and suddenly there was light.

'Can you reach?' she asked, pinching her nose against the stinky candle. 'It's quite a way up, that rope.'

'Forget it, there'll be guards posted all round this building. Listen! Can you hear that?'

'Yes. Rats.' She'd seen two so far, and that was just since the light went on. Any bigger and Gisco could harness them to his chariots.

'No, no. Can't you hear a low, gurgling sound?'

'Water?' she ventured.

'Exactly. Now hold this candle, will you?'

Arm's length was still too close for the evil pong. 'What are you looking for?'

Save your breath, Claudia. The Boy Wonder is in a world of his own. With a gleeful yelp, he pounced on a rusty iron sieve. 'We need to trace the run of the pipes.'

'What pipes?' In candlelight, she could see verdigris on her arm, rope burns all over, and a couple of scratches on her shins.

Orbilio tested the handle of the sieve. 'Sergius diverted part of his stream – those beasts need a lot of fresh water – this is the runaway.'

'Sewage, you mean?'

'Whatever,' he said cheerfully, prodding the handle into the compacted soil. 'Pushed for space,' he tried another spot, 'he laid underground pipes for his outbuildings to go over the top.'

'Do we sift our way out? That's radical.'

He looked up and grinned. 'That's what I like about you, always willing to try out new ideas.' A couple more exploratory probes. 'I know two waste pipes meet, one from the monkey house, one – '

'How do you know?'

'I always check the lie of the land, my dear. You never know when – '

' – a Gisco might be after you.'

He shot her a ha-ha-very-funny look as he prodded the soil. 'Here we are!' There was a dull clunk as iron connected with terracotta.

'I still don't get it.' It came out nasal, on account of her hand clamped over her nose.

'Well,' he proceeded to tap his way along the pipe,

'each channel is four hands square at best.' He paused to swipe the perspiration from his eyes. 'It would be far more comfortable if we could find the junction, where it widens to accommodate both outlets. Can you hold that candle steady?'

Claudia willed the muscles in her hand to change from jelly into steel. *He's talking about escaping . . . through the sewer?*

'How – ' She cleared her throat. 'How far does it go, do you know?' *They could easily get stuck! Buried alive!*

'At a guess? Two hundred paces.'

'Two hundred?'

'Maybe three or four. Look.' He pointed to a dark, damp mound.

'A leak?'

'A blockage,' he corrected, shovelling frantically. 'Which has put such a strain on the joints, we don't have the bother of how to smash our way through.'

'It's quicker if we both dig,' Claudia offered. *Any excuse to dump this revolting lump of goat fat!* As she balanced the candle on a shelf, Orbilio jumped up as though scalded.

'Holy, holy shit!' he said.

In the bright halo of light, a hand was sticking out of the earth.

As Orbilio clawed at the soil, she saw the arm was attached to a torso, and the torso attached to a neck, which still bore the deep mark of the garotte. Attached to the neck was a head with a crown of baby-fine hair, and a thin pink nose.

'Macer!' Claudia gulped.

Orbilio's expression was grim as he hauled the body out of the drainage pipe.

'Look again,' he said roughly.

For it was not the Prefect who lay dripping in his lap. It was his nephew.

XXXII

To this day, Claudia could not say how she made it out of that store room. At some stage, Orbilio must have pushed her headlong into the sewer. He must have told her to keep her head up, perhaps he showed her how to drag herself down the channel by her elbows. Certainly they were red raw when she emerged, gasping and spluttering, into the pond, as were her knees and her feet. It could even have been that he had jerked on her hair from time to time, to keep her face out of the swirling waters and save her from drowning. She just did not know.

Dawn was beginning to break in the Vale of Adonis as Orbilio tumbled into the pool after her, the air sweet and fresh and full of birdsong, as though nothing so sordid as murder could have happened under its disappearing stars. Since the goddess Aurora had not yet placed her rosy kisses on the sky, the water remained a translucent shade of grey as Claudia splashed around in it. He watched the graceful motion of her arms, the lithe movement of her long, long legs. She needed to wash away the effluent, she said, and he pretended to go along with it, and for the first time since he met her, Marcus Cornelius Orbilio did not feel a surge in his loins. True, she wore nothing but a breast band and thong, which, wet, served to accentuate her secrets, rather than hide them. But it was an overwhelming tenderness that coursed through Orbilio's veins as she splashed and swam, and the feeling took him completely by surprise. He was not entirely sure he liked it.

She had done well, he thought, hauling himself out of the water. Swoons and hysterics were not part of her psyche, but she blamed herself for Salvian's death and there was little he could do to dissuade her.

'He told me,' she'd wailed, cradling Salvian in her arms. 'He told me he knew who the murderer was. I could have saved him, Marcus. I could have saved this boy's life, but I laughed at him instead.'

Since he'd had no real answer, Orbilio reminded her sternly that time was a luxury they did not possess as he prised away a large section of the terracotta piping using a shelf as a lever. Now something was wrong. It prickled his skin and it prickled the hairs on the back of his scalp. Something was very wrong. And the danger that stalked them was almost bestial in form.

'Claudia, we have to go.' She had washed away as much of Salvian's blood as was possible. The stains that were left were all in her mind.

To his surprise, she did not protest. 'I'm cold,' was all she said, hugging her arms tight round her shoulders.

'It's still early in the year,' he replied, and his words were unconvincing.

He knew they both still saw the face of the junior tribune, rash-red from the razor, heard the clank of his ill-fitting armour. Seventeen, and almost a father. Seventeen, and more than a match for Tulola. Seventeen – yet much more of a man than he was!

'We have to tell Macer,' Claudia said, wringing her

hair with her hands. But when she looked round, Supersnoop was sprinting to the far side of the pond. His eyes were fixed on a coloured rag, dusky pink mixed with red. 'My tunic!' she cried.

He was hunkered over it. 'Don't touch it,' he growled.

But it was too late. 'I'm freezing,' she protested, grabbing it out of his hands. 'What the – ?' The red was blood. Fresh, dripping blood. And the tunic had been ripped to shreds.

There was a tenseness about him she had never seen before. 'Be quiet,' he warned. 'And don't move a muscle.'

Stealthily he padded towards the tree line, his eyes sweeping the ground. Claudia heard the snapping of a branch.

He returned with a piece of wood no thicker than her wrist, with two rough points at the ends. 'Take this,' he said. As a weapon it did not look convincing, but Claudia's nails dug into the bark as he went off in search of a more promising defence.

Her eyes scanned the valley. The slaves would just about be stirring by now, another half-hour and pans would start to sizzle in the kitchens. At her feet, the tunic seemed to have a life force all of its own. It had turned into something evil and ugly, she half expected it to pulsate, to scuttle across the grass, to . . .

From the woods behind her came the rapid whirring of a hundred wingbeats. Finches, tits, stonechats and robins. Woodlarks, jays, warblers and an owl. Claudia felt her skin crimple. Dammit, Marcus Cornelius, what's keeping you?

For a moment, she thought she saw movement. A

pale blur among the branches. Stop this! You're starting at shadows. Like dusk, dawn light plays strange tricks, and why shouldn't a flock of birds stretch their wings? No reason at all, Claudia told herself, gripping the stake with both hands.

At the far side of the villa, the gazelle would also be stretching their thin, graceful legs, and Barea would be bringing out his stallion for an early-morning gallop. What she wouldn't give to be astride that big, black horse at the moment! The fastest nag to reach Narni since Pegasus.

There *is* something moving. Up in the trees. Swinging. Swishing.

'Marcus!' she yelled. '*Marcus!*'

There was a flash of white. Muted. Soft.

'What?' He came crashing through the woods. 'What is it?'

And then he saw it. The pale underbelly. The danger in bestial form . . .

With a snarl, the cheetah pounced upon the victim it had been stalking so silently.

With no weapon to defend himself, Orbilio threw up his hands – but it was no match for a hundred-pound cat hurtling out of the canopy. He could see every sinew, every black spot on the bright yellow pelt. Her pink nose. Her long, white whiskers. He could smell her breath on his face, fishy, stale. He saw strands of saliva, saw her awesome white fangs.

They would be the very last thing he saw in this life . . .

And then . . .

In mid-leap, it twisted and jerked. The snarl changed,

became deeper, guttural. He felt a surge of liquid hot on his face. As the cheetah crashed down on top of him, a shudder rippled through its powerful frame. It convulsed twice, and twice more, then lay still. And the liquid he tasted was its blood.

Dazed, he looked round. Sticking clean through its neck was the point of his rough-hewn stake.

Marcus Cornelius Orbilio heaved the cat's corpse clear of his body and scrambled to his feet. He wanted to thank her for saving his life, he wanted to tell her how lovely she looked, hair wild, cheeks flushed, body almost naked. He wanted to ask her to marry him.

Instead he was sick on the spot.

Claudia was still shaking as she lifted the hasp on the orchard gate. It was reaction, of course. Read nothing more into it. A man's life was in danger, she had a weapon to hand at the time, that was all. She'd have done the same for anyone, and heaven knows it was easy enough. She'd seen the cheetah long before Orbilio, watched it spring. Hell, the damned cat practically impaled itself!

Smoke was rising from the kitchens and the slave barracks.

This was a set-up, start to finish, she thought. We were supposed to find Salvian. We were supposed to escape. Then – tragic accident. Cuddles gets loose and, tut-tut, two people torn to shreds. As Claudia's tunic lay in one baited heap, no doubt Orbilio's doubled the odds somewhere else, and when the cat had finished with them . . . well, that was not a pretty thought. Pallas said they start with the heart and the kidneys, but what the hell does he know? This was the man who swore it only took gazelle!

She paused to feel the first rays of the sun on her face. Her hair was almost dry now, the tangles would be excruciating. She opened the door to one of the outbuildings. It was the hay store, where Corbulo nearly came to a sticky end and quickly she shut it again. The next shed stored farm implements. Right. We're in business. A workman's coarse tunic lay discarded on a plough. Bit short on personal hygiene, Claudia thought, slipping it over her head, but not as bad as Taranis. She sauntered along the shed. Hoes, hurdles, sleds, drags – aha, what have we here? She weighted a pair of sheep shears in her hand. Probably more for the camels these days, it was a long time since sheep grazed these pastures.

Outside, Claudia stood for a moment on the terracing, listening to the yawns, grunts and chatters that seem common first thing in the morning to all creatures, whether wild, domesticated or human. While Cuddles had been stalking her victim, Claudia's mind had been completely concentrated, but the second the cat's death set in, she'd felt an inexplicable tug at her innards which owed nothing to fear and less to relief. Then when Marcus rolled out from under the cheetah, it seemed her raw emotions were mirrored on his own face! He had lurched white-faced towards her, and suddenly all she wanted was for him to open his arms and envelop her . . . Dammit, she was glad when he threw up!

Her gaze roved the Vale of Adonis, over its ordered rows of vetch and lupin. It was no good for a girl, this sudden rush of sentiment. And to hell with this workman, too, and his penchant for bloody onions. What else could be making her eyes water?

Taking a deep breath, Claudia flexed the shears. Well greased, they moved sweetly, but she did not intend to use them for haircuts.

The door to the north wing would be open by now.

Tulola, naturally, would have an alibi.

Someone to swear she had not unleashed her pet on purpose, and Claudia's money was on Timoleon. Perhaps she had drugged him the way she had drugged Orbilio?

Pausing by the leopard shed, Claudia thought of her torn and bloodied tunic. Bait, to lure the cheetah, because that's how they catch these big cats, isn't it? By staking out an animal? This time, blood was the lure, and Cuddles didn't care whether her gazelle walked on four legs or two.

'Pretty kitty,' Claudia whispered to the leopard.

She could not begin to imagine what hatred lay inside Tulola, what vitriol, but one thing was certain. Within the hour, that bitch will be spilling beans as though there was no tomorrow. Which, Claudia thought, hefting the shears, might well be the case.

'Oh, yes, you're beautiful, aren't you?'

By rights she ought to go straight to Macer, tell him what had happened, leave the army to sort out Tulola. But Claudia needed to know for herself the reason for the killings. The leopard let out a short, guttural protest, more for show than for menace. Was Tulola revenging herself on men who'd rejected her? Salvian had, and he wound up dead. Corbulo had never strayed, and he only escaped because he was rescued in time. Fronto, of course, she couldn't vouch for, but *someone* had let him inside a locked house – and didn't Balbilla say he'd been bedding some rich bitch? Suppose, then, Orbilio had also rejected her? That it was Hotshot, not Claudia, who was the victim in this latest twist?

So far, so good, but where did Claudia fit in to this jigsaw? Macer might take Tulola to trial, but she needed to hear from Tulola's own lips why she hated Claudia Seferius so bitterly that she set her up for murder . . .

Claudia looked at the long, liquid leopard, its yellow eyes blazing with anger. Who can blame you, she thought, being cooped up all your life? Having baby bunnies hop around in your cage is no compensation, is it, poppet? What life is that for a magnificent beast like yourself? She thought of the freedom Drusilla enjoyed, and smiled. By the gods, she thought, these cats are powerful weapons of war – and really you had to admire Tulola's nerve. Claudia's eyes ran from the swishing tail, over the powerful ribcage, up over the massive shoulder-blades right to its shiny pink nose.

Pink? The camel shears clattered on to the cobbles. Cuddles has a black nose. And a black tip to her tail. Cuddles has pretty black teardrops that run from her eye . . . *and Cuddles only takes gazelle.* Claudia stared at the leopard. Leopards spend most of their lives up a tree. Leopards are night hunters. Sweet Janus, leopards can *also* be trained . . .

She reached for the shears, but a hand clamped over her wrist. A red, painted, Etruscan hand.

'I can see from your expression, my dear Claudia, that you have worked out my little secret.'

The voice was quiet, barely audible. But the dark grey eyes of the trainer penetrated Claudia's very soul.

XXXIII

Claudia stared at Corbulo. His mouth was working, he seemed to be telling her what a charmed life she led, but it was not his words she was mesmerized by. Just like the night of the party, he wore his white linen kilt and his fancy, filigree torque. When the sun's rays rose above the rooftops, it would gleam and shine and glitter and reflect, Macer would be left in its shade. Again, like the night of the equinox, Corbulo's body was ritual-red, his hair looped, only this time it was bound in a dark blue fillet.

The word 'ceremony' screamed from every pore.

'Why?' she asked simply.

To struggle, to break free, to scream for help would be useless. He was strong, she could feel the calluses rough on her wrist, and all around, wild beasts roared out their hunger. It was not in Claudia Seferius to submit, to go gracefully, but the need to know held her spellbound.

'What have I ever done to you?'

She needed, godsdammit, to know.

'Too late for games, Claudia.' He pulled on her wrist. 'You've had enough chances.'

Claudia thought of the Fates, those three old crones who weave the cloth of life. One spins the thread, one determines its length and one – she shivered – snips it with her shears. Claudia looked at the sheep shears at her own feet. On no, you bloody don't, she thought. I'll tell you when to start chopping!

With her free hand, she grabbed the bars of the leopard's cage. It snarled and snapped its jaws, but what the hell? At this rate, with Corbulo tugging and the leopard salivating over its prospective breakfast, she'd probably be pulled in two. They could share the damned prize.

The trainer's expression hadn't altered, but a dagger had appeared in his hand. Insects slithered down Claudia's spine. Jupiter, Juno and Mars, this man is unhinged! Unless she released her grip, he was going to slice her fingers off!

'Let her go!'

The voice was unmistakable, she just wondered what took him so long.

'Think I haven't been expecting you, Marcus?' The Etruscan's voice was a sneer.

Relieved and off her guard, Claudia didn't realize what was happening until it was too late. With one expert movement, Corbulo spun her round and threw her headlong into an empty cage, presumably that of the late, lamented leopard in the valley. While she lay sprawled, he shot the bolt and danced round to face Orbilio. Once again, she'd forgotten how light he was on his feet.

The two men lunged at one another, each parrying the other's knife thrust. For several minutes they dodged and darted, grunting with the exertion, then suddenly Orbilio delivered a swift uppercut and blood spurted from Corbulo's chest. Reeling, his dagger knocking Orbilio's knife out of his hand, the Etruscan cried out, staggered, gasped, then pitched forward on to his face.

Orbilio bent to retrieve his weapon. And as he did so, Corbulo – trainer, trickster – bounced up, a long wooden pole in his hands. It was the vaulting pole he used for the horses, and now Claudia knew why it was here. It was another trap. This cunning, evil monster had planned this, as well. He had watched what had happened in the valley, and had waited. Even the wound was a ploy. He'd choreographed his moves in order to sustain a convincing superficial cut.

As though a ballet or a mime had been painted, frieze by frieze, Claudia watched helplessly through the bars of the cage.

Orbilio straightening . . .

Corbulo behind him, swinging the bar . . .

The bar connecting with the centre of Orbilio's spine . . .

Poleaxed, Marcus Cornelius Orbilio collapsed.

'Is he – dead?' she whispered.

Corbulo mopped his wound with his handkerchief. 'No,' he said, casting a professional eye over his shoulder as he inspected the side of Claudia's prison. 'But I doubt he'll walk again.'

Claudia's mother was not prone to dishing out advice, but then again she wasn't one for taking it either. Once, however, when Claudia was about twelve, she had prised herself off the filthy, wine-stained pallet she called bed to impart counsel and wisdom to her impressionable daughter.

'Only one thing to remember in this life, love,' she'd sobbed, wiping the corner of her mouth with the back of her hand. 'You come into it on your own, and alone is how you go out.'

Not that Claudia's mother went out alone. She was accompanied by a liver no self-respecting augur would spit on, plus 164 empty wine jugs.

Claudia knew it was 164.

She'd had plenty of time to count them while her mother's body stiffened in the coagulated blood from her slashed wrists . . .

Claudia had not thought of her mother for a long, long time, but now, inside the leopard's cage, the words shimmered back across the years. You are alone. You can rely on no one but yourself.

In a rare moment of dependence, she had waited for Marcus Cornelius Orbilio to spring to her rescue and the price she paid was heavier than she could ever have imagined possible. As a result of her selfishness, a young aristocrat lay crippled for life, his career in tatters, his pleasures just memories. No more jousting on the Field of Mars, rousting on a Saturday night. Never again would he feel the throb of horseflesh between his legs, the thrill of a woman, the pulse of a long, hard run.

It would, she reflected bitterly, have been better to let him take his chances on Thursday with Gisco and that famous gelding knife. Good grief, was it really only three days ago? A lifetime had passed since then.

Head buried in her hands as she knelt on the rough wooden floor, Claudia was denied even the luxury of self-pity. The crate, like everything else, had been planned in the most meticulous detail. It was a transport cage. It was on wheels. And Corbulo had not been inspecting the box, he'd been harnessing it.

The ceremony, whatever it might be, was about to begin.

He paused to staunch the blood from his chest by dipping his handkerchief in a barrel of drinking water and pressing it hard against the wound. As the red ochre drizzled away with the blood, Claudia could see the Etruscan's neck, unlined and unmarked. Now she knew what had happened that night in the hay store. It was Corbulo who had stolen the yellow tunic, Corbulo who had flitted so furtively round his own territory. The bastard had timed it to perfection – the gurgles, the drumming of his feet against the door. Croesus, he'd even painted the purple marks on his neck, because who'd check for treachery in the heat of cutting him down? He'd have balanced himself on a hay bale, judging his jump to the second they burst through the door.

And Salvian, young, innocent Salvian, had realized this. Macer told him about the robbery which was no robbery, and Salvian connected it with the hanging which was no hanging. Corbulo wore a scarf to the Springs; maybe it blew away a fraction for Salvian to notice the lack of evidence, maybe Timoleon's jibes set a train of thought in motion, or maybe, just maybe, Salvian was smarter than Claudia had given him credit for. She could imagine the scene, the junior tribune marching up to arrest the trainer and, tragic as the outcome was, Claudia smiled through her tears at the young man's confidence. Had he lived, he would have been a man to be reckoned with. As it is, Regina and his unborn child still have every right to be proud of him.

The cage was cramped, she could sit, kneel or crouch, but it was impossible to stand upright. Claudia scanned the compounds for other signs of life. The slaves would be well into their stride by now, the family would be up, the field workers breaking their fast for the day. But Corbulo worked alone. He was famous for it. What would bring someone here? Claudia did not believe in lucky flukes, but prayed for one anyway.

The cage began to roll forward, rumbling past bears and lions and camels. She could hear the mules whinny and snicker, and then she was bumping faster and faster. She saw the stiff neck of the giraffe, saw its silly, gormless face watching her. Did Corbulo realize the road block was still in place? Surely Macer, if no one else, would still be looking for her? Or had Corbulo taken care of that, as well? The elephant swung his trunk through the gap in his wall. The elephant? Sweet Juno, they weren't going down the hill, they were going up! Forget the Via Flaminia, he was using an old Umbrian path that went straight over the hill. Where was he taking her?

'Is this some Etruscan sacrifice you're planning?' she called out.

Not that they made human sacrifices, the gentle Etruscans, but with Corbulo's mind unhinged as it was, you could never tell. They began to bump downhill, the mules galloping at the crack of the whip. Wildly Claudia clung to the bars, her knees clattering painfully on the wooden boards.

'I've tried, Claudia,' he yelled back at her. 'The gods know I've tried to make you pay for all that you've done to us, but each time, you've escaped by the luck of the gods, you and that tosser policeman. Did he really think he could outwit me?'

No, but I did. And it's because of me he lies crippled.

Faster and faster the mules and the cage clattered down the hill. Leaves whipped the sides, weeds and grasses caught in the woodwork. Claudia's hands were bleeding from the splinters in the bars.

'This wasn't quite how I'd planned it,' he was shouting. 'I'd hoped to make you pay while I sat back and watched.' She heard a hollow laugh. 'Instead we'll have to go together, but at least I die a true Etruscan.'

Claudia pulled at the bars. They were too thick to snap. What is it, this obsession with Etruria?

'Well, if you're so damned patriotic,' she snapped, 'why don't you kill yourself on Etruscan soil?'

There was a sharp pull on the reins. 'You arrogant bitch!' he snarled, jumping down to the ground. 'To think I lowered myself to begging, as well!'

Lowered himself? It's virtually impossible to rationalize the thoughts of a madman, but when you're trapped inside a cage with a painted warrior brandishing a dagger on the other side of the bars, it wouldn't hurt to try, thought Claudia.

'Begging?'

'At Tulola's banquet. Remus, you don't think I was drunk, do you?' He rattled the blade along the sides of the bars and Claudia cowered at the back of the crate. 'I had to pretend, or you'd never have swallowed the rest of the play – but!' A hand lashed in and grabbed the neck of Claudia's rough, woollen tunic. 'I asked you for a job, I asked you to go into partnership with me.'

He jerked her towards him so hard, her cheek bruised against the wood.

'And you laughed at me. You patronized me, and then you fucking laughed at me!'

He had misunderstood her, even then. He had not recognized in her the affection she had felt, the gratitude that here was a man offering his life savings to bale her out. But how could he? As a Nubian cannot comprehend snow, how could Corbulo recognize what he did not have within him in the first place?

'And what was the next phase, Corbulo? Was I supposed to marry you, only for the poor bride to suffer an accident like little Coronis?'

As he let go the tunic, his hand lashed upwards, sending her reeling into the side of the cage. 'You think I'd marry a tramp like you?'

Claudia could feel slivers of wood in her hair, and a large bump forming on the back of her head.

'Think I don't know what's going on?' he sneered. 'First it was your bodyguard, then the policeman. What was it like, fucking the schoolboy? Did you learn much?'

Junius? Orbilio? Salvian? Mother of Hades, this man's from a different galaxy! 'More than I would from fucking a murderer,' she said evenly.

Quick as a bolt of white lightning, Corbulo's fist closed round her throat, whamming Claudia's face into the bars. 'I wouldn't waste my seed,' he spat.

As he sprang back to take the reins, Claudia pitched forward on to the floor. Blood drizzled from her nose, she could hear it, drip, drip, drip, on to the boards as the crate rumbled on down the hillside. It clattered across the valley and she could hear the mules straining with the steepness of the next hill. There was a roaring sound in her ear, from where he'd banged her head. Croesus, where was he taking her?

'Where does Fronto fit in?' she asked, wiping her face with the hem of the ploughman's tunic.

If she could only piece together the reason behind Corbulo's madness (and there had to be a reason, however tenuous!), she had ammunition. At the moment she was not only physically helpless, she was spitting into a wind which was rapidly becoming gale force.

'Him!' The derision in his voice was harsh, even through the boom inside her skull. 'Now there was a sap! Do you know, he actually believed I'd take him into partnership with me? My own land, and he thought I'd give him half. I mean,' Corbulo began to laugh, 'can you seriously believe that?'

Claudia called on the spirits of the Umbrian woodlands to trip the mares, derail the crate, make her arms grow another cubit so she could undo the bolt. In stories and the epics, Corbulo would be unseated by an overhanging branch . . .

'What land?' she shouted back. She could hear the mules puffing, and she'd never heard animals pant like that. It was almost continuous.

'*My* land, I'm talking *my* land.' His voice was ragged from working the reins. 'It was easy to persuade Fronto that it was to his own advantage, setting fire to the olive groves. I told him, if the land was burned – the olives, the vines – we could buy it cheap, him and me, and go into business together.'

'You mean, you set up me *and* Quintilian?' Whether

you liked this man or not, it was a clever sting he had going. 'Why?'

The mares had not stopped to give Corbulo a rest; this was the end of the line. The air seemed steamy, damp. Claudia half expected to hear Cinna's Cappadocian anecdotes cutting through the heavy atmosphere. *Let me help you with them buskins, duck.* Claudia felt delirium rising, the rapid welling of panic.

'Corbulo.' There was an urgency in her voice now. 'What is it that's so special about those particular plots of land?'

'Those?' he asked casually, unharnessing the crate. 'Nothing. Arson was just a means of getting you away from your precious cronies in Rome. Why do you think I paid that masseuse in the bath house to suggest the damned shortcut?'

There was a jolt as the cage settled. 'Why would you want to do that?'

Corbulo was staring at her as though she was a rather backward camel he was training. 'How else could I get my lands back?' he asked patiently. 'Now tell me, Claudia.' He lifted one end of the cage and began to turn it sideways. 'Isn't that a lovely view?'

The mules hadn't been puffing. The boom hadn't been inside her head. The dampness wasn't panic.

This was panic!

Claudia Seferius stared wide-eyed through the bars of her cage. Adjacent on the precipice, before it fell 500 feet to the valley below, churned a massive, roaring, crashing waterfall.

XXXIV

Where do you begin to describe terror? Is it this sudden inability to breathe? The gasping for breath? The shallow snatches of air? Is it the blast of freezing air that hits you? The sensation of falling? Reeling? Of spiralling into unconsciousness?

At the brink of oblivion, Claudia pulled herself back. You can't give in, a voice inside her screamed. While you're conscious, you have at least a chance.

Corbulo stood on the edge and placed his hands on his hips.

Claudia pressed her fingers to her temples and battled with hysteria.

Marble Falls, the locals called it. She remembered now. Officially they were named after the engineer who, two centuries previously, diverted the forces of two rushing torrents and a lake in order to drain the marshy uplands and put paid once and for all to the flooding which blighted this ancient landscape. But Marble Falls was more appropriate, the Umbrian people felt, because viewed from the bottom, a wall of white marble fell from the hillside.

Viewed from the top, it was awesome.

Droplets of water, breaking free of the liquid marble, rose in their thousands to cloud the valley and now, with the sun heating them in earnest, manufactured humid, claustrophobic air. Lush vegetation – birch and poplar and willow – hung over the cascade to breathe in the excitement of the raging forces, their leaves turned to silver by the swirling steam.

Even on her knees, Claudia felt herself swaying. It was wide enough to launch a ship, this torrent; one of the mighty ocean-going merchantmen, a ten-thousander as they were called. What chance a tiny crate?

Tentatively she craned her neck. Rocks, boulders, more trees, more bushes, smaller cascades where the exuberant waters split and rejoined, split and rejoined as they abandoned themselves to the forces of gravity. Her vision blurred, and not from the spray. At the bottom, although obscured by the hot, dense clouds, this mighty mass of water plunged into the river Plennia, renamed after the same engineer who built the falls and widened the stream to cope with the torrent.

Claudia hoped his ghost walked and his grave was turned over by jackals.

'I didn't – ' She stopped, took another breath and forced herself to hang on to it. 'I didn't know Etruscans were famed for leaping to their deaths over waterfalls,' she said in a voice with only the slightest tremble in it.

Corbulo turned. 'You never know when to stop, do you? You and that tongue of yours?'

Claudia forced the jellified twigs that were her legs into a sitting position and hugged her knees in a nonchalant fashion. From that angle, only she could see that her fingers were white from the fear and that her hands shook like a baby bird's wings unless she clasped them tight.

'Why? Will begging save my life? You've convinced yourself you own my lands, that by killing me you'll get them back. So go ahead. Push the damned cage. Then see where it gets you.'

'Bitch!' Corbulo ran to the crate and the bars rattled in his hands. Janus, for a moment there she thought he was going to! 'You conceited, insolent, know-it-all bitch! How dare you – you of all people – accuse me of making this up? It's my ancestors who lied buried there, *my* blood which was spilled there, *my* sweat that manured the soil, so don't you lecture me on ownership, you empty-headed golddigger, you!'

It was a dangerous line, but Claudia persisted.

'Your sweat!' she scoffed. 'How far does it travel, this precious Etruscan perspiration? How is it so different from the rest of us that it can reach from Carrera on the coast to my vineyards in the east?'

It was working, sweet Jupiter, yes, it was working. The mind that had planned and honed each meticulous detail could yet be defeated by rage.

'Carrera! Who ever lived in Carrera? We're farmers, my people, and bloody good farmers at that.' He snorted derisively. 'Your husband, Gaius Seferius. Called himself a farmer, did he? I was a lad when he bought that land, eight years old, yet I still remember the outrage among my people when he turned prime agricultural soil into vineyards. Vineyards!'

Claudia's mind made quick computations. Gaius set himself up, must be twenty-four, twenty-five years ago. That's right, Corbulo's in his early thirties. 'We've had this conversation, I believe. And I told you then, wine pays handsomely.' The Empire virtually runs on it.

The trainer wasn't listening. 'Ten years ago he added a parcel to the south. That land belonged to a man named Pollio, and he was my father – '

'Ten years ago, I was fourteen,' she pointed out, quite reasonably.

'But you know the story, don't you?'

Of course I do. Gaius trotted it out at every dinner party. 'What story?'

'It was that bloody Compulsory Purchase Scheme. Our lands for just half-a-dozen gold pieces plus some stinking slum in Rome. I ask you, Claudia, who could survive in two filthy rooms hemmed in by foul-mouthed drunks, babies crying day and night and dogs pissing up your front door? Nothing but stale sweat and rancid fats in your nostrils, and all the time, wherever you walk, that godsawful dust from the stonemasons drying the air!'

'A million of us manage quite successfully.' Some of us even love it.

Corbulo kicked the cage and she felt it lurch closer towards the waterfall. Janus! With an iron grip, Claudia hugged her knees as though conversations like this were commonplace in her calendar.

'Well, I couldn't. And neither could my father, or my mother, or my two little sisters. The girls, they were only ten and thirteen, but they died of the flux within a month. It broke my parents, watching their babies die, knowing that had we had space and fresh air and clean, running water they'd be alive today, with babies of their own, and did your husband give a damn?'

Gaius had his faults, she thought, and a sense of injustice wasn't listed among them. This story did the rounds at dinner parties not out of venom, but as a warning to others. For a start, no peasant was forced off his own land, they went voluntarily and in Pollio's case, very rapidly. Augustus was keen to stabilize the economy and men like Pollio were not only exceptionally well paid, they were given good apartments and a weekly dole. But with Pollio, it went deeper than that. He'd neglected his acres, working the land as little as possible and drinking his money away and (this was the point of Gaius's after-dinner speech) when he was remunerated for his lands, he lost the whole lot on one single cockfight. A chicken, godsdammit. Pollio sold his birthright for a chicken.

'So did he, Claudia?' Corbulo's roar was louder than the falls. 'Did Gaius give a fuck about us?'

Rumour also had it that Pollio sold his eldest daughter into prostitution. Small wonder the mother threw herself into the Tiber.

Claudia could feel her anger boil at this appalling waste of human life. If Corbulo cared about his family, he left it pretty damned late! 'For gods' sake, man, yours is not the only family who moved out under the scheme. I can name you a dozen who uprooted to Rome, and not only did they survive, godsdammit, they put their sons in the Senate. So spare me the hard-luck stories.'

She leaned forward and gripped the bars, her face barely inches from his.

'You could have gone back any time you wanted, and if land's so cheap' – it wasn't – 'why didn't you godsdamned buy some?'

Grey eyes blazed back at her. 'You've never listened to a word I've been saying, have you? How many more times do I have to tell you? I only want to work that which is mine.' He threw up his hands in a gesture of futility. 'Croesus, Claudia, I begged you, I actually fucking begged you, to let me work with you. You could have done that for me.'

'So what's the problem?' she said with a jauntiness that stuck in her throat. 'Now you've explained everything, now I understand what's behind all this, let's put it behind us and start from scratch, shall we?'

'How?' There was a glimmer of reason in the angry, grey eyes.

'Well,' she forced a laugh, 'why don't we go into partnership? Now. Etruria's not very far away.'

'You patronizing bitch,' he sneered. 'If I wrote to you once, I wrote to you a hundred times.'

I get letters from cranks all the time, how . . .? Oh, shit. The spray from the falls had soaked her tunic, water dripped from her hair. But Claudia was oblivious.

'Corbulo's not your real name, is it?' Of course not. That would have given the game away right from the start.

A long, slow, ice-cold smile spread across the Etruscan's red-painted face. 'Try Crito.'

Crito! Gaius had been bombarded with letters, he'd laughed at the insolence of a man who not asked, but demanded his lands back and at a price no sane person would consider. Each time Gaius told the little oik to get lost, although when Claudia received similar demands after her husband's death, she had not been so polite. Almost immediately, Crito's letters stopped. And she thought she'd been clever . . .

'What's the matter, Claudia? Cat got your tongue?

Wishing you'd been nicer to me?' His boot gave another menacing kick to the crate. 'Or wondering how you can talk your way out of it?'

No, I'm not. Not any more.

The cage wobbled precariously.

'Whether I'm alive or dead,' she said, praying the tremor in her voice was drowned by the crash of the torrent, 'you'll still be a craven coward.'

'Coward? *Coward*?' Corbulo shook the cage so violently they both nearly toppled over. Claudia stifled a scream. 'I'm a farmer, I'm a trainer. I am Etruscan! I am not a fucking coward.'

'What would *you* call a man who gets someone else to do his killing?' She didn't give him a chance to reply. 'Yes, you can set me up for Fronto's murder, you can set leopards on me, you can even – big deal – push a defenceless woman over a waterfall in a crate. Well, to me that's cowardice, Corbulo.' She remembered Gisco's diatribe. 'You're a lily-livered, yellow-bellied, chicken-shitted coward.'

Juno be praised, he flung open the bolt!

'Out! Out, you bitch!' He grabbed her wrist and jerked her roughly on to the stones. As she fell, the cage teetered – backwards, forwards, backwards . . . then it toppled into the torrent. For a moment it wavered, buoyed by the force, then, with astonishing speed, crashed against an overhanging tree, swirled round, and headed straight into a boulder. As Claudia watched, she felt her bones turn to chalkdust. One strong gust and they'd blow clean away. Up it rose, the cage, to stand on its end. With only an imperceptible change in the roaring in her ears, she heard it dash against the rock, saw it break into five, then ten. By the time it reached the rim of the waterfall, there was nothing left but firewood.

She could hear a demented magpie chattering, then realized it was her own teeth.

Deflected by that brush with death, Claudia failed to realize what Corbulo was up to. He'd unbound the loops of his hair and was using the dark blue ribbon to tie Claudia's wrists. Perhaps the reason she hadn't noticed was that he'd left a good cubit of space between them. Could she – wild thought – get behind him and throttle him with it?

'I've given six months of my life to get you,' he hissed, his fingers digging deep into her arms as he shook her. 'Six months, and every day with my life on the line, but did Crito flinch from the most dangerous animals on Jove's earth? Did he hesitate to put poison into the wine of those mercenaries?'

Claudia gulped the steamy air in the hope it would steady her legs. 'Poison's a woman's tool,' she rasped, but she never finished the sentence. The blow from the trainer sent her reeling to the ground, twisting her leg beneath her.

'Don't you dare suggest that,' he snarled. 'Who knifed Fronto? Who snapped that Greek doxy's neck in full view of a hundred revellers? Tell me that doesn't take balls.'

Claudia grimaced at the pain in her knee. It wasn't me Coronis was shooting nervous glances at, she realized now, it was Corbulo. Both at the elephant show and during Macer's questioning, he'd deliberately stationed himself beside me, knowing any jittery looks from the girl would be deflected by yours truly here. Callous bastard.

He snatched a handful of her hair. 'And what about the planning? Don't you think that took guts?' Claudia screamed as he twisted her curls. 'Well, answer me, my fine and fancy lady.'

'Yes! Yes,' she screamed. 'I'm sorry.'

Corbulo glanced over his shoulder to the valley shrouded by swirling steam. 'Oh, you will be,' he said. 'You will be.' Using her hair like a leash, he hauled her, whimpering, to her feet. 'You wouldn't believe what I've gone through, you and that charmed life of yours.'

'Please – '

'Doping the beasts to set the schedule back. Sucking up to Sergius and his whore of a sister. Fawning over that slimeball Fronto.'

'Corbulo, please! You're hurting me!'

'Crito. The name's Crito.' He began to drag her towards the edge. 'You may as well get used to it, because we'll be together through all eternity, Claudia. One way or another, I'll take my lands with me.'

'What – ?' She didn't need to ask the question, suddenly it was clear. Now she understood why had he left so much slack between her wrists. He intended to slip it over his head, so her arms would be round his body when he leapt from the precipice.

'This way I can watch the terror on your face all the way to the bottom.'

Frantically Claudia scrabbled on the rocks. 'Why didn't you just kill me at the beginning?'

The grip on her hair didn't waver and the cliff came ever closer. 'Revenge, you bitch. Revenge. I wanted to watch you suffer, the way my family and I had to suffer.

I wanted to see you rot in a gaolhouse. See you exiled. Penniless. Disgraced.'

He jerked her to her feet, and Claudia tasted blood from the blow that sent her flying.

'Well,' he fought to loop her arms over his, 'you denied me that pleasure, but at least I'll die happy.'

'No you bloody won't!' she yelled.

Claudia's kneecap smashed into his groin. His face, the red paint streaked by the watery air, contorted into a gargoyle as he let go of her arms. Gagging, gasping, he reached for his dagger, but for once Corbulo the trainer was too slow.

With all her strength Claudia pushed.

Like the leopard's cage, Corbulo seesawed back and forth, wobbling, wavering, teetering on the brink. But with each tremulous sway, the momentum was gaining, until slowly the balance shifted. Claudia held her breath. It could go either way . . .

Sweet Jupiter, it could still go either way!

Then, with a strangled yelp, Corbulo pitched forward into the boiling waters.

But not before he'd grabbed hold of Claudia.

Together they tumbled into oblivion.

XXXV

I am dead, she thought. I have died, and Charon is taking me across the Styx in his little grey ferry boat. I can feel it bobbing, and I am weightless.

She could feel, too, the rage of the Underworld. It throbbed, vibrated, rumbled. The fury of a hundred million souls wrenched from their bodies. She could feel their pain. In her shoulders, in her arms, in her wrists . . .

Janus, Croesus and the girl next door! Ghosts, be buggered – this pain is real. It was searing her joints and her ligaments and her tendons, and Claudia, with great trepidation, opened her eyes.

Shit!

The weightlessness, the bobbing, it made sense now. She was hanging. In mid-bloody-air, she was hanging, and the reason she was suspended, the cause of the pain shooting up her arms and biting into her wrists, was Corbulo's stupid Etruscan fillet.

Below her, two rivers and a lake launched themselves into space, and she remembered doing the same with Corbulo. What happened? She kneed him in the goolies, it made him sick, and when he reeled, she gave him a shove. She remembered that. Claudia looked down into a sea of steam, felt her head swim and looked up again. By the gods, yes. That son-of-a-bitch lunged for her, and over they went, the two of them. Corbulo, the man with a chip on his shoulder the size of a pine tree. Corbulo, who could forgive his father for gambling away the family's heritage and selling his sister for a few coppers a shot, but who could not forgive the person who bought that land fair and square in the first place. Corbulo, whose sense of duty had so warped over the years, it rotted his mind, his reason and his dignity. It had desensitized him to other people's feelings, desecrated his own emotions; he could not even see that by lowering himself, as he put it, to training wild beasts, he had unleashed a prodigious talent that would have made him rich beyond words. Rich enough to buy lands equalling Claudia's and beyond, but his rancid mind was set on one track only. Reclaiming his birthright.

It was a wonder he hadn't taken a pop at the Emperor. It was Augustus who instigated the Land Purchase Scheme. Augustus whose rapid expansionist policies stabilized the merchant classes. Augustus who, in the best possible motives, had consolidated this distinctly uneven distribution of wealth.

Not that she'd been thinking such cerebral thoughts as she toppled over the cliff! Her mind was purely on survival, and when she saw a branch – the same branch the cage crashed into – she hung on to it with both hands. She heard the woollen tunic rip, and as she clung to the tree, she saw a flash of gold as the sun caught Corbulo's torque. Then he was under, she saw his arms stiff above the boiling waters, saw a swirl of white as Corbulo's kilt was swept off in the torrent. Like a knitted doll, he was dashed from rock to rock. His tanned torso, red paint washed off long ago, was thrown up momentarily by the tumbling force, then it was pitched into the abyss. The angle of his head, the twisted limbs, told her that, if not already dead, Corbulo could not survive many more seconds.

There was a creak, a crack and she could feel the branch giving way. Desperately she swung herself to the right, into the body of the tree, but it was not strong enough to take her weight. She had crashed through the tree, a young birch, into the tree below, and then the one below that.

Where she hung now, like a pheasant on a hook, the only thing between her and certain death, paradoxically, a dark blue ribbon which belonged to the man who tried to kill her. Dammit, Corbulo, you were too lazy, too stubborn to work at the training, you never even tried to buy us out! Your contempt for me – or rather, my lands and my money – contaminated all logic. Claudia's fists closed round the fillet to ease the strain on her bleeding wrists. You thought yourself superior, manipulating Fronto, bribing a homesick Greek girl, ingratiating yourself with Sergius Pictor, setting up Quintilian and me. Did you ever, even once, wake up in the morning and see yourself as you really were? Did the mirror never throw back the reflection of the shabby, shallow, self-obsessed individual who looked in it? Did you never cringe at yourself, Corbulo?

Her fingers could take the strain no longer. She let go of the fillet and winced as the ribbon dug into her wrists. Her shoulders were on fire, her head was swimming with the pain. The woollen tunic, the one that reeked of onions and sweat, had long since slipped away. Corbulo had torn it, the branches had torn it, there was little left by the time she was caught by the canopy. She wondered what the ploughman was like, the owner of the tunic. Would he be cross at losing it? Would he thrash around looking for it? Curse the fool who stole it? Grumble all the morning? Isn't it funny, she thought, what goes through your mind at a time like this?

Everything here is white or it's green. The world is condensed. I can see spray, it washes over my face, my feet, my legs. I can see water, thousands upon thousands of gallons, rushing below me. Or I can see green, varying shades of green, from the poplars, the birches, the willows. Oh yes, and blue. That one, small, fragile piece of blue . . .

Above her, although she couldn't see it through the blur, the sky would also be blue. Not this dreary, twilight blue, it would be vibrant, fresh, the colour of speedwells. There might be a few clouds streaked across it. Mares' tails. Light, white, dancing clouds. Skittish clouds. Happy, silly, carefree clouds.

Clouds filled her eyes and dribbled down her cheeks. Dammit, I can't even see the bloody sky. Talk about irony. He gets the quick death, I just hang here until his stupid, stupid ribbon chafes through. She glanced down into the white froth and shuddered.

'Claudia Seferius, what the hell are you doing there?'

Sweet Janus, the trees are talking back! Wildly she flung her head from side to side. This is not happening. It is not, not happening.

'Couldn't you see I was in trouble back there at the villa?'

Overhead, the wavy mop of Marcus Cornelius Orbilio was being saturated in the spray. He seemed to be securing one end of the mare's reins over a branch, though the concentration couldn't wipe the grin off his face.

'I – ' She cleared her throat. 'I knew you'd be fine without interference from me.'

The tears down her face turned into a watercourse. I should have known Corbulo couldn't fell you with just one stick, she thought. For once, he'd underestimated his man. Patricians? Soft as sand, he'd have said, not stopping to consider whether any broke the mould. Whether any worked out at the gymnasium with weights. Whether any had muscles strong enough to repel the odd whack with a vaulting pole . . .

'Now I suppose you expect me to come down there and rescue you?'

Claudia gulped back her tears. 'On one condition, Orbilio.'

'Oh?'

'That after this, you leave me alone and I never have to set eyes on you again.'

Carefully he looped the rest of the reins round his shoulders. 'You've got yourself a deal!' he shouted, testing the knot.

Claudia pinched her lips together. That was the thing about Supersnoop, she thought, dangling in mid-air above a 500-foot drop while thousands of gallons of water thundered past her. He was such a godawful liar.

Hadn't she always said so?

Wolf Whistle

Marilyn Todd

Claudia's latest mystery, entitled *Wolf Whistle*, is now available in hardback from Macmillan (priced £16.99).

The opening scenes follow here.

I

Rarely do moneylenders, when faced with non-payment of debt, veer towards benevolence. But this one was in a good mood. In fact, so keen was he today to demonstrate his generosity, that he offered Claudia a head start before unleashing his dogs.

'Ratbag!' she yelled over her shoulder. That was the last time she'd do business with him!

At the first turn, she slewed the honey-seller's table across the lane behind her. Dozens of small red pots oozed their nectar on to the pavement, although Claudia was running too fast to catch the shopkeeper's exact words. He called her a something-something-little-something, she believed, and threatened that if she ever came back he'd something-something her, which seemed none too polite, but then gentlemanly conduct tended to be thin on the ground around here.

'Stop her!' cried one of the dog handlers. 'Stop that woman!' But the crowd had no intention of being deprived of their free entertainment. They cleaved a path.

Croesus, thought Claudia, haring down the street, it was a hard-boiled pack that bloodsucker had put on her tail and no mistake. Baying and slavering – you'd think they hadn't eaten for days. She skidded into a charcoal dealer, sending his coals tumbling over the cobbles. Hell, maybe they hadn't, but no way did Claudia Seferius intend to be on their menu tonight! Skirting a pile of slippery fish guts which the fishmonger had jettisoned into the gutter, she paused at the tallow man's.

'I turned left, understood?' She threw the candle-maker sufficient bronze to keep him in food (or more probably drink) for a week.

His appreciative grin showed a row of blackened teeth. 'Left, yer said.'

Good. If duff directions don't put the dogs off the scent, the stench from his rotting teeth would. Before ducking to the right, Claudia stopped to check her pursuers. The tallow man was pointing directly her way . . .

She ran and she ran, darting left, hooking right, constantly cursing the strong Judaean perfume which blazed a trail for zealous snouts. What was wrong with that moneylender? For heaven's sake, we're only talking a few hundred gold pieces (all right, a thousand; who's counting?), but it's not as though she intended to decamp with his money! It was merely that, at present, the repayment date required a modicum of flexibility . . . Surely he could trust her on that? Fine cottons, gold rings and ivory combs in her curls had been reassurance enough when he was dishing out the loan, and look how his eyes popped when she wrote down the address! Quite right, too. It was a bloody good address. Up on the Esquiline, where the patricians hang out. A rather modest house, perhaps, by Esquiline standards, with a courtyard of shade and gentle fountains and sweet singing birds. You can't miss it, she told the moneylender. It's right opposite the goldbeater's.

Which it was. It just happened not to be Claudia's address.

Jupiter, Juno and Mars! Whichever way she turned, the lanes twisted, narrowed, doubled back, and led relentlessly downhill. Damn! The dogs were not giving up, either. One had a distinctive howl – not dissimilar, she mused, to the sound her cat, Drusilla, made this morning, when her tail got caught in the door.

Kneading the stitch in her side, Claudia paused and looked around and felt a sudden chill of terror. She could not say when or where it had changed, but twisting wynds had turned into stinking runnels, sedate apartment blocks were now crumbling tenements. A standpipe dripped at the end of the street and a young mother with a child at her hip blew her nose with her fingers. Daylight was beginning to fade, too, exacerbated by the heavy grey clouds which had been building up during the course of the afternoon. Doors were being slammed, latches fastened, shutters drawn. With panic rising in her breast, Claudia knew she was well and truly lost. While the dogs still bayed close by.

'Hello?' Someone help me. Please. But only shadows and vermin roamed the alleys amid the raw sewage, the vegetation rotting on the middens and the bloated corpse of a puppy being picked over by rats. A three-legged truckle-bed sat upended where it had been dumped, broken pots crunched underfoot, and from open windows came the sounds of drunken bullies beating their wives and their children in the name of obedience. Spooked by the rankness that defines sheer and utter hopelessness, Claudia went spinning down the lanes.

Stumbling. Tripping. Oblivious to the cess trenches, the dogs, the thugs who ran with them, she had to get out . . .

'Shit!'

Swallowing hard, she blinked back the tears as she came face to face with the truckle-bed and the rats and the dead puppydog.

'Shit, shit, shit!'

Perhaps, then, it was time to use brains and not footwear? A raw-boned mongrel, grey around the face, wandered up to the broken bed, cocked its leg then lolloped off. Dear Diana! Impossible to imagine that all roads lead from Rome, reaching even the darkest outpost of our mighty Empire, while these alleys criss-cross like the minotaur's labyrinth.

'There! There she is!'

Dammit, they'd caught up! Claudia shot down the nearest passageway, then skidded to a halt. The mongrel was examining something dark and sticky on a rusty skillet. The inspection appeared to be in its early stages. Plenty of time for a girl to unclip her blue cotton wrap, rip it with the brooch pin and ram the poor mutt's head through the hole before it even had a chance to snarl its disapproval. Stung in the rump by a shard of pottery, it shot off down the street, flapping oceans of blue cotton in its wake. Blue cotton heavily scented with Judaean perfume, no less!

As she flung open the nearest tenement door, Claudia realised her ploy had failed. The dogs wanted to follow the scent, but the handlers had sharp eyes. The gap was closing. Claudia flew up the dimly lit stairs two at a time. While they searched the lower floors, she could hide. She ran along the corridor, testing door after door, until finally one surrendered.

'Anyone home?'

A toothless crone sat on a stool supping porridge straight from the crock.

'Can you hide me?' Claudia panted. 'I can pay.' She pulled off a ring set with emeralds.

Watery gruel dribbled down the old woman's chin. Sweet Janus, was she blind?

'Please!' A cupboard. Under the bed. There must be some way out of this mess! 'Will you help me?'

'Oi!' Fists pounded the door. 'Open up!' The hinges were weak. They would not stand much more rough treatment.

Rheumy eyes watched disinterestedly as the crone continued to slurp from the bowl. Bugger! Claudia ran to the window and looked down. The front door was bulging more and more with each shove from the money-lender's thug.

'No way out, luv,' he crowed. 'You're trapped!'

Really? Ignoring the dizziness, Claudia climbed on to the sill. What about that balcony over the way? She took a deep breath.

Now eight feet is not very far. Measure it out and you'd be hard pressed to fit in, say, a decent bout of shadow-boxing, half a game of hopscotch, you couldn't even rig up a funeral pyre. So, no, it's not very far. On the ground . . . Heart pounding, mouth dry, Claudia launched herself into space.

YES! As her hands connected with the balustrade, she felt a rush of such elation that she actually laughed aloud.

Until she heard the crack.

This isn't a rail. This is woodworm holding hands! Her knuckles were white as she glanced down. Janus! It must be seventy feet at the least! Waves of nausea washed over her as she struggled to swing her body on to the balcony before the rail gave way.

Too late. With a splintering sound, the balustrade began to bow inexorably downwards. Claudia closed her eyes. And wondered which great Olympian divinity owed her a favour.

MARILYN TODD

I, Claudia

Pan Books £5.99

Claudia Seferius has successfully inveigled her way into marriage
with a wealthy Roman wine merchant. But when her secret gambling debts spiral, she hits on another resourceful way to make
money – offering her 'personal services' to high-ranking Citizens.

Unfortunately her clients are now turning up dead – the victims
of a sadistic serial killer . . .

When Marcus Cornelius Orbilio, the handsome investigating
officer, starts digging deep for clues, Claudia realizes she must track
down the murderer herself – before her husband discovers what
she's been up to.

And before another man meets his grisly end . . .

MARILYN TODD

Virgin Territory

Pan Books £5.99

It just wasn't fair. When you marry a man for his money, you expect him to leave you a shining pile of gold peices. *Not* a crummy old wine business. How was the new young widow Claudia going to pay off her gambling debts now?

So when Eugenius Collatinus asks Claudia to chaperone his granddaughter to Sicily she jumps at the chance to escape Rome. It should be easy – Sabina Collatinus, she is told, has recently completed thirty five years' service as a Vestal Virgin.

Or has she . . . ?

Claudia's suspects she is escorting an imposter. And then a woman's brutilized body is discovered . . .